PENGUIN BOOKS

TIDES OF FORTUNE

TIDES OF FORTUNE

LAURYN HAMILTON MURRAY

PENGUIN BOOKS

PENGUIN BOOKS

UK | USA | Canada | Ireland | Australia
India | New Zealand | South Africa

Penguin Books is part of the Penguin Random House group of companies
whose addresses can be found at global.penguinrandomhouse.com

www.penguin.co.uk www.puffin.co.uk www.ladybird.co.uk

Penguin Random House UK

First published 2026
001

Set in 10.5/15pt Sabon LT Std
Typeset by Six Red Marbles UK, Thetford, Norfolk
Printed and bound in Great Britain by Clays Ltd, Elcograf S.p.A.

The authorized representative in the EEA is Penguin Random House Ireland,
Morrison Chambers, 32 Nassau Street, Dublin D02 YH68

A CIP catalogue record for this book is available from the British Library

ISBN: 978–0–241–68001–8

All correspondence to:
Penguin Books
Penguin Random House Children's
One Embassy Gardens, 8 Viaduct Gardens, London SW11 7BW

MIX
Paper | Supporting
responsible forestry
FSC www.fsc.org
FSC® C018179

Penguin Random House is committed to a
sustainable future for our business, our readers
and our planet. This book is made from Forest
Stewardship Council® certified paper.

For you

OSTACRE
Marble Palace
Windlands
THE RIFT
Bartell Manor
NEMETH
Firelands
Fire Mountain
VALBURN
Harglade Hall
Isolla
The Golden Palace
COR CAVAL
THE RIDGE
THE RIDGE
The Grove
Wellwall
Wildlands
Heathcross
The Greenwood
THE RIFT
Thorndale
BRAVA
Waterlands
The Lagoon
THE SECOND SEA
N
W
E
S

PART I

Tides That Break

I

Blaze

The day of the funeral dawns blood-red.

Flint and I sit side by side on a jutting stone ledge, our legs dangling, watching the stream of mourners trickle into the base of the volcano. The land surrounding Fire Mountain is barren, the terrain consisting of nothing but dark rock and hot springs, which occasionally erupt in billows of steam. I flinch each time. I'm restless, skittish. Even the air seems oppressive. Too hot. Heavy with anticipation. The figures below – beetle-sized from our high vantage point – converge from all directions, unified in their grief for their fallen queen.

My brother lets out a low whistle as he leans back on his elbows. 'Impressive turnout. I do hope there's enough finger food.'

I remain silent, knowing how much he's hurting deep down. He loved Aunt Yvainne, and she doted on him. Flint was her ward, her darling, her protégé. She'd hoped that he would be the one to replace her on her throne after the old Crowned Council relinquished their power. Only Flint didn't win the crown of golden flames, and Aunt Yvainne is dead, her body cold and stiff and wrapped in silks, waiting on the pyre.

It's been several weeks since the Binding Ceremony, yet every time I close my eyes I'm back in that chamber, watching the Earth Cleaver plunge my dagger into the emperor's heart. Though it wasn't his father Fox had intended to kill. It was his uncle, King Balen, who vanished into thin air before the knife could meet its mark, who murdered his niece on the word of a mysterious prophecy, and who has in his possession one of the three enchanted Eyes.

With the Eye of the Past, King Balen is dangerous. He has history at his fingertips, just as his father, Caius Castellion, has the future. But were he to get his hands on the Eye of the Soul, he would be invincible. Which means that someone has to find it before he does.

Flint glances at me. 'We don't have to do this, you know. We can call the whole thing off. Just say the word.'

'We might not get this chance again.'

'I'm aware of that.'

I raise an eyebrow. 'Getting cold feet, are we?'

'As if. I'm only looking out for my sister. With my one good eye, that is.'

I force a tight smile. While Flint seems perfectly at ease making jokes about his injury, I can still barely look at him without wincing. Thanks to the magic in his blood, his burns are healing well, already giving way to shiny new skin, but the leather patch obscuring the upper-left side of his face serves as a constant reminder of just what Flint lost during the third Ignitia trial, of what our cousin, Ember, took from him, and of all the ways I'm going to make her pay for it.

Flint stands up and holds out a hand. 'Come on. We'd better start getting ready.'

I take one last look at the mourners below then let him pull me to my feet. A unit of Harglade guards, their crimson uniforms emblazoned with golden cobras, escorts us back to our rooms. Since we arrived several days ago, Fire Mountain has taken some getting used to. For starters – it's a volcano. A colossal, sky-scraping, dormant volcano where the Fire Goddess Vesta, the first Ignitia Etheri, built her Court of Flames. The stone walls, intersected with glowing veins of magma, are hot to the touch, and each level is connected by steep, sweeping staircases. It's a good thing Grandmother is indisposed, as I imagine navigating the place, even with her ruby-encrusted stick, would prove an ordeal.

She's waiting for me in my chambers, her brown-gold eyes dull, her movements weary and slow. When King Balen blasted her across the Choosing Chamber, I was sure she was dead. And the Aquatori trainer, River, too. They looked so frail, lying there next to the Supreme Mother of the Valla Jakartis with her swollen, broken neck. River pulled through with only minor injuries, and Grandmother managed to hold on long enough for the physicians to attend to her. Only she hit her head, and her recollection of events seems hazy at best. She hasn't mentioned the Eyes to me in all these weeks since, to my utter relief. Because if Grandmother knew I had reason to go, she'd be doing everything in her power to make sure I stay. I wouldn't put it past her to have me fitted with a cattle bell.

I glance over to where a pretty azure dress fringed with tiny sapphires is laid out on the bed. At that moment there's a knock on the door and a timid-looking attendant enters, a red gown draped over her arm. She curtsies deeply, but not to Grandmother – to me.

It's easy to forget sometimes, what with everything going on, that I am – or at least very soon will be – a queen. The Queen of the Waterlands. Ruler of the Aquatori.

I'm still far from used to the idea. Especially since Queen Hydra is no longer here to advise me. My chest aches remembering our lessons, remembering the way her blood mingled with the water as the Eye of the Soul disappeared through that portal.

I clench my jaw, resolved. I must prove myself a worthy successor. I will not wear the crown until I have found the Eye.

Grandmother is looking the attendant up and down. 'Yes,' she murmurs absently. 'Right height, right build. She'll do nicely.'

The girl swallows.

I take a step towards her. 'Are you sure about this?'

'Of course she's sure,' snaps Grandmother. 'She's getting five gold pieces and enough food to feed her family for a year. Now, get dressed, both of you.'

I let the attendant button me into the red dress, then she slips into the blue one. I watch her run her hands over the fabric in wonder before she glances at the mirror, eyes wide as she takes in her reflection.

Grandmother sniffs. 'There will be time for admiring yourself later.'

The girl blushes and stares down at her silk slippers.

Today, I am not the Storm Weaver – she is. Posing as me, she will stand on the stone dais with the rest of my family, leaving the real me, dressed as I am in Ignitia colours, to watch the funeral with the unsuspecting crowd of mourners below. This way, if anything were to go wrong, if there were an attempt on my life, I would be safe. Though I can't say the same for the girl at my side.

I jog my knee impatiently as Grandmother braids our hair, hands us each a pair of gloves, then produces two veils – one cerulean, one scarlet.

She sighs reluctantly, then nods. 'It works. No one would know unless they knew to look. My guards will be positioned around the throne room, Blaze. As for the crowd, you must blend in. Whatever happens, do *not* reveal yourself.'

'I won't.'

She lets me go and snaps her fingers at the attendant as she moves towards the door, the skirts of her thick red gown whispering across the stone floor.

'Grandmother?'

She turns back, hands resting atop the hilt of her stick.

'I love you,' I tell her.

She looks at me for a long time, eyes glassy in the flickering candlelight, before limping from the room, her decoy granddaughter hurrying along in her wake.

I hold back a moment before crossing to the dressing table and picking up a tiny wooden figurine of a knight holding a sabre. It was a gift from my younger brother, Renly, who, after a series of tantrums, has been grudgingly left at Harglade Hall with the kittens.

For luck, he said.

Slipping the knight into my pocket, I take a long, deep breath then head out into the corridor, merging seamlessly with the tide of Ignitia courtiers.

Flint falls into step beside me. 'Everything's ready,' he mutters, without looking in my direction. 'After the service, find a way to get to the kitchens. I'll meet you there.'

Then he's gone, disappearing into the crowd.

The throne room is so cavernous that the first time I saw it I was instantly reminded of the training room in the Golden Keep. Given that we are standing directly below the mouth of the volcano, there is no ceiling, only a glimmer of blue sky far above. At one end of the room sits a towering stone throne atop a dais, and in front of it, built high with wood and kindling, a gigantic pyre, upon which lies the silk-wrapped corpse of the Fire Queen.

I keep my head down, careful not to draw attention to myself as I take my place among the crimson sea of mourners, all of them having travelled from every corner of the Firelands to offer their condolences, to express their sorrow, to say goodbye.

It's some time before House Harglade emerge. Grandmother, who cannot bring herself to look at the pyre. Aunt Hester, who appears unable to look away. Flint, with his arm round Aunt Yvainne's wife, Seraphine. And me – or rather, my decoy, who's seemingly so wracked with nerves that she stumbles slightly while taking her place on the dais.

Someone nearby snorts quietly. 'Never thought I'd see the day I pitied the Fish.'

I grit my teeth just as a second voice hisses, 'Another word and I'll torch you.'

I bite down on a gasp, because I know that voice. It belongs to my friend Elaith. And she's standing right behind me.

I force myself to remain still, keeping my eyes trained on the dais as the final member of the congregation decides to grace us with her presence. Fury slithers through me like cold water as Ember flounces into view, her rust-orange dress trailing behind her. It takes every scrap of willpower I possess to bow my head along with everyone else.

Flint's expression doesn't change, but I can almost *feel* the tension wedged between his shoulder blades. He's seen our cousin only once since the third trial – a meeting that was monitored by Grandmother, and which consisted of a sugared, insincere apology. What happened was an accident, Ember had claimed. *An accident.*

'My dear friends, my fellow mourners, I thank you for being here to celebrate the life of my beloved aunt, Queen Yvainne.' Ember's voice is girlish, sickly-sweet, honey stirred into milk that's gone bad. 'Because that is why we have come together today. To celebrate. To remember her glorious reign, and not the unspeakable circumstances that led to her death.'

It appears like a mirage before my eyes – the dagger, the golden tendrils of power, the three queens lying crumpled in pools of blood. I taste bile and swallow it down, trying to block out the murmurs spreading through the crowd. Murmurs of a name. *His* name.

The Earth Cleaver.

Queenslayer.

The last time I saw him, he was being dragged from the Choosing Chamber, hands stained red, eyes hollow. I remember the way he held my gaze, clung to it like a certainty, until the doors slammed shut between us. For I am the only one who knows what truly happened that day. That Fox is, if not entirely innocent, then not entirely guilty either.

Ever since, he has haunted me. Almost as if his absence has become a kind of presence.

'I want you to know that I share your pain, just as I shared your love,' says Ember, her gold-flecked eyes sweeping over the room. 'These past few weeks have been filled with darkness. We have been wounded. But we *will* heal. I promise each and every one of you that when I am crowned your queen, we will walk together into a new era, a new dawn.'

All around me, the crowd are nodding. I scowl. How does she know what to say? To make them listen to her, to make them feel *safe*?

'We must stand united,' Ember continues. 'We cannot tremble in the face of fear. To do so would be an insult to her memory.'

A perfect tear rolls down her cheek as she glances towards the pyre. Behind me, Elaith scoffs quietly.

Ember draws herself up to full height. 'And now, the time has come for the Burning.'

I suppress a shudder. The Burning is the death ritual of the Firelands. The head of the deceased's House is first to light the pyre, followed by the rest of their loved ones. When the pyre is at last reduced to a smouldering heap, the family each take a handful of ashes to deposit inside an urn. The Ignitia believe that the dead person's soul is carried skyward on the smoke and returned to Vesta. Like funerals, executions also take place upon a pyre. Only in these cases, the soul is thought to be damned, and the prisoner is burned alive.

The tapping of Grandmother's stick reverberates around the stone hall as she moves forward, her tread as heavy as her heart. My mind floods with images of my mother's funeral. My father, too grief-stricken to speak. Renly, squawking in the arms of the wet nurse. Flint clutching my hand tightly as it loomed before me – a dark, empty pit of pain. My own personal Rift.

There's a sudden intake of breath from the crowd as a flame springs to life in Ember's palm. I narrow my eyes. What is she doing? The head of the family is first to light the pyre. *Grandmother* is the head of the family, not Ember.

'Seeing as I am the one who will take my aunt's place on the throne, I think it only fitting that I cast the first flame. Wouldn't you agree, Grandmother?'

Ice courses through me, numbing every other feeling but cold, sharp fury. How *dare* she disrespect Grandmother like this, in front of the entire court? I know Grandmother will never undermine Ember's authority in public. No one can think our House divided.

So, Grandmother steps back.

Triumphant, Ember raises her voice and speaks the words of House Harglade: '*Flicker, flare, flame.*'

The crowd echoes her, and I watch my brother flinch as Ember sends her ball of fire shooting into the centre of the pyre. Immediately, Aunt Yvainne's body is set alight, flames arcing and crackling. Then it's Grandmother's turn, her face a careful mask. She is followed by Aunt Hester. Flint swallows hard, extending his arm. He's shaking, overcome with grief. After about a minute, when it's clear he's not up to it, a weeping Seraphine squeezes his hand, steps forward, and sends two flames shooting into the pyre – one for each of them.

My heart gives a painful jolt as Flint stares down at the floor, blinking back tears. Next to him, my decoy twists her gloved fingers together nervously. Being Aquatori, she or, rather, *I* obviously do not participate in the ritual. I am a Harglade, one of a long line of pureblood Ignitia, a descendant of Vesta herself. I should have been Flameborn – like Flint, like Ember. But I wasn't. I was born a Rain Singer, and my birth almost drowned the empire.

I think back to the Choosing Rite, when I used Syla's talisman to summon that storm and claim the gift that shaped my life – and ended so many others'. I think about the way the Eye called to me, *chose* me. I don't know why. All I know is that I need to find it.

Flint and I have spent weeks planning our escape, and now the day is finally upon us. In just a few short hours, I will be far from here.

Burying my guilt deep, I try not to look at Grandmother. Instead, I focus on the smoke dancing atop the pyre. To the surrounding provinces, it must look as though Fire Mountain is about to erupt, what with the grey clouds billowing out of the top of the volcano.

Many of the mourners are weeping. I hear Elaith give a muffled sob. I can't pretend to have had any strong attachment to Aunt Yvainne, but I always respected her, in my own way. As queen, as my mother's favourite sister, as the most powerful Ignitia in the realm.

So, as I watch the plumes of smoke curling upward towards the patch of blue sky far above, I say a silent prayer for her soul and hope that Vesta can hear me.

Suddenly, without warning, the smoke is forced back down the mouth of the volcano, engulfing the throne room. The air is dense and acrid, and I choke on it. Everyone is screaming, courtiers reduced to blurred shapes.

Another gust, and I can no longer see my hand in front of my face. I'm buffeted from side to side, crying out as figures barrel into me in their desperation to escape.

Panic takes over. Screams fill my ears.

Then, slinking through the haze, comes a voice. Smooth as silk, soft as breath, chilling me to my core.

Hello, little dove.

2

Flint

Shit. This can't be good.

Fear lances through me as the pungent fumes pour into my mouth. My eye smarts and stings, tearing up and spilling over, obscuring my vision even further.

I was watching Blaze in the seconds before the attack, several rows back from the dais, standing with her shoulders curved inwards, face hidden by that veil, gazing up at the sky. But now the world has turned grey, and I've lost her in the smoke.

The crackling flames from the pyre writhe wildly. Harglade fire – hungry and merciless, streaks of burning red across a charcoal canvas. The heat is ferocious.

A familiar tremor takes hold. My palms slicken. My heart beats out of time.

No, I tell myself. *Not now. Snap out of it. Concentrate.*

Streams of air carry King Balen's voice around the throne room. I can hear it over – no, *through* – the screams. It slices apart the din, slipping into the spaces between sounds.

I hear Grandmother too, hollering at the guards, 'Find her! Find her now!'

The words jolt me into action and I begin to move, inhaling more smoke each time I cough. Someone – I think it's Seraphine – is calling my name, but the voice is directionless and I don't stop, don't turn round, just keep stumbling blindly towards where I think the edge of the dais should be . . . and go tumbling over it.

Ouch.

I let out a grunt of pain as I push myself up, throat raw, breathing ragged.

Blaze, I think. *Where are you?*

The Etheri are charging like cattle towards the doors. I squint through the smoke, grabbing hold of arms, peering into faces.

'*Blaze*,' I hiss. 'Bla– Argh!' I cry out as I collide headlong into someone standing stock-still, as if paralysed with fright, or indecision, or both.

'Flint?'

'Blaze!' I exhale in relief as I grip her shoulders. 'There you are.' Then I take off, dragging her after me through the crowd.

King Balen's voice slithers through the tumult once more.

I know you're here, little dove.

I slam into the wall, holding Blaze's hand tightly as we feel our way towards the back of the throne room. I practically grew up at Fire Mountain, so I know all the best hiding spots, secret doors and hidden passageways. This particular passageway is used by the attendants. My friends Cole and Elaith and I discovered it years ago. I can't count the number of times we've used it to help ourselves to various desserts and bottles of wine.

Come out, come out, wherever you are.

Blaze rips off her veil and presses it to her nose. I scrabble for purchase until my fingers finally close round a stone lever, wrenching it down with all my might. A section of the wall shudders, then grinds slowly to one side, and I yank Blaze through. The deafening din is cut off as the door slides shut, the dense smoke replaced by cool, clean air.

My sister is on her hands and knees, retching, spitting out globs of grey saliva. Her voice is cracked, dried up. 'Is . . . he . . . here?'

I've been wondering the same thing. Would King Balen really risk attacking the Ignitia Court in person, or has he sent the wind in his stead? I'll say this for him: he can certainly pick his moments. Seriously, crashing a *funeral*? Talk about disrespect.

'We have to go, Flint,' Blaze chokes out, her face streaked with soot. 'Now. We have to stick to the plan.'

I grimace as I drag a hand across my streaming eye. Of all my sister's hare-brained ideas, I'm ranking this somewhere near the top. 'All right, follow me.'

I lead the way down the winding passage. Elaith once got lost down here for *hours*, just like she did in the maze at the Golden Palace. My best friend has many admirable qualities, but a sense of direction is not one of them. Nor is blending in – not with that fiery hair of hers. I spotted her standing behind Blaze during the funeral. I hope she makes it out safely. No, scratch that. She *will* make it out safely, for I refuse to consider any alternative.

A cluster of attendants gawk at us as we burst into the kitchens. They're all wielding pots, pans and knives, as though such things could protect them against smoke and wind.

I reach into my pocket and lay some coins on one of the stone countertops. 'You didn't see us here,' I say firmly, before heading for the large hatch in the corner of the room and heaving it open. This is where they get rid of all the scraps – leftovers, vegetable peelings, food that's gone stale. I turn to my sister. 'Are you sure about this?'

Grey eyes stare back at me, clear and determined. 'Yes.'

'Because if you're not, now's the time to say.'

Blaze sticks her chin in the air. 'I'm sure.'

'And *I'm* sure I'm going to regret it,' I mutter.

She ignores me, gathering up her skirts and climbing into the scrap chute.

'The space is narrow,' I tell her. 'Don't panic. Keep your arms pinned to your sides and brace yourself for landing. I'll be right behind you.'

She nods, gritting her teeth.

'Ready?' I ask.

Suddenly there's a clatter, followed by a furious, terrified voice. '*STOP*.'

We turn to find Grandmother panting hard, leaning heavily on her stick, wisps of silver-streaked dark hair slipping free of the red netting at the back of her neck. She points a finger at us, and on it I see the Harglade signet ring, shaped like a coiled cobra.

'Stop,' she orders again.

I open my mouth to speak, but Blaze gets there first. 'No.'

'*Blaze*,' Grandmother growls.

That tone still has the power to make me squirm in my boots, but Blaze doesn't flinch.

Grandmother turns to me. 'I'm surprised at you, Flint. Letting your sister put herself at risk like this, knowing just how much danger she's in.'

A low blow.

'I don't *let* her do anything,' I snap. 'She's her own person. Besides, she outranks us both now.'

Grandmother seems to deflate. 'Please,' she says. 'Stay. Whatever it is, whatever you think you have to do, we'll find another way.'

There's a long pause.

But Blaze only shakes her head. 'There is no other way.' Her voice is unsteady, but it softens as she adds, 'I'm not a child any more. You can't hide me away forever.'

A tear rolls down Grandmother's cheek. I watch it drip on to the flagstones.

Then, to my surprise, she steps back.

The look Blaze gives her is one of fierce, pure love. She glances at me one last time before disappearing down the chute. I have to hand it to her – the girl has pluck. Or a death wish. One of the two.

'I'll take care of her, Grandmother,' I say. 'I swear it.'

But the words ring hollow – less a promise than wishful thinking. Because the truth is, I'm not sure I'm capable of protecting anyone. Not any more.

I swallow hard, then plaster on a grin, tipping an imaginary cap to Grandmother before launching myself into the darkness after my sister.

3

Blaze

I hurtle downwards, each breath-stealing second carrying me further away from Grandmother, and from the expression on her face that nearly tore me in two.

Forgive me, I think.

Then I bury the guilt deep, refusing to let even the slightest crack show in my untarnished resolve. I know what I have to do.

The chute is slimy and smells *bad*, but it's a mercy compared with the acrid smoke of the throne room. King Balen's voice still echoes in my ears, a threat wrapped in silk.

The angle of the chute grows steadily steeper until I'm almost vertical, shooting towards the pinprick of light far below, pressure building and popping in my ears.

I tuck in my limbs and pray to every God I can think of – and more – that they haven't brought forward the daily incineration of the debris waiting at the bottom.

Because that could pose a problem, Flint had said. *And by problem, I mean imminent and agonizing death.*

There's a brief sensation of weightlessness as I emerge from the other end, suspended momentarily in mid-air before landing face-first in a mountainous pile of rotting food. I've barely had time to gag before Flint comes crashing down on top of me, letting out a high-pitched yelp, followed by a whoop.

'We did it,' he says, a browning banana peel stuck to his cheek.

'We did,' I agree, managing a shaky grin.

Together we scramble down the mound of kitchen waste, our clothes smeared with pulp and gravy and entrails.

A boy is waiting for us in the stables, Flint's bow and two sets of reins in his hands. The horses he's selected are not the large, snow-white, red-maned creatures belonging to the Court of Flames, but two brown mares, who nicker softly as we approach. Our supplies are stowed in a pair of leather satchels fastened to the gleaming saddles.

The stable hand frowns as he takes in the sight of us. 'Food fight?'

Panting, Flint shakes his head, slinging his bow and a quiver of arrows over his shoulder. 'We came down the scrap chute. There was an attack by the Ventalla King. Everyone else is still inside. They'll need help – water, bandages.'

He holds out a hand to help me mount the smaller of the two horses, but I bat him away impatiently before sticking my foot in the stirrup and heaving myself up.

'Thank you, Caleb,' Flint says, swinging himself on to the other horse. 'I'm in your debt.'

Caleb hands him the reins. 'Anything for you.'

'Anything?' I hear the smirk in his voice.

'*Flint*,' I hiss, incredulous.

'Fair point, sister. Time and place.'

Caleb stands aside and cocks his head towards the stable doors. 'You know, if you two die out there, they'll burn me alive.'

'Not planning on it,' I tell him, digging my heels into my horse's flank.

The clopping of hooves echoes loudly on the cobblestones as Flint and I turn our backs on Fire Mountain and set off across the barren plains.

I gaze out at the endless rocky wasteland and breathe it in – the scent of hot stone, fresh air and freedom. For this is the first time I've ever been anywhere not trapped behind walls, stuck inside a carriage, or surrounded by guards.

This is the first time I've ever been *free*.

The horse is fast and sure-footed, and I grip on tightly with my knees, half exhilarated, half expecting to lose my balance and go tumbling to the ground. My hair has come loose from its braids, dark curls streaming behind me, and when the ghost of a smile tugs at my lips, I let it bloom there. Riding feels like flying, and I like it.

We travel at lightning speed, Flint occasionally shouting instructions about my posture or my grasp on the reins, and constantly craning to look over his shoulder as we skirt bustling towns and villages. Eventually, when he's confident that we're not being followed, we slow the horses to a gentle walk. Flint reaches into one of the leather satchels and pulls out a waterskin, which he tosses to me. I catch it clumsily with both hands, letting go of the reins in the process.

'We'll make an equestrian of you yet,' my brother says as I lean down and grab them again.

I flip open the stopper of the waterskin and take a long drink. The back of my throat still burns from the smoke.

'How's your eye?' I ask Flint.

'Lonely,' he replies.

We soon reach a cluster of rocks a short distance from a gurgling hot spring. Flint slides nimbly from his horse and walks round to help me.

'Stop fussing,' I say, ignoring his outstretched arms as I swing myself down.

Only my legs feel as though they've turned to liquid, and give way as soon as my feet hit the ground. Flint sniggers. This time, I accept his hand.

'*Ouch*,' I say, registering the dull ache in my limbs, the stiffness of my hips.

'You'll get used to it.'

'Speaking of riding,' I begin as we lead the horses into the cool shadow of the rocks, 'what's with you and the stable boy?'

Flint stares at me. 'Really? That's what's going on in there?' He raps his knuckles against my head. 'We're currently fugitives after narrowly escaping an attack by King Balen, and you're thinking about me and the stable boy?'

I shrug. 'Just wondering.'

Flint drains his waterskin. 'He's a friend.'

'*Just* a friend?'

'I have lots of friends, sister. I'm a friendly boy, well known for my friendliness.'

I roll my eyes.

'Though it is true that Caleb and I enjoy a particularly close friendship,' he continues. 'You could say we know each other rather well. Intimately, in fact.'

'What about Spinner?' I ask, feeling somewhat defensive of my friend and former chaperone, who fell head over heels for my brother during our time at the Golden Palace.

'What about her? I adore her, of course I do, but we're not *married*.'

As if in response, my horse lets out a disapproving snort. Smiling, I reach up to stroke her silky muzzle. A memory jolts through me, almost knocking me off balance.

This is Cedar.

He's beautiful.

He is, but he's not why I brought you here.

I drop my hand, the Earth Cleaver's voice still echoing in my ears.

Though it was a celebration for many, news of his exile filled me with nothing but dread. For he may be callous and arrogant and sometimes cruel, but he also understands what I have to do, better than anyone. And he seems to understand *me* – more than I care to admit.

I can't help but wonder where he is. Drinking his days away at the card tables of Katteran? Sailing the Second Sea? He may have been banished from Ostacre, but try as I might, I cannot banish him from my mind. He lives there now, taking root among my thoughts, colouring them green. Does he dream of me, just as I dream of him?

Oblivious to my musings, Flint opens the satchels and begins laying out our supplies – another waterskin, enough food to last several days if we're careful, blankets, oats for the horses, chalk, a coin purse, a map, a bar of soap, bandages, burn salve, painkillers, my nightlight from Hal, a bundle of clothes and two pairs of leather riding boots.

'Was that really necessary?' I ask as Flint produces a bottle of wildfire wine from the bottom of the second satchel.

'Yes,' he says, wiggling an arrowhead into the cork and twisting it round.

It loosens with a muffled *thunk*, and Flint throws it at me. I manage to catch it, then glance down at my grimy palm, suddenly conscious of how filthy we are.

'Stand up,' I instruct.

Flint takes a gulp of wine. 'Why?'

'Just do it.'

He sets down the bottle and gets to his feet.

'Move a few paces over there.'

My brother exchanges a look with the horses but does as I say. 'Well? What is it?' He folds his arms expectantly, then yelps as he's drenched by a shower of rain.

I toss him the bar of soap. 'You're welcome.'

Grumbling, Flint shucks off his doublet and trousers until he's standing in his undershorts, and scrubs himself clean. 'You couldn't make it a bit warmer, could you?'

I shake my head. 'Still haven't figured out how to simmer, I'm afraid.'

He hands me the soap when he's done, and I follow suit, placing Renly's little figurine carefully atop a shelf of rock before moving to stand under the cool shower. Flint feeds and waters the horses, and we sit in the sun to dry off.

'So,' he says through a mouthful of bread and cheese. 'Let's go over the plan.'

I spread the map out between us, pinning the corners down with stones.

The Windlands are at the very top of the empire, as far north as you can go. The Firelands sit just below, bordering the Wildlands, which in turn border the Waterlands, occupying the south of Ostacre. Beyond the Aquatori kingdom lies nothing but the treacherous, azure waters of the Second Sea.

When I threw the Eye into Queen Hydra's portal, I wasn't thinking about where I was sending it, only that I needed to get it as far away from King Balen as possible. Yet I realized that if its location was determined by my subconscious, then it must be somewhere of significance. I spent weeks poring over the possibilities, until eventually it came to me.

The Lagoon.

The Aquatori court at the foot of the Waterlands. Where better to send the Eye than my future home, a place Queen Hydra called her haven? And what better way to earn my crown than by finding the talisman she died protecting?

The plan itself is fairly simple. It's pulling it off that's going to be the tricky part.

'Are you sure you want to go *through* the Ridge?' Flint asks, handing me his empty waterskin. 'Because I still think the Creek is our best bet for, you know, *surviving*.'

I sigh. 'We've been over this. If we go by boat, we'll be expected to present our identification papers at each checkpoint. We're hardly going to slip by unnoticed.'

'Ah, yes,' says Flint, reaching out to catch his full waterskin as I throw it back to him. 'The new Queen of the Aquatori and her dashing, half-blind brother. You're right, sister mine. Blending in never has been our strong suit.'

I roll my eyes as I help myself to a plum.

Our plan is to travel to the province of Isolla, which sits in the shadow of the Ridge – the red sandstone mountain range that stretches along the border between Queen Yvainne's lands and Queen Aspen's. Though now, I suppose, Ember's lands and . . . well, *not* Fox's. Perhaps Hal, as the new emperor, will award the Terrathian crown to Amaryllis instead. She was the runner-up, after all.

I think of the way Fox had toyed with her before his vines found purchase, dragging her through a field of nettles and stringing her up like a puppet, pulling tighter and tighter until I heard the sharp *pop* of her shoulder dislocating.

I gasp in pain as I bite right through the fruit and into my tongue. Clearing my throat before Flint can ask me what's wrong, I offer a weak 'We'll be fine.'

'Funny, I thought Caius Castellion had the Eye of the Future,' Flint says dryly. 'How can you possibly know that we won't lose our way and wander through the Ridge tunnels until we meet a very claustrophobic, very underwhelming end? *Or* get eaten alive by whatever terrifying creatures are said to live there. Snakes? Fire ants? Five-foot flesh-eating spiders? I'd rather not lose another body part, if it's all the same to you.'

'Not going to happen,' I say with far more confidence than I feel.

Once dry, we dress in the Fidra clothes Caleb managed to source for us. Fidra – those without magic – are easily distinguishable from Etheri, as they do not wear an elemental court colour. This way, we'll be able to slip under the radar. The shirts are scratchy but clean, the trousers ill-fitting, the riding boots scuffed and well worn.

Flint wrinkles his nose. 'I suspect someone may have died in this,' he says, fastening the buttons on his leather jerkin.

'You're as bad as Spinner.'

'If by that you mean I have excellent taste in clothes, then I agree with you.'

I roll up a cloak and stuff it into my satchel before tossing him the other. He catches it reluctantly, then bends down to retrieve his soiled red doublet, stroking the gold embroidery wistfully.

'Your sacrifice is noted,' I tell him, prising it from his hands and tossing it on top of my gown. 'Now, I think you should burn them.'

Flint turns away, fiddling with the arrows in his sheaf.

I frown. 'Hello? Flint? We don't want to leave a trace.'

'We also don't want to draw attention,' he says a little stiffly, swiping the clothes back and concealing them behind a large boulder.

I shrug. 'Have it your way.'

Together we pack up our supplies and set off again, riding until the sun dips low. Flint finds us a cave, and I wrap my arms round myself, my stillness making me suddenly aware of the chill in the air. That's the thing about the Firelands – scorching-hot days, icy-cold nights – both extremes having been intensified by the slaughter of the Council, which angered the elements in ways never seen before.

'Aren't you going to light a fire?' I ask my brother. 'It's freezing.' I huff out a breath for emphasis and point at the misty cloud.

But Flint shakes his head.

'Flint, we're in the middle of nowhere. There's *nobody* around.'

'You don't know that,' he says. 'Now, stop yacking. I need my beauty sleep.'

I lie down, huddled beneath my cloak, listening to the sound of crickets, the nickering of the horses, the occasional eruption of steam from a distant hot spring. For some reason, I can't seem to keep my eyes closed. I gaze out at the sliver of night sky visible through the narrow mouth of the cave.

Night.

I think of night, and I think of my former serf, Elva. Her homeland, Obsidia. The darkness that filled my chambers, lit only by an orb of light cast by the boy cradling her in his arms. The dull gut-punch of betrayal as realization dawned on me.

I wonder if Elva has told Hal the truth – that ever since I unknowingly returned the powers of her ancestors to her using the Eye of the Soul, she is no longer Fidra.

She is a Mage. A *Shadow* Mage.

My breath curls upward in silver clouds. I nestle closer to Flint.

How will Hal and Elva navigate this, I wonder? There's a cruel irony to it – an aching, hopeless sort of beauty that reminds me of the tales my mother told me as a child. But how can this one possibly have a happy ending when it is a story about what happens when light falls in love with darkness? How can they ever coexist, when one consumes the other?

I don't pretend to know much about love, but to me, that sounds an awful lot like doom.

4

Elva

I can hear my heart beating.

It pummels at my ribcage. It keeps me awake. Condemns me to consciousness when all I seek is oblivion.

The sky is a deep, velvety black, peppered with pinprick stars.

If it weren't for the opulence of this bedchamber, or the raven-haired boy sleeping at my side, I could be a thousand miles away, gazing out at the eternal night of Obsidia.

I see it when I close my eyes. Our cottage, with its thatched roof and smoky fireplace, dozens of nightshine blooms snaking up the walls. Amma, humming softly while she prepares our evening meal. Stew, maybe. Or soup – beansprout and nettle – with fresh, salty bread. Papa, whittling perhaps, or chopping wood, or counting coppers – always doing something with his hands. My older sister, Astrid, singing quietly to herself, one hand stroking Kjara, our moon panther, stretched out peacefully at my feet.

I try to ration my memories. I keep them contained, like birds in cages, and only open them one at a time. It's easier this way. In small doses they sustain me. I live off them.

But lately I've found myself consumed by thoughts of my family, of the life that was ripped away from me. Of who I was, and now, *what* I have become.

I used to dream about the Shadow Magi: my ancestors, with eyes that glowed like fallen stars, capable of wielding darkness so impenetrable it could swallow the sun. I was ten before I saw my first dawn. It broke around the same time as my heart – beams of light gilding the waves as the slave ship sailed across the Second Sea.

Nobody knows for certain why the Magi lost their magic all those years ago, just as I don't know why that magic was returned to me. All I do know is that if my secret were discovered, I wouldn't have long to wonder.

As if to taunt me, a tendril of shadow escapes from my fingertip. I ball my hands into fists, resisting the urge to shudder as fear rattles through me. I've always been frightened, for as long as I can remember.

Elva's afraid of her own shadow, Astrid used to say.

If only she knew how right she was.

My sister saw fear as a hindrance – something that needed to be stamped out.

Don't be such a baby, she'd hiss as I edged behind her, clutching her arm while the other children played, launching themselves from the rocks and into the starpools below. And when we returned home, Astrid soaking wet and glittering, me bone-dry and ashamed, my father would just smile in his quiet, gentle way and pretend not to notice.

It was my mother who would sit me on her lap, prise my hands from my face and murmur softly, *Don't shut fear out, Elva. Invite it in.*

I've tried to heed her advice – to welcome fear rather than cower from it, because fear is a response to danger. And sensing danger is key to survival.

The Earth Cleaver told me that if I wanted to survive, I'd better keep my mouth shut.

The day after my powers awoke, I remember coming to, surrounded by herbs and tinctures and vials of medicine. When I realized who was standing over me, I let out a piercing scream. He simply sighed and offered me a glass of water. Then he told me what happened. But not how. Or *why*.

Why now? Why *me*?

Hal mutters something unintelligible in his sleep and shifts his arm to cradle me. What would he say, I wonder, if he discovered that I am now . . . what? A Mage? A monster? He's a Castellion – they are the same in his eyes. I fear the truth would break him. Break *us*.

I swallow, willing away the lingering shadows, concentrating on his face. These past few weeks have taken their toll. He looks older than his twenty years.

When I slipped into his chambers to say goodnight, he kissed me like he needed me. So I stayed. It's risky, being with him like this. But as long as I'm back in the serf quarters before dawn, nobody should notice. Nobody except my bunkmate, Ingra, but she'll always cover for me, and she'd never betray me to Matron.

Matron is in charge of the palace serfs. Not much gets past her – she makes sure of that. Rewards for ratting out a fellow serf range from a fresh bedroll to an extra helping at supper, which many would do more than tell tales for. It's not that they starve us. We have enough to eat. But that's just it – *enough*, and no more. Meals are determined by our size and the nature of the labour we perform. Having inherited my mother's slender frame, and given that I am – or rather, *was* – personal serf to an Heir – meaning my duties didn't extend much beyond folding linen and braiding hair – my portions tend to make my plate look large. Of course, Hal slips me food whenever he can.

I thought I'd misheard Blaze the first time she offered to share her breakfast. Rather than feeling grateful, though, I felt guilty. She was kind, and undeserving of my deception. Yet Hal's plan, however unfair, was the perfect distraction. Their involvement provided a subterfuge, and both of them had just the right touch of shyness to make it believable. But then Blaze started to fall for him, and so every smile we shared was a sharp twist of the knife. Only the knife was buried in *her* back, not mine.

Even still, she forgave me.

When I heard about the attack on Fire Mountain, my first thought was of her. But Hal has since received reports that the Storm Weaver was unharmed, and that she and her brother will soon be moved to a safe house. In just a few weeks, Blaze's life has turned full circle. It doesn't matter that she won the Aquatori crown – she's just as confined as she has been for the last seventeen years. Trapped by circumstance, like me. Except now . . .

You could go home.

That's what she said to me, and she was right.

After the Binding Ceremony, once he'd regained the ability to form a sentence, Hal, as the new emperor, offered me a ship, as much gold as I could carry, and said that if anyone tried to stop me, he would have them killed.

I am free, and yet, here I am.

There are three reasons why I chose to remain in Ostacre.

The first is that if I were to go home, I'm afraid of what I might find there. Or worse, what I might not find. When the slavers came ashore, they set my village aflame, snatching the children and slaughtering any who stood in their way. My parents are long dead. As for Astrid, she was put on board a different ship – only she never arrived in Ostacre with the rest of the serfs, meaning she didn't survive the journey across the Second Sea. And without my family, there's nothing left for me in Obsidia. Nothing but bones and memories.

The second is that I cannot bring myself to abandon Ingra and the others. I will never truly be free until they are too.

Hal always secretly intended to find a way to liberate the serfs, long before he met me. To do what his father did not, and undo what his grandfather did all those years ago. Sometimes I wonder how someone like him was ever born into a family like *that*. Yet the timing of King Balen's betrayal has thwarted Hal's plans to end serfdom. His advisers will not hear of it. His reign is already being called into question. He has no one to support him.

Which brings me to my third reason . . .

I stroke my thumb along Hal's forearm. His father is dead, his half-brother responsible, and his uncle is intent on taking his throne. How can I leave him now, after everything? He is utterly lost. He needs me, and I . . .

I *love* him.

I wish I didn't. I tried not to. I hate myself for it. But I do.

What would the other serfs think of me if they found out about us? How could I even begin to defend myself? By telling them Hal is different? That he is good? Nothing I say would change the fact that he is their enemy. So what does that make me?

I'm so tangled up in my thoughts that I don't notice the slight shift in his breathing, and I start as he whispers, 'Can't sleep?'

I shake my head.

'Hm. Maybe I could read to you from one of my father's old trading ledgers? That'd do the trick.'

Hal's eyes are still closed, his voice husky with remnants of sleep. He's not fully awake yet – I can tell because he's smiling. I watch him remember, his smile faltering then falling, the weight of an empire crashing back down upon his shoulders.

'Hal –'

'I'm fine.' Lie. 'It's fine.' Another lie.

I don't press him. I turn on to my side so that we're face-to-face, and rest my hand on his cheek. Hal closes his eyes again, leaning into my touch. Even now, his features heavy with sleep and pain, he is beautiful.

I glance out of the window at the sky beginning to lighten. It won't be long before dawn arrives.

'I have to go soon.'

'Don't,' he murmurs. 'Stay.'

'I can't. You know that.'

A pause. 'It won't always be like this.'

'I know,' I say, though I don't – not really. We are both of us changed. The future is uncertain. It scares me even more than the past.

I kiss him once, lightly, then slide out of bed and pull on my white tunic and boots.

The solid-gold floor gleams in the waning moonlight. Hal is still living in his old chambers. He has no wish to move into his father's quarters, not while his death is so fresh. There's also the fact that Lady Kestrel Calloway, Imperial Mistress and mother to the Earth Cleaver, refuses to leave the emperor's rooms. She is, by all accounts, inconsolable. She barely sleeps, will not speak to anyone, won't eat. The serfs bring her trays of food, which remain untouched. One of the girls, Shireen, swiped a peach, thinking Matron wouldn't notice. Her foolishness cost her two days in the Pit.

'I have to go,' I say again, but Hal catches hold of my hand.

'Promise me you'd tell me if anything was wrong?' He laughs, short and hollow. 'What am I saying? What isn't wrong? Nothing about any of this is right. I just meant, you'd tell me if anything's . . . changed?'

I can hear the words he doesn't say ringing loudly in the silence.

Between us.

I don't answer, tracing the lines on his palm.

'Elva?' Soft, almost pleading.

'Of course I would.'

The lie burns my tongue. There are too many secrets. We are an ocean apart, he and I, and he doesn't even know it.

Gently, I break the bridge of our joined hands and edge behind the screen. There, I press my shoulder into a portion of the wall, which swings open. Hal whispers something into the darkness, but I don't catch it before the door snicks shut behind me.

The serf tunnels are dank and dark, but I ignore the torch crackling in a bracket. I have no need for it any more.

Ever since the shadow magic of my ancestors was returned to me, I can . . . well, I can see in the dark. And I don't just mean I have a better sense of direction or can make out shapes amid the gloom. I mean that I can see, fully, perfectly, in complete darkness. It's difficult to explain. There's no invisible spotlight. There's no light whatsoever. The dark doesn't lessen or recede. It's still there, surrounding me. Only, I can see *through* it. I slip between it, just another shadow. I'm part of it now.

After what feels like an age, I emerge from the tunnel near the kitchens. The cramped corridor is empty. Everyone is in bed. I move silently through the passageway until I reach my room – a space no larger than a few square feet, furnished with two wooden boards sticking out of the wall. Ingra sleeps on the bottom one, I on the top.

The moment I creep inside, Ingra opens one eye like a cat, smiling conspiratorially.

'Well, if it isn't fair Irabella returned from seeing her Emmeric. Tell me, how is loverboy this evening? I do hope he earned his keep.'

The Tragedy of Emmeric and Irabella was a play performed for the Court of Eyes by a travelling theatre troupe called the Bronze Buckle some years back. Ingra and I were both serving wine at the time, and so we got to watch along with everyone else. It was a tale of two lovers: rich, handsome Emmeric and poor, beautiful Irabella, who fell in love against the odds and sacrificed everything to be together. Only, Emmeric was cursed by a witch who'd lost everything at the hands of his scheming family. Hence, the tragedy.

Ingra doesn't know that the Emmeric to whom she refers is none other than the former Crown Prince, now emperor, of Ostacre.

I reach up to the top bunk and pull back my bedroll to reveal the assortment of rags beneath, all bunched together to give the appearance of a human silhouette, just in case Matron had decided to check on us.

'Thank you, Ingra. I owe you.'

'Don't mention it,' she says, waving her hand dismissively, her long honey-brown hair spilling off the side of the bed in a thick braid.

I step on the edge of her bunk and pull myself up on to my own, finally allowing myself to exhale as I lie down and close my eyes.

What feels like minutes later, the bell begins to clang.

5

Flint

'I spy with my little eye something beginning with . . .' I pause, searching for inspiration, which is notably lacking given that we're crossing a barren stone plain. 'With . . . H.'

Blaze ignores me. After almost a week of nothing but, well, *nothing*, she is tired, bored and very, very irritable.

I, too, am tired, bored and irritable. I'm also in quite a bit of pain. My burns aren't faring well in this heat, and the searing ache in my left eye never lets up. Yet despite all that, and how unappealing I suspect I look in these drab Fidra clothes, I'm trying to stay positive. They say problems should be tackled head-on, but I find that my problems are best left alone. Ignore them for long enough and you can pretend they don't exist.

'Come on, sister,' I urge. 'Play the game.'

When Blaze does speak it is through gritted teeth. '*Flint*.'

'Doesn't begin with H, I'm afraid. And to think you're supposed to be the clever one.'

'I'm not in the mood.'

'Just one guess,' I wheedle. 'Go on, it's easy.'

'*Fine.*' Blaze half closes her eyes and takes a deep breath. 'Fine. Horse.'

'Incorrect.'

'Hot spring.'

'Nope.'

I almost cower beneath her glare. Sometimes, she really does remind me of Grandmother.

'Oh, you want a word beginning with H?' Her voice is ice. 'How about hungry?'

Ah. I thought she might've moved on from our little spat this morning after I'd accidentally polished off the last of the food. It seems I was wrong.

Blaze isn't finished. 'Or how about horribly behind schedule?'

'That's three words,' I point out.

A jet of cold water shoots straight into my chest.

'How thoughtful you are, sister mine,' I splutter, shaking my head like a dog. 'I was melting in this heat.'

Blaze snarls.

'All right.' I hold my hands up in surrender. 'All right, I'll shut up.'

The next hour or so passes in silence.

'How much further?' Blaze asks eventually, flexing her wrists.

'Not long now.'

'Flint, are you sure we're going the right way?'

I consult the map. We're currently crossing Danath, which borders Isolla – the province sitting in the shadow of the Ridge.

'Well,' I say, squinting at the markings etched on to the parchment, 'if my calculations are correct, I think we'll arrive in Isolla by nightfall.'

'And if they aren't correct?'

I shrug. 'Then we're lost.'

'Brilliant.'

'How about you be the navigator, sister? I'm sure you could get us there no problem, what with your wealth of experience travelling the empire.'

Blaze holds up a finger.

I shake my head. 'Shocking. Hardly the behaviour expected of a future queen.'

'*Flint*,' Blaze breathes suddenly.

'I know, I know, you *don't want to talk about it*,' I say, folding up the map and tucking it back into my satchel. 'I get it. I do. It's a big change and –'

'No, Flint –'

'Really, it's perfectly understandable that you –'

'*FLINT*.' Blaze's voice is urgent, excited.

I glance up, frowning. 'What?'

'Look!'

I follow the direction of her finger. There, far in the distance, barely distinguishable against the clouds, is the hazy outline of mountains. Hundreds of them, dark red in colour and stretching across the horizon as far as the eye can see.

The Ridge – the border between the Firelands and the Wildlands.

I punch the air, triumphant. 'See! What'd I tell you?'

Blaze smiles. 'I take it all back.'

'And?'

'And I'm sorry for ever doubting you.'

I bow my head. 'Apology accepted. Now, come on. I'm starving.'

'You're always starving,' she says, nudging her horse onward.

By the time the sun starts painting the sky pink, the rumbling of my stomach can be heard above the clopping hooves. Smoke curls from the chimneys of the little stone cottages fringing the outskirts of Isolla, which gradually increase in both size and number as we ride through the winding streets. The noise in the centre is deafening – merchants and traders haggling at full volume, the hiss of molten metal as it meets water, children laughing and squealing as they dart through the throngs of people and pens filled with livestock.

Blaze's eyes are wide as she slides from her horse, fascinated. This rather mundane scene must seem like a whole new world to her. I dismount too, gathering my reins and leading the way on foot. We agreed to sell the horses once we got to Isolla. There's no way we'll be able to take them with us through the Ridge tunnels.

'You stay here,' I say as we untether the satchels from our saddles. I pull the hood of Blaze's cloak up over her head. 'And be careful.'

She nods, her expression bright with excitement. Leaving her to eagerly peruse the market stalls, I head off in search of someone to take the horses off our hands, taunted all the while by the glorious smells wafting from the various inns and alehouses lining the square. My burns are smarting and my limbs are heavy. Every part of me feels bruised. All I want in this moment is a hot meal and a proper bed. Perhaps a bottle of wine. Anything to take my mind off the fact that tomorrow I will be walking straight into the depths of a snake-infested mountain in order to chase some enchanted relic that I'm still not *entirely* sure isn't just a figment of my sister's imagination.

The first trader I approach is a small, balding Fidra man who waves me off, uninterested. The second, a woman dressed in strange, expensive-looking robes, shakes her head and says something in a language I don't understand. Vosti, I think. Blaze would know.

On my third attempt, the trader looks me up and down before walking round the horses, inspecting their teeth and hooves, then offers me six pieces of silver.

'*Six?* They're worth double that.'

The man snorts. 'Not a chance. Call it seven and we have a deal.'

'Nine.'

'I said seven, boy. Take it or leave it.'

I cross my arms. 'Eight.'

He considers. I try not to salivate as a girl walks past carrying a platter of roasted meat. Then the trader says, 'Very well. Eight it is.'

Smiling triumphantly, I pocket the silver and head back towards the corner of the square where I left Blaze. Only when I arrive, she's nowhere to be seen. I swallow my unease as I whip my head back and forth. I suspect she's just wandered into the centre of it all, caught up in the colourful chaos of Isolla. I adjust my satchel and plunge into the throng of travellers, tourists and traders, my good eye scanning the square for her face. Where is she? *Why* did I let her out of my sight, even for a few minutes? Panic rises, hot and clawing.

A cloaked figure stands a few yards to my right. My heart leaps.

'Blaze?' I curse myself as soon as her name leaves my mouth, but no one around me pays any attention. I try again, pushing my way through the crowd. '*Blaze?*' I almost let out a sob of relief as I feel someone tap me on the shoulder. '*There* you are.'

'Here I am.' My sister looks extremely pleased with herself as she holds aloft what appears to be a small bronze ball on a stick. 'It's a toffee apple,' she says, eyes shining.

I exhale slowly. 'I can see that.'

Blaze is undeterred. 'I bought it, just now, at one of those stalls over there.'

I raise an eyebrow, bemused. Blaze only beams. I'm about to ask her why she's acting like a five-year-old, and then I get it. She *feels* like one.

I've often wondered how she didn't go mad, shut up for all those years – first at Bartell Manor, then Harglade Hall. She was robbed of any kind of childhood because of something she did when she was barely a day old. I think of the cities I've seen, the courts I've visited. I think of the countless times I've walked into Valburn to do something as ordinary as buy a toffee apple, and I'm overcome with the urge to hug my sister.

'Come on,' I say, slinging an arm round her shoulder. 'Let's find some supper.'

We push into the heaving alehouse, the air hot from the oven fires and thick with drunken voices. Nobody gives us a second glance as we shove our way to an empty table. I toss the barmaid a piece of silver and she returns minutes later with two heaped plates and a flagon of wildfire wine. Ravenous, I fall on the food, pausing only to refill my glass.

Blaze drums her gloved fingers on the table, chewing thoughtfully.

'What?' I ask through a mouthful of guinea fowl.

'I'm just trying to remember everything I've ever read about the Ridge tunnels.'

'Well, make sure you do,' I say, pointing a bone at her, 'because, no pressure and all, but our lives depend on it.'

Blaze knocks the bone out of my hand with her fork. At that moment, a voice sounds close behind us.

'. . . the Harglade twins, Flint and Blaze.'

We both freeze.

'They survived, then?'

'It would seem so.'

I allow myself an infinitesimal sigh of relief – we're not being addressed, but rather discussed, and the group of Ignitia sharing a bowl of broth seem completely oblivious to the fact that the very people they're talking about are sitting a mere five feet away.

'I heard they've been moved to a safe house.'

Blaze makes to whisper something to me, but I tap a finger to my lips and lean back in my chair to listen to the rest of the conversation.

'And what about the Crowned Council?'

'They're not crowned yet, though I imagine they'll be summoned to the palace. Haldyn Castellion needs all the help he can get. By all accounts, the boy's too soft. And then, of course, there's his half-brother, who's quite the opposite.'

'Queenslayer,' one man mutters venomously. 'I heard he fled to Zafar.'

'Well, *I* heard he was spotted in a whorehouse in Katteran.'

My sister swallows, frowning slightly. I've been careful not to ask her too much about the Earth Cleaver and their . . . what? Alliance? Friendship? There seems to be no correct term for whatever strange connection exists between them. Blaze only told me what I needed to know about Fox Calloway Castellion and his part in all this. Yet despite what he saw with the Eye of the Past, his actions still proved fatal – to his father, to the Council, to my aunt, who I have still not allowed myself to grieve for. And though I'd never say it out loud, I'm glad he's gone. The further away he is from my sister, the better.

'Perhaps it was Prince Haldyn he meant to kill and not the emperor?'

'Some believe they were working together – the Storm Weaver and the Earth Cleaver. That they planned to assassinate both the old Council and the new.'

Blaze makes a sound I can only describe as a squawk of rage. I shake my head in warning and reach over to top up her glass. I can still hardly believe that there are those out there who think she plotted to kill the Council – and with *the Earth Cleaver*, no less.

Then again, sometimes I forget that Blaze is two people. To me, she is my twin, the girl who has a cat called Mouse and reads thousand-page history books for fun. But to them, she is an anomaly, a *threat*. She may be the rightful leader of the Aquatori, but that doesn't mean she's become any more trusted, or any less feared. Her transition to sovereignty is not going to be an easy one. She has avoided the subject for weeks. At first, I thought it was for my benefit, but now I'm not so sure. I think she's scared. I think she focused so much on winning her crown that she forgot about wearing it.

'Listen, only three people know what really happened at the Binding Ceremony. Perhaps what the Storm Weaver claims is true. But then again, perhaps it isn't. There are many who believe it was she who attacked King Balen, and not the other way round.'

Blaze, who has just taken a large gulp of wine, lets it trickle slowly back out of her mouth and into the glass. I pat her arm sympathetically. I'd assumed, perhaps naively, that if she had Hal's support, the people would accept her version of events. But these men are right – there are only three people who know exactly what happened that day. One is a monster, the second is exiled, and the third is sitting opposite me with a face like thunder.

Stony silence stretches on long after the men have paid up and left the alehouse.

Eventually, Blaze clears her throat. 'So that was a bit of a kick in the teeth.'

'I must congratulate you on your restraint,' I tell her. 'I was half expecting you to freeze their tongues like you did with Cole.'

'I was tempted.'

'Forget them,' I soothe. 'People are frightened. They don't know what to believe.'

'And that's exactly what King Balen wants, Flint,' she says bitterly. 'To sow doubt. If the people already thought I was guilty, then the news that you and I are in hiding is hardly going to convince them otherwise.'

'About that.' I lean in closer. 'If word hasn't got out about our incredibly daring escape' – my sister rolls her eyes – 'then Grandmother must be doing a pretty good job of pretending that we are wherever she claims we are. How's she managed to pull that off?'

Blaze considers this. 'If we hadn't been seen at all in the wake of the attack, we'd surely be presumed dead.'

I frown. 'But they don't think we're dead. They think we're at a safe house.'

'Exactly. Meaning that Grandmother must've made sure we were glimpsed leaving Fire Mountain.'

I take another swig of wine. 'All right, you've lost me.'

'My decoy, Flint,' Blaze says. 'She must be using my decoy. Gods, that poor girl had no idea what she was getting herself into.'

'Oh. *Oh*. Typical Grandmother.' I shake my head, suppressing a smile. Then I pause. 'Wait. What about me?'

'She must've found one for you, too.'

'And gouged his eye out for authenticity?'

Blaze grimaces. 'I wouldn't put it past her.'

We spend the rest of the meal prodding at what remains of our food. The bustle and vibrance of Isolla that had so captivated my sister appear to have worn off. Her brow is furrowed, jaw clenched. She could use some sleep. Both of us could – and in actual beds rather than huddled together on the cold stone ground.

'We should get out of here,' Blaze says eventually.

'You read my mind. Let's find an inn. I'll even let you have the top bunk.'

'No, I mean we should get out of Isolla,' she explains. 'Now. Tonight. Ours seem to be the names on everyone's lips, and I think it's best we move on.'

I stare at her, aghast. 'But . . . we've been riding since dawn? I'm *exhausted*.'

'We can sleep once we've made it through the Ridge.'

I let out a long-suffering sigh, then get to my feet. 'The things I do for you, sister.'

6

Blaze

The tunnel entrance looms before us, a cavern of impenetrable darkness. I rummage in my satchel until my fingers graze the cool glass surface of the nightlight.

Think of it as your very own sunbeam, Hal had said, his hand wrapped round mine. *As though I'm giving you a little piece of my gift.*

'Let's go,' I say.

At the sound of my voice, the box lights up, illuminating the way ahead.

I take a step forward, then another, biting my tongue so hard I taste blood. Flint mutters something – a prayer, I think – before following me into the tunnel.

The nightlight glows brightly in the gloom, casting shadows across the walls. The ground is cracked and uneven.

I tense at a scraping sound behind me, but it's only Flint with the chalk, scoring a line on the stone. It seems sensible to mark our route, especially since the passageway soon forks into three.

'What now?' Flint whispers.

I shrug. 'Trial and error, I suppose. You choose.'

We walk in silence, Flint continuing to score the walls. Twice we're required to double back on ourselves when we hit a dead end. After a while, I lose track of how many left and right turns we've taken.

Hours pass. I wonder privately if we'll ever manage to find our way out on the other side of the Ridge, or if we'll be forced to give up and retrace our steps back to Isolla.

Flint stays close, nervously plucking the string of his bow like a harp.

'Are you all right?' I ask over my shoulder.

'Oh yes, Blaze. I'm having a brilliant time. And yourself?'

I choose to ignore his sarcasm. I'm not going to give him the satisfaction of admitting that yes, maybe we should have stayed the night in Isolla. Because in truth, I'm bone-tired. If it weren't for the thought of whatever flesh-eating creatures are said to roam these tunnels, I'd be tempted to find some quiet corner and curl up.

Time stretches on. It must be almost dawn by now.

All of a sudden, and despite the fact I haven't uttered a word, Flint shushes me and moves to stand at my side. He sniffs once, sharply, then grimaces.

'What is it?' I whisper, holding the nightlight a little higher.

He doesn't respond, only beckons for me to follow him. My answer is waiting for us at the next bend. A man – or what's left of one, anyway – sitting slumped against the wall, more bone than flesh. His clothes hang in tatters, stained the deep black of old blood. His nose is missing, as well as most of his fingers, and his chest is ripped open from abdomen to throat. The stench of rotting meat hangs heavy in the air, and I can't help but gag.

'Poor bastard,' Flint mutters.

'What do you suppose did this to him?' I ask weakly.

'I don't know,' says Flint darkly. 'But I'd rather not stick around to find out.' He takes my arm and hauls me away from the bloodied corpse.

It isn't long before the passageway opens out before us, becoming a wide, cavernous chamber. A single drop of water lands on my forehead. I'm so busy looking up at the ceiling that I don't notice what lies at my feet until a crunch echoes through the air.

Bones.

They litter the stone floor – some large, some small, some grey and crumbling, others white and gleaming and undoubtedly human.

'Flint,' I whisper, but he's already moved past me, bending down to examine something lying atop the sea of carcasses, papery and translucent, like . . . skin.

Then I hear it – a blood-curdling hiss.

Flint is on his feet in an instant, bow in hand, shoving me behind him.

The sheer size of the snake steals what breath I have left, and when it opens its mouth I see a forked tongue and a pair of curved fangs as long as my forearm.

The first arrow bounces off the dark scales as easily as a skimming stone. The snake blinks its huge slit-pupilled eyes and angles its head, sizing us up. Snapping fills my ears as it slithers towards us. I try to summon my water gifts, but I'm too frightened to think clearly.

Flint takes a step backwards and fires another arrow. 'Bullseye,' he mutters.

The snake rears back, jerking its head from side to side and releasing a deafening hiss as blood begins to pour in rivulets from its right eye socket.

Triumph temporarily swamps fear, and I manage to shoot a flurry of ice shards at its head. Flint darts to the left, aiming for the snake's other eye, but the creature is writhing so wildly he can't get a clear shot. I send another burst of ice, trying to slow its movements.

A scaled monster, a stone arena – it's like the first trial all over again. Except this time I have so much more to fight for. So much more to lose.

There's a dull crack, and I glance round to where my brother stands clutching his bow, which has been split clean in half. The snake stops and turns towards Flint, who drops the useless splinters, backing away into the wall.

Why doesn't he use his fire?

As far as I know, my brother hasn't so much as lit a candle since the incident. I tried to coax a fire out of him on several occasions during our journey to Isolla, but there was always some excuse – it would draw too much attention, he was saving his strength, he preferred cold stew. Yet I'm going to need Flint to take his flames out of retirement, and soon.

The sound of my footsteps crunching over bones deflects the snake's attention. It turns again, advancing on me instead, one eye glinting furiously, the other a bloodied pulp, streaming red. I raise my hands, letting fury take hold. But the snake only sheds the ice that begins to coat its scales like a second skin.

'What're you doing?' Flint howls helplessly from the other side of the cave.

I wait until the snake is just feet away – until I can smell the carrion on its breath.

I count one heartbeat. Two.

The creature lunges, ready to devour me whole. But I'm faster, thrusting my arm upward and lodging the bone I'd been concealing behind my back into its mouth.

I become aware of a sudden searing pain in my right arm before I lose my footing and my grip on the nightlight. It bounces a few paces away, fracturing the light across the walls. The snake is bucking and thrashing as it attempts to eject the bone from its jaws. I roll to the side, grab the nightlight and scramble to my feet.

'*Flint!*' I yell.

And then my brother is there, clinging to the snake's back, an arrow clamped between his teeth. I gasp as the snake finally snaps the bone wedged inside its mouth. It bears down on me, just as Flint stabs the arrow into the side of its head. The snake lurches so violently that Flint is thrown forward. As I pull him up, I realize that I'm bleeding – my shirt sleeve is sticky with blood. I must have nicked my arm on one of the snake's fangs.

That's when my body begins to turn sluggish and leaden. The sharp pain in my arm is dulled somewhat by a strange heaviness which slackens my every movement.

Giving my head a little shake, I reach inward for my anchors but my mind is vacant. My emotions are a shifting blur, my water gifts useless, dried up.

What's happening to me?

I trip over my own feet, slumping sideways. Flint catches hold of me, shouting urgently into my ear. Only, his words make no sense – the syllables are all scrambled. He starts to back away, hauling my boneless body with him as the snake advances.

I try to speak but my tongue feels like a dead thing in my mouth.

My lips form the word.

Fire.

But Flint has begun to shake, his breaths coming in gasps, beads of sweat dewing on his brow. I think of the way he hurled a ball of flame down the throat of the cobra in the Keep. The way he dusted himself off as though it were nothing.

'Flint,' I rasp.

Our backs slam into stone. My brother turns his head to look at me, panic in his eyes. I stare back at him, willing him to act, willing a wall of fire to erupt and save us both.

My voice rises to a scream. '*Fire!*'

A split second later, the flames leap forth in a burning, billowing cloud.

The snake is thrown backwards by the force of the blast and flops down on to the bone-strewn floor, dead.

Smoke rises just as the walls start to tremble. Red sandstone dust falls from above.

I let go of Flint to shelter beneath my arms as debris begins to rain down on our heads. There's a noise like a rumble of thunder, and I look up to see cracks running along the length of the ceiling, cutting deep fissures into the surface of the stone.

A shriek rips from my mouth as the ceiling caves in. But a pair of hands shoves me hard, and I'm thrown forward, narrowly avoiding being crushed by a giant slab of rock. I slide down a wall, my body overcome by heaviness. And somewhere in the haze, I recall the snake's fangs, gleaming white and dripping with . . .

Venom.

I'm half buried in the depths of the Ridge, and I've been bitten by a venomous snake.

I can't feel my fingers. I can't feel my right arm. Is it still there? I can't tell. I can't see either, and I realize that the tunnel is now drenched in darkness, the only source of light the gentle orange glow of dying embers clinging to blood-soaked scales.

'Flint,' I croak, reaching out for him. 'Where are you?' I scrabble around, groggy and delirious, coughing on the dust floating thick in the air. '*Flint.*'

But Flint makes no reply. Because Flint isn't here.

7
Flint

It's happening again.

Every muscle in my body seems to tighten, shrink, then spasm out of control. Tremors ripple in jagged waves up and down my arms and legs. My heart hurts, beating too hard, too fast, my chest heaving, lungs screaming out for air – because I can't breathe.

I can't breathe.

I can't breathe.

My skin is slick with cold sweat, and I wish I could just rip it off. I'm squeezing the nightlight so hard I'm surprised it hasn't shattered into pieces in my hand.

I can't explain what happened back there. The desire to save my sister must have overpowered my terror, for in all these weeks I haven't been able to summon so much as a single spark. I tried my best to hide it. I made excuse after excuse, avoiding Blaze's many questioning glances – all to keep my secret. Because how could I ever confess the truth?

I don't know how much time passes before my heart rate gradually begins to slow. Hours, days, an eternity – it's hard to tell. But slow it does, and I come to as if waking from a nightmare, curled on my side, light-headed and trembling.

That was the worst it's ever been. I say *it* because I can't find the right words to describe what's been happening to me almost every day since Ember –

My stomach roils with nausea. I exhale through my teeth and begin to count.

Seconds. Heartbeats. Pebbles skittering down the smoking pile of rubble. Even the bones lying littered around me. It helps, I've found. Counting things.

And when I emerge from the haze a second time, just as shaken but more alert, my first thought is – *Blaze*.

I heave myself into a sitting position and hold the nightlight aloft, illuminating the dust motes clinging to the stale air. The centre of the ceiling has caved in.

There's no sign of my sister.

I crawl over to the towering pile of rubble, trying to find a way through. But this only dislodges more rocks. I jerk backwards as they tumble down, my spine slamming into the wall.

I think of those last moments before the explosion. It all happened so fast. One minute Blaze was wedging a bone inside the mouth of that snake, and the next she was entirely disoriented, barely able to hold herself up. If I hadn't pushed her out of the way, she'd have been crushed. But what if I pushed her too hard and she hit her head? Or what if I didn't push her hard enough and she's now buried underneath all this stone? What if she's . . .

'BLAZE!' I scream her name over and over until my throat is raw and my tongue coated with dust, but there is no response.

She's not dead, I tell myself. *She's not dead. She can't be dead.*

My face is wet with tears. The salt stings my burns, and the pain, which was temporarily suppressed by panic, comes flooding back. My skin feels as though someone is rubbing it with sandpaper. My good eye smarts and streams, and as for the other . . .

I lean over and vomit on to a mound of tiny, delicate bones. Finger bones, perhaps.

When I'm empty, I reach for my satchel, then see that my belongings are strewn across the ground. I gather them up, counting as I go.

One – burn salve.

I yank off my shirt, turn it inside out, and use it to gently wipe my face. Then I take a glob of the cool, smooth gel and apply it to my burns, letting out a low groan as the jagged heat subsides somewhat.

Two – painkillers.

I rip the stopper out of one of the vials with my teeth and tip the contents down my throat.

Three – my waterskin.

Saliva pools eagerly in my mouth as I pick it up, but my insides turn to lead as I realize there's barely more than a drop left.

No Blaze. No water. No way out.

Between the wall at my back and the debris in the centre, I have little more than a few feet of space. A tomb – that is what this is. I am literally sitting in my grave.

This time, when the panic descends, no amount of counting can stop it.

Memories plague me.

I'm standing in an amphitheatre. I can hear the roar of the crowd urging us on. I can feel the heat from the flames raining down from above. I can see my cousin, Ember, smiling. I can't hold her off any longer. She's winning. She's winning, which means I am losing. I collapse to my knees but force myself to stand. I will not kneel. Not before her.

Worry not, cousin. I accept your surrender just as I will accept your fealty.

Anger and shame twist my insides out of shape. I was aware of it, even then – the knowledge that I was experiencing a moment that would haunt me for the rest of my life.

Though it is a pity, Ember continues. *It seems you're just as pathetic as your sister.*

Rage. Heat. Tongues of flame so agonizing I wished for death.

Then nothing.

I'm shaking so violently I hear bones break beneath me. My mind is filled with fire. Crackling, smoking, burning away my future.

Fire. My gift, now my curse.

Another memory surfaces. I see a wall of flame creeping ever closer as I try to make sense of my riddle.

I am something that is felt but never touched.
You will find me at birth, I am present at death.
Submit to me and I'll hurt you.
Resist me and I'll hurt you more.
If you use me, I can make you strong.
Learn from me and I can make you wise.
Numb me, fear me, conceal me, but never escape me.
You carry me with you every day of your life.
Tell me, Flint Flameborn – what am I?

The fire was close enough to blister when the answer came to me, a spark fizzling to life in the dark.

Pain.

Another surge of tremors takes hold and I squeeze my eye shut, my outstretched hand grappling for the nightlight.

A final memory reels me in. It's my first trial this time. I'm sprinting the circumference of the stone arena, collecting flames as I go. If I'd broken my concentration, I would've scorched the skin off my palms. But I was Flint Flameborn, a son of House Harglade, Heir to the Ignitia throne. I was playing with fire before I learned to talk.

Only now, that boy is gone.

He might as well be dead.

8

Blaze

Something is crawling up my back. Lots of somethings – a series of sharp little pinpricks. It stings. Or maybe it doesn't. The problem is, I can't tell what's real any more.

I'm lost in the darkness, but there's so much I can see. I see myself in my bedchamber in Harglade Hall, with its thick scarlet curtains and large four-poster bed. I watch as the red-silk sheets begin to wrap themselves round my wrists and ankles, pulling from all sides. I open my mouth to scream, only I'm not the one screaming. It's Amaryllis, the Terrathian Heir, her limbs bound by vines that stretch and stretch until . . .

POP.

The scene changes. I'm sitting in Elaith's chambers in a beautiful midnight-blue dress, accepting a glass of champagne from the bottle my chaperone, Spinner, has just opened. But the moment I take a sip, the world starts to tilt and spin, and I'm falling down the side of a gold-capped mountain, my fellow Aquatori Heir Marina's cold laughter ringing in my ears. I hear the glass in my hand shatter, echoed by the sound of a thousand glasses shattering in a stone ballroom.

When I wake, I'm under water. In the cold blue lake of an arena, in a flooded banquet hall, in a shimmering pool, falling down, down, down until I tumble out on the other side, scrambling to my feet in a room containing a single object – a golden Eye.

It watches me. Whispers my name.

Blaze.

The voice sounds like Flint's, faint and terrified.

I blink hard to stay conscious. My whole body aches, the heaviness radiating outwards from the crook of my elbow.

I have to get up. I have to get out of here.

I must have lost the nightlight, for I am enveloped in dense gloom. As the next hallucination recedes, I manage to roll on to my side, dislodging my left hand. I catch the tip of the worn leather glove between my teeth, and pull. As it slides from my fingers, my surroundings are lit up by the soft glow of my brandmark.

Dust has settled thickly in the air. I'm lying atop a mound of rocks and bones, propped up against –

I recoil from the body of the snake, its scales charred and peeling.

Shining my brandmark into its face, I see a single drop of venom poised to fall from the end of a glistening fang. Next, I examine the bite. My arm is swollen, the skin darkened as though bruised. Blood still oozes from the wound, soaking my sleeve.

Behind me, what was once the ceiling of the chamber is now an impenetrable wall. I try to scream Flint's name, but my voice has been reduced to a slurred mumble.

Another vision tears through me – of my mother this time, her brown-gold eyes turning blood-red. I shake my head furiously, pushing it away.

I'm desperately thirsty, but I can't summon the strength to conjure so much as a mouthful of water. I glance around for my satchel, but it's nowhere to be seen.

How did it come to this? How long have I been here, debilitated by the venom coursing through my system? How long do I have before it reaches my heart? If this is really how it ends, then my soul will be trapped inside the Ridge forever, since the chances of anybody finding my body are slim at best.

The Rain Singers believed that when they died, their God, Om Shikara, cried tears of rain down upon the earth to mourn their passing. They were laid to rest high in the cliffs, close to the sky. Like the Singers, the Aquatori have their own funeral traditions. The deceased is dressed in their finest clothes, while a boat is strewn with furs and filled with gifts – offerings for Morwenna. The more extravagant the gifts, the more likely she is to allow the boat to sail over the Second Sea and pass into the First Sea, the sacred ocean of the afterlife. The Water Goddess has expensive taste, it seems.

The dead person's belongings are also put inside the boat – their most prized possessions. All my prized possessions are missing. The Eye of the Soul, lost down the waterway. The nightlight from Hal, buried beneath the rubble. My dagger, which I haven't seen since the Ceremony, scarlet to the hilt, bathed in the blood of the Council. Though there is one thing – the little wooden knight from Renly, still tucked safely in my pocket.

The thought brings me some comfort – until a series of white-hot stings pepper up the length of my back. I arch my spine, searching for the source of the pain. And then I see them, scuttling across the bones, over my legs, up my back – throngs of them descending on the dead snake, pouring into its open mouth, biting and stinging as they go.

Fire ants.

Is this real?

I cry out as I'm stung once again between my shoulder blades.

Definitely real.

With a burst of strength, I launch myself up, then fall right back down again with a thud. I try once more, gripping a boulder, slapping the ants away.

Another hallucination seizes me. My father, wide-eyed, begging my mother to *stay with him, just stay with him*, as the blood pours from between her legs. A baby squealing. My heartbeat loud in my ears.

I don't know how I'm managing to move, but I am. Not running, not even walking, but stumbling slowly over the debris and out of the chamber, straining my eyes against the darkness of the tunnel. My footsteps are loud and clumsy, and I keep bumping into the walls. If anything else is lurking nearby waiting to finish me off, it won't take long to find me.

I fall to my knees as more hallucinations descend. Cole looms over me, encircling us inside a ring of fire. River kneels by my side, murmuring softly as he gathers me into his arms, soaking wet and trembling. Then there's Renly, dressed in an oversized red doublet, giggling as he darts out of my grasp and disappears round the corner.

I start to crawl, following him. But crawling one-handed is difficult, and my body feels as though it's gone to sleep. I grit my teeth as I push on, dragging my useless arm behind me.

I hear Ren laughing again up ahead. I know it's not real, I know he's not here, but I'm overcome with a desire to reach him, fuelled by my final dregs of adrenaline and a stubborn, slightly infuriating will to live. I heave myself round the bend, then the next, then –

Light.

A tiny pocket of light up ahead, no bigger than the palm of my hand.

Real? Not real? I can't be sure, but I chase it anyway, scared it might vanish.

Renly is gone, but the light remains, growing larger as I approach, filtering through a crumbling gap in the rock.

It takes an age, but I reach it. The hole is big enough to crawl through, and I pull myself out into bright, blinding daylight.

Behind me, the Ridge towers into the sky. Before me, nothing but trees. I give my head a shake as I take in the lush green landscape of the Wildlands.

Somehow I manage to stand, but each step feels precarious, like my legs are about to snap in two. Every breath is harsh and guttural, echoing through the ringing in my ears. Grey smoke permeates the edges of my vision.

Boughs leap out at me, boulders grow and shrink before my eyes. With my senses failing me, I stumble dazedly through the forest, catching myself on branches, barely registering the pain.

That's when my feet twist in a mass of sprawling roots and I go tumbling to the ground. My reflexes are so sluggish that I don't even throw out my arms to try to break my fall. But it turns out I don't need to, because something catches me, wrapping itself firmly round my waist like a length of rope – a thick vine that is replaced moments later by a pair of arms. Strong and golden, slightly weather-beaten.

Relief. Disbelief. A spark of indignation. I feel it all as I tilt my chin to stare up at the pair of spring-green eyes looking into mine.

A small smile curves the Earth Cleaver's lips. 'We have to stop meeting like this.'

9

Elva

Of all the rooms in the Golden Palace, the Council Chamber is surprisingly modest, consisting of a round table, five thrones and nothing much else – apart from the portraits.

Lining the walls are hundreds of faces, all belonging to generations of Crowned Councils, looking down upon their successors. I spot Queen Yvainne's portrait nestled between Queen Hydra and Queen Aspen. They must've had them painted near the beginning of their rule, as all three of them are young and fresh-faced, barely older than me. King Balen is there too, lip curled amusedly. Hanging beside him is Emperor Alvar. Hal's father is almost unrecognizable in youth, so different from the man I remember. I often wondered what caused him to look so haggard all the time. He was the most powerful Etheri in the realm. He lived in a palace hewn from solid gold, and yet somehow he managed to look almost as weary and malnourished as the serfs arriving in chains into his ports each year.

A pair of eyes seems to follow me around the room as I set out a selection of wine glasses and several rolls of parchment. Raven black, beady and cunning.

Caius Castellion.

It's because of Hal's grandfather that the Otherlands fell, my people were defeated, and I am a serf, forced to serve the sons and daughters of those who tore my world apart. A cold shiver runs through me, while a thin tendril of shadow curls from my fingertip. I'm grateful that he's no longer in the palace, having disappeared without a word after the Binding Ceremony. For what would Caius Castellion do to me if he discovered my secret? Bind me in crystal chains? Burn me alive? Cut me up into little pieces and cast me into the Rift? And what could I do to defend myself? In all these weeks, I have been so desperately focused on suppressing my shadows that I don't know how to control them, let alone *use* them. It would be like trying to tame a wild animal with my bare hands.

At that moment the doors to the Council Chamber burst open and I'm almost mown down by a gaggle of Imperial advisers. Hal stands framed in the doorway, his expression tight with worry, his fine gold doublet missing a button from where he's picked incessantly at the thread. His eyes find mine and soften. I could swear that the tension in his shoulders eases, just a fraction. My heart leaps, and I make myself look away, bowing my head as he passes. Hal hesitates only for a moment before seating himself in the largest of the five golden thrones, perched like a guest, hands folded. His advisers cluster round, clucking like a brood of angry hens. They're not talking to Hal, but rather *at* him, their voices loud enough to rattle the portraits on the walls.

I edge round them and lean over to pour Hal a glass of wine – a large one.

Only when I hand it to him does he seem to forget where he is, because he looks directly into my face and says, 'Thank you.'

I freeze, my fingers still wrapped round the glass. The chatter peters out.

Hal blinks, coughs slightly, then recovers himself. 'Thank you, all of you, for your reports. But perhaps it might be best if we discussed matters one at a time?'

The room relaxes and I scuttle back to my corner.

Alator, the court official, clears his throat. He's secured himself a spot standing at Hal's right shoulder, his chest puffed out self-importantly. I remember Blaze mentioning something about his teeth. Sure enough, when he opens his mouth, I see them – two rows of gleaming gold.

'Your Imperial Majesty,' he says. 'Several of the Eyes have informed me of the support gathering for King Balen, and not just in the Windlands as we had anticipated, but across Ostacre, and even beyond to our neighbouring kingdoms.'

Hal slowly places his hands on the arms of his throne.

'I believe,' Alator continues, 'that it would be in our best interests to arrange a parley with your uncle. Perhaps then we might come to some agreement.'

Hal scrubs his palm across his face. 'This *again*? How many times must I tell you? My uncle will not consent to a parley. He knows exactly what he's doing.' I watch as Hal reaches into his doublet and produces a long, sleek feather, which he slams on to the table in front of him. 'He sent me this. It was waiting in my rooms.'

My stomach jolts uncomfortably. This is news to me.

Hal once told me of an old Ignitia king who, on the eve of battle, gave a candle to his enemy that didn't stop burning until the war was over. And of the Terrathian queen who sent flowers to those she planned to kill. That's the whole point of symbols – they have meaning. King Balen hasn't just sent a feather. He is sending a message.

Alator looks stricken. 'There must be another explanation –'

'What other explanation? How could he possibly make his position any clearer?' Hal stabs a finger at the feather. 'This right here is a promise. A challenge. He's *taunting* me.'

'The problem, sire,' Alator continues carefully, 'is that so far the king's actions have all been . . . open to interpretation.'

'*Open to interpretation?*' Hal's voice is ice. 'My uncle saw his fellow Council members lying dead around him and showed not a shred of remorse.'

A second adviser says, 'Everyone in that chamber was in shock, sire, including you. You had just watched your father –'

Hal ignores her. 'He attacked Blaze Harglade. He –'

A new voice cuts in, cold and rasping. 'You would take the word of the Storm Weaver over that of your own uncle?'

Hal turns to the man standing on his left. He's ancient-looking, with a long beard and stiff, twisted fingers.

'I served as adviser to your grandfather, sire, and your father after that. I've known King Balen since he was a boy.'

Hal grits his teeth. 'You've known me since I was a boy too, Kalf. Forgive me for thinking you might trust my judgement.'

'Not,' says Kalf, 'when your judgement is compromised. We are all aware of your . . . *relationship* with the Harglade girl.'

For a moment I think Hal might hit him. 'Blaze has *nothing* to do with –'

'Many believe she was involved in your half-brother's plot to kill the Council,' says Alator, his gold teeth flashing.

I purse my lips in protest. Of course they've selected Blaze as their scapegoat. It's hardly surprising. To many, she's been a villain since the day she was born.

Hal shakes his head. 'Impossible.'

'Sire.' Kalf places a gnarled hand on Hal's shoulder. 'Rumours about the Storm Weaver have been circulating. She is already feared by the people, fears that have only intensified since it was announced that she has been Chosen for your Council.'

'Because she *won*,' Hal almost shouts. 'She won the Aquatori crown fair and square. What was I supposed to do? Not let her compete? The actions of my half-brother, I can't excuse. Him I am not defending. But Blaze? She's done nothing wrong. I trust her. Implicitly.'

Kalf sighs. 'The problem is, sire, the people don't. And I can't say I blame them. Who would put their faith in the Storm Weaver, a girl who has brought pain and suffering to so many, rather than King Balen – the late emperor's brother, a son of the Imperial House of Castellion, and an exemplary monarch beloved by his people?'

Hal shrugs off Kalf's hand from where it still rests on his shoulder. 'Then explain to me why my *exemplary*, *beloved* uncle tried to kill Blaze at the funeral of her aunt, Queen Yvainne? It was nothing other than an act of war.'

'Or an act of vengeance,' counters Kalf. 'Many view the attack on Fire Mountain as King Balen seeking justice for the deaths of your father and the three queens. That it was his wish to apprehend the Storm Weaver and force her to stand trial for her crimes.'

Hal opens his mouth, then snaps it shut. I bite the inside of my cheek and swallow the objections that gather on my tongue.

Alator leans forward once more. 'You understand, sire, how delicate this situation is. If you continue to throw your support behind Blaze Harglade, many of your subjects will turn their allegiance to your uncle. Yet if you condemn her now, after publicly vouching for her innocence, you will appear naive and indecisive.'

'Precisely,' says Kalf. 'Which is why it is imperative we call a parley. You must listen to what your uncle has to say. You must hear what he wants.'

'I know what he wants, Kalf,' Hal growls. 'He wants to be emperor.'

'Ridiculous,' another adviser mutters impertinently from the back of the group. 'King Balen is a second son. He is Ventalla. He doesn't have the gift of light. The emperors of Ostacre are Light Wielders, descended from the Maker himself.'

'Which is why I know he doesn't intend to kill me in order to take the throne. He'll complete the Ceremony, binding himself not only to my Council but to me. To my magic.'

The silence that follows stretches taut.

Kalf breaks it, and the words that leave his mouth are unforgivable. 'Perhaps that is not such a bad idea.'

Hal's eyes burn black. '*What did you say?*'

'I meant, sire, that perhaps you should consider allowing your uncle to become regent until you are ready to take the throne yourself. I am not alone in having observed the toll your new position is taking on you, and all without even being crowned yet.'

My hands shake with anger. To my horror, a single wisp of shadow begins to twine itself round my finger. I stuff my hand behind my back, heart racing.

Eventually Hal finds his voice. 'Whose side are you on?'

'Yours, sire,' Alator assures him. 'We all of us are on your side.'

'And yet I find myself forced to ask.' Hal sighs, leaning back in his throne. 'If the people don't know what to believe, then let's give them something to believe in. Let's show them we're strong.' He pulls a sheet of parchment towards him. 'We sent envoys to all our neighbouring kingdoms weeks ago. Have there been any developments?'

Kalf grimaces.

'What about Alvora?' Hal continues, failing to keep the desperation out of his voice. 'Does Queen Celeste intend to support me against my uncle?'

'We've had no word, sire,' says an adviser in a shimmering golden cloak.

'And what of the Eastern Isles? Zafar and Katteran?'

Alator looks shifty. 'Nothing yet. Though I believe your mother's brother, the King of Vost, has sent a letter. It arrived this morning.'

He fishes it out of the pile and hands it to Hal, who rips it open, then exhales. 'King Gethen will come to my aid if required.'

My small sigh of relief is countered by a prickling sensation up my spine – the ghost of a lash upon my back. It was King Gethen's daughter, Lira, Hal's cousin, who ordered that I be whipped for spilling wine on her dress. Only, it wasn't me. It was a boy serving at the same table, Pip, whose little hands were shaking so badly that he lost control of the jug.

There are many different kinds of fear. I've felt them all twice over. But the fear I felt for that child in that moment overrode any I may have been harbouring for myself. So I took the blame. The first lash was blinding, the ones that followed worse, cutting deeper, covering my back in a series of bloody welts. I could barely move afterwards. If it weren't for Ingra, I might very well still be tethered to that post right now.

'That leaves our most important alliance,' Alator is saying. 'And most pressing.'

'King Merrick may have been a friend to your father, sire, but he's a slippery man,' says Kalf. 'He likes to be on the winning side.'

'Who doesn't?' Hal mutters.

'Quite. But unlike your father, who was an honourable ruler, King Merrick will do anything in his power to secure the best alliance, even if that means deceit and duplicity.

Even if that means saying one thing and doing another, signing a treaty but adding a hidden clause.'

Alator nods gravely. 'He's been known to switch sides at the last possible moment, just to ensure his victory.'

Hal half closes his eyes. 'What're you saying?'

'That King Merrick walks a fine line, sire. He may be your most powerful ally, but he could easily become your biggest threat. If there is going to be a war, he does not care whether you win or whether King Balen wins – only that *he* does.'

'He has informed us that during times of such . . . *political uncertainty*, he is reconsidering his position.' Kalf slides another piece of parchment towards Hal with the heel of his hand. 'This marriage treaty means nothing until you prove to King Merrick that you are the stronger ally. Only then will he consent to give you his daughter.'

My stomach tightens, then shrinks. All around, the walls seem to close in, hundreds of portraits bearing down on me. For I realize now who they are discussing. King Merrick . . . of *Thaven*. Ruler of Etheri with the power to manipulate precious metals, and father to the beautiful, golden-haired crown jewel of the kingdom – Princess Mirade.

Hal is squeezing the arms of his throne so tightly I fear his knuckles may burst through the skin. He's watching me, his face slack, eyes dull.

We don't talk about his betrothal. It's easier that way. For the thought of him with somebody else – courting her, kissing her, *marrying* her – looms over me like a taunting shadow, too painful to bear. So we pretend it doesn't exist. But if the union between Hal and the princess is the surest way to victory against his uncle . . .

For so long I have dreaded this wedding. Now I find myself dreading what might happen if it doesn't take place. One look at Hal tells me he's thinking exactly the same thing.

'Sire?' Alator prompts.

'Out.' It's barely a whisper.

'But we –'

'I said, *get out*!' Hal yells, slamming his fist on the table and knocking over his glass. Red pools on white parchment.

His advisers do as he commands, scurrying past me out of the door, led by a concerned-looking Alator. Kalf lingers a moment, seemingly unsure whether to be irked at his dismissal or pleased that Hal is finally starting to act like an emperor. When he limps after the others, not bothering to cast a glance in my direction, Hal and I are left alone.

For a time, neither of us speaks.

Then Hal says, 'I need to clean this up.'

I move across to him. 'Let me.'

'No, I'll do it. I spilled it. I'll clean it up.' He takes the rag from my hand and begins scrubbing clumsily at the documents in front of him, smearing the wine even more.

'Hal –'

'It won't – I'm just making it worse –'

'*Hal*.' I rest my hand atop his, and he stills. Gently, I disentangle the rag from his fingers and begin blotting at the parchment.

'This is such a mess,' he says, and I know he's not referring to the wine. 'My own uncle is trying to usurp me.

My half-brother murdered the Council. Which member of my family intends to betray me next? Should I barricade myself inside my rooms in case my mother decides to slit my throat on a whim?' He barks out an empty, humourless laugh. 'My House is divided. My advisers doubt me. Even some of the Eyes are spying for Balen. Sometimes I feel like you're the only person who's ever truly honest with me.'

Guilt chimes in my chest, ringing harsh and loud.

'What are you going to do?' I whisper.

'There are too many chinks in my armour,' Hal says quietly. 'And I'm going to fix it.'

IO

Blaze

I come to slowly.

My limbs are stiff and sore, my arm throbbing dully, my head still a little clouded by venom. The hallucinations seem to have subsided, yet one lingers, clinging to the corners of my mind. While the other visions possessed a hazy, dreamlike quality, this one was clear. It had been so *real*. I could *feel* Fox's arms round me, could breathe in the fresh-mint-and-pine scent of his warm skin. His voice was just as I remember – soft, slightly amused. And the way he was looking at me . . . it was as if I were the best thing he had ever seen.

I roll over, trying to claw my way out of sleep.

Only when I open my eyes, Fox is still here.

I blink hard, and yet he remains, leaning against the trunk of an overhanging willow tree, the drooping branches forming a curtain of leaves around us.

Shock hits me like a blow to the chest. Before I'm fully aware of what I'm doing, I'm scrambling to my feet, brandishing a moss-covered rock in front of me.

'Where am I?' I squeak. 'What's going on?'

Fox raises an eyebrow. 'I see your manners haven't improved, Storm Weaver.'

'*Where am I?*'

'Are you going to hit me with that?' He nods at the rock.

'Not if you answer the question.'

'Oh, how I've missed you and your questions.'

I hold the rock up even higher.

But Fox only snaps his fingers, and it crumbles to dust in my hand. 'Sit down.'

I stare at him, furious and bewildered.

'I said, sit down. *Please*.'

I count an entire minute before I concede. I lower myself unsteadily to the ground, letting out a groan as I gingerly probe my brow. 'Everything's spinning.'

'Put your head between your knees.'

Reluctantly, I do as he says, resurfacing a minute later to resume my accusatory glare. 'What's going on?' I demand. 'Why am I here?'

'What's going on is that you were bitten by a venomous snake, managed to stumble your way out of the Ridge, and then collapsed in the forest,' he tells me matter-of-factly. 'You're here because I found you and patched you up. You're welcome, by the way.'

I stare at him, then glance down. Sure enough, my shirt sleeve has been ripped to the shoulder, the wound on my forearm thickly bandaged. Several pots and tinctures are neatly arranged on the carpet of moss, each labelled in lazy, looping handwriting.

Of course. I remember now.

Cleaver. Slaver. Hunter. *Healer.*

Fox watches me, his expression unreadable. It's strange seeing him dressed like the Fidra and not in Terrathian green. Yet even in a pale fawn-coloured shirt and ragged trousers, he is still utterly, *irritatingly* beautiful. His sun-gold skin is a shade deeper, his dark hair slightly longer and just as untidy as ever, and his eyes, fringed by thick lashes, manage to make the bright hue of the leaves overhead appear dull. He still wears that little hoop earring, though I'm not surprised to see that his signet rings – one engraved with the Castellion raven, the other with the Calloway falcon – are absent. Too conspicuous.

'But – but what are you doing here?' I ask. 'How did you even find me?' Taking a deep breath, I try to piece it all together, retracing my steps back through the Ridge tunnels. I recall a rubble-strewn chamber, a smouldering beast, a burst of flame . . .

My stomach plummets.

'*Flint*,' I breathe. 'Flint. He's still in there. He saved me. We have to go back. *Now*. He could be hurt, he could –'

But Fox holds up a hand, silencing me. 'Your brother's alive.'

'What? Is he here?' I look around frantically, as if half expecting to find Flint curled up like a cat beside the bag of medical supplies.

'No,' Fox says, snuffing out my brief spark of hope. 'But he's not dead. I promise.'

'What are you *talking* about?' I almost yell. 'How can you *possibly* promise that?' Confusion turns to rage. I grit my teeth, hauling myself to my feet once more. 'Actually, I don't have time for your games. Now, if you don't mind, I'm going to find my brother.'

Fox rolls his eyes. 'Storm Weaver.'

I ignore him, drawing back the curtain of branches.

'*Storm Weaver*.'

I hesitate for a moment, then turn back. Fox watches, with an undeniable air of satisfaction, as my face floods with shock.

He grins, letting the Eye of the Past swing back and forth on its chain. 'You didn't really think I let my uncle take the real one, did you?'

11

Flint

If this is what dying feels like, then I wish death would stop being such a tease. Come and get me already. Come and take me somewhere safe and quiet. A lush green meadow. A comfortable room. Perhaps my mother will be there, waiting with Aunt Yvainne. Maybe Blaze is there too, sitting cross-legged in an armchair, her nose buried in a book.

Strange. It's almost as if I can hear voices speaking softly. If my mouth weren't all dried up, I'd call out to them.

More time passes and I wait patiently, letting my life drift away slowly, like smoke.

A light breeze flutters gently across my face. There's a strange scraping sound, followed by a grunt. This must be it – the end.

'Mother?' I whisper.

'Hmm,' says a familiar voice. 'You know I like it when you call me *baby*, but I think *Mother* might be a step too far.'

I open my eye. '*Spinner?*'

'Hello, lover.'

I stare at her, stunned. I blink once, twice, three times, and yet she's still there, grinning down at me, her pretty, pointed face illuminated by the nightlight.

'I've always liked how you look when you're sleepy. Wouldn't you agree, Sheen?'

My chaperone steps out from behind her. His white-blonde hair looks even paler against his smooth russet skin. His violet eyes are fixed on me, unblinking. My stomach tumbles at the sight of him. Both of them wear modest travel clothes and thick boots. There's not a scrap of gold in sight.

'What're you *doing* here?' My voice is a rough croak.

Spinner laughs. 'We've come to rescue you, silly.'

'But –'

'But what?'

'*Blaze*,' I say. 'Blaze. She's on the other side. You – you have to get her out.'

'No need,' Spinner tells me.

'What d'you mean, *no need*?' I demand. 'I pushed her out of the way. She could be under the rubble . . .' I trail off, my body wracked with coughs that sound a bit like sobs.

Spinner shakes her head. 'I said no need, Flint, because she's already gone.'

'That's impossible.'

'Tell that to the trail of footsteps we found leading out of the tunnel.'

I let her words sink in. 'She got out?'

'Yup.'

'And I'm not dying?'

'Nope.'

'And you . . . you're not just in my head?'

Spinner leans down and presses a soft kiss to my mouth. Her lips are sugar-sweet, comforting and familiar. 'Feel that?'

I nod slowly.

'Don't worry,' Spinner says gently, looping my satchel over her shoulder and straightening up. 'We're going to get you out of here.'

My head pounds. 'How? And how did you even get in?'

Spinner glances at Sheen, who hesitates briefly before stepping forward. Before I can let out so much as a squeak of protest, he gathers me into his arms.

'Like this.' Spinner winks at me.

The next moment she's gone, vanished into thin air.

My jaw drops. I look up at Sheen, his face so closed off, so close to mine. I open my mouth to say something – I'm not entirely sure what – but I don't get the chance. There's a sudden rush of wind, an unpleasant squeezing feeling, a sense of weightlessness. When I open my eye seconds later, I'm no longer trapped inside a rubble-filled, bone-strewn chamber in the Ridge tunnels but on a grassy bank, breathing cool, sweet air.

I twist my head from side to side, taking in my surroundings. Rolling hills, blue sky, midday sun beating down hot – and a whole lot of green.

The Wildlands.

Spinner beckons us over into the shade, where a few branches have been bent and bound to form a haphazard little shelter. Beside it sit three waterskins and a steaming cooking pot. One whiff of the contents sets my stomach growling.

I become aware of two things in quick succession. First, I'm not wearing a shirt. Second, I'm still cradled in Sheen's arms, which are surprisingly muscular despite his lean frame. And what's more, I'm clinging to him so tightly I've lost some of the feeling in my fingers.

Heat blooms in my face and neck. In an attempt to preserve a shred of dignity, I stick out my chin and fold my distinctly less brawny arms across my chest.

'Put me down.'

Sheen raises an eyebrow.

'*Now*,' I command, with considerably more authority.

'My pleasure,' he says dryly, and lets go of me.

I hit the ground with a thud, letting out a traitorously high-pitched yelp. I glare at Sheen. The ghost of a smirk quirks the corners of his sullen mouth. I'm too weak to stand, so I swallow my pride and start crawling over to where Spinner is holding out a waterskin.

'Slow down,' she says mildly as I drain it in a few gulps.

I lean back against a boulder. 'How did you even find me?'

'We may have been . . . observing you these past few days.'

'You were *spying* on us?' I exclaim, outraged.

'We were simply checking in on you, that's all,' Spinner says, raising her hands defensively. 'We just dropped by occasionally to make sure you were both all right. You and Blaze – well, you're important. And you're important to me.'

I soften, just a fraction. Then a thought hits me. 'My grandmother didn't hire you to keep tabs on us, did she?'

Spinner giggles. 'Gods, no. Your grandmother terrifies me.'

I snort. 'Join the club. You should've seen the way she looked at me at Fire Mountain, as though I were *encouraging* my sister to put herself in harm's way.' I pause, rolling a vial of painkiller between my fingers. 'I promised her I'd take care of Blaze . . .'

'Blaze is alive,' Spinner says gently. 'We'll find her, I promise.'

'Then what are we waiting for?' I ask, hauling myself up.

'Don't be a fool,' says Sheen, sounding bored.

'There's no time to waste,' I snap over my shoulder.

'Look at you. You can barely walk.'

As soon as I turn back, Sheen is there, standing right in front of me. I let out a hiss of irritation before side-stepping him and carrying on. But he just does it again, and again, until I'm overcome with the urge to punch him in his stupid, surly face.

'Listen,' he says curtly. 'Your sister could've emerged from any of the Ridge tunnels. Rather than wandering around like an idiot, you have to think logically. You don't know where she is, so head to where you think she'd go.'

I frown, puzzled.

Sheen pinches the bridge of his nose in exasperation. 'Are you really as dim as you are vain? You and Blaze – where were you going?'

I consider not telling him, then tell him anyway. 'The Court of Waves.'

'Well, then,' he says. 'There's your answer.'

I hesitate, mulling over his words.

'He's right, Flint,' says Spinner.

'I'm always right,' Sheen tells her matter-of-factly.

I scowl, drawing myself up to full height, though Sheen still towers over me by several irritating inches. 'Fine. I'll go to the Lagoon.'

'Excellent.' Spinner beams. 'I've always wanted to see it.'

I glance round at her. 'You're coming with me?'

'Of *course* we are,' she says. 'You think we'd leave you to fend for yourself? Besides, I've missed you, Flint Flameborn. I don't intend to let you out of my sight.'

I return her smile. I've missed her too. Being with Spinner makes me feel like my old self again. Or at least, it's easier to pretend to be.

Then I turn back to Sheen. 'And you?'

His eyes shutter, tightening at the corners. 'I'm your chaperone,' is all he says.

I arch a brow and reach up reflexively to strum the string of my bow before remembering that it's now just a pile of matchsticks in the Ridge tunnels. My arm falls loosely to my side, and I experience a begrudging spark of gratitude for my companions, sullen or otherwise. If it weren't for them, I'd have met the same fate as my weapon, my remains buried forever inside a rocky tomb. I try not to shudder.

Spinner ladles some soup into a bowl. 'You should eat.'

I return to the camp and descend on the food. Sheen watches me with only mild disgust, picking at a loose thread on his ill-fitting shirt. Like Blaze and me, he and Spinner have chosen to pose as Fidra too. It's strange seeing them like this. Toned down. Disguised. Only, they've really just traded one disguise for another, because as members of the emperor's court, they're always in disguise. Unlike the rest of the Etheri, Eyes never wear their gift colour, only Imperial gold. That's what makes them dangerous – their unpredictability. Their power lies in the fact that we don't know which element they wield.

Except, I do know which element Spinner and Sheen wield, because they showed me. Vanishing in one place, reappearing somewhere else entirely. Travelling through the air. *Flitting*, just like King Balen.

'So,' I venture, scraping my bowl clean and holding it out for more, 'when were the two of you planning on telling me that you're Ventalla?'

A long pause.

'Er . . . soon?' Spinner suggests.

'Never,' says Sheen.

'Well, that's too bad,' I tell him smugly. 'But the good news is, now I know your secret, we should make it to the Waterlands in record time.'

Spinner shakes her head. 'No.'

'What d'you mean, *no*?'

'We're not flitting,' she says firmly. 'We have to go on foot.'

'*What*? Why?'

'Because it's too risky,' she says simply. 'The wind still belongs to King Balen. It spies for him, listens for him. Flitting can only be a last resort. Besides, it's awfully draining.'

I let out a long-suffering sigh and get to my feet. 'I'm going to wash.'

'Thank the Gods,' mutters Sheen.

I shoot him a dark look before ducking through a leafy canopy of trees, emerging next to the Creek. The water is bracing and blissfully cool. It eases the heat in my burns.

I emerge sometime later, cold but clean. A neatly folded pile of clothes waits for me on the bank. I pull them on, step into my boots, tug my eyepatch back over my head and return to the camp, where Spinner leads me by the hand into the makeshift shelter. Sheen sits at the entrance, playing absent-mindedly with a small current of air.

'Aren't you going to ask what we were doing?' I say. 'Blaze and me?'

Spinner shrugs. 'We already know.'

I stare at her. 'You know? About the three sisters? About the talismans?'

'Mm-hm.'

'*How?*'

Spinner smiles, her dark-green eyes sparkling. 'I have friends in high places.'

I let out an exasperated huff. 'Anything else you'd like to share?'

She tuts. 'Someone's a little grumpy.'

'That's because someone's had a long day.'

'Then why doesn't someone get some rest?'

I do feel tired, come to mention it. I'm still weak, and my head aches. It's exhausting, almost dying. Really wears you out.

'Maybe . . . maybe just a couple of hours,' I concede. 'And then –'

'I know, I know, and then we head to the Lagoon.'

'And find Blaze.'

'And find Blaze,' Spinner echoes, patting my arm.

Settling myself down on a pile of thick furs, I drift off slowly with my head in Spinner's lap. For someone who started his day on the brink of death, this is certainly not the worst outcome in the world.

12

Blaze

The Eye of the Past winks at me in the dappled light filtering through the branches.

I stare at Fox in disbelief. 'You . . . you have . . .'

My mind is spinning. I feel like I might throw up. Is this just another hallucination? Somehow I think not. While my head still pounds painfully, the fog that clouded my every thought has cleared, as though I've emerged on the other side.

'Explain,' I order, a little breathlessly.

And so he tells me about the replica he had made in case anything were to happen, about how he let King Balen believe it was the real one, when all the while Sifa's Eye was safely wedged down the side of his boot.

I blink. 'So what you're saying is that your uncle . . .'

'. . . does not, in fact, have the Eye of the Past in his possession?' Fox finishes. 'Yes. All he has is a useless lump of gold. I wouldn't want to be anywhere near the Windlands when he figures it out. That sort of rage could warrant a hurricane.'

I grimace. 'I take it you know about the attack on Fire Mountain?'

He nods. 'Very resourceful on your part, escaping down the waste chute. Less impressive was your decision to travel *through* the Ridge tunnels. What were you thinking?' His tone is more amused than chiding.

I exhale as I sit down and cradle my bandaged arm. 'That's how you found me, isn't it? Using your Eye. You knew where I'd be because you knew where I'd *been*.'

Fox nods, tucking the pendant back beneath his collar.

'What about Flint?'

'I told you, he's alive.'

'Truly?'

Fox reaches out. 'Give me your hand.'

My heart lurches. 'Why?'

'Because I can prove it.'

I hesitate. One by one, I count the lines on his palm.

Fox sighs theatrically. 'Do you want to see your brother or not?'

He already knows my answer. 'Yes,' I say, finally moving closer. 'Yes, show me.'

'Please?'

'*Please*,' I grit out, and slip my hand into his.

It feels much like it did when we danced together at King Balen's ball, his skin warm and callused, his grip firm. I'm suddenly keenly aware of how filthy I am. My clothes are grimy; my hair matted with sandstone dust and blood.

'*What now?*' I don't know why I'm whispering – we're the only ones here.

Fox shushes me, his eyes closed. 'I'm concentrating.'

I resist pulling a face and cast my eyes around the willow tree. Is this really where he's been living? My gaze lands on the bedroll, medical supplies, pungent herbs and plants, until, quite suddenly, I don't see them any more. I see a boy wearing an eyepatch. He's walking beneath a leafy canopy, his dark curls wet and glistening.

Flint.

It's him. It's really him.

Then he's gone. My surroundings fade back in, and I'm once again sitting face-to-face with the Earth Cleaver.

I feel overcome with the urge to cry – or laugh. 'Flint's alive.'

'Told you.'

'How . . . how did you do that?' I breathe.

'Practice.' Fox smirks infuriatingly, dragging the pad of his thumb across my palm. He does it again, his touch feather-light, sending small shivers down the nape of my neck.

I draw my hand back quickly. That's when another realization hits me. 'The Ceremony,' I say. 'When the Eye gave you that vision . . .'

It's instantaneous the way the amused expression slides off Fox's face.

'I was able to see it too,' I continue, 'because I – I touched you.'

'I'm aware.' His entire demeanour has changed, become cool and emotionless. 'It's how I discovered I'm able to let others see what I see, if I wish it.'

I open my mouth, then close it again, thinking of what he saw that day. His sister, Freya, a little girl no older than

Renly is now. I remember the way her green eyes had bulged as she choked, wild and desperate, then glassy and unseeing.

'Who else knows?' I ask quietly. 'About what your uncle did?'

'Very few, I imagine.'

'What about Hal?'

Fox shakes his head, then cracks his neck.

'Why didn't you tell him?'

'You don't think I tried?'

'But now you can prove it,' I say. 'You can use the Eye to show him the whole story.'

'I think you're forgetting one small detail,' says Fox. 'I've been exiled.'

'But you're not in exile,' I point out. 'You're still here in Ostacre.'

'As ever, Storm Weaver, your observational skills are second to none.'

I scowl, growing impatient. 'He's your brother –'

'*Half*-brother,' Fox corrects. 'And I assure you, whatever familial bond existed between us has long since been severed.'

'I don't believe that,' I say, remembering the way they had looked at one another in my chambers the night I returned Elva's magic – Fox's offer of help, Hal's reluctant acceptance, a flicker of an old trust, fragile yet unbroken.

Fox leans forward. 'Then tell me, would *your* brother ever turn you away? Refuse to hear you out? Threaten to have you killed if you returned?'

I stare at him. After the Ceremony, many called for the Earth Cleaver's execution, demanding his life as payment for the deaths of the Council, but I never for one moment imagined that Hal would consider such a thing. And not just because killing an Heir is an insult to the Gods, but because, for better or for worse, Fox is his family.

I think of my own brother. He would never do anything to hurt me, even if I were the one who had hurt him.

'I have to find Flint,' I say so loudly I startle even myself.

'And how do you propose to do that?' Fox drawls. 'Stroll into the forest and call his name? Ask any low-flying birds if they happen to have seen him?'

I glower, any last dregs of sympathy drying up and turning to dust. 'Strangely enough, no. What I'm going to do is stick to the plan and make for the Lagoon.'

'Ah, so that's where you were headed,' says Fox, wiping his hands on his shirt. 'I take it you're searching for the missing Eye?'

'I'd have thought you'd have worked that one out for yourself by now, what with all the spying you seem to have been doing on us lately.'

Fox rolls his eyes fondly, then tosses me a waterskin. 'Here.'

I hadn't realized how thirsty I was until I take a drink. A sudden whinnying sound causes me to choke in surprise.

'It's just Cedar,' Fox says as I turn to him in panic, water running down my chin. 'You should really eat something. We have a long ride ahead of us.'

I stare at him. 'We? What do you mean, *we*?'

Fox leans back against the trunk of the willow. 'You thought I'd let you just wander out alone into the Wildlands?'

I hesitate. I've heard tales of creatures roaming the mountains, people going missing on the moors, beautiful flowers that secrete deadly toxins in the meadows, even a haunted forest called the Greenwood, filled with bandits and dryads.

'You think I can't do it alone?' I challenge.

Fox clicks his tongue and mutters something in Veridian. '*Syrath velena*.'

Stubborn girl.

'*Fazari velen*,' I bite back.

Stupid boy.

'Nice pronunciation.' He grins, impressed, then changes tack. 'Listen, you may be a future queen, but that doesn't mean you know how to navigate without a map, or forage for food. Your chances of survival are far greater by my side.' He dips into a mocking half-bow. 'I am but your humble servant.'

'*Humble* is not a word I associate with you,' I say waspishly.

'What about *handsome*?' Fox muses.

I blush, scowling, remembering what I'd said to him the first time we met, woozy with painkiller.

'Face it, Storm Weaver,' he says. 'You need my help.'

I waver, conflicted.

The sooner I get to the Lagoon, the sooner I find Flint. Plus, Fox has a horse, which should make the journey to the Aquatori Court a whole lot faster. He also has the Eye of the Past. Fox told me once that the Eyes are sisters, just like their original owners – that they're drawn to one another. What if staying close to Sifa's talisman could help me find Syla's? I may not have complete faith in the superiority of his moral compass, but what I do know with absolute certainty is that whatever happens, he won't let the Eyes fall into King Balen's hands. Surely a shared enemy is all the foundation needed to build an alliance?

Besides, he's right. By all accounts, the Wildlands can be treacherous. And as the Heir once destined to rule over them, perhaps he might prove useful.

Perhaps it really would be safer to remain with the most dangerous Etheri in the realm.

13

Blaze

As I watch the Earth Cleaver pack away his various tinctures and vials of medicine – meticulously, for there seems to be some kind of order – I find myself thinking that he looks far more content out here in the forest than he ever did at the Golden Palace, with all its gilded pomp and ceremony. I think of his private chambers – that unruly jungle, the carpet of wildflowers, a bed nestled among the entwined branches of a towering tree.

He hands me a bowl of oats, which I reluctantly accept, keenly aware of the hollow ache in my stomach.

'How long was I out?' I ask between mouthfuls.

'A day or so,' Fox tells me.

I make an impatient sound, letting my head tip back against the trunk of the willow.

Fox smiles a little at my petulance. He pulls off his left glove, severs its fingertips with his knife, then tosses it to me. 'Here.'

I catch it warily and hold it at arm's length, as if he'd thrown the knife rather than the glove. 'What's this for?'

'To conceal your brandmark. It somewhat ruins your cover.'

'I must've left mine in the Ridge,' I mutter, sliding it on and fastening it at the wrist, concealing the soft glow. As expected, it's too big for me, but it'll have to suffice.

'Are you feeling well enough to travel?' Fox asks.

I nod. 'Yes.'

'And you're sure about that?'

'Yes.'

'And you promise to do everything I tell you?'

'Yes – *Hold on*.' I narrow my eyes. 'I'm not promising that.'

'Too late,' he points out.

'In case you'd forgotten, I'm going to be queen,' I snap. 'Doesn't that mean you have to promise to do everything *I* tell *you*?'

A smirk tugs at the corners of Fox's mouth. 'Pulling rank already, I see. Forgive me, *Your Majesty*, but given that your safety is now my responsibility, I'm going to need you to let me take the reins on this one. And speaking of, I'd better start tacking up.'

I glower into my bowl before following Fox between the branches into a small clearing. Cedar is there, snuffling through the undergrowth, his dark mane shining in the dappled light.

Fox clicks his tongue in greeting. 'Storm Weaver, you remember my horse?'

I reach out a tentative hand to stroke Cedar's muzzle, thinking back to when I first met him that night in the stables, when Fox gave me the kittens.

'What news of my younger brother?' I ask, experiencing a fresh wave of relief that Renly was not permitted to attend Aunt Yvainne's funeral.

'Your grandmother sent for him before she left Fire Mountain,' says Fox. 'He was taken to the safe house along with the decoys. Genius plan, by the way. Let's hope it works long enough for us to reach the Lagoon, or else we'll have half of Ostacre – and my uncle – on our tails.'

I frown, because he's right. I have to find the Eye before anybody realizes I'm missing, which can only be a matter of time.

What would the people make of it, I wonder? The Storm Weaver, a runaway queen. A *fugitive*. Many already question my account of the Binding Ceremony. They would never believe my intentions to be noble. And if I were discovered with the Earth Cleaver . . .

'Do you know what they're saying? About you and me?' I grimace, recalling the conversation Flint and I overheard in Isolla.

A muscle twitches in Fox's jaw. 'More or less. Neither one of us has an excess of admirers, as I understand it.' He chuckles humourlessly. 'My uncle is taking advantage of the people's doubt. He's using their uncertainty to win their support.'

'How?'

'By giving them a villain,' says Fox. 'Or in this case – two.'

Despite the sunlight glinting through the branches, I feel suddenly cold.

Fox sets to work packing the rest of his belongings, sliding his gold dagger into the sheath at his hip, strapping his satchel securely to Cedar's flank.

It's only when he offers me a leg-up into the saddle that the reality of our situation dawns on me. There is only *one* horse. I roll my shoulders uncomfortably in my soiled shirt, painfully conscious of the layer of grime coating my skin.

'What's the matter?' Fox asks.

'I'm filthy,' I mutter.

'You've certainly looked better,' he concedes mildly. 'But we should make a start. You'll have a chance to clean up later.'

Ignoring his proffered hand, I heave myself reluctantly into the saddle, inhaling sharply through my nose as my injured arm takes most of my weight.

Fox hesitates, looking up at me. Maybe he's having second thoughts too.

'Well, aren't you coming?' I ask impatiently.

He clears his throat and bows his head in mock deference. 'Right away, Your Majesty.'

I tense as Fox swings himself up behind me, looping his feet into the stirrups. The hard planes of his chest press against my back as he leans forward to grab the reins, the corded muscles of his legs digging into mine as he nudges Cedar forward.

Fox glances upward occasionally, checking the position of the sun as a means of navigation, since the towering outline of the Ridge has long been swallowed by the trees.

Neither of us speaks for a while. I concentrate instead on trying to ignore the continual graze of our arms.

It makes me nervous – being this close to him.

In fact, everything about this situation makes me nervous.

The forest is wild and overgrown, a tangle of roots and vines, filled with all manner of woodland creatures that crawl and croak and leap from branch to branch. I sit poker-straight, flinching at every creak and snap, in a constant state of high alert.

I can sense Fox biting his tongue, but when a butterfly flutters past and I lurch so violently I nearly topple to the ground, he can't seem to take it any longer.

'*Relax*, would you? You'll give yourself a heart attack.'

'I *am* relaxed,' I protest, righting myself.

'How foolish of me. You positively ooze serenity.'

The way ahead gradually grows denser, then denser still. Fox flicks his wrist carelessly, and a path begins to form, thickets parting down the middle, trees bending gracefully as we pass. Shoulders rigid, I focus on a fixed point ahead.

At a sudden rustle in the canopy above, I jerk my head up so fast that the back of my skull collides with Fox's face. 'What's that?!'

'That,' he says thickly, pinching the bridge of his nose, 'is a very rare, very dangerous creature known as a squirrel.'

Cedar huffs amusedly. I scowl, embarrassed.

'Look, I understand your trepidation,' says Fox. 'This is all new for you. It's only natural for you to be on your guard. But you're forgetting you're with me.'

His arms encircle my waist as he gathers the reins into one hand.

'Not likely,' I mutter.

14

Elva

I hardly dare breathe as Matron paces slowly along the line of serfs, inspecting each of us in turn. Her beady eyes linger on me, scanning from head to toe before she lifts a hand. I flinch involuntarily, but she only tugs the collar of my tunic straight before moving on to Ingra, who doesn't lower her gaze to the floor like the rest of us but stares back defiantly.

I hate it when she does this. Most of us spend our time trying to be invisible, but not Ingra. I've often wondered if it's because of her age. Ingra was sixteen when she was snatched from Veridia – an isle of hot, rolling deserts. Of all the chained-up children arriving in Ostacre's ports that year, she was among the eldest. The other serfs have always looked to her for guidance. She raised half the people in this room.

It's yet another means of punishing the Otherlands for the War of the Empires – enslaving the children of the vanquished. A cruel method of oppression, and a practical one. Because children are easier to catch. Less trouble, more *malleable*. They're also more likely to die on the long journey across the Second Sea, but that's why the slavers always make sure to take extra as spares to replace the tiny, limp bodies they toss overboard.

I was only ten when I was brought to this place, out of my mind with terror. So I kept my head down. I learned to be small and silent, and how to cry without making a sound.

Ingra was different.

'Why?' I once asked when she came back to our bunk, grimy and shivering after spending another night in the Pit. 'Why do you do it? Drawing attention to yourself, antagonizing Matron like that. Why do you always have to do . . . *something*?'

And I remember the way she smiled at me – softly, sadly – her split lip bleeding afresh. 'Because if I did nothing, I'd become nothing.'

The words weren't said with venom, but they still stung. For she was brave, unbroken. But me? I was broken before I had the chance to be whole.

I glance to my left, where Ingra is still caught up in some kind of staring contest with Matron. Gritting my teeth, I elbow her gently in the side. Ingra lets out a little huff of air but answers my silent plea, lowering her head with deliberate slowness.

For a moment I think about how different things would be if Ingra were in my shoes. If the magic of our ancestors had been returned to *her* instead. *She* wouldn't have been frightened. She wouldn't have tried to hide. She wouldn't have wasted her gift. She would've *used* it.

The people of Veridia once controlled and harnessed the power of the desert. I imagine Matron would be neck-deep in quicksand by now.

When the inspection is over, duties are assigned. It comes as little surprise that Ingra will spend the best part of the afternoon mucking out the stables.

For some reason, Matron leaves me until last. I clasp my hands behind my back, willing my shadows to remain hidden.

'You've been granted a new position. Requested personally, I believe.'

I stare at her, uncomprehending. Matron clicks her tongue impatiently and I straighten up, blinking. 'By – by who?'

'Don't ask questions,' she scolds. 'Report to the Ignitia Wing, first door on the right.'

The Ignitia Wing? Requested personally? I frown, confusion swamping fear.

'What're you waiting for?' Matron snaps.

I jump, nodding hurriedly, then head to the serf tunnels. There are thousands of them, all interconnected, leading to every floor of the palace. Some, though they're well hidden, even have direct access to individual chambers – like the ones belonging to the Earth Cleaver, who's clearly been using them to navigate the place for quite some time, and Hal, who unsealed the secret door behind the screen in his rooms for my use alone.

I wend my way through the pitch-black tunnels. Just as my eyesight has become sharpened, so too have my other senses. I've started hearing sounds in the dark that my ears wouldn't normally pick up. The soft scurrying of mice beneath floorboards. The slow, rhythmic breathing coming from bunks halfway down the corridor. Everything smells stronger, too. Roses in the palace gardens. The musty, metallic scent of the serf quarters, which sit just above the dungeons, cut into the golden bedrock of the mine. Unfortunately, this heightening of my senses also applies to taste. Food that was once stale is now inedible, the tea leaves swirling at the bottom of my cup unbearably bitter, and fruit even the slightest bit overripe carries the cloying sweetness of rot. Ingra keeps eyeing me suspiciously each time I push my plate away unfinished.

I'm out of breath by the time I emerge into the Ignitia Wing. The first door on the right is ajar. I realize that I've been to these chambers before, readying Blaze for what turned out to be her second trial. Cautiously, I reach out and rap twice.

'Come in,' trills a familiar voice. 'It's open!'

The room beyond is almost identical to Blaze's, except while hers was blue, this one is red. Crimson tapestries, scarlet cushions and chaises, and *clothes* – mountains of them.

I startle as a figure emerges from a pile of sparkling vermillion jumpsuits. The girl is tiny, not five feet tall, with periwinkle eyes, freckled skin and a mass of fiery hair.

'Elva!' Elaith cries. Then, a little anxiously, 'It is Elva, isn't it?'

'Yes, my lady.'

She pulls a face. 'Oh please, none of that. It makes me sound about a hundred and three. Besides, technically, I'm not actually highborn. My family are just obscenely rich. My father bought us all titles though he's not fooling anyone. Money can buy nobility, but not noble blood. Anyway, forgive me. I'm rambling. I do that a lot.'

'You . . . you wanted to see me?' I say, a little bemused.

Elaith snaps her fingers. 'Right, yes. I hope you don't mind, but I wanted to ask, since Blaze isn't here, would you consider helping me instead?' My astonishment must be evident, for Elaith hurries on, 'It's just, I know she was fond of you, and her hair always looked *so* beautiful. And between you and me, I swear my last serf was stealing my rings.'

This doesn't surprise me. Clover is known for being a tad light-fingered. I only hope Matron never finds the collection of trinkets hidden beneath her bedroll, or she'll be facing a far worse fate than the Pit.

'In any case,' Elaith continues, 'what with most of my friends back at Fire Mountain, the twins locked up in a safe house and Spinner nowhere to be found, I could use some company.' She eyes me hopefully. 'So, what about it?'

It's sweet of her to position it as a request though we both know I couldn't refuse. I muster a tentative smile. 'Of course.'

'Yay!' She bounces up and down with delight, barely clearing my shoulder.

Despite my protests, Elaith helps me unpack and put away all of her belongings.

'Gods,' she groans afterwards, falling theatrically across a red-silk chaise, 'I'm stiff as a board from that carriage journey. But I couldn't disappoint Hal.'

My head snaps up involuntarily, but Elaith is too busy fishing something out of her pocket to notice. It's a crumpled piece of parchment. On it I recognize Hal's spidery scrawl, though I can't make out the words since they're written in Ostacrian. I might've been forced to learn how to speak the language, but I was never taught to read it.

Elaith smooths out the letter with her fingers. 'It was delivered right into my hands. Doesn't say much, though. I still haven't a clue what he actually wants.' She clears her throat. '*Elaith*,' she reads in a deep voice. '*I have need of you. Come to the palace? Hal.*'

My brows knit together. Hal tells me almost everything, yet he never mentioned this.

At that moment, there's a knock on the door.

'Enter,' calls Elaith, stuffing the letter back into her pocket.

A boy appears in the doorframe, tall and chiselled with dark skin and eyes the colour of honey. I recognize him as Zephyr, the Ventalla Heir who won the Choosing, and one of Hal's closest friends. Unlike the rest of the new Council, Zephyr does not have a court to reside in, since King Balen is still occupying the Marble Palace.

'Hello, Elaith.'

'Zeph! How are you?'

He dips his head, grinning. 'Still in one piece. And yourself?'

'Mildly traumatized,' muses Elaith. 'To what do I owe the pleasure?'

Zephyr shifts on his feet. 'I'm not . . . entirely sure.'

She arches an eyebrow. 'Come again?'

'I have instructions to fetch you and tell nobody.'

'How mysterious,' she says. 'Where are you supposed to be taking me?'

'The observatory.'

'Now?'

Zephyr nods.

'Very well, consider me intrigued,' says Elaith before smiling at me. 'Thank you, Elva. That'll be all.'

But Zephyr shakes his head. 'She comes too.'

My stomach drops. Fear courses through me, and I clasp my hands behind my back.

'Er . . . what?' Elaith asks, perplexed.

Zephyr sighs as he props open the door. 'Are you coming or not?'

Elaith looks as uncertain as I feel, but she only shrugs, springing lightly to her feet. 'All right, then. Let's go.'

I have no choice but to follow.

Zephyr glances from side to side before swinging open the entrance to the serf tunnels. 'Discretion,' he explains. Then he turns to me. 'I take it you know the way?' His tone is polite though he seems unable to hide the confusion creasing his brow.

I feel myself flush pink. Nodding once, I slip silently into the darkness beyond.

'Hold on,' says Elaith, reaching up on her tiptoes to heave one of the torches from its golden bracket. 'Won't you be needing this?'

I take it gratefully, inwardly cursing myself.

Since our destination sits at the very top of the palace – a colossal golden tower adjacent to the Choosing Chamber – there are a lot of stairs to climb. I can hear Elaith panting behind me as the steep steps stretch on and on.

Eventually, joints aching, we come to a stop. Elaith is bouncing again, whether from excitement or nerves I can't tell. My heart is beating so loudly I don't hear what she whispers in my ear as Zephyr shoulders open the door.

The observatory is a vast domed chamber, opulent and echoing. A portion of the ceiling has slid open to allow a wedge of sunlight to spill in across the solid-gold floor, which is emblazoned with the Imperial emblem. The curved walls are carved with constellations, and the table in the centre is scattered with an array of telescopes, astronomical maps, sky charts, and even what look to be small urns filled to the brim with stardust.

Sitting at this table are two people. The first is a beautiful girl with bronze skin and dark hair pinned back with silver clips shaped like fish. Marina Kalpara, the Aquatori Heir who lost to Blaze during the third trial. The second rises to greet us. The dark circles beneath his eyes contrast starkly with his pale complexion, yet his mouth tugs upward into a smile.

'You made it,' Hal says warmly. 'Good. Please, take a seat. I have something I wish to discuss with you all.'

I gape at him in shock. I don't understand. What's going on? What is he *doing*, bringing me here?

His gaze lingers on mine, but his face reveals nothing.

Zephyr watches this silent exchange, shooting another bewildered glance in my direction before throwing himself into the nearest chair. 'All right, let's hear it.'

'What's with all the secrecy?' Elaith chimes, plonking herself down beside him.

'And could you explain *this*?' Marina's voice is a sharp lash. She's staring straight at me, her eyes narrowed.

'All in good time,' Hal soothes, pushing out the remaining chair with his foot.

I hesitate for a long moment before perching lightly on the edge, my arms wrapped tightly round my chest.

'As I'm sure you're aware, we face times of political unrest,' Hal begins. 'The people are scared, and fear tends to divide rather than unite. It's come to my attention that . . .' He pauses, his jaw clenched. 'There are many – more than I had perhaps anticipated – who would see me step aside in favour of my uncle, to allow him to rule as regent in my place.'

Marina makes a disgusted sound.

'It seems,' Hal continues, raven eyes shuttering with barely concealed fury, 'that some of my advisers are also in favour of this idea.'

'But what about the attack on Fire Mountain?' Elaith asks, outraged.

'Or what happened at the Binding Ceremony,' Zephyr adds. 'King Balen watched the Council die, and he . . . he was *smiling*. Like it was all some big joke.'

'You hit your head,' Marina reminds him. 'Everyone did.'

'Yes, Marina, I hit my head – I didn't *lose my mind*. I know what I saw.'

She holds up her hands in surrender. 'And I believe you. I only *meant* that's why people's recollections differ. Why the evidence is contestable. Everyone was knocked unconscious, so nobody knows for sure what went on in that chamber. Nobody except . . .'

Zephyr nods. 'He wanted something from them. From Fox and Blaze. Wanted it *bad*. A brooch, maybe? Or was it a necklace? I can't remember.'

'Only they know what truly happened,' says Marina. 'And with Fox exiled . . .'

'It's Balen's word against Blaze's,' Elaith finishes. 'Only, unlike her, he has the people's respect. That's why he's able to twist the truth to garner support.'

Hal nods. 'And that support is growing every day. Not just among the commonfolk, but the courts. My own court, especially. The Eyes are supposed to be the emperor's spies, but I believe some are working against me – intercepting my letters, watching my every move, spreading lies about my ignorance, my inability to lead, even my health.'

I take in his gaunt appearance, the tremor in his hands as he grips the table. There's no denying how ill he looks. But if the people start questioning whether he's fit to rule . . .

'If I can't prove to our neighbouring kingdoms that I'm the stronger ally, then there's a high likelihood that they could side with my uncle. King Merrick of Thaven will not consent to my marrying his daughter until he can be sure of my victory.'

I feel a sharp twinge in my chest at the mention of Princess Mirade.

'What's this got to do with us?' Marina asks.

Elaith glares at her. 'She *means*, what can we do to help?'

Hal takes a deep breath, knitting his fingers together. 'My Crowned Council are scattered across the empire, my advisers don't have faith in me, and some of my Eyes have turned traitors. I can't trust anyone.' His gaze flickers from face to face. 'But I can trust you.'

Elaith leans forward in her chair. 'What d'you want us to do?'

'It's more a question of who I want you to be.'

The four of us stare at him blankly.

Hal smiles a little, then points at Zephyr. 'My Council, naturally.' He nods at Marina and Elaith. 'My advisers.' Then he turns to me, his voice as soft as his gaze. 'And my spy.'

I stiffen, my mouth falling open a second time. Did I just hear him right?

'I'm alone in this,' Hal says. 'I need you – all of you. If you're willing.'

Zephyr grins at him. 'Been a long time coming, my friend.'

Elaith beams. 'You already know my answer.'

Hal inclines his head then glances at Marina. She may be a difficult sort of person, and she was no friend to Blaze, but Hal has always made allowances for her. They've known each other since infancy, and despite her rather frosty demeanour, her loyalty runs deep. She would never betray the crown.

'Of *course* I'll advise you, Hal,' she says. 'But a *serf* spy? *Really?*'

'I confess, I've been wondering the same thing,' Zephyr admits. 'Why her?'

I sink further into my chair.

'Isn't it obvious?' Hal asks, his dark eyes never leaving my face.

My heart lurches. I hold my breath, bracing myself. Surely he's not going to . . .

'Anonymity,' he says abruptly. 'Her ability to slip unnoticed through a crowd. The three of you are high profile, easily recognizable. You can't blend in the way she can.'

I'm so shocked that all I can do is blink at him.

'But how d'you know you can trust her?' Marina presses.

The pause before Hal speaks lasts only a fraction of a second. 'Because Blaze does.'

'And so do I,' says Elaith, smiling.

'But I am giving her a choice,' Hal continues, turning back to me. 'What do you say? I'm not asking you to engage, just observe. I want to know who's trustworthy and who's treasonous. I want you to be the Eye watching the Eyes. My shadow, hiding in plain sight.'

Oh, Hal, I think. *If only you knew.*

15

Blaze

The next few hours pass in terse silence.

Of course I'm not *relaxed*. How could I be? I just woke up from a fever dream after being bitten by a giant snake. I lost my brother and, seemingly, my mind, because somehow I agreed to travel through this strange, overgrown maze of a kingdom with the very same boy who broke the empire in half. I can feel him leaning away from me, sitting as far back in the saddle as he can. Maybe he's regretting his offer to escort me to the Lagoon, or maybe it's that I could really do with a wash. Either way, as pairings go, the two of us are exceedingly ill-matched. It's not just the way he speaks to me, his every word infused with that mocking pleasantness, or worse, that maddening softness. It's that . . . well, he *saved* me. And of all the things he's ever done, it's this I find hardest to forgive.

We reach a slight incline, and I'm forced to grab a handful of Cedar's mane to avoid tipping backwards into Fox's chest.

Perhaps I'm being ungrateful. Perhaps I should be thanking him. I imagine that's generally the response one gives in such circumstances. But doing so will only affirm out loud what we both already know – that I owe him, now.

I'm beginning to wish he'd just left me there in the forest. Getting eaten by wild dogs or slowly decomposing into the undergrowth seem like vastly preferable alternatives to being in the Earth Cleaver's debt.

Oblivious to the whirlpool of self-loathing swirling inside my head, Fox clears his throat and asks, 'How're you feeling?'

His voice is neutral, almost bored. Gone is any trace of that lingering smirk. Is he intent on making another gibe, or does the question indicate a temporary ceasefire?

'Better,' I concede.

We lapse back into silence, but this time it's not as heavy. Maybe it's my turn to break it? I rack my brains for a question of my own. As usual, I have plenty. But there's one in particular I've been burning to know the answer to ever since that night in the dungeons:

'Tell me how you found the Eye of the Past.'

More of a demand than a question, I admit, but it's a start.

'Only if you ask nicely,' Fox replies.

I toss my hair over my shoulder, hitting him in the face with it. 'Fine. Tell me how you found the Eye of the Past, *please*.'

'That's better.' He spits out a stray curl. 'Now then, let's see. Four years ago, I was sailing around the Eastern Isles.'

A sharp gasp escapes my lips as he brushes my fingers with his own, and just as they had before, my surroundings fade and transform. Suddenly I am no longer riding on horseback through the dense wilderness of the Wildlands but clinging to the rigging of a ship, Fox at my side. I can feel the coarse bristles of the thick rope in my hands, the wind in my hair, the sun on my face. I hear gulls cawing, wood creaking. The ocean stretches out before me like swathes of cerulean silk, glittering, endless, foaming waves curling up to slap the helm of the boat. The salt air tastes like freedom and I savour it, breathing deeply as a lump forms in my throat. How long have I dreamed of sailing the Second Sea?

I start in surprise as a second boy climbs up beside us, telescope in hand. Fifteen-year-old Fox stares right through me at a fixed point in the distance. His green eyes are just as piercing, his dark hair even more untidy, yet there's a boyishness to him. Gone is the ghost of the stubble on his jaw, the corded muscle of his forearms, the hard contours of his chest. He's slighter, softer. His threadbare shirt billows in the breeze as he leans backwards, one hand holding the rigging while the other raises the telescope.

Letting out a sudden hoot, he begins climbing down the rope, but before he can jump the last few feet to the deck of the ship, the vision changes.

I'm standing in what appears to be a busy shipping port. All around, people dressed in brightly coloured robes are calling out to one another in a language I don't understand, selling from stalls groaning under the weight of jewellery, armour and weapons. Fat silver fish are packed in barrels spilling over with flakes of salt, and the smell of ripened fruit and cooking meat fills the air, which is uncomfortably hot and heavy with smoke and incense.

'Zafar – one of the Eastern Isles,' Fox murmurs in my ear.

His younger self stands a little to the right of us, flanked by his crew, whom he sends off in pursuit of various goods – food, fresh water, soap. He possesses the easy authority of someone twice his age despite appearing at least a decade younger than the most junior of the men. Yet they clearly respect him – seem fond of him, even. Young Fox watches them lumber off into the throng, then begins to peruse the stalls, keeping one hand on the hilt of his gold dagger. We follow him, and I marvel at all manner of exotic curiosities – necklaces made from human teeth, talking birds, unbreakable chains. He buys what looks like an orange from a cart, except this orange is purple, and proceeds to peel it slowly.

Soon we reach the outskirts of the city.

'Where are you going?' I whisper.

'I'd heard a rumour about a woman,' Fox replies. 'A Mage. One believed to have retained her magic after the war.'

'But *how*? That's impossible.' Yet the words have barely left my mouth before a memory tugs at me – a boy bound in crystal shackles, hidden deep in the palace dungeons.

I jump as a gaggle of children runs by, the eldest of them no older than eight or nine. They're dressed in rags and pitifully thin, their faces streaked with grease and dirt. Young Fox catches hold of the boy at the rear of the group and says something to him in Zafarian. I find myself wondering just how many languages he can speak. As many as me? More,

I'd wager. He's travelled extensively. I envy the opportunities he's had to put his skills to use.

There's something about the way the little boy nods that reminds me of Renly. He glances around nervously, mumbles something, pointing left, then right, then left again. Young Fox smiles and tosses him the fruit. The boy's face lights up. He holds it in both hands, carefully, as though it were an object of great value, then scampers off after his friends.

'What did he say to you?' I ask Fox. I'm not sure exactly why I'm speaking so quietly. To those in this memory, we seem to be mute as well as invisible.

'He told me where I could find the *mahala*. That's Zafarian for witch.'

As we round the next corner, I know instantly this must be the place. A small hovel at the end of a row of abandoned buildings – a part of the city left to decay. The doorframe gapes and the window glass has long since shattered. The empty spaces are hung with scraps of thin fabric that ripple gently despite the lack of a breeze.

Young Fox hesitates, adjusting his dagger before stepping inside. We follow him, my heart rattling in my chest.

At first, the hovel appears empty. There's no furniture, no flooring of any kind. The ground beneath my feet is littered with silt and discarded food – chicken legs, apple rinds. I wrinkle my nose as I pick my way across, reminded of the waste chute at Fire Mountain.

Then, as my eyes adjust to the gloom, I see her, propped in a corner on a pile of blankets, unmoving. For a moment I think she might be dead, but then she lifts a wizened hand and makes a shooing gesture, baring a set of cracked, blackened teeth.

'As you can see, she wasn't the most welcoming,' Fox observes.

'Well, you did just walk into her house,' I mutter.

In front of us, young Fox bows his head respectfully, then begins to speak in Zafarian.

'What are you saying?' I ask.

'That I mean her no harm. I merely wish to ask some questions.'

The old woman burbles an angry response, shaking her fist. She's a sorry-looking creature, frail and sallow, her tattered hood pulled over her head like a shroud.

'If she's a Mage, then that means she's from the Otherlands,' I point out.

'A most astute observation, Storm Weaver.'

I resist thrusting my elbow into his ribs. 'Then wouldn't it help to speak to her in her own language? Which of the seven isles is she from?'

'Thresk.'

Thresk. An isle carpeted in grassy plains and green, moss-draped forests.

I can speak Threskan. It's a tricky language, full of vowels and double meanings. It took years to learn, but I persisted. I had nothing better to do, after all.

Eventually young Fox holds up his hands in surrender, half turning to leave. Only, his parting words are not in Zafarian.

'*Al ici daan cera solina?*'

Not even for a bag of silver?

The old woman's head snaps up. Her beady eyes narrow, flicking to the leather pouch at his belt. Young Fox smiles triumphantly. Slowly, he sits down opposite her. We watch as he reaches into the pouch and pulls out a slender coin stamped with a three-pronged crown – the Thavenian royal seal. The old woman licks her lips.

'Is it true?' he asks in Threskan. 'Are you a Mage?'

The old woman remains expressionless. Then she smiles.

Young Fox rolls the coin between his thumb and forefinger. 'Prove it.'

There's a long, precarious pause, during which the only sound is that of bells ringing far off in the distance, accompanied by the wheezing rasp of the old woman's breath. Then, all of a sudden, they're gone, replaced by dead silence. I turn my head this way and that, snapping my fingers beside my ear, yet I hear nothing.

Young Fox remains perfectly still, his gaze fixed on the old woman. She grins, and then she's gone too. Everything's gone. I can't see anything. I can't *see*.

I stumble forward into something solid and slide to the ground. I'm screaming, or at least I think I am. Sound and sight evade me. I am deaf and blind and terrified.

Then, quite suddenly, my hearing returns, followed by my vision.

The old woman is cackling softly. I flinch as she leans towards young Fox, extending her hand. He presses the coin into her palm. If he's shaken, he doesn't show it.

'What *was* that?' I hiss, as his older self pulls me to my feet.

'She's a Mage with the power to manipulate the senses,' he murmurs.

'Proof enough for you, boy?' The old woman slips the coin into the folds of her filthy robes. Her accent is thick, native. It takes me a moment to translate.

'How?' Young Fox asks bluntly. 'How did you retain your magic after the war?'

The old woman picks up a discarded animal bone. It's picked clean, but she nibbles on it anyway, sucking out the marrow. 'It is the past you seek, not me.'

'And where do I find the past?'

'The past does not wish to be found. That is why she hid it.'

Young Fox spins a coin on the dusty ground. 'Who is *she*?'

The old woman waits until the coin begins to slow, teetering jerkily from side to side. Snatching it up before it can fall, she breathes, 'The first sister.'

The vision fades out.

'What're you doing?' I demand, turning round in the saddle to face Fox. 'Make it come back. I want to hear what she said.'

'Her story is one you've heard before, Storm Weaver,' he says, taking a swig from his waterskin. 'The story of the three sisters and their enchanted Eyes. Except the Mage knew something my grandfather did not. That nobody knew, bar a handful, and most of that handful were dead. A small detail, but a crucial one. A secret whispered among friends.'

Anticipation drums into me. 'What secret?'

'She told me that Sifa was in love with a Threskan boy.'

I frown. 'So?'

Fox brushes my arm, and suddenly I see a girl, only a few years older than me, her dark eyes alight with eagerness as she hurries along a moonlit path.

'Sifa,' I whisper, as the vision fades.

'The very same.'

My breath hitches as Fox's fingers encircle my wrist. In the time it takes to blink, we're standing waist-deep in a sea of long grass swaying gently in the warm breeze. This must be Thresk.

Fifteen-year-old Fox is already wading through the stems, his gaze fixed on something up ahead where the ground begins to slope upward.

'Under an oak tree on top of a hill – that's where Sifa used to meet her lover.'

We follow young Fox until we reach the summit, where a large tree stretches high into the sky, its gnarled branches casting long shadows.

'Pretty little spot, don't you think?' Fox's voice is tinged with amusement.

We watch as his younger self drops to his knees at the base of the tree, closing his eyes in concentration. A moment later the carpet of grass trembles then splits, and soil begins to bubble up like water. Young Fox reaches his hand into the earth, a triumphant grin blooming across his face as he pulls out something small and gold.

That's when the pieces start to fall into place. 'You're not telling me . . .' The Wildlands flood back in once more, and I swivel to stare at Fox. 'But . . . but . . . I thought she was supposed to have hidden her Eye where she believed it would never be found?'

Fox shifts slightly in the saddle and cracks his neck. 'You see, Storm Weaver, people are predictable. They have a compulsion to attach meaning. And that was Sifa's mistake.'

I exhale. 'So what you're saying is that you now possess one of the most powerful enchanted talismans in the world all because its previous owner was a romantic fool?'

Fox smirks as he runs the tip of his finger along his chain. 'Essentially, yes.'

We're silent for a time as Cedar continues to pick his way among the trees.

My mind spins, thoughts tripping over themselves. 'And what about Seera?' I ask. 'Assuming she didn't also have some secret lover, how do you suppose your grandfather found the Eye of the Future?'

'I don't know,' says Fox grudgingly.

I swallow my disappointment. 'Then what about the Mage in Zafar? Did you ever discover why she was able to retain her magic?'

The pause before Fox responds lasts a fraction of a second too long. 'I've searched for answers, but there's nothing concrete. Nothing easy to prove.'

'But you have a theory?'

'I never said that.'

'You once told me that you *always* have a theory,' I point out.

'And you once told me that you wanted nothing to do with the very talisman you're risking your life to search for.'

I grit my teeth, irritated. Why must he close off after being so open?

'People change,' I reply with a shrug.

I hear the smirk in his voice as he leans in close to my ear. 'Oh no,' he says. 'That's one thing people never do.'

16

Blaze

We ride until the sun begins to set.

Ignoring Fox's outstretched hand, I slide clumsily down from Cedar's back and wince as my feet hit the ground. My whole body feels bruised.

'Are you hungry?'

I hesitate, leaning heavily against the trunk of an ash tree, trying to work out why an admission of hunger feels tantamount to a declaration of weakness.

'A little,' I concede at last, combing my fingers through my tangled curls.

'How about I find us some food while you wash up in the Creek?' Fox suggests.

I frown, waiting for the catch. That's the problem with the Earth Cleaver – he's not an easy person to trust. He's not especially kind either.

As if on cue, he changes tack. 'My apologies, that sounded like a suggestion, but really it was a request. Look at the state of you. Do us both a favour and bathe.'

I glower at him before heading off towards the sound of running water.

'Wait,' Fox calls, rummaging in his satchel before tossing me a bar of soap and a spare change of clothes.

I hold up the shirt. 'I don't want your clothes. I have my own.'

'Yes, and they're filthy.'

'So I'll wash them,' I bite back, irritated.

'And what will you wear while you wait for them to dry?' Fox asks innocently. 'Forgive me, *Your Majesty*, but I always considered you the modest type. Though do feel free to prove me wrong.'

A furious blush blooms across my cheeks.

'Fine,' I spit, tucking the bundle under my arm and ducking through the trees.

I glance back in time to see Fox untacking Cedar, chuckling quietly to himself as the horse nuzzles his shoulder, as if the two of them were sharing some private joke.

The Creek is a welcome sight, the water bracingly cold. It soothes the angry fire-ant stings peppered along my spine. I scrub myself clean as best I can, then pull on the borrowed set of clothes, rolling up the trousers and rolling my eyes at the low-cut shirt.

Shivering a little, I return to the camp and drape my own clothes over a branch to dry.

Fox appears several minutes later. He takes in the sight of me, tilting his head in apparent bemusement. 'Any particular reason why you're wearing that shirt back to front?'

I glance down. 'Oh, I thought I'd try something new. Why? Do you like it?'

Fox blinks, taken aback. 'I . . . I mean . . .' He clears his throat uncomfortably, seemingly at a loss for words. That's when he notices my withering expression. 'As the future Queen of the Waterlands, you certainly have a very dry sense of humour, Storm Weaver,' he remarks. 'What's your quarrel with my shirt? Not quite to your taste?'

I run a finger along the slightly fraying hem. 'While *you* clearly have a liking for shirts that gape open practically to your midriff –'

He scoffs. 'Hardly.'

'– I'd really rather not wander around only half-dressed,' I finish scathingly.

A grin slides on to his face. 'Well, I for one wouldn't be complaining.'

I scowl darkly. 'Remind me again why I agreed to stay with you?'

Fox shakes his head fondly. 'Storm Weaver, most girls would trade just about anything for a mere hour of my company.'

'That I very much doubt, unless they'd paid a visit to the Mage in Zafar. I imagine I would find your company entirely tolerable, provided I could neither hear nor see you.'

His grin widens, and he tosses his satchel down at my feet. 'I brought you something.'

I narrow my eyes suspiciously, but reach inside, unable to turn down a direct challenge, only to draw my hand back moments later with a yelp. Hissing in pain, I empty the clump of stinging nettles out on to the ground, then glare at Fox.

'They made me think of you,' he tells me.

Seething, I hold up a finger.

Fox tuts. 'How vulgar you are, Your Majesty.'

'Stop calling me that,' I snap, massaging my palm.

Still smirking, Fox sets to work building a fire, placing the pewter cooking pot on a large flat stone in the centre. I watch as he meticulously cuts and cleans the roots he foraged, adding them to the pot alongside the nettles to blanch, followed by a sprinkling of wild herbs. As the steel sparks and the kindling catches, my thoughts turn to Flint.

There was a moment in the Ridge tunnels, before the explosion, when I almost believed he wasn't going to do it. I'd never seen him so helpless. He looked . . . terrified.

I'd screamed at him, begged him, *willed* the flames to spring forth – and then, mercifully, they did. He saved us. And now he's out here all alone.

Fox watches me gaze uselessly into the flames. 'Your brother can handle himself,' he says, as if I'd spoken aloud.

I look up in surprise, and he holds out a bowlful of sorry-looking stew.

After his stunt with the nettles, I consider not taking it. Or throwing it back in his face. But hunger tips the scale, and I pick up my spoon, blowing gently on the steaming concoction before taking a small sip. I pull a face. It tastes as bad as it looks. Worse.

'Don't worry, Storm Weaver,' Fox tells me, grinning as he settles himself against a tree stump. 'There's more than enough for seconds.'

Silence resumes as we both choke down the stew. When I push away my empty bowl, Fox tosses me the waterskin. Reflexively, I catch it with my injured arm and wince. The bandage is damp and fraying, and most of the salve was washed away in the spring.

'Want me to take a look?' Fox asks.

I wrestle with my response. Pain battles pride. Pain wins.

I shuffle closer to him, extending my arm and avoiding his gaze. He encircles my wrist to examine the bite. His touch is warm, gentle.

'So?' I say rudely, unable to help myself. 'How does it look?'

'Not bad,' he responds, applying some poultice.

I flinch at the sound of his dagger being slid from its sheath and watch as he uses it to sever the end of the bandage.

'That dagger,' I begin.

'What about it?'

'It's the same one you had in Zafar.'

'It is. I won it in a game of cards.'

'You didn't have it at the Binding Ceremony,' I say quietly.

A flicker of something dark and wretched passes across his features. 'No,' he agrees. 'I didn't think I'd need it.'

I remember the moment he snatched my own dagger from my belt – that curved silver claw cut from the beast in my first trial. I remember the moment it was plunged deep into the emperor's chest. I can still smell the blood spreading slowly across the dais.

Fox says nothing as he finishes tying the bandage, then turns away to stoke the fire. Dusk has fallen, and the flickering light glances off his face, which is carefully neutral – a mask of indifference. Well, almost. I watch a muscle pulse in his jaw, recalling his expression that day. The horror. The guilt.

When I speak, my voice is softer than intended. 'I don't blame you, you know.'

Fox begins packing away his medical supplies. 'Then you're on your own with that.'

'Only because people don't know the truth.'

'They know I murdered my father and the three queens.'

'But not that you didn't *mean* to,' I say, frustrated.

'That doesn't matter.'

The fierceness in my tone takes me by surprise. 'Of *course* it matters.'

At long last, Fox looks at me. Green eyes gaze into mine, unblinking. 'Careful, Storm Weaver,' he murmurs. 'Anyone would think you cared.'

I swallow self-consciously, then change the subject. 'You said you won it?'

'What?'

'The dagger,' I clarify.

'Ah.' Fox runs his finger along the blade. 'Yes, it used to belong to Magnus Aurelian.'

Recognition stirs. 'Is that –'

'The Prince of Thaven,' he finishes. 'Sadistic brute. Soon to be brother-in-law to the emperor – that is, if Haldyn can drag himself away from our friend the Shadow Mage.'

'Elva,' I correct stiffly.

'Elva, yes. Honestly, I've never seen him so smitten. But even he wouldn't be stupid enough to jeopardize the alliance with Thaven over an infatuation.'

I don't respond.

'I wonder how he'll manage it,' Fox muses. 'Juggling them both.'

'It's not like he hasn't had the practice,' I snap, unable to help myself as I recall, with a dull pang of humiliation, the night I learned of Hal's betrayal, when I found him on his knees in my darkened chamber, cradling Elva to his chest.

Fox frowns, as though he's remembering it too. 'About what my brother did –'

I cut him off. 'It's getting late.'

I might have forgiven Hal his deception, but it appears it hasn't entirely lost its sting. Though if the Earth Cleaver suspects I'm still harbouring any unrequited feelings for his brother, then he's mistaken. I only hope Princess Mirade will be smarter than I was.

Fox tries again. 'If this is because I knew and didn't tell you –'

'It's got nothing to do with you,' I say bluntly.

He leans back against a tree, one hand on his chest. 'You wound me, Storm Weaver.'

I scoff, using a branch to pull myself to my feet. 'Goodnight.'

'I can't protect you from over here, you know,' he calls as I snatch the blanket from his bedroll and make my way to the other side of the clearing.

'I can protect myself.'

'Not without your water gifts you can't.'

I grimace. The temporary absence of my magic makes me feel uneasy. Off-kilter, as though I were missing a limb, or rather something far more intrinsic – a part of myself I can no longer live without. For seventeen years I was utterly defenceless, and I resented it.

Fox folds his arms behind his head. 'Look, you're still weak, which means your powers are weak. Right now, you're a sitting duck.'

'And you're insufferable,' I grit out, grudgingly edging back towards the fire and lying down with my back to him.

Cedar nickers quietly, as if to say, *She's got a point.*

17

Elva

It's the darkest part of the night, and the Golden Palace is as silent as the grave.

I steal through empty hallways, ears pricked for the slightest sound – hushed voices emanating from any of the opulent chambers, a clandestine meeting of traitorous Eyes. I figured that if such gatherings were taking place, then this would be a good time to convene. Those operating under the cloak of darkness often have something to hide.

I should know.

A ribbon of shadow curls from my fingertip and begins to twine round my wrist. I shake it off, cursing, and it fades into nothing.

I spent the day slipping into the rooms of some of the courtiers Hal suspects may be working for his uncle, armed with a mop and bucket for plausibility, searching for anything that might confirm his suspicions, yet I found no incriminating evidence. When evening arrived I helped ready Elaith for the feast, weaving tiny red fire-opals through her hair, then joined the other serfs in the banquet hall, pouring wine and fetching platters of food from the kitchens. I mostly lingered at the Eyes' table, listening in on conversations, paying attention to particular groups and pairings, to who was whispering in whose ear.

Ingra wasn't in our bunk when I returned to the serf quarters just before midnight. I couldn't account for her absence. I began to worry that she'd been tossed in the Pit, though if Matron catches me out of bed, at least Ingra will have some company.

The Pit is exactly as it sounds – a damp, dark hole. The space is cramped and narrow. You just have to stand there, or sit, hugging your knees tight to your chest. The walls are uneven, filled with footholes used to climb back up again once you've served your time – if you're strong enough to climb, that is. Ingra once spent three days down there without food or water. She was barely conscious and had to be hoisted back up.

I was eleven years old the first time I was thrown in the Pit.

There was this little girl – she couldn't have been more than seven or eight. She was from Obsidia too. I remembered her from the ship. She'd cradled this sorry-looking piece of sack that I think was supposed to be a doll, and would whisper to it over the creaking sails. One time, I found her crying in a stairwell. Matron had confiscated her doll, claiming that it could be carrying any number of diseases. I crouched beside the girl, speaking softly and comfortingly, just like my mother would have. Only, I didn't realize that I wasn't speaking Ostacrian – the language of our oppressors we were forced to learn upon our arrival here. No, I was speaking in my native tongue, Obsidian. And I was overheard.

Matron dragged me by my hair to the Pit. I was too scared to scream, but I recall making this awful whimpering noise as she selected a key from the bunch jangling ominously on her belt. She reached down to unlock the hatch, swung it open, and then shoved me inside. I fell and hit the ground with a jarring thud. Moments later, the trapdoor was slammed shut behind me, and I was swallowed by the darkness.

I was left in the Pit all night. It was to teach me a lesson, Matron said. So that I would never do it again – speak my own language. And I didn't. At least, not out loud. I *think* in Obsidian all the time. Right now, in fact. My thoughts are my own, and so are my memories.

All of a sudden, I hear footsteps heading in this direction. In a crowd I might be inconspicuous, but wandering the corridors alone in the dead of night – not so much.

I spot a door up ahead and slip inside.

The candles are still burning, the flickering light dancing across the walls of the room, which have each been designed to represent a different Crown Court – one carved with golden flames, another with crashing waves, the next with towering trees, and the last with hundreds upon hundreds of feathers. In the far corner sits a grand piano hewn from solid gold.

The Golden Palace is always sparkling. That's because every day it's cleaned by an army of serfs. The floor is so well polished that I can see myself reflected in it. Sometimes, when Blaze was at training, I would sit in front of the mirror in her bedchamber. Though it wasn't an act of vanity. It's because I can see my family in my face. Astrid's straight nose and cornsilk hair. My mother's high cheekbones. My father's eyes – dark amber, like the sunset.

I tense as I remember what the Earth Cleaver told me about my eyes, about how they glowed in the dark that night that changed everything. Just like my moon panther Kjara's did. Just like my grandparents' had in the years before the war.

The footsteps are louder now. I will them to keep moving down the corridor, but to my horror the door handle begins to twist.

It's instantaneous the way the darkness springs from my fingertips. Trembling, I shrink back against the wall, melting into the shadows. I didn't call upon them – I didn't will them to appear – and yet here they are, tendrils of dark mist wrapping themselves round me. Perhaps if I weren't so afraid I'd feel something close to wonder.

At that moment the door swings open, and someone steps inside. I hold my breath, then exhale in relief. It's Hal. Only, as his eyes slide over me without a flicker of recognition, the comfort I feel at the sight of him is swamped by a chilling realization.

He can't see me.

Shock roots me to the spot, rippling up my spine.

The shadows – they must be concealing me from view. They're *hiding* me.

I clamp my hand over my mouth to muffle the choked gasp that catches in my throat as understanding sparks to life amid the gloom.

The Earth Cleaver called my magic a gift, but it didn't really feel like one. I never asked for it. I still don't understand how it happened. I've spent these past few weeks terrified of accidentally revealing myself, since I never knew when those ribbons of darkness would emerge, or why. I couldn't see a connection – until now. Or could it just be a coincidence that the shadows seem to appear when I'm *frightened*? Almost as if my fear wakes them up, like they can sense I'm in danger and want to protect me.

I think of what my mother used to say.

Don't shut fear out, Elva. Invite it in.

The idea is strangely comforting. I feel the knot in my chest loosen slightly. For if I'm right, then maybe I have a shot at controlling my power. Maybe I could . . . *use* it.

I watch as Hal crosses to the piano and sits down. He opens the lid and flexes his hands before positioning his fingers gently on the keys. He plays very well. Sometimes he follows the sheet music; other times he creates his own. Today it's the latter. He pours himself into every note. The music echoes through me, beautiful and soulful and sweeping. There's a desperation to it, too – the difference between wanting to play and *needing* to.

It soothes me, listening to him, and after a while the shadows slowly recede into nothingness.

Steeling myself, I step out into the light.

Hal startles as I lay a hand on his shoulder, and the music stops so abruptly that my caress feels more like an assault.

'Elva.' He smiles softly. 'I didn't see you.'

I feign nonchalance. 'You're the one who said I'd make a good spy.'

His expression turns slightly sheepish. 'I'm sorry for springing it on you like that. I know it's a lot to ask.'

'I want to do it,' I assure him. 'I want to help. And you were right, about me going unnoticed. None of the Eyes gave me a second glance at the feast. I'm invisible.'

'Not to me,' says Hal. 'Never to me.'

He shifts to the side. I glance warily at the closed door before sitting down next to him on the piano stool.

'Why aren't you in bed?' I ask. 'It's late.'

'Too much on my mind. Anyway, I could ask you the same question. Why are you wandering the palace during the small hours?'

'Why do you think? I'm your shadow, remember?' My lips quirk in spite of myself.

'I didn't mean for you to not get any rest,' he says reproachfully.

'I like the nighttime,' I reply with a shrug. 'It's peaceful, and it reminds me of home.'

The lines on Hal's brow cut deeper. 'You know you didn't have to accept, don't you? You know that you're free to go, whenever you choose.'

'I do, and I choose to stay.'

His voice is strained. 'I understand why, and that it's not only for me that you've decided to remain.'

My heart thumps painfully. He's talking about the serfs.

'I won't abandon them,' I say quietly. 'I couldn't live with myself.'

Hal rakes a hand through his hair in a manner that reminds me of his half-brother. 'You know I always planned to free them when I came into power,' he says. 'To take action where my father did not. But my advisers still won't even entertain the idea. They think me too soft. If I'm to make them listen – *really* listen – I'll have to target them separately. Appeal to them one by one. Bribe them, if I have to.'

I've seen the way they look at him – Kalf, Alator and the others. They see him less as a leader and more as a boy. A figurehead. I think back to a time not so long ago, when Hal was just a prince, powerful in name but powerless when it came to facilitating real change. I thought everything would be different when he took the throne. Yet now, even as emperor, he walks a fine line, subject to public opinion, governed by his own advisers.

'Can't you just . . . overrule them?' I ask tentatively.

His face twists with anguish. 'I wish it were that simple. But I have to tread carefully. I can't give my enemies, or my allies, any more reasons to question my judgement.'

I hate it. I reject and resent it with every fibre of my being, but he's right. Thanks to King Balen, the political climate is unstable. If Hal were to liberate the serfs now, the entire system might collapse. A decision like that could bury him. And then where would we be?

I make no reply, lightly tracing the dark circles beneath his eyes. He looks even more gaunt than yesterday, his lean frame verging on thin, his cheekbones jutting out, sharp and angular. It scares me, seeing him like this. I remember what he said in the observatory, about the Eyes spreading lies regarding his poor health. Only, they don't appear to *be* lies. Hal *does* look ill. I assumed it was stress-related at first, but now I'm not so sure. And no matter how many times I ask him about it, he just shakes his head and says, *It's nothing*.

Hal threads his fingers with mine. 'I've been thinking about . . . about the other reason you're reluctant to return to Obsidia.'

I feel my throat tighten.

'I know your parents died in the raid, and that you think your sister didn't survive the journey over here.'

I glance down at our joined hands, grief tearing at my insides.

'For days, I've been poring over old ledgers and treaties,' Hal continues. 'And tonight . . . I found something.'

My head snaps up. 'What?'

'The year you were . . . taken, my father made a deal with our neighbouring kingdoms. Rather than trading gold, he decided to trade serfs.'

My breath catches. I pull my hand from his grasp and brace it on the piano. 'What're you saying?'

'That two of the slave ships departing from the Otherlands were not bound for Ostacre, but for Thaven and Vost.' He pauses, swallows, looks me right in the eyes, then says, 'Elva, there's a chance your sister may still be alive.'

His words take a moment to land. But when they do, they hit me with the force of a falling star, lighting up the world with joy so bright it's blinding.

Astrid.

Tears well up and spill over. A flood of relief breaks free from the carefully constructed dam inside my chest and cascades through me in dizzying waves. I sway where I sit, and Hal reaches out to steady me before I topple right off the stool.

'Help me discover which Eyes are still loyal to me and I'll send them as emissaries to make discreet enquiries,' he says. 'I can't promise to find her, but I can promise to try.'

I make a sound somewhere between a sob and a laugh, and the next thing I know my arms are round Hal's neck and I'm pulling his mouth down to mine. His lips are cool and soft, always a little hesitant at first, as though making sure this is really what I want. Then one of his hands moves to cup my waist as the other slides gently through my hair.

For once, I don't object to my heightened senses. His touch is as warm and welcome as sunlight caressing my skin.

Suddenly Hal pulls back, his face twisted in pain, a fist pressed to his forehead.

'What's wrong?' I ask, startled.

He stifles a low groan, his jaw clenched. Then, with obvious effort, he straightens up, his expression smoothing over.

'What was that?' I demand.

He shakes his head dismissively as he tucks me under his arm. 'It's nothing.'

I let him lie, let it slide, let him brush a tender kiss to my temple – but I don't let it go.

I take the tunnels back to the serf quarters, and when I slip into my room, I find Ingra fast asleep and snoring, sprawled across her bunk. Wherever she was, it wasn't the Pit.

In my dreams, I see Astrid, as beautiful as the night, beckoning me home.

18

Blaze

The forest at dawn looks like something out of the fairytales I read to Renly.

Curling tendrils of silver mist snake through the undergrowth as I walk among the trees, the leaves glittering with early-morning dew. All around, wildflowers compete for space on this canvas of green, blooming in varying shades of deep blue, bright yellow and heartbreak-red, their petals sprawling and feathered – nothing like the perfectly uniform bunches of golden roses Hal used to leave in my chambers.

I lean down to pluck a thick stem from another patch of flowers. It's pretty, if a little peculiar, heavy with a dozen thimble-shaped purplish blooms.

'I like these better anyway,' I mutter, as if Hal could hear me.

It's not long before sunlight begins to filter through the branches, and I come to a stop in a small clearing. After ascertaining that I'm not about to be set upon by a pack of hungry beasts, I take a long, deep breath, then close my eyes. Injured or not, I resent the exhaustion seeping through my body. Without my gifts I'm vulnerable, and I'd rather not keep it that way, particularly since the idea of aiming a jet of icy water at Fox's arrogant face is becoming increasingly appealing. I tug moodily at the collar of his shirt, which digs uncomfortably into the underside of my throat. It would be far more practical to just wear it the right way round, but I meant what I said about the neckline gaping open to a frankly indecent degree.

All of a sudden, I'm seized by an unwelcome memory of a cold blade on hot skin, a dagger sliding down my chest punishingly slowly, cutting the buttons off my shirt one by one as a pair of green eyes bored into mine, piercing and hungry and . . .

I give my head a little shake, attempting to expel the Earth Cleaver from my mind.

I hate that I'm wearing his clothes, and I hate how much he likes it.

Clearing my throat, I force myself to concentrate on my anchors, deciding to start with rain. When I'm ready, I reach inwards for that familiar sadness – grief that became a gift, pain that became power. But all I manage to produce is a weak flurry of drizzle.

Exasperated, I roll my neck and try again.

I picture my mother telling me a story, kissing a scraped knee, teaching me to swim in the cove below Bartell Manor, holding me tightly after I'd had a bad dream.

Tears spring into my eyes and I feel the drizzle intensify, turning to raindrops. Yet it isn't long before they subside.

How long will it take before my magic returns to its full capacity? A day? A week? The idea is torture. Letting out a hiss of frustration, I aim a kick at a nearby tree stump.

That's when a voice overhead drawls, 'What a nasty temper you have, Storm Weaver. Have you ever tried counting to ten?'

Startled, I look up. Fox is draped ceremoniously across a branch several feet above me, rolling a ripened blackberry between his thumb and forefinger. His dark hair gleams as though he's recently bathed, and his unkempt shirt gapes open, exposing the smooth golden planes of his chest. He looks perfectly at home up there in the trees, idly regal, an outlaw king as dazzling and dangerous as the Wildlands themselves.

'What d'you want?' I ask waspishly.

Fox smiles. 'And good morning to you too.'

I scowl. 'Do you enjoy sneaking up on me?'

'I could ask you the same question,' he says. 'Have you ever considered the possibility that perhaps it's *you* who sneaks up on me? For all you know, I was just out here engaging in a spot of light birdwatching.'

'Somehow I find that hard to believe.'

Fox tosses the blackberry into the air and catches it again. 'How shrewd you are. All right, perhaps I may have been checking in on you, but that's only because you ventured beyond the bounds of screaming distance.'

'*Screaming distance?*' I repeat.

'Yes,' he replies. 'Say I was back at the camp and you were all the way out here, and say you happened to run into trouble, I'd be too far away to hear you scream for help.

And while I admit the notion of your screaming my name appeals to me –'

I glare at him.

'– I'd really rather not spend my morning searching for your mangled corpse, or parcelling up various limbs to send back to your grandmother.'

In one lightning-quick motion, Fox drops from the branch and lands directly in front of me, his face tilted downward, mere inches from mine. My stomach lurches and I take a stumbling step back.

He smirks. 'Fancy some breakfast?'

I watch as he slips a hand into his pocket and pulls out a handful of dark berries. I eye them distrustfully.

'Ah, yes,' Fox drawls. 'Because I saved your life, tended to your wound, gave you my clothes, shared my food, and even offered you safe passage through the Wildlands all just so I could poison you with a berry.' He holds his arms up in surrender. 'You got me.'

My cheeks flush and I instantly feel foolish. But then again, can he really blame me for hesitating? He's still the Earth Cleaver. It's not as if he hasn't killed anyone before. Besides, he's entirely unpredictable. For all I know, he could have changed his mind about the missing Eye and decided that he does in fact want it for himself. And how easy it would be to dispose of me here in the woods, weak and feeble as I am.

'Trust me,' says Fox, in a voice that doesn't inspire me to trust him at all. 'If I wanted you dead, you'd be six feet under. And I assure you that if I were ever to kill you, my methods would prove a vast deal more interesting than this.' He holds up the berries.

'Of course,' I respond dryly, determined not to let him win. 'How could I ever overlook your twisted desire for spectacle?'

'Twisted desire?' Fox echoes, a vicious glint in his eyes. 'And what do you know of my *twisted desire*, Storm Weaver?'

I refuse to blush, jutting my chin. 'I know that you take pleasure in others' pain. That you enjoy hurting people.'

Fox mulls this over, then says softly, 'Only people who deserve it.'

A small shiver skitters along my spine. 'That doesn't make it right.'

He looks unmoved. 'I admit there are times when I do find enjoyment in watching my enemies suffer. Though I'm not the only one, it seems.'

I feel my skin grow cold. In my mind I see Ember's hands dripping blood, Marina suspended inside a frozen wave, the gargled, choking sounds Cole made as he tried desperately to prise his frozen tongue from the roof of his mouth. I remember how I felt during those moments. Not horrified, not regretful, but powerful. Triumphant.

I think about the way Fox looked at me then, and I think about the way he's looking at me now, and suddenly I no longer find him merely insufferable. I find him *infuriating*.

In the time it takes to blink, the handful of berries crystallize in Fox's palm.

I'm breathing heavily – whether from rage or exertion, I can't be sure. To my surprise, Fox just grins and pops a berry into his mouth. There's a crunching sound as he bites down on the frozen fruit, chews slowly and then swallows, his eyes never leaving my face.

Emboldened by my small surge of power, I do the same, taking a berry and cracking the thin layer of ice with my teeth.

'Impressive,' Fox says, as sweetness explodes on my tongue. 'Only, if you're going to produce some real ice, you'll have to channel a lot more anger than that.'

The sweetness turns sour the second his words land and their implication slams into me, knocking the air from my lungs. 'I . . . You . . .' I spit out the berry. '*How do you know that?*'

'What?' Fox asks innocently. 'About your ice making specifically or the fact that your water gifts are anchored to your emotions?'

I stare at him, utterly aghast. How can he possibly know about Melding? It's a secret the Rain Singers protected for thousands of years, one they took to their graves. Only a handful of people know the truth, and I doubt that either River or Queen Hydra would ever have entrusted it to Fox. I consider briefly whether his grandfather may have told him, but what would Caius Castellion have to gain from offering up that information?

There's nothing about Melding in any of the stories about the Singers, nor is it mentioned in any of the history books – save for the mysterious volume that appeared to me in the Golden Library, River's handwriting scrawled in the margin. But I'm having a hard time believing my trainer would have just left it lying around.

At last, I find my voice. 'I don't understand.'

'Then you're forgetting something, Storm Weaver,' Fox says, casting his eyes down. I follow his gaze to the talisman round his neck.

Of course.

Nobody told Fox about Melding. He didn't hear about it in a story or read about it in a history book. Why would he? He has history at his fingertips. History *belongs* to him.

'So, you used the Eye of the Past not only to unearth the secret of the Rain Singers but to discover my anchors?'

Fox considers this for a moment. 'If I said no, would you believe me?'

I take a step closer to him, incensed. 'Do you know how *personal* . . . how much of an *invasion* that is? I haven't even told Flint about Melding.'

'Well, perhaps you should,' Fox muses. 'Provided you manage to find him.'

A jet of cold water hits him square in the chest. I blink, momentarily stunned, as I watch rivulets streak down his torso, soaking his shirt. I feel it then – *power.* Magic stirs, as though waking up, growing stronger, just like my fury.

'Don't talk about my brother,' I snap.

'You're the one who brought him up. And speaking of brothers, would you rather we discussed mine instead?'

Another stream of water barrels into Fox's legs.

'I'll take that as a no,' he says, smiling deviously. 'Only it seems you felt differently last night. You said his name in your sleep, you know.'

Heat blooms across my cheeks. 'Liar.'

'You say lots of things in your sleep, Storm Weaver.'

This time, when the water shoots straight at his face, he sidesteps out of the way. 'It really was most unlike Haldyn, manipulating you like that. Out of the two of us, he's always been the more chivalrous one. I don't blame you for falling for his lies.'

Gleaming icicles, ragged and sharp, begin to form on the underside of the branch where Fox had been sitting.

His expression turns suddenly tortured. He clutches at his shirt theatrically. '*It kills me, Blaze*,' he imitates, '*knowing I can't have the one that I want*.'

Every vein in my body seems to turn to ice. He's gone too far.

'Stop spying on my life!' I yell. 'Stop snooping through my memories! They're *MINE*!'

No sooner have the words left my mouth than the first icicle falls. It catches Fox on the side of his shoulder. Blood slides down his arm, pooling in his palm. He's still holding the berries, which are now no longer black but stained crimson.

He holds them out to me. 'Want one?'

I stare at him, my chest heaving.

'What?' he says. 'I've tasted your blood. Why don't you try mine?'

The coldness spreading through me turns to heat as I recall once more that night in the dungeon – the press of his body, my own dagger held to my throat, how I'd struggled so much that the blade had nicked my skin, drawing forth a bead of blood. Fox had leaned in close enough for me to feel his warm breath on my neck and licked it away.

I shake my head and cross my arms over my chest.

'Pity,' he says, throwing a bloodied berry up and catching it in his mouth.

'You're repulsive,' I tell him.

With a snap of my fingers, a second icicle begins to fall. But Fox is faster this time, catching it in his hand and squeezing until it splinters into pieces. Seconds later something thick and green snakes round my leg. I shriek as my foot is pulled out from under me, but rather than go crashing to the ground, I'm hoisted into the air by my ankle.

Blood rushes to my head as I dangle upside down from the vine wrapped round the icy branch above.

Fox prowls closer until our faces are level. He looks as though he's trying not to laugh. The vine grows tighter, then tighter still, causing me to yelp.

'Let me down,' I snarl.

Fox brushes a stray curl from my face. 'Has anyone ever told you that you're beautiful when you're angry?'

I clench my jaw. 'Nope. Just you.'

'You know, Haldyn and I have always been a little competitive,' he continues. 'I imagine most brothers are. And so I've often wondered . . .' He's so close that I can see the small smear of blood on his lower lip. 'Which one of us was the better kisser?'

I forget how to breathe. His words are flames that devour me, scorching my skin.

'*Let. Me. Down.*'

Fox chuckles softly. 'As you wish.'

The vine releases me and I hit the forest floor with an agonizing thud. Pain barks along my joints, jarring and hot.

Then Fox is there, bent over me, pinning me to the ground, and I'm enveloped by the scent of him – pine and fresh mint and triumph. His eyes graze my face, glittering, ravenous.

'What do you think, Storm Weaver?' he whispers. 'You said I enjoy inflicting pain. Am I *enjoying* myself now?'

I gaze up at him, breathless. My stomach tumbles as something burning and treacherous takes root, clawing at my insides. For a moment I forget which it is I'm supposed to be fighting – him, or that feeling.

Fox has gone very still. I wait until his gaze drops to my lips. Then I bring my forehead up and crack it hard against his.

White light blinds me, then recedes to a dull throb. Fox rolls off me with a grunt and I scramble to my feet, ignoring the ache of protest from my limbs.

'I've had enough,' I spit.

'Enough?' Fox repeats, sounding almost sulky as he pulls himself up. 'But this is the most fun I've had in weeks.'

I take a small step back, then another.

Power still hums through my chest, pulsating and eager, like a muscle longing to be worked. But I meant what I said. I'm done.

Drawing myself up to full height, I say, 'You know, I might not always agree with Hal, but it seems there's one matter upon which he and I see eye to eye.'

Fox takes a step closer. 'Oh really? And what's that?'

I don't hesitate. 'Wanting you *gone*.'

With that, I turn on my heel and stride away from the Earth Cleaver.

'Do give Haldyn my regards once all this is over,' he calls after me. 'Make sure to tell him that if he's playing at being emperor even half as convincingly as he played at being in love with you, no doubt the people will soon be throwing themselves at his feet.'

I freeze mid-step.

Fury spikes.

Power erupts.

And it's as though the world turns to ice.

The forest now resembles a winter painting. I watch my shaking breaths curl upward in shimmering clouds. Sunlight elbows its way through the branches overhead, making the frost sparkle. And there, standing in the middle of it all, a satisfied smile etching at the corners of his cruel mouth, is the Earth Cleaver.

My heart beats so loudly in my ears that I wouldn't be surprised if he could hear it too. What have I done? And *how* did I do it?

Fox leans against a glistening tree, crossing one ankle behind the other. 'I'd say you're welcome, but I have a feeling that wouldn't go down particularly well.'

My brows shoot up. '*You're* taking credit for this?'

'In part. I gave you what you wanted. Your power was weak – now it's not, and seemingly it's even stronger than before.'

I make to respond but a sudden wave of dizziness washes over me, causing me to sway on my feet. Fox is there in an instant, holding out a steadying arm.

I shake him off, some of my anger returning, battling through the shock. '*Don't.*'

For a moment, so fleeting that I can't be sure whether it happened at all, he looks almost wounded.

Good, I think.

I start to march away but the slippery ground lurches violently then turns spongy. My limbs feel like liquid.

'Easy,' says Fox. His voice is soft. Gone is any trace of arrogance or amusement.

I try to frown at him but it proves rather difficult, for there now seem to be two of him. My head spins and I make a small, feeble sound. Everything hurts.

This time, when he reaches out, I surrender. Fox scoops me up, cradling me with surprising tenderness as he carries me through the frozen forest.

'I don't like you,' I mumble into his chest.

His lips are on my hair as he murmurs, 'I know.'

19

Flint

The moor seems to go on forever, purple heather stretching in all directions.

The Wildlands are made up of four principal landscapes – moors, meadows, mountains and forests. Having already grown tired of the endless moorland, frankly, any of the others would be preferable. At least then there would be some variation – trees, grassy plains, pretty flowers, not-so-pretty swamps. Even cliffs. I would honestly rather be hiking up a cliff right now, if only to fantasize about pushing Sheen over the edge.

He's walking several paces in front, shoulders back, spine poker-straight, really milking those few inches of height he has on me. He tends to do that – walk slightly ahead. I've never been able to work out whether it's because he likes that I'm forced to trail along behind, or that he hates being in my company so much he needs just a couple of yards of distance between us in order to tolerate it. Perhaps both.

It's been this way since the day we met. Sheen seemed to take an instant dislike to me, and as someone who has spent their entire life being more or less *adored* by everyone, I admit I find it . . . well, rather infuriating, actually. I'm not used to people not liking me. It's not that I expected it to feel *good*, but I just never expected it to feel this *bad*. Several times I've come close to asking him outright. But it just always sounded a bit stupid.

Why don't you like me?

All right. Pathetic, even.

Though maybe I shouldn't take it too much to heart, because Sheen doesn't seem to like anyone. He's so different from the other Eyes, with their court gossip and glamorous parties, living so vivaciously, carving out a space for themselves in every room.

In any case, Spinner's delight at being in my company more than makes up for Sheen's distaste for it. Unlike him, she was never immune to my charms. Things between us started just before the second trial, but I knew how she felt about me only days after arriving at the palace. I have this way of drawing people into my orbit, of making them fall fast and hard. It's not intentional. It's inherent – just a part of who I am. Or *was*.

Yet while I may have a long list of lovers, I don't *do* love. I'm not one for grand gestures or soul-bearing declarations. I only hope Spinner doesn't see this, *us*, as more than it is – a bit of fun, a casual, mutually satisfying arrangement with no strings attached.

She's currently swinging merrily from my arm, chattering about a multitude of people I've never heard of.

'. . . and *then* he found out that she was *already married*. Can you believe it?'

Spinner is, as always, unfailingly cheerful, her face cycling through its repertoire of expressions, which under usual circumstances would cause the tattoos on her cheeks to twist into all manner of different shapes. But since she was forced to accept that most Fidra don't, in fact, have swirling golden whorls inked into their skin, I helped her paint over them with a dark shade of panstick – the kind used by actors in theatre troupes.

'So, I asked him what he was going to do –'

'And what did he say?' I ask mildly. I'm only half paying attention to the story but I like listening to her talk. Spinner is so sweet, so lively, so animated. So unlike Sheen.

He adjusts the satchel on his shoulder. I don't think I've heard him speak today. I barely know anything about him other than that he's an Eye and my chaperone and chronically unpleasant. But wait – that's not all. I do know something else about him, something he never intended for me to find out.

'Isn't it only the most gifted Ventalla who're able flit?' I direct the question at Sheen's back, interrupting Spinner's steady stream of chatter.

Sheen doesn't even turn round as he says, 'Correct.'

'So what does that make you, then?'

'Play nice,' warns Spinner.

I hold up my hands in surrender. 'It's just a question. Questions start conversations, Spinner dearest. I figure that if I'm going to be spending the next however many weeks with my darling chaperone, the very least we could do is get to know one another.'

Spinner rolls her eyes. Sheen says nothing.

'*Well?*' Antagonizing him in this way is perhaps as unnecessary as it is unprovoked, but in my defence – I'm bored. And I'm bored of Sheen's morose silence. Maybe I'll never break through that steadfast wall of composure, but I take considerable pleasure in chipping away at the brickwork. Anything to pass the time.

'I suppose that would make me exceptionally gifted,' says Sheen eventually.

'Someone's a little full of themselves.'

Spinner elbows me in the ribs in Blaze-like fashion.

'I have another question,' I say, wincing.

Sheen sighs. 'Then by all means, ask away.'

'What other tricks can you do, besides flitting?'

'I'm not a performing monkey, Harglade.'

'Oh, come on,' I wheedle. 'Give us a show, why don't you?'

I watch Sheen's shoulders rise and fall as he marches across the heather, his white-blonde hair gleaming in the afternoon sun.

'Not a fan of that question? All right, here's another. Aside from Spinner and me, who else knows you're Ventalla?'

Sheen glances to the side, but doesn't turn round. 'Keep your voice down.'

I raise an eyebrow. 'Why? We're in the middle of nowhere.'

'Yes, I'm aware of that. I just don't want to listen to it.'

Now it's my turn to feel irritated.

Spinner loops her arm through mine again. 'A word to the wise, Flint, my love. Don't bother trying to take on Sheen. He'll eat you alive.'

'Sounds intimate,' I tell her.

After several more endless hours of hiking, my feet are beginning to hurt.

'My feet are beginning to hurt,' I announce plaintively.

Sheen continues to march ahead as though I hadn't spoken at all. Gods, what is his *problem*? And how is he managing to walk like that? The soil beneath the heather is covered with a spongy layer of moss. Twice Spinner has fallen flat on her face. But not Sheen. His tread is as light and graceful as ever, as though he were walking on air. Typical.

I reach up reflexively to readjust my bow, forgetting it's no longer there. I feel defenceless without it. Magically impotent *and* unarmed. In other words, useless.

My thoughts drift to Blaze. I wonder where she is. I wonder if she thinks I'm dead. I hope she's safe. *Please* let her be safe.

My burns smart and sting as another bead of sweat rolls down my forehead. I'm running low on supplies. My vials of painkiller are almost entirely depleted. There's only a small amount of salve left and I'm trying to save it for when the pain becomes truly unbearable, as if it were a treat for special occasions. The dull ache in my eye is only made worse by the eyepatch, which traps heat in and rubs uncomfortably against my skin.

All in all, I'm having a brilliant day.

I think of Harglade Hall, of my huge stone bath with taps shaped like little cobras, my four-poster bed with its red-silk sheets and mountain of pillows, a tray piled high with all my favourite things – roasted duck, honey-glazed carrots, apple pie and custard . . .

'I'm *hungry*,' I moan. 'And I'm tired.' I glance at Spinner for support. 'What about you? You're tiny. You must be exhausted.'

She shrugs. 'I have a lot of stamina.'

I smirk in spite of myself. 'Now *that* I can confirm.'

A few steps ahead of us, Sheen pretends to shudder.

'Prude,' I mutter.

With my request to stop and rest denied, and the pain in my burns increasing with every uneven step, I fall into a prickly silence. This lasts only a minute or two, however, because I'm struck by a sudden realization – that sometimes, in order to get your way, you have to make yourself absolutely *insufferable*.

I clear my throat. 'Are we there yet?'

'Oh, *please* don't start that again,' Spinner groans.

'But are we there yet?'

'*Flint*.'

'*Spinner*.'

'Shut up, will you?'

'No, I won't. Sheen? D'you know if we're there yet?'

No answer.

'Are we there yet?'

Still no answer.

'*Are we there yet are we there yet are we there yet are we there yet are we* –' I stop abruptly, or rather, I *am* stopped, as something in the air around me shifts.

Bemused, I try to speak. But it's no use. It's as if my voice has been stolen, the sound of it vacuumed into nothingness.

What the –

Then, as Sheen glances round at me, a satisfied smile playing at the corners of his usually sullen mouth, I understand.

'There,' he says blithely. 'That's better. Wouldn't you agree, Spinner?'

Spinner is looking at the ground, trying very hard not to giggle. I scowl, furious. Sheen turns round again, leading the way across the heather.

Bastard, I mouth at his retreating back.

20

Blaze

The frozen forest has begun to melt.

I can hear the soft patter of water droplets dripping from the trees overhead. One lands in the corner of my eye and slides down my face like a tear. I don't wipe it away but remain very still, listening to Fox murmuring quietly to Cedar over the crackling fire.

I don't want him to know I'm awake yet. I don't wish to speak to him at all.

How long, exactly, has he been spying on me?

With Sifa's Eye, Fox holds the key to the secrets of the past. But never did I imagine he would use it to steal *my* secrets, to eavesdrop on *my* memories, to callously bear witness to some of the most private, most personal moments of my life.

I concentrate on keeping my breathing even.

How dare he? How *dare* he? What he's done . . . it's an abuse of power. An *invasion* of my mind. How am I expected to trust somebody who treats my past like their property?

Who provokes me into unleashing dangerous magic just to prove a point?

Fury splinters once more, eager for release. I clamp down on it hard, suddenly wary.

I can't explain what happened. The power humming through my veins had felt so *potent*. I might've found it exhilarating, had it been intentional. Only it wasn't, and that's what frightens me. I thought I had my gifts under control, but it appears I was wrong.

Despite the heat from the fire, I'm desperately cold. I shiver, clenching my teeth to stop them from chattering.

Cedar, as if sensing my discomfort, nickers forlornly.

'I know, I know,' Fox murmurs. 'I'm sure she's fine.'

My eyes snap open. 'Fine?'

He looks up sharply, meeting my gaze.

'You goad me into freezing half the forest and you think I'm *fine*?' I hiss.

Fox arches a brow. 'I wasn't talking about you, Storm Weaver.'

I frown. Who else could he be talking about? Come to think of it, why is he *talking* to the horse in the first place? Perhaps he's deranged as well as sadistic.

'Besides,' Fox continues, '*you* don't look fine at all.'

'Speak for yourself,' I retort, taking in the blood-stained bandage wrapped round his shoulder and the purplish-blue bruise blooming on his brow – twin to my own. I wince as my fingers probe at the bulbous lump, remembering the blinding crack as our foreheads collided, remembering the moments before, breathless and burning, caged by his body.

I look away quickly.

This forest is denser than the last. The darkening sky is partially obscured by thick fir trees, and the ground is hard, carpeted with browning needles.

'Where are we?' I ask.

'The Wildlands,' Fox replies.

I glare at him. 'I'd worked that out for myself, funnily enough.'

'A few hours' south of the previous camp,' he adds. 'I didn't want to waste a day's travelling.' A smirk tugs at the corners of his mouth. 'You drooled on my shoulder.'

My cheeks heat. 'I did not.'

'Whatever you say, Your Majesty.'

'I told you already, *stop* calling me that,' I growl.

He holds his hands up. 'All right. Wouldn't want to get on the wrong side of that temper of yours. I can think of better ways to go than freezing to death.'

Silence descends. It feels a bit like being doused in cold water. I rake a hand through my curls and nibble at my lower lip.

Fox edges closer, sitting down next to the fire.

'I . . . I don't know what happened back there,' I confess eventually. 'I've never done anything like that before. I never knew I could.'

Fox eyes me thoughtfully for a moment, then pushes a bowl of soup towards me. 'You should eat.'

'I'm not hungry.'

'I didn't ask if you were hungry; I said that you should eat.'

I stare at him. 'Am I really expected to believe that you're concerned for my well-being after what you did this morning?'

He shrugs. 'Believe it. Don't believe it. That's not really the issue here.'

I wrinkle my nose as I peer into the bowl. The soup is cold and looks like bog water, and I imagine it tastes much the same.

'I appreciate it's not exactly what you're used to,' Fox says airily. 'You may have grown up a glorified prisoner, but at least that prison was a castle with a pastry chef.'

I bristle. Then, with a grim surge of determination, I pick up the spoon.

Fox watches with mild satisfaction as I eat, screwing up my face with every mouthful. 'Good?' he asks innocently.

I swallow, shudder, then mumble something incoherent.

He raises an eyebrow. 'Storm Weaver, why is it that you would spill my blood yet won't insult my cooking?'

I purse my lips.

'Well?'

'I don't know,' I say, exasperated. 'It just seems –' I search for the right word, recalling Grandmother's endless lessons in etiquette – '*impolite.*'

Fox laughs, then catches sight of my nettled expression and laughs harder. 'And slicing my shoulder open doesn't?'

I drop my gaze, a guilty blush creeping up my cheeks.

'It's all right,' he tells me. 'I probably deserved it.'

'For spying on my memories?' I drive the end of my spoon into the packed earth. 'Yes, I'd say you did deserve it. In fact, I'd say you got off easy.'

Fox has the decency to look a little sheepish. 'About that,' he begins.

I fold my arms expectantly.

'I told you before, this thing is unpredictable,' he says, gesturing to the talisman round his neck. 'Just because it shows me something doesn't mean I was searching for it.'

'And I'm supposed to believe that, am I?' I ask sharply. 'That the Eye of the Past just *happened* to reveal my most guarded secret? Or that it gave you a vision of a private conversation that took place between your brother and me purely *by chance*?'

Fox cracks his neck. 'It wasn't just a conversation though, was it?'

My blush deepens while my voice turns icy. 'Why do you even care?'

'Who says I do?' His own voice is perfectly even. Almost toneless.

I laugh, harsh and empty. 'Of course. How foolish of me to think that you might ever view somebody as anything more than a pawn in whatever game you seem to be playing.'

'But that's where you're wrong,' he says. 'You're not a pawn. You're the queen.'

My heart trips over a beat.

'Not yet I'm not,' I mutter.

'You know, I've been sensing some apprehension about your impending sovereignty,' Fox continues. 'Tell me, is it the responsibility that frightens you, or the knowledge of just how much time you'll be forced to spend with my dear brother?'

I exhale deeply.

For weeks, the thought of becoming queen has loomed over me. I've tried to ignore it, to focus solely on the task at hand, but every passing day, the coronation creeps closer and my doubt continues to grow, an ever-present thorn in my side.

Perhaps I've avoided this conversation for long enough.

'I can't help wondering if it's all some big mistake,' I say at last.

'In what way?' Fox asks.

'Well, for starters, I don't know the first thing about ruling a kingdom. I don't know if I have what it takes.' *And I don't know if it's what I want*, a small voice whispers. I banish it quickly with a little shake of my head. 'Besides, you said it yourself – the people think me a villain. Many will never accept me as queen, and in truth I can't blame them. Take what happened back there. My gifts can be . . . temperamental. Dangerous.'

I think back to the third trial, remembering the screams as my storm rained down upon the earth. For me, power is a double-edged sword, both a blessing and a curse. I have long been condemned for my magic, yet my magic is what won me the crown.

Fox leans back on his elbows, mulling this over.

'And by the way,' I add pointedly, 'if you're under the impression that I'm really so hung up on Hal, then maybe you don't know me as well as you think you do.'

He blinks in surprise, and I experience an unexpected spark of satisfaction.

I clear my throat and draw my knees up to my chest. 'I want you to stop.'

'Stop what?'

'Poking around in my past. Just stay out of my head, all right? Promise me.'

Fox runs his tongue over his teeth as he considers this.

'Do it,' I say. 'Or this alliance is over.'

He hesitates, then nods.

At last, I drop my gaze. It lands on the fire, crackling brightly amid the gloom. Something catches my attention. I peer closer, frowning as I reach towards a pile of ash.

'What the –' I hold up the charred remains of a button. 'What is this?'

Fox feigns innocence.

'Is this from my shirt?' I demand.

'What shirt?'

'*My* shirt. The one I was wearing in the Ridge tunnels. The one I washed in the Creek and hung out to dry.'

'Oh, *that* shirt,' he says. 'Yes. Yes, it is.'

I speak through gritted teeth. 'You *burned* my shirt?'

Fox looks unmoved. 'It was cold. You were shivering. And the firewood was too damp to be of any use, so I improvised. It proved to be excellent kindling. Besides, my clothes suit you better, even if you are wearing them back to front.'

I shake my head incredulously and hurl the button back into the fire. '*Unbelievable*.'

Fox takes a mint leaf from his pocket, pops it into his mouth and grins at me while he chews. 'I've been thinking,' he says. 'Given this morning's little outburst, you really need to be more careful. A girl who turns the forest to ice when provoked will have a hard time convincing somebody that she doesn't possess any magic. If this plan is going to work – if we're going to make it to the Lagoon without detection – then you'll have to find a way to defend yourself that doesn't involve your water gifts.'

'Such as?'

Fox pushes himself to his feet and walks across to Cedar. Puzzled, I follow him, wincing at the stiffness in my muscles.

'Have a look under there,' he says, gesturing to the saddle.

So I do, and my eyes widen with horror as I take in the object strapped beneath. Small and silver and curved like a scythe.

'My dagger,' I whisper. 'Why . . . why do you still have this?'

'I kept it for you.'

I shake my head slowly. 'I – I don't want it. How could I ever want the weapon that killed the Council? It's *twisted*.'

There's a long, drawn-out pause, punctuated by the violent thudding of my heart.

'I'm . . .' Fox clears his throat. 'I'm sorry about your aunt.'

I dip my chin, slightly taken aback. 'Aunt Yvainne only ever cared for Flint. I grieve for his loss, and for my grandmother's, but it's Queen Hydra I mourn. She taught me so much. She was always . . .' I trail off, my voice unsteady. 'She was always kind to me. I'll never be able to repay that kindness.' My chest aches, and I will away the cloud of drizzle threatening to form above my head. 'And if it weren't for her, King Balen would have the Eye of the Soul.'

It was Queen Hydra's final act – opening and closing that portal. Her parting gift to me. It's why I feel sure that wherever I sent the Eye must be connected to her in some way. The Lagoon is a place of meaning to us both. It's *home*. Her former, my future. An everlasting bridge between us.

Fox strokes Cedar's flank. 'What Queen Hydra did was honourable, and I have no doubt you'll find a way to honour her,' he says. 'I understand why you don't want this dagger back, and I don't blame you. But while it may be the murder weapon, *I'm* the murderer. The Council are dead because of me. It was never my intention, yet their blood is still on my hands, and will be for the rest of my life. It's *my* burden to bear, not yours.'

Something flickers in his green eyes, something dark, almost wretched. I watch warily as he unsheathes the dagger from the saddle belt.

'Look, it belongs to you, whether you want it or not. I took it from you, and now I'm giving it back. At any rate, you'd be wise to learn how to fight without magic.' Fox's gaze rakes over me, lingering on the leather glove concealing my brandmark. 'You want to pass as Fidra? Then stop acting like an Etheri. Because pull another stunt like this morning's and you'll bring my uncle's soldiers down on us faster than you can blink.'

I glance at my feet, conflicted. Perhaps he has a point. We're supposed to be undercover, after all.

Fox slips the tip of the blade underneath my chin, tilting my face up to look at him. 'I'll even teach you how to use it,' he says.

My mouth parts in surprise. 'Really?'

He shrugs, then flips the dagger round and holds it out to me, hilt first. 'Why not? Consider it a peace offering.'

I almost smile. 'Your peace offering is proposing to fight with me some more?'

He almost smiles back. 'It's what you and I do best.'

21

Blaze

Over the following week Fox is as good as his word. Our days begin to fall into a pattern, though it's nothing like the monotonous routine of my childhood, in which hours were measured by mealtimes and page numbers. Here, we rise at dawn, ride until late afternoon, set up camp, and then train until sundown. By the time night falls I'm so ravenous that I eat every mouthful of whatever root-based concoction I'm presented with, and I'm so bone-tired that sleeping on the forest floor no longer feels like some sort of punishment.

We began with footwork. Fox would bark instructions while I ran through a sequence of steps, learning how to keep my tread light in order to better dodge, duck and lunge.

'Fighting,' he said as he walked in a slow circle around me, correcting my stance, 'is a bit like dancing. Your opponent is your partner. Wherever they go, you go. Whenever they move, you move. Except rather than trying to spin you, they're trying to stab you. You must always be anticipating what they're going to do next. Remember, every step counts.'

I would repeat the series of drills over and over while Fox lounged against a boulder, chewing lazily on a sprig of mint, braiding Cedar's mane, or shaving with his dagger.

At long last, I was allowed my weapon.

'You should always name your blade,' Fox told me.

'Really?' I asked sceptically. 'I thought people only did that with swords.'

'Who cares what other people do? Give it a name.'

I racked my brain, but nothing sprang to mind. 'What's yours called?'

'Soulkiller,' he replied.

'Oh, lovely,' I said dryly. 'Were Spiritbreaker and Dreamcrusher already taken?'

This made him laugh. 'Precisely. Now, go on.'

I looked down at the dagger in my hands. 'Silverclaw,' I decided.

Fox nodded approvingly. 'Nice choice. A little on the nose, perhaps, but I like it.'

During the last few lessons, he created a kind of assault course for me to practise on. I'd sever vines that sprang out at me, swerve away from moving branches, and leap over large stones that rolled across the forest floor. He even scored the outline of a body into the trunk of a tree, marking the places where I would find the vital organs.

This evening, as I retrieve my dagger from Cedar's saddle, I'm surprised to see Fox pull out his own.

'What're you doing?' I ask warily.

'What does it look like? You said yesterday you wanted a real opponent. Well, today is your lucky day.'

My stomach clenches nervously. I may have said it, but now, when actually faced with the prospect . . .

Fox smirks, flexing his shoulder. His cut has long since scarred over – one of the many advantages of being Etheri, who heal in a mere fraction of the time it would take the Fidra – but he seems to enjoy reminding me that I was the one who inflicted it. I tell myself he deserved it for goading me into freezing half the forest. Yet this does nothing to ease the disquiet I feel when I recall his insinuation that he and I are more alike than I care to admit.

'What're we waiting for?' I say, tugging at the collar of my borrowed shirt, which I still insist on wearing back to front. 'Shall we begin?'

'Not yet.' Fox angles his head as he takes me in, his eyes raking over my body with such unabashed scrutiny that I almost blush. 'Come here,' he says softly.

My insides turn to vines, twisting and coiling around themselves. 'Why?'

'Just come here.'

I know he's not going to hurt me. So why am I hesitating?

Green eyes gleam with amusement. 'Scared, Storm Weaver?'

Yes.

'No,' I scoff.

I walk cautiously towards him, wondering if perhaps this is a trick – some kind of lesson about not trusting your opponent. When I reach him, I square my shoulders and meet his gaze. For a moment he is perfectly still. Then he raises his dagger and slashes it through the air so fast I don't even have time to scream before it meets its mark.

Fox dangles the severed collar of my shirt in front of my nose. 'Better?'

'*Better?*' I repeat. 'You almost slit my throat!'

He rolls his eyes. 'Don't be so dramatic. But if that had been my intention, you'd currently be choking on your own blood. Your reflexes are sloppy at best.'

Much to my annoyance, I find that the shirt does in fact feel better. The new neckline is still modest, cut to just below my collarbones, yet far more comfortable.

Scowling, I follow Fox out of the treeline and over to the Creek, where we take up our positions upon the grassy bank. We start off slowly, with him teaching me how to block.

'It depends on the angle of the blade,' he tells me, taking hold of my forearm and positioning it in front of my face. Like his shoulder, my arm has also healed, the snake bite reduced to nothing more than a small purple welt. It's a miracle the venom didn't kill me. Though I suppose I have Fox to thank for that.

'Again,' he says, and our daggers clash loudly as they slide together.

This goes on for some time, until my wrist is aching and beads of sweat begin to trickle down my back. It was strange at first, fighting without my water gifts, but I was forced to admit, grudgingly, that Fox was right, and not just about passing as Fidra but about being more cautious with my magic. I still can't wrap my head round what happened that day in the forest. The power humming through my veins had felt so . . . eager. So *alive*.

Fox clamps Soulkiller between his teeth as he rolls up his sleeves, exposing a pair of strong golden forearms flecked with little white scars. For a brief moment I recall what it felt like to be held in those arms as he carried me through the frozen forest. And I recall waking hours later, still furious but less disorientated, to the sound of Fox murmuring softly to Cedar.

'Who were you talking about the other day?' I ask, unable to help myself.

Fox removes the dagger from his mouth. 'When?'

'After my . . . outburst. You said, *I'm sure she's fine*. But you didn't mean me.'

He aims another swing at me. I manage to dodge it, but stumble.

'Remember your balance,' he says mildly. 'Find your centre.'

I plant my feet. 'Answer the question.'

'I was talking about Scout,' he says, lifting my arm back into position.

'Scout?' I repeat, frowning. 'Who's Scout?'

Fox smiles mysteriously. 'A friend.'

I can't help arching a brow. '*You* have friends?'

He smirks. 'Does that surprise you?'

'Truthfully? Yes.'

'What about us, Storm Weaver?' Fox asks, slashing Soulkiller so close to my ear I can hear it slice through the air. 'Are we friends?'

'No, we're not *friends*,' I snap, a little too viciously. 'We're . . .' I pause. 'We're two exceedingly ill-matched individuals who just so happen to share a common goal.'

He chuckles as though I've said something perfectly charming. I adjust my grip on Silverclaw and take a swipe at him, which he sidesteps with maddening ease. We circle one another, our daggers gleaming in the late-afternoon sun.

'Besides,' I continue, using my forearm to wipe the sweat from my brow, 'friends don't spy on each other's memories.'

Fox looks unmoved. 'You know, during my time in Katteran, I came across a rare bird,' he says. 'It was an ill-tempered creature which would peck at you if you got too close. The trader told me it could talk, and indeed it could. Only, it kept reciting this one line, just repeating the same thing over and over. It grew rather tiresome after a while.' He grins. 'You remind me of this bird.'

I glower at him. I have every right to be furious about what he did, and I'm far from ready to forgive and forget.

'Tell you what,' Fox says, sounding amused. 'Let's strike a deal.'

I narrow my eyes, ducking as he aims another lazy swipe. 'What kind of deal?'

He twirls his dagger. 'We're both aware that if this little duel were real, you'd be dead. I'm not asking you to best me, only that you put up a good fight.'

'And what's in it for me?'

'A question. We both know how much you love those.'

'A question about what?'

'Me,' he says simply. 'It seems only fair, after all. I snatched a glimpse of your past, albeit unintentionally, and now I'm offering you a chance to do the same. Then we're even, and you can do us both a favour by finally getting rid of that chip on your shoulder.'

I hesitate, mulling this over. While I imagine it would be difficult letting go of this particular grudge, I can't deny that his offer intrigues me.

'Fine,' I tell him. 'Deal.'

In truth, I thought I was doing rather a good job of putting my new skills to use. But as the pace begins to pick up, I realize I wasn't. Fox is still holding back, but even now, using a mere fraction of his strength, he's a formidable opponent. His movements are precise and instinctive, his reflexes impossibly fast – always one step ahead.

'How do you make it look so effortless?' I pant.

'With a great deal of effort,' he responds, not even slightly out of breath. 'I used to practise for hours every day with my crew. I'd switch hands too, so my opponent would never know which one was dominant.'

'And which is?' I ask, taking another swing.

Fox blocks it before my arm is fully extended. He grins as he tosses Soulkiller into the air with his right hand then catches it in his left. 'Both.'

I flip my hair over my shoulder and concentrate, remembering what he taught me. Wherever he goes, I go. Whenever he moves, I move. Although Fox seems to be intent on driving me backwards. The soft mud stretching along the bank of the Creek proves slippery underfoot. I slide around in it, cursing, while he remains entirely centred.

'Balance, Storm Weaver.'

'I'm *trying*.'

I swipe, he blocks. He feints left, I nearly lose a boot in the mud.

When I finally manage to right myself, he's already closing in, his eyes glinting as brightly as the talisman round his neck. I tighten my grip on Silverclaw as he leans in close, then closer still – almost as if he's going to whisper something, as if he's going to . . .

I seize my chance. Drawing my arm back in one smooth arc, I lunge for him. Only Fox is quicker, darting out of reach, while the force of my swing is enough to throw me off balance. All I can do is gasp as I trip, slip, then topple backwards into the Creek.

Coldness closes over my head. For a moment I'm so shocked that I just allow myself to sink. Then I come to, kicking my legs and breaking the surface. Water sluices off my clothes as I heave myself up and on to dry land, dagger clamped in my fist.

Staggering up the muddy bank, I catch sight of Fox. He's standing a few yards away, Soulkiller dangling loosely at his side, laughing so hard he's doubled over.

'You think this is funny?' I growl, suddenly conscious of the way my wet shirt is clinging to every inch of me. I fold my arms across my chest in an effort to keep some dignity intact.

Fox only laughs harder.

Seething, I attempt to storm away, only my waterlogged boots sink further into the quagmire with every step. I glance down, then back at Fox, struck by an idea.

The clump of mud hits him square in the face, stunning him into silence. He even drops his dagger.

My methods may have been unconventional, but I've succeeded in disarming him. I watch him wipe away the mud with his gloved hand, blinking it out of his eyes. He bends over to retrieve his knife, and for one foolish, fearful heartbeat, I wonder what he might do.

Then, to my surprise, he grins.

'So, Storm Weaver,' he says. 'What is it you wish to know?'

22

Elva

Every evening this week Hal has called a meeting in the observatory, and much to my ongoing frustration, I've had very little to report. The Eyes certainly know how to be discreet.

Yet the revelation that my sister may be alive has only strengthened my resolve, and I've combed the palace from top to bottom trying to determine which members of the Imperial Court are loyal and which are treasonous. The dark circles beneath my eyes could almost rival Hal's, though not quite. His health appears to have declined even further since his uncle announced his official bid for regency.

King Balen is playing a very clever game. For if he were to usurp the throne, the people would rally to Hal's cause. But instead, by offering himself as regent, he is sending a clear message – that Hal is in need of one. Rumours continue to spread across the empire, calling Hal hesitant, soft, weak-willed, and as yet unwed. An alliance with Thaven is his best chance at victory, but King Merrick has made it plain that he will withhold his support and his daughter until Hal proves himself the stronger ally. That's part of the reason he decided to invite the Court of Flames to Cor Caval. Hal doesn't care much for Ember Harglade, but, flanked by two members of his Council, he is presenting a united front.

The Ignitia Court's arrival yesterday morning threw the palace into disarray. Matron was barking orders, arranging for chambers to be readied, food to be prepared, and bottles of wildfire wine to be fetched from the cellars. Much to everyone's amusement, Ingra managed to swipe a couple when Matron wasn't looking. Despite how occupied I've been lately, I haven't failed to notice Ingra's pattern of unexplained absences though whenever I ask her what she's up to, she only asks me the same question, and of course, I can't answer.

Tonight, Hal is throwing a banquet in Ember's honour.

Elaith seems more subdued than usual as I help her dress. Perhaps it's all the time she's been forced to spend with Marina. The dislike between them is evident, though not as blatant as Marina's contempt for me. Zephyr, meanwhile, seems to have mellowed. Several nights ago he winked playfully at me before flitting right in front of Elaith, causing her to jump about a foot in the air then burst into peals of tinkling laughter.

She's not laughing now, though. Her expression is tense, and she keeps rubbing absent-mindedly at her wrists.

'Is something wrong?' I ask.

'What?' Her head snaps up. 'Oh no. No, I'm fine.' She peers at me in the mirror. 'You look tired, Elva. Just because you're now an Eye doesn't mean you can't shut yours.'

I manage a half-smile. 'I'll bear that in mind, my lady.'

She arches a flame-red eyebrow.

'Elaith,' I correct myself.

Her scarlet-silk dress trails behind her in a delicate train. I select a handful of ruby-studded hairpins and sweep her hair back over one shoulder, pausing as I catch sight of a series of marks adorning her fair skin. It looks as if someone's gripped her by the throat.

She flushes, reaching up to tug her hair back into place. 'It was a necklace. The clasp was too tight. Clumsy.'

Maybe I would've believed her if this brief action hadn't exposed her wrists. They too are covered with marks – a bracelet of angry purple bruises.

'It's nothing, really,' she says hastily, slipping on a pair of crimson gloves.

That's exactly what Hal says whenever I ask what's ailing him.

Nothing.

That word is a weapon. I'm defenceless against it. So I bite my tongue, brush a little golden powder over Elaith's freckled cheeks, and follow her to the banquet hall.

It's sweltering in here, the torches burning fiercely in their brackets, candles dripping wax on to the floor. Hal is sitting in his father's throne on top of the dais, Zephyr on his left, Ember on his right. Blaze's cousin is a tiny creature, almost as small as Elaith. She's not yet sixteen, her heavily lidded eyes, alight with malice, ill-suited to such a youthful face. She's wearing a gown studded with garnets, so many that they reflect the flames, making it look as if the whole dress is sparkling. The cost of the hem alone would be enough to feed my village for a year.

Even after all this time, the wealth and splendour of Ostacre never fail to astonish me. Compared to my plain, bone-coloured tunic, Ember's dress is outlandish. But next to the suffering and poverty of the Otherlands, it is utterly grotesque.

Snatching up a tray of glasses, I begin to make my way around the room. The Aquatori, Terrathian and Ventalla tables are more or less empty, while almost every chair at both the Ignitia's and Eyes' tables is occupied. Voices ricochet off the walls, and I screw up my face as the noise overwhelms my newfound bat-like hearing. Gritting my teeth, I attempt to extract individual conversations from the din, tuning in to different frequencies.

Poor Flint Harglade, he lost the Choosing and his good looks in one fell swoop.

Pity the Storm Weaver didn't choke on all that smoke at Fire Mountain.

Pass the salt, would you?

Marina appears in the doorframe, looking elegant in a silver fish-scale dress. If it weren't for the remarkable quality of my eyesight, I likely wouldn't have noticed that several scales appear to be missing, or that the hoops round her wrist are tarnished with age. I watch as she makes her way up on to the dais to embrace Ember.

Apparently, the Earth Cleaver was last seen in Alvora with the Prince of Thaven.

I heard he fled to the Eastern Isles.

I spot Elaith sitting with the Court of Flames. A conversation is taking place around her, but she's too absorbed in the boy at her side. He's roguishly handsome, stocky and muscular, with fair hair and hazel eyes. I recognize him as one of the Ignitia Heirs – Cole, I think. His arm is slung possessively across the back of Elaith's chair, and he's nursing a glass of dragon whisky. My gaze lingers on his large hands before flickering to Elaith, to the curtain of fiery hair shielding her neck, to the pair of fine gloves concealing her wrists.

More conversations compete for space in my head.

He looks a little peaky perhaps, but then he has just lost his father.

The King of Vost has pledged allegiance. That's something, at least.

Ventalla soldiers have been cropping up in every province, so I hear. Rallying support, handing out food to the commonfolk. King Balen's influence is spreading by the day.

Abandoning my tray, I reach for a decanter of wine. Yet the second my skin grazes the surface, an awful sensation takes hold, so achingly cold it seems to numb my very bones. I jerk backwards, bewildered. It takes a few moments before I understand.

The decanter is made from crystal, and crystal weakens Magi.

Suddenly an unfamiliar voice cuts through my realization.

Tonight's the night.

It belongs to an Eye sitting at the furthest end of the centre table, a tall, pasty-faced man whispering quietly in his companion's ear. The urgency in his tone catches my attention. Grabbing a golden flagon of ale, I slowly make my way towards them.

The Pyros' arrival is the perfect distraction.

I still don't understand what he wants with a bunch of half-starved prisoners.

Keep your voice down.

My heart thuds violently, though I can't make sense of what I'm hearing. Distraction from what? Which prisoners are they referring to? And who is *he*?

At that moment, Hal gets to his feet, and a hush falls over the room.

'Thank you all for being here tonight,' he begins. 'It's a great pleasure to have the Court of Flames back in our halls, particularly their future queen.'

The Ignitia cheer, banging their fists on the table, wine sloshing out of their glasses.

Ember smiles, her voice little-girlish. 'Your Imperial Majesty, the pleasure is ours.'

Hal attempts to return her smile, but I watch in alarm as his face suddenly crumples in pain, his mouth twisting into a grimace, his jaw protruding sharply.

All around, courtiers are murmuring.

He blinks hard and straightens up. 'A toast,' he grits out through clenched teeth.

The Etheri raise their glasses.

'To . . . to the future,' says Hal. 'Let it be –' He breaks off again, wincing, two fingers pressed to his temple.

I swallow nervously. Several of the serfs exchange looks. Zephyr places a hand on Hal's arm, but Hal shakes him off, wiping his brow with the sleeve of his doublet.

He looks like a ghost.

'Let it be brighter . . . than the past,' he finishes weakly, then collapses on to the table in front of him.

My piercing shriek is drowned by the uproar that ensues. I move forward instinctively, but Hal is already surrounded. Blood rushes in my ears, and I clench my fists tightly in case my shadows decide to descend, sensing my fear.

All night, I sit in the serf tunnels outside Hal's chambers, listening as the physicians try and fail to determine what's wrong with him.

Worry eats away at my insides. I feel colder than I did when I touched the crystal.

I must've fallen asleep at some point, because I'm awoken by Alator's reedy voice on the other side of the door, informing the emperor that in the early hours of the morning, a large number of prisoners were freed from the palace dungeons.

All that was left in their place was a single black feather.

23

Blaze

'Tell me how you became a Healer.'

I'm sitting cross-legged on a tree stump, watching as Fox forages through the undergrowth. His hair is still wet from bathing, damp strands framing his face.

'Really?' He tries not to smile. 'That's your question?'

I nod, resolved.

Fox slides Soulkiller from his belt and uses it to slice a few long stems before stuffing them inside his satchel. Then he says, 'My grandmother was a Healer.'

I gasp as he brushes his fingers against mine. The woman in the memory looks remarkably like Kestrel Calloway, only older. Green eyes, auburn hair streaked with grey, sleeves rolled up to her elbows. She wears a leather apron with a dozen pockets of varying shapes and sizes. I edge closer to discover that each contains something different – flower cuttings, soil samples, a handful of emerald-coloured beetles, even a baby mouse.

The woman smiles softly, then fades into nothing.

Fox clears his throat as he draws back his hand. 'She taught me everything I know. About medicinal herbs, edible plants, how to treat a wound. I was younger than your brother Renly when she first took me out into the forest. I'd help her dig for roots, gather pine cones, scrape sap from tree bark. Then we'd take it all back to her workshop.'

Another light graze of our hands and I see it – a poky little hut lit by firefly lanterns, the shelves crammed with pots and potions.

'She made all sorts of remedies – elixirs and tonics, tinctures and salves,' Fox continues. 'And she would take them to those in need.'

'She didn't sell them?' I ask.

He shakes his head as he kneels to inspect a patch of wild mushrooms. 'My grandmother never charged. Most of her patients were Fidra, and many couldn't afford to pay for medicine. But often they would give her something in return, anything they could spare – a loaf of bread, shoelaces, that kind of thing.' He smiles a little, remembering. 'And she didn't just treat people; she helped animals, too. A wild dog that had been mauled, a bird with a broken wing. She would take them in and nurse them back to health.'

'She certainly sounds very different to my grandmother,' I muse, biting back a grin.

'She was different from everybody,' he says. 'She was one of the most extraordinary people I ever knew, and yet she lived so simply. Lived off the land. She used to tell me that the forest has everything we need to survive, so long as you know where to look.'

'And how do you know where to look?'

Fox pauses, considering the question, then shrugs. 'I can show you, if you like.'

I return the shrug in what I hope is a nonchalant manner. 'All right.'

Fox chuckles as Cedar nudges him gently with his muzzle.

'If I didn't know any better, I'd think you could speak to that horse,' I mutter as we set off through the trees.

'What a vivid imagination you have, Storm Weaver,' Fox says mildly.

The morning air is cool and fresh, heavy with the scent of wild garlic. I pick my way across the forest floor with newfound ease, having gradually grown accustomed to the tangle of roots and twisting plants that once threatened to trip me up at any given moment.

I catch Fox watching me. 'What?'

'You just seem like you've got used to it, that's all,' he says. 'Being here.'

'Being here in the Wildlands or being here with you?'

'Both, I suppose.'

I smile sweetly. 'I confess that I now consider you to be merely aggravating as opposed to wholly insufferable.'

Fox lays a hand on his chest in mock gratitude. 'High praise indeed.'

'As for the Wildlands,' I continue, 'I can't say that I hate it here. In fact, I find it strangely . . . peaceful.'

'Peaceful,' he murmurs.

The dappled white-gold light filtering through the branches dances across his face. I watch as he absent-mindedly reaches out his gloved hand to skim every tree we pass, as though marking an invisible trail.

It's not long before we slow to a stop.

'This is as good a place as any,' Fox declares, crouching to examine a patch of jagged purple plants. 'Shall we start with roots?'

'Ah, so it's your grandmother I have to thank for all those root stews,' I say dryly.

'Precisely.'

I kneel beside him in the undergrowth, close enough to breathe in the scent of fresh mint and pine.

'Now, this one is called burdock,' he begins. 'Not only can you eat the root but it can also be used to draw out toxins in the blood.' His voice is animated, almost boyish. 'Then over here we have bull thistle, which is similar in appearance and good for joint pain.'

Arrowroot. Evening primrose. Mandrake. Goldenseal. Wood sorrel.

I listen intently as Fox explains the healing properties of each, telling me which parts are edible, which aren't. Some he digs up and shows me, then pockets for later use.

I point at a cluster of pinkish flowers. 'What's that?'

He pulls the stem from the earth, exposing the slender roots beneath. 'Valerian. Grind it up into a powder and it can help you sleep. Helps with headaches, too.'

'And that one?'

'Cowslip. Reduces swelling. And see over there? The white ones? That's wild carrot. Not to be confused with poison hemlock. It's important, when learning which plants are edible, to make note of the ones that are deadly – particularly those that appear deceptively similar to others. You know those currants you like?'

I nod. I couldn't help noticing that the fruit has been in regular supply ever since I mentioned my partiality. More peace offerings.

Fox produces what look like three identical berries from his pocket and holds them out to me. 'Pick one out of the line-up.'

I frown uncertainly. 'The . . . left?'

Fox shakes his head. 'Moonseed.'

'Middle?'

'Nightshade.' He smirks a little at my disgruntled expression. 'False familiarity. Never underestimate nature's ability to trick. Some weapons are made; others grow.'

'You sound almost admiring.'

'I suppose I am. I admire the fact that a tiny berry can kill as easily as a knife, and sometimes faster.'

He tosses the berries over his shoulder.

I shake my head incredulously. 'Your grandmother really taught you all of this?'

He nods, twirling the stem of a fern between his fingers.

'And what of your grandfather?'

'He was a woodcutter,' Fox tells me. 'He built her workshop, built her a home.'

Once again, I find my hand in his. I see a little cottage by the Creek, with a smoking chimney and crooked stained-glass windows.

'We used to spend whole summers there,' he says. 'My sister and me.'

I watch a girl with hair like autumn leaves swinging upside down from a branch, toasting bread on a bonfire, sleeping soundly underneath a chequered quilt. All of a sudden Fox's grip tightens, and the warm glow of memory is replaced by a gust of ice-cold wind. Another vision swims into focus – Freya, eyes bulging with terror, suffocating to death.

Fox drops my hand as if it burns him and takes an unsteady step back, his expression tight, tortured, a muscle throbbing in his jaw. I can almost see the cracks beginning to form, fault lines spreading across his chest from the gaping hole in his heart. For a moment I think he might be about to break. I don't know what to say, so I opt for a distraction.

'Oh, I like these ones,' I blurt out, pointing at a group of the tall thimble-shaped blooms I'd preferred to Hal's roses. 'What are they?'

It works. Fox blinks and exhales, and I watch as the pain slowly drains from his features. 'Those?' He leads the way to the patch of wildflowers. 'These are foxgloves.'

The corners of my mouth twitch.

He arches a brow. 'What is it?'

'*Please* tell me that's your full name.'

Fox stares at me. Then, as if he can't help it, he laughs.

I'm about to smile back when, all of a sudden, the air is filled with the unmistakable sound of voices.

'You should've seen the size of its teeth!'

'Please, it's no match for my spear.'

'Take it easy. Remember, the Baron wants it alive.'

'I reckon one that big is worth ten pieces of silver.'

'Then we'd better catch it, hadn't we?'

Through the trees, I can just make out a group of burly men heading this way.

Fox swears under his breath. We weren't expecting to encounter anyone this deep into the woodland. The nearest province is still several days' ride away.

My stomach lurches with panic.

'Hunters,' Fox mutters. Then, 'Want me to deal with them?'

'Are you asking me if I want you to kill them?' I clarify, horrified.

He shrugs. 'That or severely incapacitate.'

'*No*. No, I do not want you to do either of those things. Besides, I thought we weren't supposed to be using our gifts.'

Fox looks a little disappointed, but nods grudgingly. He may be handy with a dagger, but I imagine even he would struggle to hold off five heavily armed men without magic.

'Then we hide,' he says. 'This way.' He grabs my arm, pulling me into a dense thicket.

'*Ouch*,' I hiss as a branch rebounds off his shoulder and hits me in the face.

But Fox doesn't stop, tugging me further into the bushes as the men draw nearer. I let out a gasp of pain as my hair catches on several thorny briars.

He turns at the sound. We're pressed together, so close I can feel his heart beating.

'Hold still,' he murmurs.

Gently, he untangles my curls one by one.

All of a sudden, the sharp *snap* of a twig causes me to violently whip my head round. I stumble forward into Fox, who catches hold of me before taking a small step back as he tries to steady us both. Only the ground is uneven, and he loses his balance, falling flat on his back and breaking several branches on the way down. I land hard on his chest a split second later, knocking the wind out of us both.

'Did you hear that?' The man's voice is uncomfortably close.

'What?'

'Listen.'

I freeze. The copse is thick, but I can just make out a pair of boots trampling through the patch of foxgloves, coming to a stop less than five yards away from where we lie tangled in the undergrowth. Instinctively, I raise a hand, sparkling white frost already glistening at the ends of my fingertips, but Fox grabs my wrist and pins it tightly to his chest. I glare at him as I try to wrench it free, but he just shakes his head in warning and presses a finger to his lips. Against my own better judgement, my gaze lingers there. For a moment I allow myself to remember what those lips felt like that night in the maze – crushing into mine, trailing down my neck, teeth grazing lightly across my jawline, my pulse point, my collarbones.

Then I push the memory away. Because it never should have happened. It was a case of mistaken identity, nothing more. I thought he was Hal. I would never have kissed Fox like that had I known it was him beneath the mask. I would never have kissed him at all.

The ice coating my hand has slowly melted into his shirt. I can feel his heartbeat under my palm, the hard planes of his body under my own. Our faces are mere inches apart. I can't escape. I can barely move for fear of being discovered.

I glance away, inwardly cursing the blush creeping up my neck. My arm shakes with the effort of propping myself up. I don't have long before it gives out.

Careful not to make a sound, I grit my teeth and shift my weight ever so slightly.

I hear Fox's sharp intake of breath as I move against him.

His gaze locks with mine. He swallows.

That's when a gruff voice sounds, startling us. 'We're wasting time. Let's go.'

'But I swear I heard –'

'Must've been a squirrel or something. Come on, this way.'

We listen as five pairs of boots begin to retreat, heading west through the forest.

Slowly, Fox releases his grip on my wrist. 'That was close,' he says.

'Too close,' I agree, privately wondering whether we're referring to our run-in with the hunters or the proximity of our bodies.

Fox is looking at me expectantly. I blink, blushing harder, then scramble to my feet.

'What do you think those men were looking for?' I ask as he pulls himself up and follows me through the tangle of branches.

'How should I know?' His voice sounds a little rough. He clears his throat. 'But I suggest we head back to the camp before whatever it is makes an appearance.'

I nod, ducking out of the thicket, then stop dead in my tracks.

'I think you might've spoken too soon,' I whisper.

For there, framed among the trees, its muzzle stained with old blood, is an enormous wolf. It's a beautiful beast, as grey as a winter's day. As it moves closer I notice a pattern of distinctive silver markings on its brow, as well as the row of razor-sharp claws protruding from each of its four paws. A pair of yellow eyes fixes on us, unblinking.

Fear lances through me, scattering my anchors. My breathing turns ragged as I fumble for my dagger.

'No,' Fox says.

I glance at him, stricken. 'What're you –'

He takes me by the shoulders and pushes me firmly behind him. 'Stay here. No sudden movements.'

Then he turns back to the wolf. Its hackles are up, teeth bared in a snarl, incisors gleaming in the dappled sunlight.

It growls in warning as Fox begins to inch forward.

'*Stop*,' I hiss, but he holds up a hand to silence me.

What does he think he's doing?

Suddenly the wolf tilts its head, its ears pricking, as though listening to something, then begins to prowl closer.

I gasp as Fox slowly drops to his knees.

For a long, breathless moment, they stare at one another. Then, quite inexplicably, the wolf turns and darts away through the trees.

'How . . . *how* did you do that?' I stammer.

Fox gets to his feet, dusting himself off. 'Call it a gift.'

My mouth opens and closes in bewilderment.

'What?' He shrugs. 'I'm good with animals.'

My tone drips disbelief. 'So you're an animal tamer now, too?'

'Oh, I wouldn't say that. There's nothing to stop it coming back here and tearing us to pieces. But don't worry. That wolf is far from the most dangerous thing in the Wildlands.'

I narrow my eyes. 'Then what is?'

Fox grins as he reaches out to pluck a stray thorn from my hair. 'I'm looking at her.'

24

Flint

The sun is beginning to set, painting the sky honey-gold. There are no trees on this part of the moor that we could use to help build a shelter, and no gorse to protect us from the cool breeze blowing in from the north.

I watch as Sheen walks in a perfect circle around our camp, his hands outstretched.

'He's creating a wind shield,' Spinner informs me as she unhooks the cooking pot from her satchel. 'It'll keep us warm while also acting as a sound barrier.'

'Well,' I say, making a conscious effort not to sound impressed. 'That answers my question about what other tricks he can do.'

'*Would you like me to make you a list, Harglade?*'

I almost jump out of my skin as Sheen's voice whispers into my ear, despite the fact that he's standing more than ten feet away from me.

There is only one other person I know capable of such a thing – King Balen.

'How are you *doing* that?' I gasp, unable to suppress the shiver that crawls up the back of my neck.

'*I told you*,' Sheen murmurs, barely moving his lips. '*I'm exceptionally gifted*.'

I clamp my hands over my ears. 'Stop it.'

He turns back to finish his wind shield, smirking slightly. I bristle, peeved at being bested yet again. I wonder whether he secretly enjoys our sparring. It's the only time I've ever seen anything slightly resembling amusement flicker across that face – which is, I might add, entirely wasted on him. Unpleasant people don't deserve to be beautiful.

'Flint? Come here and light a fire, would you?'

I wince. Every night Spinner asks the same question, and every night I give her the same feeble response. 'Too tired.'

'*Again?*'

'Yup. It takes up a lot of energy, you know, being me. Use the flint and steel – they're in here.' I slip my satchel from my shoulder and toss it to her.

Grumbling, Spinner begins rummaging through the contents. She pulls out my last few vials of painkiller. 'There aren't many left. Have you got reserves?'

'Those *are* my reserves,' I tell her.

'Oh,' she says, looking troubled. 'Well, maybe we'll pass an apothecary soon and you can get some more.'

'Yes,' says Sheen dryly, glancing round at the deserted expanse of moorland. 'I'm sure I glimpsed one just up there by that patch of heather.'

I manage to ignore him though it's getting harder and harder to ignore the pain radiating from my burns.

Spinner pats the ground beside her and holds up the pot of salve. 'Why don't you let me put some of this on for you?'

'*No*.' I say it too quickly. Both of them are looking at me. 'I mean . . . no, thank you.'

'Why not? You haven't let me help you at all.'

'I – I just prefer to do it myself.' I shrug. 'It's no big deal.'

Spinner looks slightly wounded. 'Well, all right, then. But burns take a while to heal. You need to take proper care of them. The physicians said –'

'Yes, yes, I know. I'll get right on it.' I snatch the supplies out of her hands and start picking my way across the uneven terrain.

'Where are you going?'

'Nature calls,' I yell cheerfully over my shoulder.

When I'm far enough away, I sit down and remove my eyepatch. I take a long time applying the burn salve, letting out a low hiss of pain mingled with relief, then ration out half a vial of painkiller, swallowing it down along with the lump in my throat.

I know I should be thankful. My burns are healing. But while the physicians were able to save my skin, they couldn't save my eye.

Half-blind. Half my vision gone, just like that.

I'm still not used to it. Sometimes someone will start speaking and I'll jump because I didn't see them standing there. I have no peripheral vision on my left side. You don't realize how much you can see – until you can't any more. Now I have to swivel my head round like some skittish owl. My sight is impaired, and it's . . . well, it's terrifying.

But there's something else, too. Something I'm afraid to admit, because it makes me sound superficial and conceited, and maybe that's because I am.

It's like this – I have spent my whole life being someone people enjoy looking at. Yet now, I'm damaged. Disfigured. An eyesore with a missing eye.

Sheen was right to call me vain. Only since the third trial, I've had no reason to be. Where there was once vanity there is now shame and a crippling self-consciousness.

I never realized before just how much of my happiness, my identity, my sense of self-worth, was so tragically dependent on how I looked. I took such pleasure in it, seeing the effect I had on people. Only now, that's undoubtedly a thing of the past. I'm not sure the phrase 'bedroom *eye*' has quite the same ring to it.

But then there's Spinner. The way she smiles at me, the way she kissed me in the Ridge tunnels . . . it was like nothing had changed. Am I a fool for wanting to believe she feels the same attraction to me? Or am I just so insufferably shallow as to imagine she wouldn't?

Grandmother always used to say, *It's what's on the inside that counts.*

Except I'm just as screwed up on the inside as I am on the outside. But unlike my burns or my blindness, at least I'm able to hide it.

Nobody knows about the times when the panic descends. When my lungs stop working and I feel like I'm dying and part of me . . . part of me doesn't care.

And nobody will.

In my dreams, I see Ember.

The world burns as firebombs rain down from the sky. I throw up my arms to shield my face, and when I lower them, it's no longer Ember standing in front of me but Blaze, a flame igniting in her palm. She smiles, then launches the fire straight at my head.

I scream as agony explodes across my skin.

'Flint? Flint!'

I wake to Spinner shaking me. It takes me a moment to realize I'm still screaming.

'Flint, what is it?'

I make out her face in the light from the smouldering fire, shadows dancing along her tattooed cheeks where some of the panstick has been rubbed away.

'I . . . I'm fine,' I croak. 'I just . . . I had a bad dream, that's all.'

Spinner looks unconvinced. 'Are you sure?'

I will my hands to stop trembling as I find hers and squeeze it. 'Go back to sleep.'

At last she relents, kissing me lightly before lying down again. I wait until her breathing turns slow and rhythmic before carefully disentangling myself.

I take a few shaky steps away from the camp, far enough that I'm sure I've gone beyond the wind shield, then collapse to my knees and vomit into the heather.

I retch and heave until I'm empty and shivering, then return to the camp, seeking Spinner's warmth. She mumbles something incoherent, pulls my arm over her and snuggles into me, yet somehow, I feel more alone than ever.

I lie awake, clenching and unclenching my fists, and begin to count.

My fingers.

My heartbeats.

The clicking of insects in the undergrowth.

The soft snuffling sounds Spinner makes in her sleep.

Two violet eyes, fixed on me from across the dying embers, unblinking and unreadable.

My breath catches. The thought of Sheen witnessing me like that – weak, vulnerable . . .

A memory stirs. I'm lying in the medical wing, bandages obscuring half my face, drifting in and out of a drug-induced stupor. A figure sits at my bedside, head tipped forward on his chest, white-blonde hair gleaming silver in the flickering candlelight.

I look away quickly, banishing the image from my mind and burrowing under the blanket beside Spinner. Only when I glance back sometime later, Sheen is still watching me. And maybe it's my competitive nature, or maybe it's that the intensity of his gaze offers some reprieve from the ceaseless torment inside my head, but I watch him back.

I watch him right back until I fall asleep, and in the morning I don't look at him at all.

25

Blaze

The seven Magi ambassadors sit side by side along a grand golden dining table. Across from them, leaning back in his throne as though to better take in the scene, his resplendent spun-gold robes shining almost as brightly as the orbs of light floating lazily around the ceiling, is a young man who looks startlingly like Hal. But of course, this isn't Hal.

It's his grandfather, Caius Castellion.

While the Maker – God of Gods who created Etheri – decreed that the four elemental crowns should be won rather than inherited, he ensured that his own crown, the Imperial Crown, would be passed down only to the first-born sons of his line. It was a way of continuing his legacy and, rather chillingly, immortalizing his face, for the men of House Castellion all bear an unsettling resemblance to their forefather: sleek black hair, porcelain skin and raven eyes. Caius's eyes flit between his guests, alight not with kindness, like Hal's, or amusement, like King Balen's, but with anticipation, as though he were waiting for something.

Fox and I stand over by the far wall, watching.

It's not long before several attendants file into the room, each carrying a golden platter complete with a domed lid. I count seven – one for each ambassador.

'Ladies and gentlemen,' says Caius, his voice smooth and pleasant, so different from the grating rasp of the old man I met in the library. 'You honour me with your presence. For too long our great empires have remained divided. Let us come together to heal the rift of the past. Let us unite and forge a new future, one rich in trade and friendship.'

As the platters are placed in front of the Magi, unease curls round me like a fist. I already know how this memory ends – with all seven ambassadors dead. But what I don't know is how they were killed. Perhaps the food is poisoned? Or the wine?

That's when my gaze snags on the attendants. I'm struck by just how burly they are – disconcertingly muscular, standing straight-backed and alert behind the ambassadors, almost as if they were soldiers rather than servants.

My heart plummets.

Caius smiles widely. 'And yet,' he says, swilling the dregs in his glass, 'I've often found alliances to be such fickle, fragile things. It's unfortunate, really, but in my experience, spilling blood is far more effective than breaking bread.'

Seconds later the supposed attendants yank the lids from the platters to reveal seven vicious-looking blades. The ambassadors leap to their feet, but they aren't quick enough. I swallow a scream as every last one has their throat cut from ear to ear. Blood pools on the table, dripping to the floor, so much that I can smell the iron in it.

The last thing I see before the vision changes is Caius Castellion pouring himself another glass of wine.

We soon find ourselves in a different chamber. Five thrones are positioned round a circular table in the centre, and the walls are lined with portraits, hundreds of them, each depicting a different king, queen or emperor – generations of Crowned Councils. Fox leans against a portrait of a rather cantankerous-looking man wearing the Ignitia crown of golden flames. In one hand the king holds a sceptre, in the other, a pile of ash.

'Where are we?' I ask.

'Welcome to the Council Chambers,' says Fox. 'Where you'll soon be spending an awful lot of time. It's now the morning after the secret assassination of the ambassadors.'

I open my mouth to say more, but Fox puts a finger to his lips and points towards the far window. His grandfather is standing silhouetted in a beam of buttery sunlight, as though he were some kind of fallen angel rather than a murderous, bloodthirsty monster. He's clutching a scrap of parchment, scanning the contents greedily. I move closer, trying to peer over his shoulder, but at that moment a set of towering golden doors fly open to reveal a beautiful woman dressed in a billowing red shirt and fighting leathers. Her dark hair is unbound, her downturned lips painted a rich shade of crimson, and her eyes – deep brown, flecked with gold – burn with unconcealed rage as she hisses, 'What have you *done*?'

I'm rooted to the spot, my jaw slack with shock. I know those eyes. I know that voice. Everything about this woman is familiar to me. She looks like my mother, only her face is sharper, more severe, more striking.

Then it hits me.

'*Grandmother?*' I whisper hoarsely.

And so it is. My grandmother, Leda Flameslinger, matriarch of House Harglade, standing right in front of me, barely a few years older than I am now.

Utterly dumbfounded, I sag against Fox then leap away as if scalded, hastily turning my attention towards Grandmother's companion, whose hand is still raised as though he were about to knock before she decided to burst in. Dressed in a simple blue tunic, the young man is clearly Aquatori. He's achingly handsome, with high cheekbones, close-cropped snow-white hair, and eyes the colour of deep water. He, too, is familiar. But it's not until I clock the small silver trident strapped to his belt that I realize why.

'Leda, River,' says Caius, seemingly unperturbed by Grandmother's livid expression. 'Come in, my friends. I have something I wish to discuss with you.'

I turn to Fox, wide-eyed. Ever since I saw them speaking together on my Name Day, I've suspected that Grandmother and River knew one another, a suspicion confirmed at the Binding Ceremony when they united to fight King Balen. So it comes as little surprise to me that they were friends, once. But what does surprise me – horrify me, even – is that Grandmother was seemingly also friends with none other than Caius Castellion. Though the way she's glaring at him in this moment is far from friendly.

'It would appear our grandparents have history,' Fox murmurs.

'You have something to discuss with us,' Grandmother repeats, stalking into the room. 'And would that have anything to do with the blood leaking from beneath the door to your private dining chamber? Or the fact I saw seven of those boorish brutes you call your Imperial Guard dressed as attendants for some inexplicable reason?'

'Have you been keeping tabs on me, Leda?' Caius asks mildly, as River closes the double doors and moves quietly to Grandmother's side.

She points at Caius, and several sparks shoot from her fingertip, landing on the floor with a dull hiss. 'Where are the ambassadors?'

'Dead,' he says matter-of-factly, picking a speck of lint from the sleeve of his robes.

River looks stricken. 'All of them?'

Caius nods laboriously, up and down, up and down, like a solemn child.

'Are you out of your mind?' Grandmother snarls. 'You know what this means, don't you? This is all it'll take to start a war.'

'Precisely.'

Grandmother glances at River, and something unspoken seems to pass between them. She sits down heavily in one of the five thrones. 'Caius, what are you doing?'

'I'm creating a distraction.'

'You're starting an imperial war to *create a distraction*?' Grandmother half shrieks.

'A distraction from what?' River asks calmly.

Caius slaps the scrap of parchment on the table. 'From obtaining the most powerful weapons in the world and destroying the Magi once and for all.'

On the parchment are three identical drawings. As the scene begins to recede, I can just make out the words scrawled beneath each sketch.

The Eye of the Past, *The Eye of the Future* and *The Eye of the Soul.*

I jerk myself back into the present. I'm sitting upon a carpet of moss, my arm extended towards the hammock above, which is made from vines and slung between two low-hanging branches. It sways slightly as Fox glances down to look at me, his gaze lingering on our joined hands. I pull mine away quickly. It's cold and clammy and trembling.

'My grandmother,' I mumble.

'I certainly see where you get your looks from,' Fox muses, chewing on a mint leaf.

I ignore him. 'She was *friends* with your grandfather, she *knows* about the sisters' talismans, she –' That's when another thought collides into me. 'After the third trial, she sat by my bedside and she saw it – she *saw* the Eye of the Soul round my neck.'

I remember Grandmother reaching out to touch it.

An Eye, she'd murmured softly.

'I told her it belonged to Spinner,' I continue. 'She didn't question it.'

'Of course she didn't – then she would've had to explain how she knew what it was.' Fox pauses. 'If it makes you feel any better, I believe your grandmother is deeply ashamed of the past, and of the part she played in it. I believe she wants to make things right. And I think letting you go was her way of proving that.'

I think back to escaping Fire Mountain. Grandmother had come after Flint and me. She'd begged us to stay. But Fox is right. She'd *let* us go.

He holds out a hand. 'Shall we continue?'

The following visions are like something out of a nightmare.

The severed heads of the Magi ambassadors are returned to the Otherlands on golden platters.

A fleet of a thousand ships sails across the Second Sea, bearing the flags of Thresk, Obsidia, Nepta, Veridia, Serolia, Havar and Al Sh'ib – seven isles united as one.

The Ostacrian armies march to meet them. My gaze lands on the Ignitia High General. That must be my mother's father. Grandfather looks remarkably like Aunt Hester, wiry and graceful astride his horse, his thin mouth set in a grim line.

A war-torn hellscape greets me next.

Screams pierce through the din. The air is thick with magic and blood. Bodies are piled high, pecked at by birds. The Creek runs red.

Back in Cor Caval, Caius Castellion paces through the Golden Keep as his Imperial Guard ride for the harbour.

His words echo in my ears.

You know what to do.

Nausea rises in my throat.

'Want to stop?' Fox asks.

I shake my head. The next moment we're in a cottage. The walls are painted sunshine yellow, peach-pink, forget-me-not blue – bright, happy colours that clash garishly with the terrified girls standing in front of us.

My stomach flips. The three sisters.

No, the *four* sisters.

One girl is standing a little apart from the others, her expression far away as she clutches the Eye round her neck.

When she speaks, it is a language I recognize – Threskan.

'They're coming,' she breathes. 'We have to hurry.'

I turn to Fox, who nods before the words have even left my mouth.

This must be Seera.

'Let's go,' says another. I recognize her from a previous vision, hurrying along a moonlit path to meet her love. Sifa adjusts the hood of her cloak and beckons to the smallest girl. Senna looks no older than Renly. She's crying, tears dripping down her heart-shaped face as she looks up at the final sister – a beautiful girl with long auburn hair.

My breath catches.

Syla.

I watch Syla wrap her arms round her younger sister, holding her tightly. 'We'll be all right. We'll find somewhere safe. Just stay close.'

The vision changes. The sisters are running for their lives through a darkened wood. Behind them comes the sound of pounding hooves, the Imperial Guard jeering and hooting as if this were a hunt and these girls were the foxes.

Syla hurls spell after spell over her shoulder, blasting the men off their horses. One is impaled on a tree branch then torn in half as his mount charges on, feet still wedged in the stirrups. I gasp as another knight lifts a crossbow and takes aim.

The bolt strikes Sifa in the back of the head. She's dead before she hits the ground.

Her sisters scream.

That's when another bolt soars through the air and buries itself in Seera's chest. She crumples to her knees, her last word a strangled, breathless scream: '*GO*.'

Syla chokes on sobs as she half drags, half carries a wailing Senna onward. Neither of them sees the tree root jutting into their path. They tumble to the ground just as the Imperial Guard descend. Senna is lifted on to a horse, while heavy crystal chains are clamped round Syla's neck, wrists and ankles before she can unleash her power.

One of the soldiers uses his foot to roll Sifa's and Seera's bodies over, and I watch in astonishment as their talismans vanish before he can seize them.

The vision changes a final time.

Caius Castellion is sitting smugly on the Imperial throne. At the bottom of the golden steps, peering blearily up at him from inside a crystal cage, is Syla.

'Such a prize,' Caius purrs.

'What do you want?' Syla spits.

'What I *want* is for you to do exactly as I tell you from here on out. And you can start by winning me the war.'

Syla blanches. 'How?'

'By stripping your people of their power.'

She barks out an empty laugh. 'Never.'

Caius smiles. 'I thought you might say that. Only you haven't heard what I'll offer you in return. Something tells me it might change your mind.' He raises his voice, addressing someone beyond the door. 'Bring in the girl.'

My heart twists violently as a knight drags Senna into the throne room, whimpering with fear. I don't realize I'm shaking until Fox touches me lightly on the shoulder.

Syla's eyes are wild, her hands gripping the bars of her cage. '*Let her go.*'

Caius presses the tips of his long fingers together. 'Only if you do as I ask. Submit to me. Strip my enemies of their magic.'

At his words, Syla turns very still.

'And be warned,' Caius continues pleasantly. 'If you're pretending to comply only so that I will free you from that cage, you would be unwise. For I had one of the Magi prisoners of war cast a rather ingenious enchantment in exchange for his freedom. If you ever disobey me, young Senna here will die. So I ask one more time – *take away the powers of the Magi.*'

Silence falls like an axe. Past, present and future hang in the balance as Syla looks up at Caius, then over at Senna. The expression on her face is one of pure agony and pure love. It stays with me even when the vision fades. I suspect it'll stay with me forever.

When I open my eyes, I'm back in the Wildlands, drizzle falling softly overhead.

'Had enough?' Fox asks quietly.

I nod, blinking away tears before they can fall. Tremors rack my body. My mind is full, but I feel only sick and hollow.

In order to save Senna, Syla agreed to give up her freedom and use her power to betray her own kind. She condemned her homeland to ruin, her people to a life of poverty and servitude. That was the cost of her sister's life – *everything.*

And it was a price Syla was willing to pay.

26

Blaze

I yelp as Fox's dagger slices a shallow cut along my thigh. 'That *hurt*.'

'Oh please, I barely scratched you,' he drawls, dodging another of my ill-aimed swipes. 'And maybe if you were paying attention, it wouldn't have happened at all.'

'I *am* paying attention.'

'No, you're miles away. Come back to me, then we'll fight like civilized people.'

He's right – I am distracted, not to mention short-tempered, and so tense it's difficult to achieve any degree of agility as we circle one another in the ring Fox has fashioned from several intertwined saplings. I've barely slept. I'm still reeling from those visions of the past. And is it any wonder? It's not every day you come face-to-face with your adolescent grandmother, or witness a war that took place more than fifty years ago.

Eventually, I give up and toss Silverclaw to the ground. Fox does the same, driving the point of Soulkiller deep into the earth and hitching himself up on to a fallen tree.

'Come, sit,' he tells me, patting the patch of moss beside him as though it were a silk chaise. 'I've been told I'm a good listener.'

I arch a brow. 'Really?'

'No.'

Rolling my eyes, I clamber up on to the tree.

'I'm guessing this –' Fox gestures at my brooding expression – 'has something to do with this?' He holds up the Eye of the Past.

'I can't stop thinking about it,' I say quietly. 'Our grandparents, the war, the sisters, Syla. It's all so much *bigger* than us. I suppose I've been reminded of how much is at stake.'

Fox angles his head. 'Are you worried we won't find the missing Eye?'

'Yes,' I admit, glancing at him. 'But I'm also worried about what'll happen if we do.'

I recall Syla's face, the pain that seemed to rip her apart from inside out as she made her choice. I understood then, more than ever before, that power is a burden as well as a gift. And wielding power itself is a burden almost too great to fathom.

A heavy silence smothers us until Fox says, 'There's something else, isn't there?'

His shrewdness is disarming.

'You know the old woman you met in Zafar?' I ask. 'The one who told you about the Eyes?'

He nods.

I swallow hard as a memory surfaces – a boy bound in crystal chains, imprisoned in the cell next to Syla's. I did not know him, but he knew me.

S'ai nova sempara, Voya Ishraki.

I will remember this, Storm Weaver.

Despite the heat of the day, I shiver.

I clear my throat. 'If the Magi were truly stripped of their magic, then how do some still retain it? I know you have a theory. I want you to tell me what it is.'

'Is that an order, Your Majesty?'

I glare at him.

Fox rakes a hand through his hair, then exhales. 'So, it's like this,' he says. 'We know Syla's spell worked. The Etheri won the War of the Empires, and the powers of the Magi were sealed inside the Eye of the Soul. Only sometimes, with enchantments that powerful, it seems a lack of *specificity* can lead to a . . . loophole.'

I frown. 'What d'you mean?'

'Bear with me, all right? Think of the Noble Houses. Take your family, for instance. House Harglade prides itself on being pureblood. Generations of Ignitia, descended from Vesta herself. Though of course not everyone cares about that sort of thing. You'll find that most people tend to marry for love rather than *ancestral purity*.' He doesn't bother to disguise the derision in his tone. 'Intermarriage between Etheri with different gifts isn't discouraged. But what is discouraged, forbidden even, is intermarriage between us and . . . others. If an Etheri were to marry a Fidra, for example, they would be accused of diluting their bloodline. They'd be branded a blood-traitor. An outcast.'

'Go on,' I say slowly, failing to see his point.

'For centuries, Etheri and Magi were estranged. Or so we thought.'

I shake my head. 'I'm not following.'

Fox traces patterns across the tree bark. 'Over the years, there've been cases – very rare cases – of children born half Etheri, half Magi.'

My mouth tips open. I stare at him, wordless.

'Children born to those children would then be *part* Etheri, part Magi, and so on, forever tainting a bloodline,' he continues. 'Generations of Etheri could be descended from one single Mage, and vice versa. The point is –' he takes a breath, as though steeling himself – 'my grandfather told Syla to strip the Magi of their magic. He didn't tell her to take away the powers of anyone with Magi blood.'

The hairs on the back of my neck stand on end. 'So ... so what you're saying is ... these people, they're Magi, but not *full* Magi? They're descended from Etheri, directly or distantly ... and that's why they were able to retain their magic when Syla cast her spell?'

Fox inclines his head. 'Like I said – a loophole.'

'But ... if somebody is Etheri *and* Magi, then what does that make them?'

'Both,' he says. 'They're called Demari. Many will have been hiding their whole lives, even before the war. Others may not know the truth about who they really are.'

'And they're able to wield the gifts of both Etheri and Magi?' I ask slowly.

'Some, yes. For others, the gift they inherit seems to depend on the dominant bloodline. Except mixing Etheri and Magi blood can have ... consequences.'

'Meaning?'

'Meaning someone with dual ancestry might only inherit one gift,' Fox says. 'They may appear to be either Etheri or Magi. But their gift could be . . . distorted. Too strong. Too dangerous. Hence the need for concealment.' He pauses, as if weighing his next words. 'These people . . . they were never supposed to exist. They inherit too much power.'

'*Gods*,' I whisper, eyes wide as I try to take it all in. Then a thought strikes, followed by a wave of panic. 'Your grandfather. He *has* to know about Syla's loophole.'

'You're right,' Fox tells me. 'There are dozens of Demari down in the dungeons. I suspect he's been hunting them for years.'

Bile burns my throat as I recall the hollow-eyed prisoners hidden in the darkest depths of the palace.

'What about King Balen?' I ask. 'How much does he know?'

Fox grimaces.

My voice is stricken. 'Tell me.'

'After the Binding Ceremony, it was like a door had been opened in my mind. The Eye gave me vision after vision.'

'And?'

'And it seems my uncle's been . . . *collecting* Demari for some time.'

'*What?*' I splutter, horrified. 'Why?'

'Think about it. If he's planning to take the throne, he'll need a bigger army. And what better way to ensure his victory than to infuse his ranks with Demari soldiers.'

'But *why* would they agree to fight for him?'

'Some may not, it's true. But others might. Because Balen's offering them something they've never had – legitimacy, security, protection. To be valued and rewarded for who they are, rather than ostracized or imprisoned for it. And with an army of Demari at his disposal, if he were then to get his hands on the missing Eye . . .'

For a moment I think I might vomit.

'I keep thinking about it,' I whisper. 'The way he looked at the Eye. All he's got planned for it. For me. *This is only the beginning* – that's what he said.'

'He's just trying to scare you.'

'Then it's working. Take what happened at Fire Mountain – he attacked the entire Ignitia Court just to get to me.'

'I won't let him hurt you, Storm Weaver,' Fox says quietly.

I glance up, and the intensity of his gaze roots me to the spot. I'm not sure I could move if I tried.

'It's not just me I'm worried about,' I say at last.

'Your brothers?' Fox guesses.

I nod, winding a stray curl tightly round my finger. 'I was the one who insisted we go through the Ridge tunnels, I'm the reason Flint and I were separated, and now he's out there, all alone. I *hate* not knowing where he is.'

'You know he's alive,' Fox points out.

It's true – he's been using the Eye of the Past to check on my family every day at my behest. Grandmother and Renly are holed up at the safe house with the decoys, while Flint appears to be making his way across some endless stretch of moorland.

'But what if he runs into trouble? What if –' I cut myself off, afraid I might speak some unfavourable future into existence. 'And then there's Ren . . .'

'He's safe,' Fox reassures me as I pull the little wooden figurine out of my pocket.

'Maybe. But for how long? We both know your uncle isn't above killing children to further his own agenda.'

The words are out before I can snatch them back. Ugly and insensitive, they linger in the space between us.

Fox has turned very still. I can almost feel it – the quiet agony, the coiled, all-consuming rage.

'I'm – I'm so – I don't –'

'Know how to form a sentence?' His voice is cool and clipped.

I twist my fingers together, cursing my own thoughtlessness. It's some time before I manage to speak again. 'I'm sorry. About your sister.'

'Why?' Fox says flatly. 'You didn't kill her.'

I wince. 'I mean, I'm sorry for your loss. I can't even imagine –'

'Then don't.'

'I . . . I know you prefer not to talk about it.'

'How perceptive you are, Storm Weaver.' Fox drops to the ground. The saplings bend to let him pass, but something makes him turn back and face me head-on. 'What do you want me to say?' he demands. 'That I loved my sister? That I'm *sad* she's dead? Well, I did, and I am. Every day. But what good will that do? It won't bring her back.'

'No, it won't,' I agree. 'But keeping it to yourself, going through something like this alone . . .' I pause self-consciously. I don't often share this part of myself, not with anybody. But I've realized, with more than a little surprise, how painful it is – seeing him in pain.

'I . . . I know what it's like to lose someone you love,' I murmur softly. 'And it's enough to break anyone.'

Drizzle kisses my cheeks.

Fox hesitates, torn. Then he closes the distance between us in two strides. My breath hitches, my knees grazing his hips as he plants his hands on either side of me. For a long moment, we stare at one another. Green eyes bore into mine, tearless yet brimming with such torment that I want to look away. But I don't. I force myself to meet his gaze, because he needs something to hold on to, even if he won't admit it.

Grief is a language I understand. It's the very worst kind of pain. An ache that never really goes away. There's no cure, no remedy or antidote. Not even for a Healer.

And I meant what I said – it is enough to break anyone.

But broken things are sharp. So maybe that's why Fox takes my concern and my vulnerability and throws them back in my face. Why he *recoils* from my sympathy as though it were a loaded weapon pointed straight at his heart.

The fallen tree beneath me begins to quiver, then quake. I gasp as it snaps clean in half, the deafening *CRACK* causing birds to take flight from the branches overhead.

I freeze as Fox leans in close, eyes cold, lips brushing the shell of my ear. 'I'm the one who does the breaking, remember?'

Then he yanks Soulkiller from the earth and walks away without a backward glance.

27

Elva

I remember that the week following the whipping passed in an indistinguishable haze of pain, each day blending into the next. Ingra had done her best, but my back still resembled a slab of raw meat, latticed with lashes. The heat of the omnipresent Ostacrian sun only worsened matters, with the makeshift bandages sticking to my skin with blood and sweat.

I was polishing a vase in the corner of a glittering parlour. It was filled to bursting with golden roses, and I was reminded of what my father used to call my sister and me. Astrid was his star, and I was his petal. They were just pet names, little terms of endearment, but fitting nonetheless. For Astrid was always bold and bright and dazzling. Whereas I was delicate and fragile, easily wilted.

I recall reaching out to touch one of the silken blooms, then drawing my hand back quickly at the sound of someone clearing their throat behind me. I turned to find a pair of raven-black eyes fixed on mine. The boy was impossibly handsome – tall and lithe, with marble-fair skin and sharply chiselled, dark features. Only this wasn't just any boy.

This was the Crown Prince of Ostacre.

Panic reared, and I stumbled backwards, nearly knocking over the vase.

Concern creased his perfect face. 'I'm sorry. I didn't mean to startle you.'

I began to tremble, flinching as the movement aggravated the welts on my back.

The prince shook his head apologetically. 'No, please, I'm not – I just wanted to –' He cut himself off, took a deep breath and smiled. And it was such a shy, sweet smile that I felt the frenzied clamour of my fear fade to a soft echo. 'I'm . . . I'm Haldyn,' he said.

I stared at him, utterly bewildered. Why was he introducing himself as if I didn't know exactly who he was? Why was he talking to me at all?

Hal took a small step forward. 'I saw what you did for that young boy, at the feast.'

Terror flared once more. Was Pip to be punished for spilling the wine? Was I to be punished twice over for taking the blame?

Hal must've sensed my alarm, for his expression softened, his voice smooth and deep and achingly gentle. 'You were really brave.'

Nobody had ever said that to me before.

My heart stuttered, then almost stopped entirely as he added, 'I want to apologize.'

I blinked, convinced I'd misheard him. The future Emperor of Ostacre was apologizing . . . to *me*?

'My cousin was out of order,' he continued. 'I tried to reason with her, but my father overruled me.' He grimaced, his jaw flexing. 'And I . . . I also wanted to give you this.'

In his outstretched hand sat a small silver pot.

'It's a salve. For your back. I got it from my broth– from a Healer. You're supposed to apply it twice a day. It should ease the pain and minimize the scarring.'

My lips parted in surprise. For a long moment, we just looked at one another. I scanned his face for a sign – that this was all some trick, a cruel joke designed to taunt me. I searched for hate and found only kindness. His gaze was steady and true, his eyes as dark and beautiful as the eternal night of my homeland. Hardly daring to breathe, I unfurled my palm and accepted the salve, watching his throat bob as his fingers brushed against mine.

After that, I found I didn't despise the sun so much any more. In fact, I found myself hopelessly drawn towards it. Towards *him*.

A lot has changed these past two years, but never that.

I perch on the edge of Hal's four-poster bed, watching him sleep.

One of his hands is curled into a fist round the bedsheets, while the other lies flat upon his chest, which rises and falls in time with the low ticking of the clock on the wall. It's late – past midnight. *Witching hour*, my sister would call it. She used to love telling ghost stories. Singing them, too. Many Obsidian ballads are rooted in eerie folklore, and were made a hundred times more haunting when sung by Astrid, her voice pure and mournful, almost otherworldly. I can still hear her, even now. Perhaps, some day, I'll hear her again.

Hal's eyelids flicker while he dreams, muttering a word that sounds a little like my name. I reach for him and smooth his hair back from his face. He's been this way since he collapsed during the banquet.

The palace is awash with whispers, and not only concerning the emperor's ill health but also the unexplained break-in – and break-out – down in the dungeons. King Balen's motive remains a mystery. And what's even more puzzling is how selective he was. He didn't free all the prisoners, only some. What was it about those ones that rendered them of such value to the Ventalla King? What does he know that we don't?

In light of Hal's condition, it was with Zephyr I shared the information I'd gathered in the banquet hall. The two Eyes I overheard discussing King Balen's plan – the nature of which I didn't understand until after it was carried out successfully – were arrested. When both refused to talk, Marina suggested torturing them for answers. I didn't relish the idea, traitors or not, but I had no say in the matter. So far, neither has cracked.

With one last look at Hal, I slip behind the tapestry and through the concealed door into the serf tunnels.

My bunk was empty when I left to check on him. Ingra still hasn't told me what she's up to, and what with her pattern of unexplained absences, roaming the palace at night has become even riskier. I can only hope Matron doesn't decide to perform an inspection.

I take a left at the next fork, then a right.

The significant downside to arresting those Eyes is that it's let other traitorous members of the Imperial

Court know that we're watching, and their discretion has reached new heights. I haven't managed to ascertain anything useful these past few days, nor have I found any evidence of clandestine meetings taking place inside the palace.

I pause, my brows knitting together as an idea begins to form.

What if such gatherings aren't taking place *inside* the palace at all?

I follow the tunnels down to the lower levels before stepping out into cool night air, glancing round at the moon-bleached grounds. Often, when they first arrive here, the youngest serfs are assigned unskilled labour such as polishing cutlery or sweeping floors, but many are put to work in the palace gardens. I remember looking around at these perfectly manicured lawns, sweat dripping down my brow, and thinking that just a handful of Terrathian and Aquatori Etheri could keep them in flawless condition with a mere flick of their wrists. But instead, the serfs are forced to plant, weed and water, cutting the grass, clipping the hedges, breaking our backs beneath the indifferent sun.

A pair of sentries rounds the corner, the Castellion raven emblazoned across their golden uniforms, swords glinting in their sheaths. Immediately, my shadows emerge, cloaking me in darkness. Pressing my back to the wall, I hold my breath as the sentries pass by, engaged in muttered speculation about the cause of the emperor's illness. Neither of them so much as glances in my direction.

'Thank you,' I whisper as the darkness recedes.

I wander through the orchard, the trees swollen with golden apples. There was an apple tree by our cottage. Astrid used to swing me up on to her shoulders to pick them.

I strain my ears for the faintest murmur of conversation, but there's none. Disappointment and frustration twist painfully in my chest.

I'm so lost in thought that I barely notice where I'm headed until I arrive. Hundreds of eyes watch me from all sides, carved into the faces of statues so unsettlingly lifelike it looks as though the bodies were merely dipped in molten gold, the features perfectly captured to immortalize each of Ostacre's former emperors.

In the weeks following his father's death, this is where Hal would come. I used to find him sitting by Emperor Alvar's statue, which was erected just days after the Binding Ceremony. It's no secret that their relationship was strained by the emperor's dismissal of his wife and infatuation with his mistress. But in spite of everything, he was still Hal's father, and Hal mourned him quietly, in his own way.

My gaze lands on the statue, which looks nothing like the haggard, weary man Emperor Alvar became – a pale imitation of his former self. He was rarely seen without Lady Calloway on his arm, but towards the end I remember thinking that it looked more like she was propping him up. I asked Hal about it once, but he just changed the subject.

As I continue to stare, my mind makes alterations, and for a moment I don't see smooth golden perfection but a skeletal frame, hollow cheeks, trembling hands and dark bruise-like shadows lingering beneath the eyes, so similar to . . .

I drag in a breath. Could there be a connection between the emperor's peculiar affliction and Hal's own condition? What if the physicians can't tell what's wrong with him because he's not suffering from some common illness, but from something . . . hereditary?

'Hello, girl.'

I lurch with fright as a rasping voice sounds startlingly close.

Slowly, I turn, willing my shadows to remain hidden. But all I see is a statue. This one is smaller than Emperor Alvar's, the subject's mouth twisted into a crooked smile. Something about him makes my skin turn cold, the same way it did when I touched that crystal decanter – a numbing, bone-deep kind of dread.

The old man who steps out from behind the statue is dressed in plain golden robes that trail behind him on the ground. His shoulders are stooped, hunched forward with age, and his hands are tucked into a pair of delicate gloves. The skin on his face sags loosely, almost as pale as the wispy white beard stretching down to his navel.

Realization turns my insides to ice.

For I am looking into the beady black eyes of Caius Castellion.

He inclines his head pleasantly before glancing round at the statue behind him. 'A good likeness, wouldn't you say? I was younger then, of course. Barely entering my prime.'

I stare at him, wide-eyed and terrified. This man conquered my homeland and enslaved my people. He is a *monster*. Nobody's seen him since the Binding Ceremony. What is he doing here? And what answer will I give if he asks me the same question?

His mouth curves into a mirror image of the smile adorning his statue, as though he can hear the cogs of my brain ticking and whirring and is amused by it.

Fear prickles down the back of my neck, sweat dewing on my brow. Before I can clamp down on them, my shadows spring forth to defend me.

No.

I stumble backwards, colliding with another statue.

Caius Castellion looks neither shocked nor scared nor outraged. He just continues to smile pleasantly, utterly unfazed by the darkness swarming around me.

I wonder briefly about his eyesight, then his mental faculties. I consider whether to make a break for it. It's not like he'd be able to catch me. But what if he were to tell someone about this? What if he were to tell *Hal*? He is his grandfather, after all.

The old man sighs. 'Don't be afraid, girl. I mean you no harm.'

Surprise slices through fear, and my shadows begin to melt away. He can't be serious. This is the emperor who sought to eradicate the Magi, who revelled in the loss of their magic. Why does he look so calm? And why is he *smiling* at me?

'Come now,' he says dismissively. 'If I was planning on killing you, I would have done it the second your powers were returned to you, if not before. Or, if I'd wanted to avoid this scenario altogether, I could have just killed *her*. Kind of you, to bandage her cut hand. Kindness that was rewarded in ways neither of you could've imagined.'

I shake my head slowly, perplexed.

'But I digress,' the old man continues. 'Reports of Haldyn's ill health have reached far and wide. It is for my grandson that I have returned, not to murder the girl he loves.'

My insides turn from ice to stone. The game is up. He knows. He *knows*. But *how*?

I blink, trying to clear my head. 'I . . . I don't . . . understand.'

'No,' he says thoughtfully. 'I should imagine not.'

'How . . . how do you . . .'

'I could wait for you to stumble to the end of your sentence, but it seems unnecessary, for the answer would be the same. I know many things.' He presses the tips of his gloved fingers together, thumbs forming an arch. 'I once thought I knew everything, but it seems I was wrong. The future is not a fixed entity. It twists and alters every passing day. Just as I'm beginning to see it clearly, *she* does something to change its mind. For she is the key, and keys unlock many doors, each of them leading to myriad different fates, infinite possibilities – some good, some bad, some catastrophic, but all equally plausible.'

I stare blankly at him. This man speaks in riddles. 'You . . . you said you came back for Hal,' I stutter. 'Do you know what's wrong with him?'

He ignores me. 'Shall I tell you a story, girl?'

My voice is breathless. 'Please, if you could just –'

He cuts me off. 'Are you familiar with *The Tragedy of Emmeric and Irabella*?'

My mouth tips open, then snaps shut. Of course I'm familiar with that particular tale. Ingra even teasingly refers to me and my *secret lover* by the names of the titular characters. But what does it have to do with anything? And why does Caius Castellion wish to tell it to me? I was right. He must be senile.

The old man doesn't seem to require a response, for he clears his throat with a dragging cough and begins. 'Noble, handsome Emmeric was born into a powerful family. He was heir to a large fortune and wanted for nothing. Yet our tragic hero was lonely. He wished for only one thing – to find true love.'

He pauses to grin crookedly at me.

'Irabella was a rare beauty, with hair like cornsilk and eyes as bright as jewels. But she was also penniless, a mere servant, and because of this, nobody ever really *saw* her. Nobody, except for Emmeric. Their love was pure and unselfish, soul-deep and star-crossed. And yet with love comes sacrifice. Emmeric could not allow his family to discover the truth for fear of what they might do, and so his relationship with Irabella had to be kept secret.'

The old man starts walking among the statues, limping a slow figure of eight.

'Despite those who sought to keep them apart, all the young lovers wanted was to be together. Only their plans were foiled. Do you know why, girl?'

I wet my lips. 'Because Emmeric was cursed.'

'Indeed he was,' the old man agrees. 'He was cursed by a vengeful witch who blamed his family for her people's ruin. Every story needs a villain, you know.'

I frown slightly, having long considered Emmeric's power-hungry relations to be the villains of this tale.

'She cursed the first-born sons of their House,' Caius Castellion continues. 'In destroying their legacy, she took away their dominion. *An eye for an eye*, as the Fidra say.' For some reason, this expression seems to amuse him, and he lets out a wheezy chuckle. 'Irabella was forced to watch her love sicken and die, knowing there was nothing she could do to stop it.' He sighs wistfully, stroking his beard. 'A tragedy indeed.'

I shrink backwards as he comes to a stop in front of me.

'I told your friend Blaze a different story. She knows the beginning, you know the end. Though of course, there are no beginnings and endings. As one thing ends, another begins – a perpetual cycle, an eternal existence, a life thread that stretches on forevermore.'

A shiver travels down my spine. I can hear my heartbeat accelerate, a pounding frenzy next to the old man's rattling plod. 'What does *Blaze* have to do with any of this?'

His black eyes are depthless, as dark and cold as death. '*Everything*.'

I grit my teeth against the mounting confusion. 'I . . . don't . . .'

'Come now,' he scolds. 'Use that pretty head of yours. Who do you think has the power to break the curse?'

'The curse on . . . Emmeric?' My eyes narrow. *Definitely senile*. 'But that's just a story?'

Caius Castellion smiles. 'We are all stories, girl,' he murmurs. 'Just as we are all of us bound by this curse of blood.'

PART II

Tides That Bind

28

Blaze

In my dreams, I scrabble desperately at the bars of a crystal cage, panic rising like the tide.

Far above me, perched smugly upon the Imperial throne, is Caius Castellion. Only he is no longer the young emperor from Fox's visions but the old man I met in the library: sallow-skinned and frail, his narrow frame shrouded in robes of pale gold. Held in his hand is the Eye of the Future. I can sense its power pulsing in time with my own, like a second heartbeat. His voice is quiet and yet his words echo through my head.

Your enemy is close, girl. If only you knew what he has in store for you.

And suddenly it's not Caius smiling down at me but King Balen, his raven eyes glinting with amusement. My insides twist with fear just as the doors to the throne room burst open and a child is dragged inside. Except this time, it's not Senna.

It's Renly.

I wake with a start, my breathing ragged. It's almost dawn – the slivers of sky among the trees are a hazy golden orange. As I push myself upright, I register the dull ache in my lower stomach. I look down to find the front of my trousers stained with blood.

My heart sinks. *Not now.*

I try to stand, but a surge of nausea courses through me, stopping me in my tracks. The pain spikes. I feel it in my legs, my hips, the base of my spine – a series of sharp, violent spasms. Letting out a low groan, I lean over and vomit into the undergrowth.

When there's nothing left, I slump back against a tree, shivering, cold sweat beading on my brow. That's when I catch sight of Fox standing a few yards to my right. We haven't spoken since my careless blunder involving his sister. I'd remained sitting on that broken tree long after he disappeared into the forest, cursing my own thoughtlessness.

Heat stains my cheeks as he takes in the sight of me. He clears his throat uncomfortably, then abruptly turns and strides off into the trees.

I shrink with shame, but it's not long before another wave of pain arrives. I take several deep breaths, trying not to think about Fox – hating that he saw me like this, hating how much it hurts that he just walked away.

I must've eventually dozed off because when I come to the pain has eased somewhat, and there's a blanket draped over me. I turn my head to discover Fox sitting in front of the fire, stirring the contents of a pot. He pours the concoction carefully into a tin cup and offers it to me. I reach out to take it, peering down at the liquid within.

'What's this?'

'Ginger tea,' he responds. 'I added some fennel and raspberry leaf too. It should help with the pain.'

I blink, taken aback. So *that's* why he disappeared.

Fox's eyes meet mine, and I'm startled by the softness I find there. 'Drink up.'

The tea is tangy and sweet. I sip it slowly, unsure what to say. I thought it had made him uncomfortable, seeing me in this condition, and perhaps it did – only not because he was embarrassed but because I was suffering.

Fox fills the silence. 'I can wash your things in the Creek, if you like.'

I stare at him, half astonished, half horrified. 'You don't have to do that.'

He shrugs, unfazed. 'I don't mind. I'm a Healer. I'm no stranger to blood.'

I run my finger along the rim of the cup, avoiding his gaze.

'Look, you can wear these in the meantime,' says Fox, fishing my old pair of tattered trousers from his satchel. 'I'll turn round.'

I hesitate, then shuck off my soiled garments beneath the blanket, remembering to snatch Renly's figurine out of the pocket. Fox takes them without comment, pausing only to toss me a scrap of cloth and several rolls of gauze before winding his way through the trees. I glance at Cedar, as if he might be able to offer some explanation for this unexpected display of chivalry, but he just continues to graze half-heartedly at a clump of weeds.

By the time Fox returns, the tea seems to have done its job. The pain has passed, and I feel more like myself again.

'Better?' he asks, draping my clean clothes over a branch to dry.

I nod. 'Much.' Then I add quietly, 'Thank you.'

He sits down to stoke the fire. 'You were tossing and turning all night. Bad dreams?'

'I can't get it out of my head,' I say, grimacing. 'I can't get *her* out of my head – Syla. All she sacrificed, just to save one life.'

Fox leans back on his elbows, sensing I'm not finished.

'It scares me,' I admit. 'What she did. It scares me because . . .' I take a breath. 'Because I know, deep down, that I would do the same thing.' I force myself to meet his gaze, my voice little more than a whisper as I ask, 'Does that make me a bad person?'

'It makes you a good sister.'

My heart twists. He didn't even hesitate.

'I want . . . I wanted to say that I'm sorry. About yesterday.'

Fox half closes his eyes. 'You don't need to apologize.'

'I wasn't thinking, and I feel awful –'

He cuts me off. 'I don't want your pity, Storm Weaver.'

'Fine,' I say defeatedly. 'Forget it.'

'It's not that I –' Fox stops, grinding his jaw. 'It's just, I find it . . . *difficult*. Talking about her. About what happened to her.'

'Of course you do,' I say softly. 'She was your sister. She *is* your sister.'

Something flickers in his gaze. There's a long, strained pause. Then he says, 'Haldyn prefers to act like she never existed.'

I rest my chin on my knees and look up at him. 'What about your mother?'

He exhales. 'Sometimes I'll find her sitting in Freya's room. She wouldn't let them clear it out after. Everything is exactly as it was. Untouched.'

I remember that room. It was overflowing with flowers. Lilies, mostly. Pearly white and beautiful. Lady Calloway's favourite, Spinner told me.

'As for my father . . .' Fox swallows. 'Well, because of me, his grief died with him.'

'You don't have to talk about it,' I mumble, ashamed of my intrusion.

But now Fox has started, he can't seem to stop.

'They said Freya must've caught the sweating sickness. There was an outbreak in the citadel, with many of the courtiers dropping like flies. It was some time before a falcon arrived at my grandparents' cottage, summoning me back to the palace. When I got there, my mother didn't even need to tell me. I saw it on her face. That's when . . .'

But I already know what happened next. I've known ever since the Binding Ceremony. There was a reason King Balen murdered his niece. It set in motion a chain of events that changed the course of history. It was the trigger to destruction.

I taste bile as I recall what Fox told me about his uncle hunting down those with both Etheri and Magi heritage. *Demari*. The isle of Al Sh'ib was once home to a number of prophets. It would appear that some of their Demari descendants have inherited that gift, one the Ventalla King used to further his own gain.

The words of the prophecy echo in my ears.

To break the world, you must first break his heart.

'The Cleaving . . . it was because of Freya, wasn't it? Her death caused the Rift.'

A long, strung-out silence follows. Then Fox says, 'Yes.'

I lean back slowly against the tree.

'I didn't mean to do it,' he continues quietly. 'The power – it was too strong. All-consuming. I – I couldn't stop it.'

So it's true. My suspicions confirmed. Fox never meant to create the Rift, just as I never meant to summon that storm. Both were tragedies, yet both were unintentional. Uncontrollable.

'And nobody ever suspected?' I say weakly.

A muscle flexes in his jaw. 'The palace had already moved on. In their minds, Freya was just one of the emperor's bastards. Not worth mourning. Not worthy of respect.'

I shake my head. 'That's . . . awful.'

'There was a time the Calloways weren't exactly held in high esteem. The court did their best to disguise their hostility, but I still felt it, even as a child.'

His words strike a chord, and I glance away. Because I know that feeling all too well – to be an outsider stuck on the inside.

'In short, my sister and I were considered to be nothing more than the consequences of my father's ill-advised infatuation with a lowborn Terrathian girl,' says Fox.

I think of his adoring bunch of sycophants who hang on his every word. The awe he inspires among the courtiers – part admiration, part terror. It's difficult to imagine that their fawning deference was once scornful contempt.

'It made me angry,' he continues. 'I resented their resentment. The way nobody seemed to care when Freya died.'

His voice cracks. Without thinking, I reach for him. Fox catches hold of my hand. For one breathless moment, I wonder if he's going to snap my wrist. But he only runs a finger over my scar, briefly caressing the waxy, mottled skin – the remnants of my first brandmark.

'The Cleaving changed everything,' Fox continues, his tone now infused with bitter triumph. 'Afterwards, when all eyes were on me, I knew I had a choice to make. I could grovel and cower and beg for the people's forgiveness. Or I could own it.'

A memory stirs.

Sometimes we must claim our accidents. Intention can define you. And better to appear wilful than witless, wouldn't you say?

'I knew I couldn't make them accept me, but I could make them *fear* me.' Fox shrugs. 'And that's what I did. Little did I know I was playing right into my uncle's hands. What I'd done, who I became – it was all by his design.'

My gaze flickers upward, latching on to his.

'I'm going to kill him,' he says quietly. 'I'm not going to stop until I've made him pay for what he did. To the Council, to my sister, to me.'

I nod. I'd guessed as much. 'So that's why you're still in Ostacre – to find the Eye?'

'Yes,' Fox admits. Then he adds softly, 'But that's not the only reason.'

I feel it in my chest: fragile roots that begin to spread, a seed that sprouts into something gentle and curious, unfurling like flower petals in the sun. I have no name for it, the feeling. It's unlike anything I've ever known. And for a moment, as I look into a pair of eyes the colour of spring, I'm torn between ripping it out or letting it bloom.

Fox moves forward, or perhaps it's me. I can't be sure. All I know is that suddenly he's close enough for me to see the tiny freckle at the corner of his mouth. His eyes scour my face, as though searching for a sign, something to tell him what I want. Only the trouble is, I don't know what I want. Or maybe it's that I do know, and I just won't admit it.

All at once, something small and coppery-red comes darting into the clearing. I scramble backwards in fright, but Cedar tosses his mane happily and Fox's face lights up. I stare, nonplussed, as the creature curls up in his lap, its beady green-gold eyes fixed on me.

'Storm Weaver, meet Scout.'

'*This* is Scout?' Laughter bubbles up my throat as I try, and fail, to hide the amusement in my voice. '*Of course* you would have a pet fox.'

Fox grins. 'Too subtle?'

'A little on the nose, perhaps,' I reply, echoing what he said about Silverclaw.

'Then tell me,' he says, smirking, 'because I've been desperate to know. What did you name that kitten I gave you?'

I clamp my mouth shut.

Fox looks jubilant. 'Let's hear it.'

'Mouse,' I mutter under my breath, blushing crimson.

He cups a hand to his ear. 'Speak up, Storm Weaver.'

'*Mouse.*'

Fox tips his head back and laughs.

'What?' I say haughtily. 'She's scared of mice. I thought it was sweet.'

He only laughs harder. I fold my arms across my chest defiantly, but can't suppress the smile tugging at my lips.

I feel it then, unexpected yet unmistakable – *warmth*, as well as heat. And in that moment, the Earth Cleaver just became a thousand times more dangerous.

29

Flint

After what feels like several decades, Spinner, Sheen and I reach the foot of a small hill near the border between the moorland and the Greenwood. I've heard stories about this particular forest. Many believe it's haunted, swarming with unfriendly spirits – something I've chosen to ignore, given that it's a shortcut to the Waterlands.

Besides, it'll take more than a bunch of ghost stories to stop me from finding my sister.

A village sits at the top of the hill. I let out a triumphant whoop, elbowing past Sheen to get a better look. 'Thank the *Gods*. I'm starving.'

'Me too,' says Spinner.

But Sheen shakes his head. 'No. We said no detours. No stopping off anywhere you might be recognized.'

'Oh, come *on*,' I say exasperatedly. 'I may be something of a socialite, I grant you, but I can't claim to have had many dealings with a bunch of sheep farmers from . . .'

'Heathcross,' Spinner supplies, consulting the map.

'Precisely. And even if I had,' I continue, stabbing a finger at my eyepatch, 'I doubt any of them would recognize me now anyway.'

My words dangle in the air, the tone all wrong. I'd meant to sound self-deprecating, but my voice comes out tinged with a bitter acidity I usually succeed in swallowing down. I cringe away as Spinner reaches out to pat my arm, her face flooded with sympathy. Sheen says nothing, his violet eyes unreadable. And just for a brief moment, I hate them both. One for their pity, the other for their lack of it.

'In any case,' I hurry on, 'I'd rather gnaw the leather from my boot than eat another bowl of Spinner's revolting soup.'

Spinner lets out a theatrical gasp of indignation and launches herself at me. 'Why, you rude, ungrateful –'

We fall backwards into the heather, her half tickling, half punching me, our laughter shattering the tension. I roll her over, pinning her wrists to the ground while she squeals and struggles and does a poor job of pretending she's not enjoying every second.

Sheen looks as though he'd rather be anywhere else.

'Fine,' he says eventually, as a giggling Spinner leans up to kiss me. '*Fine.* If you two get up and stop acting like idiots, then we'll go. But if anything happens, it's on you. Happy?'

'Delirious,' I tell him, scrambling to my feet.

I hold out a hand to Spinner, and together the three of us start making our way up the hill towards Heathcross.

I picture a quaint little hamlet filled with all manner of delights – a bakery selling fresh bread, children dancing joyfully around a maypole, thatched cottages covered in honeysuckle with shutters painted cornflower blue.

Yet when we arrive, the reality is . . . quite different.

There's no bakery. There's no maypole either. Instead, a series of treacherous-looking spikes are wedged into the earth around the village perimeter, and all windows are boarded shut, bristling with iron nails.

I glance around, scratching the back of my neck. 'This is . . . cosy.'

We refill our waterskins from a nearby well, and I splash some water over my face in an attempt to cool my burns.

Several people eye us suspiciously as we approach. Some even pull their children away, doors slamming behind them, while others rest their hands on the weapons slung from their belts. The *weapons*. I stare in surprise – not just because they seem out of place in a small Fidran village in the middle of the Wildlands but because of how magnificent they are. Axes, maces, longswords – all expertly crafted.

I think of my bow, snapped to splinters in the Ridge tunnels.

'What's with this place?' Spinner whispers. 'Why are they looking at us like that?'

'I don't know,' says Sheen. 'But I don't like it.'

'You don't like anything,' I tell him.

My gaze rests on a woman with a kind face. She's throwing scraps into a pen built high with steel railings, a few pigs milling about aimlessly inside.

I clear my throat, preparing to turn on that famous Harglade charm. 'Afternoon,' I call cheerfully. 'May I ask –' But I don't get to finish my sentence, because the woman takes one frightened look at us and bolts in the opposite direction. 'I'll take that as a no,' I say, just as a burly man lumbers towards us, a gleaming crossbow strapped to his back.

'What's your business here?'

I bow my head. 'We are but poor travellers come to seek a hot meal and a bed for the night. Would you be so kind as to point us in the direction of your best alehouse?'

The man snorts. 'Don't got one.'

'Ah.' My stomach growls. 'That's unfortunate.'

'Leave it,' says Sheen. 'Let's just go.'

I ignore him. 'What about an inn? D'you have one of those?'

'I *said*, let's go.'

'Or perhaps a brothel?' I continue. 'My friend here could certainly use one. Truly, I've never known someone so uptight in all my life.'

Sheen looks as though he'd like to summon every current of air he can muster and blast me into the middle of next week.

A few of the other villagers are listening now, forming a circle around us.

'*Flint*,' Spinner mutters under her breath.

I hold up my hands. 'Fine. If there's nowhere for us to eat, or sleep, or in some cases *not sleep* –' I wink, which really doesn't go down as well as anticipated – 'then what I want is one of those weapons you're all carrying. I've never seen such fine craftsmanship.'

A stream of murmurs ripples through the crowd.

'What're you doing?' Sheen hisses.

I shrug. 'I want a new bow.'

The man considers me for a moment, then turns to a woman holding a mace. 'What d'you think? He doesn't strike me as one of them.'

I glance at Spinner and Sheen. Is he talking about Etheri? I wedge my hands firmly into my pockets, grateful for the thin leather gloves covering my brandmark. It no longer glows, of course. Not since I lost the third trial. But if these heavily armed villagers are looking for an Etheri, the triple flame of the Ignitia branded into the back of my right hand is still a *pretty* big giveaway. Then again, if they are questioning whether or not we're Fidra, wouldn't it be a whole lot simpler to just ask us to prove it?

'You're right, Glen,' the woman replies. 'Not with that accent.'

My *accent*? Etheri can be found in almost every province across Ostacre. Apart from carrying the faint lilt of the Firelands, my accent reveals little else.

'They could be spies,' muses another, tapping her fingers along the hilt of her sword.

Spies? Spies for whom, exactly? Who on earth would care about the goings-on in this dump?

'No,' says the boy next to her, sizing us up. 'They're too clean.'

Too clean? I'm positively filthy. I'd sell a kidney for a hot bath. Are they under the impression that Etheri don't wash?

The man, Glen, sucks his teeth. 'All right,' he says eventually, and I allow myself a small exhale of relief. 'You can have your bow. But I warn you, it won't come cheap.'

'I should hope not,' I tell him genially. 'I have very expensive taste.'

Glen jerks his head, signalling for us to follow him.

We're led past a barn, its doors barricaded by a thick piece of wood. What are they protecting themselves from? Are they afraid the spirits haunting the Greenwood are going to emerge from the treeline and charge up the hill to attack? Though even if this were the case, I doubt such defences would do much to deter them.

'This way,' says Glen.

Heathcross isn't particularly big, and we soon come to a stop outside a rundown little workshop. The chimney belches out smoke, and the walls are carved with Fidran runes.

Glen knocks on the door – four sharp raps. There's a scuffle from inside followed by a faint clattering. After a minute or so, the door swings open to reveal a woman wearing a dress made entirely from chainmail. She has on thick gloves that stretch almost up to her elbows, and there's a streak of coal dust on the tip of her nose.

'This is my wife,' says Glen. 'Iris, meet your new customers.'

Iris looks me up and down. 'You got coin?'

I reach my hand into my satchel and pull out a handful of silver. 'Will this suffice?'

She raises an eyebrow, then moves back to let us enter.

The forge is cramped and cluttered. Weapons litter every available surface – delicately crafted axes scattered across workbenches, gleaming longswords hanging from the walls. The air is hot and heavy, thick with the tang of metal. Various tools are laid out on the table in front of us, and in the corner a fire burns brightly. My stomach tightens. Forcing myself to sit round the campfire Spinner begrudgingly builds every night is bad enough, but at least then it's out in the open. Here, it's too close. I'm hemmed in, just like I was in the throne room at Fire Mountain when Ember lit the pyre, setting Aunt Yvainne's body alight.

A familiar tremor ripples through my hands and I clasp them behind my back, leaning against the far wall, the handle of a mace digging into my spine.

I begin to count – knives, hammers, marks on the table.

'So,' says Iris, tying back her corn-gold hair with a scrap of cloth before picking up a long pair of tongs. 'What can I do for you?'

'I'd like a bow,' I tell her. 'A good one. And some arrows. Please.'

She points to her husband's crossbow. 'One like that?'

'Mm, I was thinking something a little more . . . classic?'

Iris smiles as she draws a red-hot blade from the flames and plunges it into a vat of water. She sets to work gathering what she needs from her stores, occasionally barking orders at Glen, who does as she asks without comment, his gruff, hardened demeanour dissipating like smoke from the fire.

Sheen stands by the door, stiff and alert, poised to combat any potential threat.

Spinner skips past me and perches on the sill of a boarded-up window, running her hand along the shutters. 'Can I ask who you mistook us for when we arrived here?'

There's a pause, in which husband and wife exchange a look.

Then Iris says, 'For some time our village has been targeted by a group of brigands. They come in the night, silent as ghosts. They steal from us – taking our grain, our tools, our livestock – attacking anyone who gets in their way. We never know when they'll strike.'

'That's awful,' says Spinner.

I practically jump as Sheen, who has been silent since we entered the forge, clears his throat and asks, 'Who are they? These people?'

'They call themselves the Green Bandits,' says Iris darkly. 'I've never seen such barbarism.' Her gaze flickers to me. 'Speaking of, what happened to you?'

It's as if her words open up a hole in the centre of my chest, and for a moment all I can hear is the fire snapping and crackling in the corner. My stomach heaves.

Sheen is watching me.

Hold it together, Flint.

I plaster on a smile – the smile of a boy who wins, and keeps winning.

'This old thing?' I say cheerfully, gesturing to my eyepatch. 'I wear it to look tough.'

Glen, who's busy fletching the shaft of an arrow, scoffs. Iris raises an eyebrow as she brushes a pile of wood shavings off the table and on to the floor, but doesn't press me.

'You don't happen to know a physician, do you?' Sheen asks.

'I'm *fine*,' I mutter, irritated.

Iris shakes her head. 'Afraid not. Physicians are hard to come by in outlying villages. They tend to flock to the central provinces, big towns and cities where they're more likely to find work. The more people, the more sick people.' She finishes carving the riser and sets it down on the table. 'Here, we make do. We learn to live with pain. You survive or you die.'

'Ever thought of moving?' Spinner suggests.

Iris selects a wicked-looking arrowhead from a pile in front of her. 'This is our home.'

Spinner nods politely, but I can tell she's thinking about the Golden Palace. For her, home means opulence, luxury, high society and pretty dresses, not struggling to get by in a poky cottage surrounded by sheep and heather.

'Where are you lot headed, anyway?' Iris asks.

I see no reason not to tell the truth. 'The Waterlands.'

'Then I take it you're planning to travel through the Greenwood?'

I nod.

'You'll need more than that bow to protect you in there,' says Glen.

I take a swig from my waterskin. 'Perhaps. But I suspect the constant threat of death will keep things interesting.'

Sheen gives me a look.

Iris takes a freshly fletched arrow shaft from Glen and tests its balance. Watching them together – her spirited and resourceful, him doting and dependable – reminds me of my parents. I was ten when my mother died giving birth to Renly. My memories are somewhat hazy, but something I recall with absolute clarity is the way my father used to look at her. It was an expression of utter contentment coupled with just a little dash of surprise, as though he couldn't quite believe he was getting to breathe the same air as her, let alone spend his life with her. That is, until he couldn't. Her death shattered him beyond repair.

Since then, I suppose I've always found the idea of *love* a little terrifying. From what I've seen, it only ever ends in pain. I think of my father's silent grief, of Seraphine's keening wails, of the way Elaith's spark dulls every time Cole passes her over for another.

Hearts are fragile, so easily broken. It's why I choose to keep things light, casual. To have fun, without having to worry about *feelings*.

I glance over to where Sheen is speaking quietly with Iris, having moved across to examine her work. The fire casts strange shadows along his sharp cheekbones.

Spinner snaps her fingers in front of my face. 'Flint?'

I blink. 'What?'

'I *said*, we should leave before nightfall, give ourselves time to set up camp.'

'Sure,' I say, as she entwines her gloved fingers with my own.

It's not long before Iris presents my bow, complete with a full quiver of arrows. It's beautiful – sleek, lightweight, delicate, yet entirely robust. It's a far superior model to my old one. For the first time in weeks, I don't feel utterly defenceless.

I nock an arrow and draw back the string.

'Careful!' Spinner yelps.

'Relax, I'm just testing it out.' I turn back to Iris. 'How much?'

I'd have paid double what she asks for a bow like this, so I hand over several pieces of silver, which she's not too proud to accept.

Though I've barely set one foot outside when a voice behind me calls, 'Wait!'

Iris appears in the doorway, holding a small packet. Upon closer examination, I see that it's filled with a number of dried leaves.

'What's this?'

'Dillweed,' she replies. 'For your eye. Whenever the pain gets too much, chew on a couple of these.'

'Oh,' I say, first taken aback, then touched. 'Thank you.'

'Be careful,' Iris says as Sheen marches off into the pale evening light, Spinner and I following in his wake. 'There's more than just bandits to contend with in the Greenwood. It's home to tree nymphs, commonly known as dryads, though some call them sirens of the forest. They'll try to trick you, lure you in so deep you'll never find your way out again. Remember, never eat anything that grows in there, and try to vary your path. If you hear your name, don't respond. Turn and walk away in the opposite direction.'

'And whatever you do, keep your wits about you,' warns Glen.

'Don't worry,' I call over my shoulder, slinging an arm round Spinner. 'I have more than enough wit for the three of us.'

30

Blaze

After the peaceful tranquillity of the forest, the bustling province of Wellwall is something of a shock to the system. All around us, the air is thick – from the acrid grey smoke funnelling out of crooked chimneys to the sweet-smelling, multi-coloured vapour lingering above stalls selling anything from love potions to honeycakes. Terrathian men in green waistcoats spill out of taverns, puffing on cherrywood pipes, or stand gathered round fires built to ward off the cool breeze blowing in from the north.

Judging by the unseasonable chill in the air, it appears King Balen is growing restless.

My gaze lingers on the chain round Fox's neck, trying not to smirk as I picture his uncle holed up in the Marble Palace, puzzling over a useless replica. I only wonder how long it'll take him to find out the truth – about the Eyes, and about Grandmother's decoys.

We wouldn't have risked coming here at all if it weren't for Cedar throwing a shoe. He's plodding along grumpily, muzzle twitching as we pass a cart of shiny pink apples. Fox gives in and buys him one, tossing another to me. I catch it deftly in one hand.

He nods approvingly. 'Your reflexes are getting better.'

'I know,' I reply, a little smugly.

The corners of his mouth quirk upward. I'm just raising the apple to my lips when he snatches it right out of my grip and takes a large bite.

'But there's always room for improvement,' he adds, grinning at me while he chews.

I snatch it back, trying my best to scowl.

I can't help noticing that things between us have felt . . . *different* these past few days. Grief is heavy, and ever since he told me about Freya, Fox seems lighter. He was reluctant at first, defensive to the point of anger. Yet it wasn't me he needed to confront, but rather his own loss. His refusal to let himself feel it. I looked at him, and I saw myself. For years, I bottled up my grief as though it were poison in a glass vial. I swallowed it down again and again, in the hope that one day it would run dry. But I was wrong.

Sometimes, the only way to survive pain is to accept it.

Scout pokes her head out of Fox's satchel and licks his hand. Her unexpected arrival is yet another reason for his good humour, though I can't seem to account for her absence.

'She's a wild animal – she goes where she pleases,' Fox had insisted, as said *wild animal* curled up to sleep in his lap.

The road is wide and winding and lined with all manner of stores – apothecaries and butchers, glassblowers and cobblers, even a tailor claiming to sell the finest Vosti silks.

It's not long before the sign we're seeking swings into view. The blacksmith, a squat man with an unkempt beard, stands outside his forge, hammer in hand.

'My horse requires a shoe,' Fox tells him.

'Please,' I add pointedly.

The blacksmith shakes his head. 'Won't be ready till tomorrow.'

'No, you don't understand,' Fox says firmly. 'We need it now.'

'Can't be done. I'm snowed under. The Baron's ordered a ton of new weaponry for his fighting pit.'

'Fighting pit?' I repeat.

'Mm-hm. There's nothing the Baron of Wellwall enjoys more than a brawl. Come back in the morning at first light.' He gestures vaguely. 'You'll find an inn round that corner.'

Fox frowns and tugs me aside to talk privately. 'I don't like this,' he mutters.

He's right to be cautious. We were supposed to be in and out before anyone gave us a second glance.

'It's not ideal,' I agree. 'But you said yourself that without a properly fitted shoe, Cedar could end up injuring himself.'

Fox rakes a hand through his hair, his expression torn.

'Besides,' I continue, 'the people believe that you're on a ship bound for the far corners of the earth and that I'm holed up in a safe house.'

I glance in the direction of the inn. Foolish or not, I can't deny that the idea of a few hours of comfort appeals to me. 'Just think, a meal that doesn't involve digging through soil. Proper beds. Pillows. Pudding . . .'

Fox rolls his eyes, but I can sense his resolve beginning to weaken.

'It's just one night,' I add.

'Fine,' he says, handing Cedar's reins to the blacksmith. 'Just one night.'

The inn itself appears fairly rundown – a patchwork of crumbling bricks threaded with moss and covered in browning ivy. Yet the view beyond the doors is a vast deal more inviting. The hall is littered with stools and spindle-legged tables piled high with food and wine, and suspended from the beamed ceiling are several cast-iron chandeliers dripping wax. A fire crackles in the hearth, enveloping the room in a delicious wave of heat.

Patrons crowd the bar, while others are hunched over tankards of mead. A group of young men sit with their heads together at the far side of the room, half obscured by a large barrel of ale. I edge round a cluster of raucous old women towards a table tucked in the corner, directly underneath a portrait of Queen Aspen. The likeness is impressive, with the artist even having managed to capture her slightly dreamy countenance.

By all accounts, the Grove – the towering forest the queen called home – is in mourning for its fallen leader. Leaves whisper and wail, the trees drooping under the weight of their grief. Being Terrathian, she was buried – laid to rest in the earth for all eternity.

It's only then I notice Fox's expression, the guilt creasing his brow.

'Want to sit somewhere else?' I ask.

He swallows, then shakes his head and drops on to a stool.

I take the seat opposite and begin to pick at a bit of dried wax, avoiding his gaze. I wonder what the people of Wellwall would do if they knew the boy who killed their queen was sitting in their midst.

'What was she like?' I ask. 'Queen Aspen.'

'Gentle,' he tells me. 'Powerful. Unfailingly kind, even to me. Though I always suspected she was a little scared of me, too.'

I huff a laugh. 'The whole palace was scared of you.'

Fox drops his voice to a whisper. 'And you, Storm Weaver?' The grin spreads across his face as slowly as the blush spreads across mine. 'Were you scared of me?'

Yes.

'No,' I lie.

At that moment the innkeeper – a sturdy, ruddy-cheeked woman in a gravy-splattered apron – plonks a flagon of floral-smelling ale on the table between us. 'Pleasant evening, my dears. What brings you to Wellwall?'

Fox bestows upon her his most dazzling smile. 'Just passing through.'

The innkeeper beams back at him and pours us both a cup of ale before winking at me. 'He's easy on the eyes, isn't he?'

Feeling myself turn from pink to crimson, I reach for my cup and take a large gulp as an excuse not to answer her.

'You know, I've been told I look like the Earth Cleaver,' Fox says mildly.

I choke on the ale and begin to cough.

The innkeeper pats me on the back. 'Really? Well, he's a devil, no doubt, but I've heard he's a handsome one.'

Fox jerks his chin at me. 'She certainly thinks so.'

If looks could kill, he'd be six feet under.

That's when the three of us become aware of a disgruntled growling sound. It appears Scout is beginning to lose her patience.

Clearing his throat, Fox pushes his satchel further under the table with his foot and rubs his stomach theatrically. 'I seem to have worked up an appetite.'

The innkeeper bustles off to fetch us some food.

I glower darkly at him, but the severity is somewhat discredited by an uncontrollable bout of hiccups.

'What?' Fox says innocently.

'You –' *hiccup* – 'are –' *hiccup* – 'unbelievable.'

Though I find myself mellowing considerably when the innkeeper returns with plates heaped with roasted rabbit, salted rye bread, potatoes swimming in butter and sprinkled with rosemary, carrots, cabbage and green beans, and, for dessert, two helpings of gooseberry pie and cream. I close my eyes while I eat, savouring every mouthful.

'Sure you're not missing my root stew?' Fox asks.

'Quite sure.' I crack open an eye and watch him slip the rabbit off his plate and into his satchel for Scout. 'Aren't you keeping some for yourself?'

'I don't eat meat,' he tells me.

'Ever?'

He shakes his head.

'Why not?'

'I don't believe in killing animals.'

I arch a brow. 'Only people?'

He shrugs, stabbing a carrot. 'People can be cruel, and inherently selfish. But not animals. A wild animal kills because it's in their nature. A person kills because they choose to. For them, it's instinctive. For us, it's personal.'

I frown, chewing slowly. 'But . . . but they say you're a hunter. That you hunt magical creatures for sport.'

'Yes, they do,' Fox agrees. 'They also say I'm a slaver. That I snatch innocents and condemn them to a life of servitude.'

'And you're telling me you don't do either of these things?'

'You seem unconvinced.'

'Can you blame me?'

'No,' he says. 'I can't.'

I study his face as I swirl the contents of my cup. 'Just because the Cleaving was an accident doesn't mean you haven't done other deplorable things.'

'True. And believe me, I've done *many* deplorable things.' He smirks a little. 'But I have nothing to gain from refuting these claims, especially since I had a large hand in concocting them. All the best lies have an element of truth. It made concealing what I was really doing so much easier.'

'Which was?' I eye him sceptically.

'I did hunt magical creatures,' he admits, spearing a potato. 'But not to kill them, or turn their bodies into trophies.'

'Then why?'

'Because I wanted to study them. Most of the books you've read about the Otherlands are outdated. Countless native species have gone undiscovered for years, and not just animals, but plants, too. A great number are deadly, but many possess healing qualities that outrival anything I could forage here. Like lachrymortis, for instance.'

'What's lachrymortis?' I ask.

'According to legend, there was once a Magi warrior who died bravely in battle,' Fox says. 'Yet he was favoured by the Gods, and as his wife wept over his body, from her spilled tears grew an ancient tree. It was said that if you drank from its veins, it could heal any wound. It was destroyed during the war, but I possess the two remaining vials of elixir.'

'Oh.' I blink, taken aback. Then my eyes narrow once more. 'And . . . and what about the slaving? How do you explain that?'

Fox takes a deep breath. 'Ever since my grandfather won the war, the people of the Otherlands have lived in fear of the slave ships that arrive every year to take their children.'

I grimace, thinking of Elva.

'It's true that my own ship was used to transport slaves,' he continues. 'But I wasn't *taking* them, I was . . . returning them.'

I stare at him.

'I knew the routes the Ostacrian slavers followed,' he continues. 'It wasn't difficult to hijack their ships. My crew and I styled ourselves as pirates. We took everything. Sometimes we'd even take the slavers themselves and abandon them on a distant isle with no means of getting home. Other times . . .' He trails off, reaching across the table to brush his fingers against mine. I catch a glimpse of blood-slicked decks, the sound of desperate pleas before the men are tossed overboard, their screams swallowed by the sea as the waiting sirens drag them under. 'Well, as you can see, they got what they deserved.'

My lips part in surprise. 'And the slaves?'

'We took them back to the Otherlands. Left them in boats just off the shore.'

'How often did you do this?'

'As often as I could, but never enough to be noticeable,' says Fox. 'A handful of alleged shipwrecks could slip under the radar, but not dozens. I had to be careful. I couldn't save them all, but I could save some.' He catches sight of my incredulous expression and shrugs a shoulder. 'I told you before, I abhor injustice. To enslave another person, to take away their freedom – there is nothing more unjust, more immoral, than that.'

Slowly, I set down my knife and fork and fold my arms, my mind spinning. Fox watches me, his green eyes scanning my face.

Eventually, I mutter, 'I can *never* figure you out.'

Which makes him smile.

We finish our food, scraping up every mouthful of gooseberry pie. I even save my last piece of rabbit for Scout.

The inn continues to fill up around us, a cacophony of voices and laughter. It doesn't escape my notice that several heads turn in our direction, gazes snagging on me and lingering. With relief, I realize that it's not recognition I see in their eyes, nor the hatred or fear I've learned to expect as a result. Instead, the looks are oddly . . . appreciative.

I'm not so naive as to be unaware of my own appearance. I am my mother's daughter, after all. It's just that in my experience, the way I looked never had any bearing on how

I was treated. With a reputation like mine, beauty proved of little consequence. In truth, I considered it wasted on me. But here, I'm not the Storm Weaver. These people don't look at me and see a murderer, or a changeling, or a freak. They don't see a future queen or a fugitive. They just see a girl. Someone to be admired, not reviled.

Yet while flattering, I admit I find even this favourable attention somewhat uncomfortable, and so, it appears, does Fox.

I watch as one boy nudges his friend and whispers something, then pales as he catches sight of Fox's expression.

I sip my ale, not entirely sure whether this possessive display is all part of the act. Yet I soon find myself at risk of choking a second time, for when the innkeeper shuffles over to refill my cup, Fox leans back in his chair and announces, 'We'd like a room, please.'

'Two rooms,' I correct, glaring at him.

The innkeeper smiles knowingly. 'Lovers' tiff?'

I blush.

'Something like that,' Fox says breezily.

'What're you doing?' I hiss, kicking him under the table.

'You really want to risk being separated?' he whispers back, wincing. 'Besides, my brother didn't exactly offer me the keys to the treasury before I was hounded from the palace. I can barely afford this meal, let alone Cedar's shoe.'

The innkeeper clicks her tongue. 'Well, then, what's it to be? One room or two?'

'One.'

'*Two*.'

The woman plants her hands on her hips, clearly amused.

I change tack, glancing admiringly round the inn. 'You seem like you run a respectable establishment here.'

Fox raises an eyebrow.

The innkeeper puffs out her chest. 'That I do, dear.'

'Then I'm afraid we can't possibly share a room,' I declare triumphantly. 'Because we aren't married.'

'Well, not *yet*,' says Fox.

I stare at him, dumbstruck.

He smiles affectionately at me. 'My bride-to-be is understandably concerned for her reputation, but I simply can't allow her out of my sight. Especially not with these vultures circling. It would be only a matter of time before one of them carried her off.'

I could *strangle* him.

The innkeeper winks conspiratorially at us, then taps her nose and passes Fox a large bronze key. 'One room it is.'

He barely has time to hand her a few coins before I've snatched the key and stormed off towards the staircase. I've barely made it halfway when I'm stopped in my tracks by a low whistle, followed by an unfamiliar voice. 'Wait! You there.'

The speaker is one of the men in the opposite corner, those partially concealed by a barrel of ale.

My heart plummets into the soles of my boots. For crowded round the table, their silvery-grey armour reflecting the flickering candlelight, are four Ventalla soldiers.

31

Elva

Ever since meeting Caius Castellion in the statue garden, I have been left with nothing but questions – mainly about his sanity. The old man is surely senile. What other explanation could there be for his utter lack of surprise when my shadows burst forth? Or his frankly unbelievable assertion that he means me no harm?

Yet if his unwillingness to mount my head on a spike was not evidence enough of his instability, then there was his bewildering recital of *The Tragedy of Emmeric and Irabella*. And what was it he said about Blaze? That she possessed the power to break the curse? Clearly he is unable to tell the difference between fiction and reality.

I wander aimlessly through the serf tunnels, trying to make sense of it. I'm painfully on edge. I can't sleep, can't sit still; I just have to keep moving or else risk being crushed under a landslide of unanswered questions. They swirl round my head, taunting, incessant.

How does the old man know about Hal and me? How

long has he known? And is he planning on telling him my secret?

Hal awoke this morning. He's still weak, but the physicians have prescribed several vials of opium, which should ease the pain and have him on his feet soon enough. His condition is still a mystery, but if I'm right, and it's the same as the one his father was suffering from, I have to find out what it is – and fast, for the idea of losing him . . .

I swallow, nauseated, and redirect my thoughts back to his grandfather.

He said he'd returned for Hal, but he never said why he left, or what he's been doing. I overheard an Eye whispering that the ship the old man arrived on had travelled to Ostacre from Thresk. Yet this information only succeeded in confusing me further, for what was Caius Castellion doing in the Otherlands?

Up ahead, the tunnel splits into three. I choose the fork on the right and pause to catch my breath. Something moves in the corner of my eye. I jolt with fright, but it's just a mouse, scampering through a crack in the wall. Perhaps it's time I emerge, too. I peer through the next door and find myself in the Aquatori Wing. Old habits, I suppose. I'm about to slip into the corridor beyond when the sound of a door handle turning makes me stop short. Marina appears, a dress draped over her arm. She glances furtively around before darting along the hallway and into her chambers.

I frown, puzzled. For the room Marina has just so swiftly exited is one I know as well as my own bunk – Blaze's. The dress is Blaze's too. I remember the way the pearls Spinner selected for the bodice would gleam teal blue in the candlelight. Whatever would Marina want with Blaze's dress? I imagine she must have a thousand of her own, given that the Kalparas are said to be one of the richest families in the empire.

Not wanting to risk running into her, I make myself scarce. Perhaps helping Elaith prepare for bed might pose a welcome distraction. But as soon as I turn the corner into the Ignitia Wing, I see she already has company.

Cole is lounging against her doorframe, though it appears he's really using it to prop himself up, for he's clearly extremely drunk. Even slouched, he towers over Elaith, who seems to be blocking his path with an outstretched arm. I spot a fresh bruise blooming across her skin, this one right below her collarbone. Her mouth is set in a determined line, but her pale-blue eyes are fixed on Cole, gazing at him with a mixture of hurt, defiance and unquestionable longing.

'You know I never meant to hurt you, don't you?' His voice is soft, slightly slurred. 'You do know that, Elaith?'

She bites her lip. 'I . . . It doesn't –'

'I don't know what came over me,' Cole continues, cutting her off. 'It was a mistake. Just a stupid mistake. It won't happen again, I swear.'

My heart sinks. I remain out of sight, willing Elaith to slam the door in his face.

But she only hangs her head. 'Cole . . .'

'You know I love you, right?' He reaches out, sliding his fingers through her fiery hair. It might've been a tender gesture if his hand hadn't come to rest on the back of her neck, angling it a certain way to get her to look at him. 'And I know you love me.'

Her eyes shutter and her shoulders stoop as any resolve drains out of her.

'I need you,' he whispers. 'You're the only person I care about. Just let me in. Please.'

No, I think desperately.

But it's too late. Elaith nods wordlessly. Cole moves forward, his other hand wrapping round her waist, drawing her to him. She doesn't fight, doesn't push him away, just turns limp in his arms, as pliant as a doll. My insides twist with rage as Cole backs her slowly into her chambers, using his foot to nudge the door closed behind them.

Sickened, I turn away and slip back into the serf tunnels, gritting my teeth so hard my jaw begins to ache. It's little wonder Elaith wouldn't tell me how she got those bruises. How could she, when she's in love with the person who's hurting her?

Perhaps Hal would send the Court of Flames back to Fire Mountain, were I to ask him. I could invent some excuse. Lie, if I had to.

Suddenly I hear a voice. Quiet, muffled. My pulse quickens. Could this be what I've been searching for? A clandestine meeting of traitors intent on sabotaging Hal?

I strain my ears as I edge closer to the source. A different voice sounds. The pitch is lower, growing louder as I approach the door up ahead. Only this door doesn't lead to a wing of the palace or an echoing chamber – just a broom cupboard.

This is where the Eyes have been meeting?

I draw level, listening. The voices are clearer now. I can make out several of them, all talking excitedly.

'It works.'

'You're sure?'

'Course I'm sure, stupid.'

'Give it here, then.'

'I still think a dagger would be easier to conceal.'

'Nah. Nothing at close range. She'd have to be standing right next to him. A bow means she'd be far enough away to make a break for it.'

'I still think *I* should be the one to do it.'

'No, me!'

'Don't be an idiot, Pip. You're twelve years old.'

'Who're you calling an idiot?'

'Oh, just shut up, all of you. I can barely hear myself think.'

My mouth falls open. Because I know that voice. I know them all. And one thing is for certain – these are no Eyes.

Without thinking, without pausing for breath, I reach out and swing open the door.

Five startled faces turn to stare at me, illuminated by the light of a single candle. Two girls, three boys, all of them dressed in white tunics.

In the centre, leaning against a shelf stacked with polish, her dark eyes wide with surprise, is Ingra.

'Elva?' Her tone is relieved, then defensive. 'What d'you think you're doing?'

I glance pointedly at the congregation. 'I could ask you the same question.'

For a moment we all just stand there, looking at each other. Then the oldest boy, Seth, grabs my arm and yanks me inside the cupboard.

I shake him off, rubbing my elbow as he shuts the door behind me.

'Hello, Elva,' beams a dimpled, sandy-haired boy in the corner as he lowers the feather duster he'd been brandishing like a blade.

I manage a half-smile in return. 'Hello, Pip.' Then I turn back to Ingra. 'Well?'

She glances shiftily at Seth.

'So I take it this is where you've been sneaking off to?' I press. 'What's going on?'

Ingra sighs and uncrosses her arms. 'All right. All right, but you can't breathe a word.'

Another girl, Clover, shakes her head. 'No.'

'We can trust Elva, I promise.'

'Then why didn't you tell her in the first place?'

Ingra shoots me a look that is part wounded, part accusatory. 'Because she has her fair share of secrets too. I barely see her any more.'

A pang of guilt.

'What if she rats us out?' Seth growls, turning what looks like a key over in his hands.

'She's on our side,' Ingra assures him.

I watch this exchange, wary, suspicious and utterly bewildered. 'What're you up to?' I demand with as much authority as I can muster. 'Why have you been meeting in secret? And why were you talking about *weapons*? What is it you're planning?'

Everyone looks at Ingra. A triumphant smirk tugs at her lips. She glances from side to side before leaning towards me and whispering, 'We're going to kill the emperor.'

32

Blaze

This can't be happening.

My whole body turns rigid, fear spiking as the Ventalla soldier gets to his feet. He looks only a couple of years older than me, his boyish face peppered with stubble. I watch his eyes rake over me, his expression alight with . . . what? Victory? Disbelief?

Several onlookers are watching the proceedings with interest.

I swallow hard. My cover is blown. The game is up. And now that they've found me, what do they intend to do? Capture me? Bind me with chains and drag me to the Windlands? I could fight them. I could win, too. I know I could. But that would only reveal my identity, and word of my whereabouts would spread like wildfire.

The soldier strides towards me, one hand resting on the hilt of his longsword.

There's nothing else for it. Taking a shaky breath, I jut my chin to meet his gaze just as ice begins to coat my palms.

But to my surprise, the soldier merely grins. 'Where d'you think you're going, sweetheart? Fancy a drink?'

I'm too stunned to do much more than blink at him.

Slowly, realization dawns. He doesn't know who I am. *Of course* he doesn't. As far as anyone knows, the Storm Weaver is hidden away at a safe house in the Firelands. This man doesn't recognize me because he isn't looking for me. Then there's the fact I'm dressed like a lowborn Fidra girl as opposed to the future Queen of the Waterlands.

I sag with relief just as someone slips an arm round my waist.

Fox smiles pleasantly as he appears at my shoulder, tucking me possessively into his side. 'Ready, love? Our room's upstairs.'

I glance sidelong at him, my heart tripping. Did he just call me *love*?

The soldier's face falls and he clears his throat uncomfortably. 'Ah, I see that you have – Right. Well. Sorry to trouble you.'

Fox waves his apology away as his thumb traces lazy circles along the curve of my hip. 'You're a long way from home,' he says casually. 'What brings you to the Wildlands?'

The soldier's response sounds scripted. 'His Majesty King Balen, Ruler of the Windlands and rightful Emperor Regent, wishes the people of Ostacre to feel safe and protected during these uncertain times. In his wisdom, he has sent a number of his most loyal soldiers to every province across the empire in order to –'

Intimidate the commonfolk? Spy on the Etheri? Ensure his influence extends far and wide beyond his kingdom in order to seize the Imperial throne under false pretences?

'– keep the peace,' the soldier finishes.

It takes everything I have not to scoff.

'It's true, then?' Fox says. 'There's to be a war?'

The soldier's eyes are a little clouded from drink. They keep coming to rest on me, and perhaps I'm imagining it, but every time they do, I feel Fox's arm tighten.

'Not as long as the Castellion boy does his duty to the realm and names his uncle regent.' The soldier raises his voice, slurring as he chants, 'Long live King Balen!'

His comrades echo him. Several of the onlookers join in, raising their glasses.

Fox's voice is as tense as his grip as he grits out, 'Long live King Balen.' Then he takes my hand and pulls me up the staircase.

I glance back to see the Ventalla soldiers calling for more ale before proceeding to entertain themselves by sending little jets of wind up the innkeeper's skirts.

I don't dare breathe until the door to our room is locked behind us. The space is cramped, the furniture modest: nothing but a rickety table, a small chest of drawers and, over by the far wall, its headboard carved from the bough of a tree – the bed.

My stomach swoops nervously.

Fox places his satchel carefully on the floor and Scout tumbles out, along with a few bones. He curses, rakes a hand through his hair, then crosses to the window. 'I'm not sleeping until my uncle's lapdogs have gone.'

I exhale slowly as I recall the soldier's words. 'So that's King Balen's plan. He's not usurping Hal's throne – he's campaigning for regency.'

Fox nods. 'A temporary position he no doubt intends to make permanent. My uncle understands that politics is a performance, and one's success depends on how well they play their part. He knows he could never succeed in tarnishing Golden Boy with the same brush as you and me, so his attempts to discredit Haldyn are of an entirely different nature. He's not turning him into the villain, but something far worse.'

I frown. 'What?'

'The *idiot*,' says Fox. 'Weak, foolish, easily led, the hapless young emperor, brother to the Earth Cleaver, and by all accounts, still infatuated with the Storm Weaver.'

I grimace.

'All in all, the three of us are hardly endearing ourselves to the people,' Fox continues. 'It's little wonder support for Balen grows by the day.'

Nausea churns in my stomach.

For a while, neither of us speaks. Fox keeps watch while I roll rabbit bones across the floor for Scout to chase.

After about an hour, just as my eyes are beginning to droop, Fox jerks his head down towards the courtyard. 'They're leaving.'

I push myself to my feet and watch the four Ventalla soldiers mount their horses and ride away down the winding road.

'We should get some sleep,' says Fox.

I glance behind him at the bed. The swooping feeling returns, and I resent the heat that floods into my cheeks. It's stupid, really. I've spent weeks sleeping next to Fox. Well, not *next to*, exactly. There was always a few feet of space between us, or a fire, or even branches if he'd fashioned himself a hammock from vines. But this is different.

'We're not sharing the bed,' I say, a little too loudly.

Fox shrugs. 'Fine by me.'

I blink in surprise. That was easy.

I watch as he swipes a pillow and blanket and tosses them on to the floor. He kicks off his boots, and I slip out of the door, heading along the narrow corridor to the bathing room at the end of the hall. After weeks in the forest, even these slightly grubby facilities feel luxurious. Yet as I scrub myself clean, I'm surprised to find I miss the cool waters of the Creek, the scent of Fox's pinewood soap, the trill of birdsong overhead.

I take a deep breath and glance briefly at my reflection in the cracked mirror before returning to the room, ready to collapse into bed. Only when I push open the door, I discover that it's already occupied.

Fox is sprawled on his back, shirtless, one arm tucked behind his head. Scout is curled up at his feet, fast asleep.

'What d'you think you're doing?' I demand. 'We agreed we weren't going to share.'

'And we aren't,' says Fox, nodding to the corner of the room where he flung the spare pillow and blanket.

I narrow my eyes. 'You can't be serious.'

'What?' Fox smirks. 'It's not me who has a problem with sharing. Did you really expect me to volunteer to sleep on the floor?'

'Honestly? Yes,' I snap.

'Why? Because you're a girl? Or because you're the queen?'

I glare at him.

'Goodnight, Storm Weaver,' he says smugly, closing his eyes.

Bastard.

For a moment I just stand there, seething. Then, with as much dignity as I can muster, I turn and stomp away, resolved not to let him win.

The floor is hard and a little dusty. There's no fireplace, and the blanket is thin and slightly moth-eaten. It's not long before the oil lamp burns itself out. I listen out for slow, rhythmic breathing but hear nothing. Fox must be lying awake too.

The low rumble of voices drifts up from a couple of floors below. I wonder what the innkeeper would say if she knew exactly who she'd welcomed into her establishment. Yet in spite of the risk, and the not-so-comfortable sleeping arrangements, I find myself revelling in the anonymity of it all, in the freedom of pretending to be someone other than myself, just like I did at the masquerade ball after the second trial.

I swallow, digging my nails into my palms. I can't think about that night without thinking about what happened in the maze. About that kiss. What it had felt like. What *he* had felt like. The heat of his skin. The muscles in his shoulders. The pressure of his mouth on mine. He was a headrush. He was risk and danger and honey wine. He was a bad decision, one I cannot – *will* not – make again.

And yet, the memories linger.

My legs round his waist. His hands in my hair.

Growling with irritation, I roll over to face the wall, the chill in the air now exacerbated by my flushed cheeks.

I wrap my arms round myself as another cool draught blows in from under the door, my whole body wracked with shivers.

All of a sudden, there's a long-suffering sigh, followed by the twang of mattress springs. I let out a feeble squeak of protest as I'm lifted effortlessly off the floor and dumped unceremoniously on to the bed.

'What're you *doing*?' I hiss.

'How am I supposed to sleep with all that teeth-chattering going on?' Fox retorts, climbing in the other side.

The bed is by no means large. He lies mere inches away from me in the darkness. I can just make out the steady rise and fall of his chest.

This is a bad idea. A *very* bad idea. I have every intention of returning to my spot on the floor. But perhaps . . . perhaps I should stay and warm up, just for a minute or two.

The moon emerges from behind a cloud, briefly illuminating the room. Fox stares up at the ceiling, turning the Eye of the Past over and over in his palm. Moonlight glances off his cheekbones, the bow of his lips, the cobbled muscles of his chest, turning his sun-kissed skin silver. And I just lie there, looking at him.

Fox Calloway Castellion. The Earth Cleaver, whose broken heart ripped the realm in two. The sadistic killer with Healer's hands. The hunter who has never slain an animal. The Prince of Slavers who liberates the enslaved. He truly is the perfect conundrum. Every time I think I've got him figured out, he obliterates the blueprint and I have to start again.

His eyelashes are so long they cast their own shadows. For a moment all I can think about is the way they brushed against my neck as he trailed soft kisses down my throat.

Fox's eyes meet mine, and I forget how to breathe.

'You're thinking,' he says quietly. 'What are you thinking about?'

And maybe it's because it's easier to be honest in the dark, or maybe it's because I'm not convinced I'll have the courage to, but I hold his gaze like a grudge, then tell him, 'You.'

Fox grows very still, as if that one word had the ability to turn him to stone.

'Why do you let everyone believe all those terrible things about you?' I whisper.

He shifts on to his side, facing me. 'It serves a purpose,' he says, his voice gentle. 'People see what you want them to see. Act the part and you become the part.'

'*We all have our roles to play*,' I murmur, recalling his words.

Fox smiles, and I can feel my heart beating. 'This way, I was untouchable. *Free*. I could do as I pleased, go anywhere I wanted.'

'I always envied you that,' I admit. 'I used to think it so desperately unfair that you were off sailing the world while I was locked up in Harglade Hall.'

He's silent for a moment, mulling this over. Then he says, 'I'll show you, if you like.'

'Show me what?'

His hand finds mine in the darkness, callused and warm. 'The world.'

And suddenly I'm no longer lying in a rickety bed in the Wildlands, but standing at the crest of a sand dune in Veridia, gazing out at miles upon miles of endless desert.

The visions melt into one another, each more breathtaking than the last. We scale the canyons of Havar, wade across the saltmarshes of Nepta, walk through the vibrant rainforests of Serolia. I watch a phoenix burst into flames. I see kelpies and sirens and sea dragons, moon panthers and starpools, flowers as tall as trees, and trees as tall as mountains. It's everything I've ever dreamed of and more. The stories of my childhood come to life, words on a page given form. Mythic and treacherous and utterly beautiful.

I don't remember falling asleep, but when I wake, sunlight is streaming into the room, and Fox is still holding my hand.

33

Flint

The Greenwood is enveloped in a dense shroud of gloom and carpeted with a thick layer of moss.

There's not so much as a faint trill of birdsong or rustling of leaves. It's a dead, empty kind of silence, as though this part of the world has been forgotten, and yet I can't shake the feeling that we're not alone. I'm thankful for the comforting weight of the bow slung across my back. Whatever danger lurks among the darkened trees will not find me defenceless.

'I'm starting to understand why people avoid this place,' Spinner whispers.

'Yes,' I say with false joviality. 'Cold, silent and distinctly off-putting. It's little wonder Sheen looks right at home.'

My attempt to lighten the mood does not go as planned, however, as the sound of a twig snapping close to my ear causes me to emit a high-pitched yelp of terror. Sheen lets the broken pieces fall from his hand with a smirk. I feign innocence, turning to stare at Spinner as if she were the one who'd screamed. She only raises an eyebrow at me, unimpressed.

We soon reach a small clearing. The forest floor is spongy and almost entirely covered with leaves.

'This seems as good a place as any to set up camp,' I say.

Spinner nods, but Sheen, standing a few paces ahead, frowns curiously at the ground then shakes his head. I sigh. Of course he'd find fault with my suggestion. I grab Spinner's hand and push roughly past him.

'No,' he hisses, lunging for us.

But it's too late.

At that moment the leaves beneath our feet quiver, grow still, then shoot upward in a rapid flurry alongside the large net they were concealing. I cry out as the three of us are ensnared, our heads knocking together.

We're now dangling several feet above the ground, swinging gently from side to side, limbs sticking out of the net at various angles.

I make a face. 'Oops.'

'*Oops*,' Sheen repeats, his expression livid. 'What were you playing at?'

'How was I to know?' I protest.

'Did it not strike you as odd,' he spits, 'that there were no leaves on any other part of the forest floor but here?'

I grimace. Truthfully, no. I just thought he was being a prick.

I'm suddenly all too aware of how close we are, our faces mere inches apart, legs intertwined. After weeks of hiking across moors, how does he manage to smell that *good*? Crisp and clean, like fresh snow.

I clear my throat. 'Look, I'll get us out of here, all right?'

'And how do you propose to do that?' Sheen growls.

'Where's your knife?' I ask Spinner.

'At the bottom of my satchel.'

'Which is . . .' I follow the direction of her gaze down to the ground. 'Ah. Well, anytime either of you feels like flitting, just let me know.'

'Harglade –'

'Alternatively, I could always try and . . . I don't know . . . chew through the rope?'

'Flint, shut up, would you?' Spinner's eyes are on Sheen, a finger pressed to her lips.

That's when I hear it – a low three-note whistle. I can't tell where it's coming from. Above? Below? Inside my head?

The hairs on the back of my neck stand on end as the signal is answered. More whistling fills the air, shrill and eager. I struggle frantically in the net, but only succeed in further entangling myself. All I can do is raise my head to watch as our captors approach, moving soundlessly through the forest. They're so shrouded in shadow that for a moment I wonder if the stories are true, if there really are spirits come to trap our souls for eternity.

One by one, they step out of the trees.

I blink, taken aback. For these are no spirits – they're *children*. Two dozen of them at least. Some look around my age, while others are as young as Renly, yet all are armed. Their clothes are ragged, their feet bare and grimy. They stare up at us, excited, suspicious.

'Well, would you look at what we have here,' says a tall girl, grinning as she thumbs the hilt of her gleaming cutlass. 'Talk about easy pickings.'

Spinner shrieks as yet more children swing down from the branches overhead. One of them begins rifling through her satchel.

I swivel my head round to take them in, my terror morphing into bemusement.

'*Ohhh*,' I say, finding my voice. 'So *you're* the ones terrorizing Heathcross. What d'you call yourselves again? The Purple Pickpockets?'

'The Green Bandits,' snarls a boy wielding a hatchet.

I click my fingers. 'That was it. Well, lovely meeting you all, but if you don't mind letting us down now, we'd best be on our way.'

The girl brandishing the cutlass steps forward. She looks as sharp and angular as her blade, her dark hair cropped short, jaw set, mouth stretched in a thin line. She seems to be the eldest, and given the way the others are looking at her, I'd imagine she's the leader too.

'People don't tend to stray this far into the Greenwood,' she says. 'Either you have a death wish, or you've got something to hide.'

Sheen's voice is strained. 'Look, we mean you no harm.'

The girl narrows her eyes. 'What d'you think, Darrow?'

The boy with the axe scoffs. 'Not a chance. I don't like the look of them. Especially the mouthy one with the eyepatch.'

I tut self-righteously. 'Now, that's just discrimination.'

There's a giggle from among the congregation, the sound as sweet and silvery as a windchime. A little girl of about five or six skips into view, her wispy hair tied in bunches.

'I like him, Briar,' she says to the older girl as she tugs on the hem of her tattered shirt. 'He's funny. Maybe you should let them go.'

'Stay out of this, Posy,' cautions Darrow.

Posy pouts. I wink at her and she giggles some more, waving her tiny slingshot.

Briar deliberates for a moment. The others clutch their weapons, waiting for her verdict. 'All right,' she says at last.

Beside me, Spinner lets out a sigh of relief.

'But in return, you can give us some information. It's been a while since we left the Greenwood, and I like to stay up to date with current affairs.'

I can hardly begin to imagine it, living here in the darkest depths of the Wildlands, entirely cut off from civilization. 'Deal.'

Darrow rakes a grubby hand through his long, straw-coloured hair. 'What if they're –'

Briar cuts him off. 'If they were, they'd have used their magic on us, wouldn't they? In any case, they're outnumbered.'

I exchange a furtive glance with Spinner, my brandmark tingling beneath my glove. Best we keep up the pretence and let them think we're Fidra.

'Fine,' Darrow growls before slicing his axe through the air and severing the rope.

We land in a tangled, breathless heap, my face buried in Sheen's stomach. I'm sure I'll have bruises to add to my collection of burns, because it's surprisingly rock-solid. He quickly slides out from under me just as little Posy prances over and takes my hand.

'My name's Posy,' she sing-songs. 'What's yours?'

'I'm . . . Renly,' I decide. 'Pleasure to meet you, Posy. Tell me, why are you and your friends out here all alone? Where are your parents?'

She looks at me sadly with big blue eyes. 'Dead.'

Oh.

So it would seem the Green Bandits are not a group of vicious cut-throat brigands. They're just orphans running wild.

'Where are we going?' I ask as Posy begins to tow me through the trees, the others following in our wake.

'You'll see,' she says.

The trouble is, I can't see very well at all. The forest grows darker and denser by the minute, not to mention that I only have the use of one eye. I hear Spinner stumbling along behind, murmuring her thanks as Sheen holds her steady. The Bandits possess none of his easy grace, yet rather seem to be entirely in tune with the forest itself, predicting every wayward root, branch and boulder.

I'm suddenly distracted by the sight of flickering lights up ahead. Posy pulls me through a thick copse of trees and my mouth falls open as I take in what lies beyond.

Treehouses. Nine – no, ten – of them, crooked but sturdy, curved round the trunks of several towering maples and connected by a series of rope bridges. Firefly lanterns hang from the lower boughs, illuminating the reddish-gold leaves.

It's like something out of a storybook.

'*This* is where you live?'

Briar nods.

'But what about the . . .' I screw up my face as I try to remember what Iris had said. 'The . . . tree people?'

'The dryads?'

'That was it. I thought this place was supposed to be overrun with them.'

'Oh, it is,' she replies, grinning fondly at Posy as the little girl scampers off. 'But we don't interfere with the spirits, and in return they leave us be.'

I raise an eyebrow. 'And why's that?'

Briar shrugs. 'Because we don't fall for their tricks.'

It's not long before the Bandits are assembled, sitting cross-legged on the earth like schoolchildren as I proceed to fill them in on recent events, doing my best to make it sound as though I'd merely *heard* about them rather than experienced many first-hand. Darrow leans against a tree, twirling his hatchet while pretending not to listen. There are several gasps as I speak of the Choosing Rite, even more as I reveal what happened at the Binding Ceremony. At the mention of Blaze and Fox, several of the congregation cry out in rage. Some even spit on the ground, their faces twisted with fury.

I tell them of King Balen's betrayal and Hal's elevation to emperor, Aunt Yvainne's funeral and the attack on Fire Mountain. Afterwards, Sheen, Spinner and I are handed bowls of stew, which we readily accept. My stomach has barely stopped growling for weeks.

As I eat, I realize I'm not entirely sure whether this is supposed to be supper or breakfast. The canopy above is so thick it blocks out any dregs of moonlight or glimmers of dawn. Come to think of it, how long has it been since we left Iris's workshop? Hours? A day? More? I can't seem to tell. I can't shake this strange, warped feeling of detachment. It's as if the deeper one travels into the Greenwood, the more time bends.

'That's a fine bow you have there,' Briar tells me, her eyes appraising.

'I got it in Heathcross,' I say. 'You know, that village you plunder from time to time.'

Several conversations peter out, their participants turning to stare at me defensively.

Briar's face darkens. 'We do that out of necessity, not malice. We only take what we need to survive.'

'What happened to your families?' Spinner asks.

'Some died in the storm,' says Briar flatly. 'Most died in the Cleaving.'

I feel my stomach drop. These children are not just orphans – they're Storm and Rift Orphans. It's little wonder their hatred for Blaze and Fox is so visceral.

'How old were you when . . .'

'Four,' answers Briar. 'My mother had me scale a tree to escape the flooding. She tied me to a branch, then climbed down to fetch my little brother. She never came back.'

My throat tightens. 'I'm sorry.'

'For the next few years I was all alone. I lived off scraps. Nobody helped me. People were too busy rebuilding their own lives to care. Until one day, I met Darrow.'

Darrow's hard gaze softens momentarily.

'Together we discovered other Storm Orphans. We became a family.' Briar smiles at the oldest Bandits. 'We travelled from province to province, looking for work where we could find it. Then, six years ago . . .'

'The Cleaving,' I finish.

She nods grimly. 'As if we needed another reason to hate the Etheri. Needless to say, our numbers grew. Posy was only a few weeks old when it happened.' Briar pulls the little girl into her lap. 'I found her in the wreckage of a City of Buried Souls, under a shelf of rock surrounded by rubble and bodies, right on the edge of the Rift. After that, we decided we had to protect ourselves. So we came here, to the Greenwood, where nobody can hurt us.'

'You really hate all Etheri?' I ask, unable to help myself.

Sheen shoots me a warning look.

'Of course we do. Look at what they're capable of. And to think, they're crowning the Storm Weaver Queen of the Fish,' Briar spits.

'Look, I'm sorry about your parents,' I say softly. 'And that the world was so unkind. But surely you can't blame every Etheri for the actions of only two of uh– *them*.' I catch myself just in time, biting down hard on my tongue, but the damage is already done.

Darrow straightens up, angling his chin, his voice low and dangerous. 'Knew it.'

Shit.

I feel my bow dig into my shoulder blades as I cringe back against the tree.

'Take off your gloves,' Darrow orders.

I glance at Spinner, who looks stricken.

'I *said*, take *off* your gloves.'

'Darrow.' There's a note of warning in Briar's tone.

I swallow. 'What're you accusing me of, exactly?'

'I think you're one of *them*,' Darrow growls. 'I think you're Etheri.'

I shake my head, my mouth as dry as sand. 'I assure you, you're mistaken.'

Darrow grins, baring his teeth. 'Well, I suppose there's an easy way to find out.'

'What d'you –'

But I don't get a chance to finish my sentence, because Darrow has already raised his arms, his hatchet gleaming as it soars through the air.

I can't move. Can't think. All I can do is screw my good eye shut as everything goes quiet.

34

Blaze

Cedar is waiting for us outside the forge, freshly shoed. Fox takes his reins, tossing the blacksmith a few coins before we set off down the winding road, Scout tucked out of sight inside Fox's satchel.

Wellwall is just as vibrant and bustling as it was the day before, yet I barely notice. Visions of the Otherlands still cling to the corners of my mind, dangerous and magnificent. For hours I'd gazed with childlike wonder at a world I thought beyond my reach, a world so vast it made everything else feel small, even if just for a night.

What Fox gave me . . . it's a gift I can never repay. A taste of the freedom and adventure I've dreamed of all my life.

He keeps stealing glances at me, and I keep pretending not to notice, trying not to think about the way he looked while he was sleeping – all long lashes and softened edges, his untidy dark hair strewn across the pillow. I swing my arms as I walk, flexing my right hand as if to shake off the memory of his fingers entwined with mine.

It meant nothing, I tell myself firmly, even as my heartbeats patter like raindrops against my ribcage.

At that moment, a clamour of voices rises up ahead. I crane my neck to glimpse a large wagon trundling along the road. People begin spilling from doorways to watch it pass.

'What's going on?' I ask an elderly woman selling broth from a copper cauldron.

She sniffs as she stirs the contents with a ladle. 'Looks like the Baron's new toy has arrived.'

Perplexed, I glance at Fox, who's gone rigid, his brow furrowed in concentration.

As the wagon draws nearer, I see it's not a wagon at all, but a large cage on wheels. Inside – hackles raised, teeth bared, grey fur matted with blood – is a wolf. I notice with a pang of recognition the distinctive silver markings round its eyes.

'Is that . . .'

Fox nods grimly.

Before the cage walk the hunters, each armed with a spear. I recall their words that day in the forest: *Remember, the Baron wants it alive.*

There were five of them before, yet now I count only three. The wolf must have put up a good fight – just not good enough.

I turn back to the old woman. 'What do you mean, *new toy*?'

'Every month the Baron selects a new contender for his fighting pit. Sometimes man, sometimes beast.' She sprinkles a handful of herbs into the bubbling broth. 'There's a fight tonight, I hear. Perhaps you should stay and watch. It's quite the show.'

My insides curl in disgust. ‘Come on,’ I say, nudging Fox. ‘Let’s get out of here.’

He blinks dazedly, unable to tear his gaze from the wolf as the cage rolls past. ‘Where are they taking it now?’

‘To the Baron’s estate, I should think,’ replies the old woman.

I look at Fox. He looks back at me. I shake my head. ‘No. Whatever you’re planning, you can forget it.’

‘How d’you know I’m planning anything?’

I raise an eyebrow.

He takes my arm and pulls me into a nearby alleyway. ‘Listen –’

‘No, *you* listen,’ I say, shaking him off. ‘That wolf is not our responsibility.’

Fox’s expression is inexplicably pained. ‘I can’t just leave it.’

‘Why?’ I splutter. ‘Because it decided not to *eat* us that one time?’

He shrugs. ‘Something like that.’

I lean against the wall. ‘You can’t be serious.’

‘’Fraid so.’

‘*No.*’

‘Yes.’

‘You’re impossible,’ I growl.

‘I prefer *daring*.’

I fix him with a glare. ‘This is a stupid idea.’

‘I never said it wasn’t,’ says Fox. ‘Go with Cedar and wait for me in the treeline.’

I snort, folding my arms across my chest. ‘Like that’s happening.’

He mirrors my stance. ‘Meaning?’

I sigh, half exasperated, half resigned. 'We're allies, remember? And if you're really insisting on this ludicrous rescue mission, then I'm coming with you.'

For a moment I think he might be about to kiss me.

Instead, he just grins. 'Then what are we waiting for?'

The Baron of Wellwall lives on a sprawling estate at the very edge of the province. The manor itself is reminiscent of a child's dollhouse, with butter-yellow brickwork and diamond-paned windows. A twelve-foot wall encircles the manicured grounds, accessible only by way of towering wrought-iron gates which clang shut behind the wagon.

'So what's the plan, exactly?' I ask sceptically.

'We go round the back,' says Fox. 'Scale the wall.'

'Brilliant,' I mutter. Yet still, I sense it beneath the coiled spring of apprehension – that strange, giddy rush that accompanies recklessness, the thrill of doing something I know I shouldn't. Like escaping Fire Mountain or walking straight into the Ridge tunnels. Perhaps, deep down, there's a part of me that *likes* risks. Even ones with green eyes and a death wish.

Fox murmurs something, and Scout darts away in a flash of copper, slipping easily through the bars of the gate, while Cedar trots obediently towards the trees.

'How do you propose we get over the wall?' I ask Fox as we skirt the perimeter.

He snaps his fingers, and a host of vines spring forth, creeping up the stone.

'I thought we were supposed to be acting like Fidra,' I point out.

'A necessary exception,' he tells me as he laces his fingers together.

I place my foot carefully in his cupped hands and grip his shoulder as I hoist myself up. He follows suit, scaling the wall with ease. Together, we peer over the top.

The rear of the manor is just as grand as the front. Opposite are a row of empty horse stalls. The wolf's cage is stationed next to them, a scrap of tarpaulin draped over it. I suspect the hunters are off claiming their reward. About thirty yards away, I spot a lone attendant pruning a rosebush, his back to us. There is no one else in sight, except for Scout, standing guard at the bottom of the wall.

Fox lands lightly beside her, then glances back up at me. 'Jump,' he orders.

I swallow, steeling myself, and wonder what it would feel like to break both my legs. Fortunately, I don't find out, for Fox catches me before I hit the ground. I stare up at him, a little breathless, a little indignant.

'This way,' he says, setting me back on my feet.

'I can't believe we're doing this,' I hiss as Fox tugs the tarpaulin off the cage.

The wolf shrinks back warily, a low growl rumbling in its throat. I watch its yellow eyes linger on Fox and, just as before, something unspoken seems to pass between them, as though they were engaged in a wordless conversation.

'Storm Weaver,' Fox says, without looking at me. 'Freeze the lock.'

'But what if –'

'He won't hurt us, I promise. Just do it.'

I take a deep breath and concentrate. A moment later

the large brass padlock is encased in a thick layer of ice. Fox smashes it with the hilt of his dagger, and it falls to the ground. I back away as he slowly opens the door to the cage.

The wolf springs free, landing silently at Fox's side. It stares up at him one last time, then, in a streak of grey, it's gone.

'Let's go.'

We follow Scout round the back of the stalls, where we discover a crumbling cleft at the base of the wall, just wide enough to crawl through.

Fox jerks his head. 'After you, Your Majesty.'

I've only made it halfway when an enraged cry splits the air.

'Hurry,' Fox urges.

But it's too late. I scream in fright as hands clamp down on my ankles and drag me back under the wall. Fox barely has time to pull Soulkiller from his belt before he's surrounded by the three hunters. A fourth man hauls me up by my hair. I struggle frantically, but he pins me tight to his chest. Fox snarls, lunging at him, but the hunters brandish their spears. Scout curls around his legs protectively, but my captor aims a kick at her.

'Go,' Fox whispers.

She shoots him a mournful look before bolting through the hole.

'Well, well, well,' says a reedy voice. 'What do we have here?'

I look up to see a fifth man waddling towards us, his fair hair thin and oiled, his large nose purple with broken blood vessels. Round his neck he wears a plum-coloured silk cravat, and stretched across his portly frame is a green-velvet waistcoat that looks in danger of popping a button.

He peers at us through watery-blue eyes, one of which is oddly magnified by a gold-rimmed monocle.

'We caught them trying to escape, Baron,' my captor responds, twisting my arms painfully behind my back.

'And what of my wolf?'

'Gone,' Fox says bluntly.

For a moment I think one of the hunters might spear him through the throat.

The Baron tuts. 'A pity. It would have made an excellent addition to my fighting pit.'

My captor sneers. 'Do you know what happens to thieves in Wellwall?'

'I don't,' Fox tells him. 'But I'd wager it's not pleasant.'

'Now, now, Garrick,' says the Baron. 'No need to be hasty. I agree they must be punished, but there's more than one way to skin a cat.'

'You would know,' Fox mutters.

'One more word,' says Garrick, gripping me so tightly I cry out. 'Just one more word and I'll snap her neck.'

Fury spikes. How *dare* he? I could end him right here, without so much as lifting a finger. I could drown him where he stands.

Fox's eyes are dark with rage, but when he speaks, his voice is calm. 'She did nothing. It was all me.'

The Baron tilts his head. 'And who are you, boy?'

'No one of any consequence.'

'And yet you break into my grounds and steal my property. That sounds rather consequential to me.'

'All right,' Fox concedes. 'Then I'm someone who believes that men who slaughter innocents for sport are not men at all.'

I tense as a spearhead grazes his neck.

The Baron chortles as if he's said something amusing. 'You certainly have a great deal of backbone for a common thief. I should hate to see such courage go to waste. But Garrick is right – no crime should go unpunished. So I'm going to offer you three choices.'

'Which are?'

'First, the standard sentence for stealing – having one's hand cut off.'

Nausea curdles in my gut.

Fox merely grimaces. 'Pass.'

'Second, I ask Garrick to kill your pretty little friend here.'

'He can try,' I mutter.

Garrick chuckles, and I recoil as he reaches down to stroke my cheek. Fox watches him with an expression that suggests he'd like to sever each of Garrick's fingers and feed them to him one by one.

'Again, I must decline,' he tells the Baron.

'Then what do you say to putting that admirable courage to the test?' the Baron asks.

'In what regard?'

The Baron grins. 'By winning your freedom,' he says. 'You stole my wolf, thus robbing me of an evening's entertainment. My offer is this – take his place in my fighting pit.'

I suck in a breath, feeling the whole world shift beneath my feet. '*What?*'

Fox tilts his head to the side, mulling it over.

'*No*,' I hiss.

He ignores me. I scowl and stamp down hard on Garrick's foot. We should end this. Now. Escape while we still have the chance. Cover be damned – I'll turn the lot of them to ice statues if I have to, then leave them locked up in the stalls to melt.

Fox shakes his head, as if he knows what I'm planning. I glare furiously at him. What other choice do we have?

Deep inside, my power stirs, hungry and impatient, longing to be released. Only . . . only if I were to dispense with the Baron and his henchmen, how long would it take for word to spread? For rumours to be picked up on the breeze and carried back to King Balen?

I chew the inside of my cheek.

Fox is right. In order to maintain our ruse, we can't use our magic. The Baron hasn't once questioned our being Fidra, nor does he seem to care where we come from. What he wants is a show. And if there's one thing Fox knows how to do – it's perform.

'Deal,' he says.

I let out a low groan.

The Baron claps his hands, jubilant. 'Until tonight, then.' He nods at Garrick, who begins dragging me towards the manor.

'Stop!' Fox yells. 'What're you doing?'

'You didn't think I'd just let her go, did you?' The Baron snorts. 'It's not only your freedom you're fighting for, boy.'

Fox clenches his jaw. Neither of us thought to clarify the terms of the deal. He goes rigid, as if struck by a second realization. I watch, puzzled, as his expression clears and he turns to glance beseechingly at the Baron. 'At least let me say goodbye.'

The Baron's lip curls. 'How touching. Very well, then.'

Garrick gives me a shove and I stumble forward into Fox's arms as the rest of the men guffaw. For a moment he holds me close. I breathe in the scent of him, heart thudding in my chest, before he lowers his mouth to my ear and murmurs, 'Take the Eye.'

Understanding washes over me. Of course. In my panic, I'd almost forgotten about the Eye of the Past.

I hesitate, then hook my arms round Fox's neck, cursing the heat flaring in my cheeks. He leans down a little, resting his brow against mine. My fingers find the clasp of the chain beneath his collar, and after some fumbling, I feel it come loose. Fox reaches up to encircle my wrists, and my hands skim the solid planes of his chest as he guides them back down between us before carefully extracting the talisman from my fist.

My breath hitches as he pulls me closer, then, slowly, slides his palm down the length of my spine and slips the talisman into my back pocket.

I swallow hard. My skin burns and burns, but I don't pull away.

'All right,' a voice drawls. 'Time's up, lovebirds.'

Fox brushes his lips to my forehead. 'Whatever happens,' he whispers, 'promise me you won't reveal yourself.'

Seconds later we're wrenched apart. I yelp in protest as Garrick tosses me roughly over his shoulder.

'Wait!' Fox calls as the hunters begin herding him away. 'Who is my opponent?'

The Baron's expression is one of pure glee. 'Tonight, the thief will battle the bear.'

35

Flint

It must've been a quick death, for I don't feel a thing. I wonder briefly whether I'll be made whole again in the afterlife, or if I'll be half-blind *and* have an axe sticking out of my face.

I suppose there's only one way to find out.

Cautiously, I crack open my eye, expecting a fanfare, golden streamers and fireworks, angels drinking merrily from a river of wine.

The reality, however, is quite a bit different.

I'm not dead, as it turns out. I'm still in the Greenwood, surrounded by the Bandits, who appear to be engaged in conflict, screaming and shouting, stabbing their fingers in the air or brandishing their weapons. Only, I can't hear them. It's as if I'm behind glass.

I frown, puzzled, and glance around for my companions.

Spinner's eyes are wide and frightened. Beside her, Sheen is on his feet, one hand raised defensively towards the Bandits, the other directed at me.

And at last I understand.

The moment he drops the forcefield, a deluge of voices comes pouring in.

'I *knew* it,' snarls Darrow, retrieving his hatchet from where it must have rebounded and buried itself in the trunk of a tall maple.

'All of you, stay *back*!' Briar hollers.

'Etheri!' Posy shrieks, recoiling from Sheen, Spinner and me as if we were her nightmares come to life. 'Etheri! Etheri!'

I stagger to my feet, my arms raised in surrender. 'Easy.'

'Not another step,' Darrow warns.

'Look,' I say, gritting my teeth. 'Yes, we're Etheri. No, we didn't declare ourselves.'

'Why not?' Briar moves to stand protectively in front of Posy and the little ones.

'We thought we'd be less conspicuous travelling as Fidra. And because you made it quite clear that you despise our kind, which, I might add, is rather generalizing.'

'Flint,' Spinner hisses.

'What? It is. Holding hundreds of thousands of people accountable for the actions of only two.' I take a deep breath, watching Sheen's violet eyes flick among the Bandits. 'Listen, I'm not going to stand here and defend the Earth Cleaver. The boy's a sadistic prick –'

'Harglade,' cautions Sheen.

'But as for the Storm Weaver,' I continue brazenly, 'I can promise you that she did not drown the empire deliberately. How could she? She was only a baby. It wasn't her fault, but believe me, she still hates herself for it. She carries it with her every day.'

There's a long, stunned silence. Even the trees seem to be staring at me.

Sheen half closes his eyes. 'Let me guess,' he mutters. '*Oops?*'

Briar's voice is barely a whisper. 'You *know* her?'

I square my shoulders, resolved. 'Yes, I do. Rather well, in fact. And I know that she'd be devastated to learn of your situation.'

At that moment, I hear a voice.

Her voice.

It's unmistakable. As familiar to me as my own.

'Flint?'

My heart races.

But for some inexplicable reason, Briar shakes her head in warning. 'No. Don't listen. It's not who you think it is.'

'Flint?' Blaze calls eagerly. 'Flint, is that you?'

My feet kick into gear before my mind does, propelling me forward. I have to get to her. I have to find her, *now*.

'Stop!' Spinner yells. 'Somebody grab him!'

But the Bandits seem reluctant to touch me and shrink back as I pass.

'Let him go.' I barely register the smug smile in Darrow's voice.

'*No*,' wails Spinner as I duck among the trees, the light from the firefly lanterns fading with every step.

Branches tear at my arms and face as I plunge through the darkened forest, stumbling blindly, tripping over roots in my haste to reach my sister.

'Blaze!'

'Flint!'

I can't see a thing. Twice I fall headlong, then pick myself up and charge on.

All of a sudden the way ahead is illuminated by a series of tiny green orbs. They sputter to life amid the gloom, lighting a path through the trees. I follow them, not stopping to question what they are or who might have sent them. My thoughts are all for Blaze.

'Flint, where are you?'

Her voice sounds so close and yet far away. I whip my head round frantically, straining my ears.

'Hold on!' I call. 'I'm coming!'

The trail of lights leads me deeper into the forest, driven on by my sister's voice. What is she doing here? Did she manage to track us as far as Heathcross and then lose her way? Or has she been stuck in the Greenwood for days, terrified out of her wits?

'Blaze!' I scream again. 'Bla– *Argh!*'

Something slams into my back so hard that I'm sent sprawling in a patch of moss. The air is knocked from my lungs and I begin to cough.

'Blaze?' I roll over, blinking dazedly. 'Is that you?'

The something – or rather *someone* – pins me to the ground, the hard lines of their body pressing into mine.

'Of course not, you *fool*.' Sheen's violet eyes flash furiously in the pale-green light.

'Get off!' I protest, wriggling frantically beneath his weight. 'I have to find her.'

'She's not here, Harglade.'

'What do you mean, *she's not here*? I may be half-blind but I'm not *deaf*. Listen!'

Yet to my dismay the forest is silent.

'Blaze? Blaze!'

Sheen covers my mouth with his hand, smothering my cries. I scrabble furiously at his fingers, scratching and tugging until he snatches both my wrists and slams them into the ground above my head, his face just inches from mine. 'Shut. *Up*.'

I've never hated him more than I do in this moment. 'Let go of me.'

'Not until you stop.'

'But Blaze –'

'It's not her, Flint,' Sheen hisses, my name uncertain on his tongue. 'It's not real. Don't you see? Were the will-o'-the-wisps not clue enough? We were warned about the spirits that dwell in the Greenwood, but as always you were too arrogant to listen.'

Iris's words come back to me.

If you hear your name, don't respond. Turn and walk away in the opposite direction.

Ice-cold dread lines my stomach.

And why's that? I'd asked sceptically, when Briar told me the dryads did not interfere with the Bandits.

Because we don't fall for their tricks, she'd replied.

They might not, but I certainly did – and what a cruel trick it was.

Blaze isn't here.

Disappointment barrels into me, barbed and stinging. To my horror, tears of frustration prickle in response, but I banish them before they can fall.

Sheen scrutinizes my face for a long moment, then relaxes his grip.

I keep my voice light, trying not to wince as I rub my wrists. 'You know, when I said I enjoyed being manhandled, this is not what I had in mind.'

He makes no reply, only rolls his eyes in disgust. Yet perhaps it's just my imagination, but his smooth russet skin seems to flush a shade darker.

Slowly, we get to our feet. I clutch the stitch in my side, still panting. Sheen, meanwhile, appears barely out of breath.

'Where's Spinner?' I ask, staring past him into the gloom.

'She couldn't keep up.'

My tone is accusatory. 'So you left her behind?'

'She can handle herself.'

'And I can't?'

Sheen shoots me a particularly withering look. 'Evidently.'

I grind my teeth together. 'Let's go. We'll find Spinner and head back to the Bandits' camp. I'd rather risk another axe to the face than stay here with only you for company.'

'And how d'you propose we do that?'

I gesture at the greenish orbs. 'We'll just follow the . . . thingamajigs.'

'Will-o'-the-wisps.'

'That's what I said. Come on, what're you waiting for?'

A muscle in Sheen's jaw pulses. 'Take a look around, Harglade.'

So I do, and what I see causes my heart to nosedive.

The flickering lights that lit my way are gone. Or rather, they're now entirely indistinguishable. For they have been joined by countless others – hundreds of them – spreading out in all directions and casting ghostly shadows across the forest floor.

'Ah,' I say, grimacing. 'In that case, you'll have to flit us out of here. This counts as an emergency, surely?'

Sheen sighs. 'Fine. Take my hand.'

'I never knew you cared.'

'Just shut up and do as I say.'

I shut up and do as he says. His hand is stiff in mine, as cool and smooth as marble. After the red-hot panic of my chase, it feels . . . soothing. Oddly familiar too – the tight rigidity of his grip, the grooves of his palm, though I can't explain why.

I clear my throat and brace myself for that strange squeezing sensation and the deafening *whoosh* as I'm transported through the air. But it doesn't come.

I click my tongue impatiently. 'Any time today.'

Sheen frowns. 'I . . . can't do it.'

'What're you talking about?' I ask, a note of alarm creeping into my voice.

'My magic,' he says. 'It's not working. Something's . . . blocking it.'

'What? What could be . . .' My brows knit together as the realization hits me.

Those blasted nymphs.

I slip my hand out of Sheen's and glance at the trees as a phantom breeze whispers through the leaves. 'Well played.'

I gasp in astonishment as the will-o'-the-wisps flare even brighter than before, turning purple, then blue, then back to green. Sheen's cold mask is beginning to crack, his forehead creasing. Fear tugs at my edges, but I push it away. I nock an arrow, take aim at a gnarled old oak and let it fly. It lodges deep in the trunk, dead centre.

'You've had your fun,' I snap. 'Now let us be.'

Somewhere high in the canopy above, I hear the faint ghost of a giggle.

They'll try to trick you, lure you in so deep you'll never find your way out again.

I swallow hard as the Greenwood presses in from all sides, dark and ominous and swarming with troublesome spirits.

Just my luck.

36

Blaze

The fighting pit is built from stone and lined with flaming torches. A few rusted spearheads lie littered across the sawdust-strewn ground, which unnervingly appears stained with dried blood from previous brawls. At opposite ends are two steel portcullises. My eyes dart between them, my insides twisting themselves in knots.

I stand at the edge of a wooden platform raised several feet above the pit, wrists bound in front of me with a length of rope. I can feel the Eye of the Past tucked safely inside my pocket, while Silverclaw is stuffed down the side of my boot. Behind me is the Baron's brutish henchman, Garrick. In the centre of the pedestal, lounging on a plush gold-silk divan, is the Baron himself, his left eye freakishly enlarged by his monocle, which he keeps polishing impatiently on his cravat, eager for the fight to begin. Perched on a stool beside him is his wife – a silent, waifish girl who looks no older than me.

The crisp night air is filled with excited chatter as the crowd of spectators continues to grow in both size and exuberance. A host of loud, insistent voices rises above the din as a queue of punters clamour to place their bets.

A *bear* – that's what the Baron said Fox would be fighting.

Cold dread sits heavy in my stomach. There's no denying that Fox is a skilled fighter. Strong, quick and handy with a weapon. But bears have size on their side. I read somewhere that they have the strength of five men, not to mention claws designed to rip their prey from limb to limb. Can Fox really hope to defeat such a creature without magic? And what's more, would he even want to? He doesn't believe in killing animals – he said it himself only last night. But would he really sacrifice his life, his future, his quest for revenge, just to uphold his principles? It's certainly possible, I suppose. After all, the only reason we're in this mess in the first place is because he insisted on saving that wolf.

I think of Fox's peculiar affinity with animals, as mesmerizing as it is bewildering. What if he could use that gift now? Forge whatever kind of strange connection that might allow him to convince the bear not to attack?

I take several deep breaths, trying to remain calm. But this proves rather difficult, given the knife currently pressed to my throat.

'What's the matter, sweetness?' Garrick murmurs in my ear, his breath hot and sour. 'Worried your boy doesn't have what it takes?'

'No,' I say, with far more confidence than I feel. 'In fact, quite the opposite. If I were the Baron, I'd be worried for my bear.'

Garrick sneers. He pulls a deerskin hipflask from his pocket and takes a swig, and I comfort myself by imagining turning the liquor in his bloodstream to ice.

A sudden hush falls over the crowd. I turn my head a fraction to see the Baron on his feet, his hand raised for silence.

'As some of you may know, this morning my hunters returned with a highly coveted new contender for my fighting pit.'

There are several gasps among the spectators.

'However, no sooner had it arrived than my wolf was stolen from me, set free by a young man intent on spoiling our fun.'

The gasps are replaced with booing.

'Bring out the boy,' orders the Baron.

There's a loud scrape and screech of metal as the first portcullis is raised, the steel grate rising slowly to reveal Fox. My heart flips at the sight of him, then sinks as I take in the raw skin round his neck that suggests he's been shackled like some wild animal. His gaze latches on to me instantly, travelling from my face to my bound wrists to the knife at my throat. He is armed with a simple longsword. I'd wager the blacksmith will never want for business so long as the Baron lords over Wellwall.

He peers down at Fox through his monocle, his mouth twisted in a gleeful smile. 'Being a generous man, I offered this thief three options. Lose his hand . . .'

There's the sound of jeering.

'Lose his girl . . .'

Fox clenches his bruised jaw as the Baron points a stubby finger at me.

'Or –' the Baron pauses, presumably for effect – 'to give us a show twice as good as the one he sought to sabotage.'

The crowd cheer, and I think about how innate it is – this insatiable appetite for violence. How bloodshed becomes a spectacle. Punishment by way of entertainment.

'Tonight, he will fight my reigning champion, as yet undefeated. Ladies and gentlemen, behold the Bear!'

I watch with bated breath as the second portcullis is raised.

Yet it's not an animal that lumbers out into the pit, but a man – the most enormous man I have ever seen, so mountainous I wouldn't be at all surprised if he were descended from giants. His beard is thick, his head shaven and scarred and oddly disproportionate to his vast frame, which is bedecked in fighting leathers, the material severed at the shoulders to reveal biceps the width of my body.

'*That's* the Bear?' I say weakly.

Garrick chuckles. 'Fitting, don't you think? Given that he's killed so many of them. Loverboy doesn't stand a chance.'

Fox's face remains impassive, but I watch him grip his sword a little tighter as the Bear advances, brandishing a wicked-looking mace in one hand and waving to the crowd with the other. To my horror, I see that he's wearing a pair of spiked brass knuckles.

'Every tooth is from a different kill,' Garrick crows. 'He rips them from the jaws of the beasts as a momento.'

Sure enough, as I look closer, I realize that they're not spikes protruding from each knuckle – they're teeth. *Bear* teeth.

Nausea writhes in my stomach.

The Baron calls for silence once more. 'The rules are simple,' he says. 'The fight is hand-to-hand combat, and it's to the death.'

My heart is a fist, punching me repeatedly in the chest.

'If the boy wins, he and the girl go free. And if he loses . . . Well, he'll be dead.'

The crowd roar. It's like being back at the third trial, when I snuck out of my tent to watch Fox fight Amaryllis. Except this time the spectators are rooting against him, and he's not competing against a fellow Terrathian Heir but an eight-foot-tall bear-killer with a mace. Garrick is right. Fox doesn't stand a chance – not if he's going to fight like a Fidra. I think about what he whispered before the Baron's guards dragged him away.

Whatever happens, promise me you won't reveal yourself.

But how can he expect me to keep that promise after seeing his opponent? Is concealing our identities really more important than saving his life?

I have to do something. I have to act now, before Fox is beaten to a bloody pulp.

The coldness is already there, frost and fury crystallizing at my core. Slowly I allow it to spread as my eyes scan the crowd. I could freeze them where they stand. I could skewer the Baron with icicles, engulf the Bear inside a monstrous wave, drown Garrick in his own liquor-steeped blood. I could get us out of here.

But then, just as he did before, Fox stares straight at me and shakes his head.

A split second later the Baron claps his hands. 'Fight!'

Fox turns to face his opponent and bows – customary before a duel. The Bear grins at him. They begin to circle one another, Fox testing his sword by swinging it through the air in a series of twirling arcs.

Please, I think helplessly. *Please don't die. I can't watch you die.*

The Bear takes the first swipe. I suck in a breath but Fox dodges the mace with ease, his reflexes as sharp as a knife. This goes on for some time, the Bear lunging and Fox darting out of the way. The crowd grow impatient, stomping their feet and chanting.

Fight.

Garrick sniggers into my ear. Next to us, the Baron is pouting, his patience already waning. They don't know that this is how Fox operates on the battlefield, getting the measure of somebody while revealing nothing about himself.

I watch him analyse the Bear's movements and footwork.

Fight.

Another swing of the mace, another evasion. The Bear snarls.

Fight.

The Bear swipes left; Fox darts right. The Bear swipes right; Fox darts left. The Bear lifts the mace above his head and brings it down hard, but Fox has already rolled between his legs and slashed the back of his knees. The brute roars in pain as blood streams down his calves. Fox smiles, having reached his conclusion – and I think I know what it is. Strength and size are one thing, but speed is quite another. The Bear is bigger, but Fox is faster.

A spark of hope ignites in my chest.

Fox keeps his tread light, making every step count. He's conserving his energy while slowly depleting his opponent's. Those who placed bets are beginning to look uneasy.

I let out a shaky huff of laughter as Fox uses his sword to trip the Bear, sending him sprawling into the sawdust.

Garrick grips me tighter. 'Show's not over yet.'

It seems the Baron is in agreement. He's bouncing on the soles of his feet like an overeager schoolboy as he addresses the crowd. 'Who here thinks I should up the stakes?'

The Bear heaves himself off the ground, panting heavily. I frown, confused. What higher stakes could there possibly be?

The Baron's gaze falls on me. The look on his face is so revoltingly slimy that I feel sullied by it. He raises his voice above the din and declares, 'Whoever wins gets the girl.'

Everything slows as his words land, and my heart beats out of time. Magic hums through my veins, sparking like flint on steel, begging to be unleashed. It takes everything I have, and more, not to turn the entire province to ice.

Down in the pit, Fox has gone very still. Something primal flashes in his eyes – rage so powerful I can almost feel it pouring off him, red-hot and ferocious.

I watch as the Bear peers up at me, his mouth twisted into a toothless smile. To my utter disgust, he licks his lips. The crowd hoot and jeer. I struggle in Garrick's grip and he presses his blade harder into my throat. I fear if I swallow, it'll break the skin.

Fox cracks his neck as the Bear advances once more. The Baron's announcement seems to have given the brute a new lease of life. His mace flies through the air with precision and catches Fox on the arm. Blood soaks the sleeve of Fox's shirt and he snarls. I barely have time to blink before his own weapon slashes out in a blur of silver.

The Bear howls and Fox decides to switch hands, tossing the sword high with his right and catching it in his left. The crowd respond with enthusiasm. I shake my head incredulously. Even now, with his life on the line, he can't resist putting on a show.

Yet to my surprise, Fox begins to back off, retreating slowly until he collides with the lowered portcullis. He's hemming himself in, making himself vulnerable. But why?

The Bear grasps his opportunity. He raises the mace above his head and throws it with all his might towards Fox – who ducks before it can meet its mark. With a deafening clang, the mace collides with the portcullis and lodges in the steel grate.

Fox darts out of the way as the Bear lurches towards it. But try as he might, the Bear can't pull it free. Behind me, Garrick curses. The Bear whirls on Fox, but Fox is ready for him. I watch, open-mouthed, as Fox plunges his sword deep into the Bear's abdomen.

The crowd gasps. The Baron is on his feet, his monocled eye blinking in disbelief.

Fox takes a step back, breathing heavily, his sword still protruding from the Bear's flesh. I wait for the Bear to keel over. Instead, he grips the hilt of the sword and pulls. Blood bubbles from the wound in his stomach and drips on to the ground. With a savage cry he tosses the weapon across the pit. It collides with the stone wall and breaks in two.

My relief is quickly replaced by horror as the Bear takes a staggering step forward, then another. He's bleeding out, but he's still standing. He's going to fight to the end. Except now Fox has no weapon.

The Bear flexes one hand, his set of brass knuckles glinting in the torchlight, studded with the razor-sharp teeth of his victims.

Fox dodges the first swipe and the second, but then he stumbles over a pile of broken spears and almost loses his footing. The third blow catches him on the shoulder. Grimacing with pain, he reaches down and snatches up a rusted spearhead.

He's covered in blood, green eyes blazing, and in this moment all the feelings I've tried to drown and burn and bury come shooting to the surface, almost painful in their intensity. I can deny them no longer.

Fox has to win. He has to win because . . . *because I don't want to lose him.*

The Bear staggers, succumbing to his wound. Fox seizes his chance. As the Bear lunges, Fox drives the spearhead up towards his neck.

That's when Garrick slices his knife along my collarbone.

I let out a piercing scream, which causes Fox to whip his head round in alarm – just in time for the Bear's gleaming brass knuckles to pierce his chest.

The crowd erupts, but all I can hear is ringing silence as the Bear drags his fist down, slicing Fox's skin to ribbons.

Fox stares at the blood pouring from the puncture wounds. Swallows.

Then falls to his knees.

Suddenly Garrick lets out a howl of pain. I look down to find Scout, her teeth sunk deep into his calf. Adrenaline surges through me, the sensation as potent as magic. I barely know what I'm doing before I've done it. Raw instinct kicks in and takes control.

I drive my hips back into Garrick's groin. As he doubles over, I whirl round and thrust my wrists up to meet his knife, severing the rope that binds them. Then I pull Silverclaw from my boot and launch myself into the pit below.

The impact shudders through my joints, but the pain barely registers. My eyes are trained on the Bear. He's looming over Fox, fist raised, ready to deliver the killing blow.

But he doesn't get the chance, for I've already plunged my dagger into his back.

Hot blood spurts on to my face. The Bear roars in agony.

My heart beats loud in my ears as I look up at the Baron – at the man who conflates brutality with merriment, the man who saw me as nothing more than a prize to be won. His face is flushed with shock, and his monocle dangles loosely from its chain.

I grip Silverclaw's hilt and twist hard. My hands are shaking but my voice is steady.

'Nobody *wins* me.'

37

Blaze

The Bear is dead before he hits the ground.

There's a crunch as he falls flat on his face, my dagger sticking out of his back. His eyes are blank and staring, and the ghost of his last scream is still etched on his face. He lies with his arm outstretched, hand curled into a fist. The brass knuckles gleam in the torchlight, the inlaid row of bear teeth all dripping blood.

The noise from the crowd sounds distant and distorted, as though I'm in a dream. The Baron is apoplectic with rage, hollering at Garrick, who is utterly incapacitated – rolling on the wooden platform, clutching his bleeding leg. My stomach lurches as I place one foot on the Bear's spine and yank Silverclaw free.

Fox's jaw is clenched tight, but choked, rasping sounds fight their way out of his mouth. I kneel in front of him to inspect the wound. It's bad. The skin on his chest is shredded right down to his navel, the flesh torn and streaming. I can only hope those incisors didn't penetrate deep enough to puncture an organ.

'Can you stand?' I yell over the din.

Fox nods dazedly and grits his teeth as I help him to his feet. He doubles over, then staggers, drunk with pain.

I spot a flash of copper darting among the crowd.

'This way.' I pull Fox over to the portcullis. 'Time to climb.'

He places one foot on the bottom rung, glances up and swallows. It's barely ten feet yet it might as well be a hundred.

I take the lead and look back when I reach the top. Fox's golden skin is ashen, with sweat beading on his forehead. Every movement looks excruciating. Twice he appears to almost lose consciousness. I haul him up the rest of the way, gasping with the effort.

'Seize them!' cries the Baron.

Those nearest to us begin to close in, then shrink back as I brandish my dagger. But I can't fight off an entire province with a single weapon. We're entirely surrounded. And if we reveal ourselves now, it'll have all been for nothing.

Suddenly the crowd begins to part down the middle as people throw themselves aside to make way for something racing towards us at speed. My heart leaps as the air rings with the unmistakable clattering of hooves.

Cedar.

He skids to a halt in front of us. Fox leans heavily on my shoulder as he clambers into the saddle. I waste no time before swinging myself up behind him.

The Baron is howling with fury. 'Stop them! Don't let them get away!'

Cedar rears on his hind legs, tosses his head, then bolts through the crowd and out of the square. I cling on for dear life, my arms wrapped tightly round Fox. He's clutching his wound as if attempting to hold his torn skin together. My nose fills with the metallic tang of blood. I burrow my face into Fox's back as we ride, and squeeze my eyes shut.

When I open them again, the winding streets of Wellwall have been replaced by towering trees. Moonlight leaks through the branches, illuminating the path ahead. I flinch as something darts across it, but it's only Scout – a streak of rust-orange fur.

'That's far enough,' I say, pulling gently on the reins. 'They won't find us here.'

Cedar slows to a halt, and I slide off his back. Fox lets out a low groan as his feet hit the ground, and I thrust an arm out to steady him.

His slightly unfocused gaze comes to rest on my collarbone. 'You're hurt.'

I blink, incredulous. 'Never mind *me*,' I say, using the sleeve of my shirt to blot hastily at the thin gash left by Garrick's knife. 'I think your wound takes precedence here. Tell me what to do.'

'Satchel,' he murmurs.

I nod, then unfasten the bag from the saddle with trembling fingers and empty the contents on to the forest floor. Fox leans back against a tree, panting through clenched teeth.

I yank off my glove and drop to my knees, illuminating the pile of medical supplies with the glow from my brandmark.

Fox's voice is gravelly. 'I need essence of fenhallow.'

I rifle through the various vials, pots and pouches. 'Come on, come *on*,' I mutter. Then, mercifully, 'Got it!' I call, almost tripping in my haste to reach him.

'I need to assess the damage,' he grits out. 'Could you . . .'

In the pale-gold light I watch his throat bob as he swallows. I nod, understanding. I pocket the bottle of fenhallow and take a deep breath as I begin to unbutton his tattered shirt, which is so stained with blood it looks as though he's dressed in Ignitia colours. I fumble clumsily over every button before carefully easing the fabric off Fox's shoulders. At my command, rivulets of water begin to stream down his chest, and I press my lips tightly together as we take in the full extent of the mutilated mess.

'Now the fenhallow.'

I remember Fox telling me about this particular tincture. It's used to clean wounds. It doesn't damage the tissue in the same way liquor would, but it burns just as badly. I hesitate, but already the blood has begun to pour afresh.

'Wait,' Fox says as I pull out the stopper. He tears a thick piece of bark from the tree and bites down on it hard before nodding.

The moment the fenhallow makes contact with his skin, Fox screams. He grips a branch for support, the agonized sounds muffled by the bark between his teeth. Tears leak from the corners of his eyes and track their way through the flecks of blood on his face.

My hands are shaking so badly I drop the bottle. 'I'm sorry,' I whisper. 'I'm so sorry, I'm –'

Fox doubles over, staggering away through the trees.

'Don't,' I implore as I follow him deeper into the forest. 'Come back, Fox –'

He turns sharply. Somewhere through the red-hot haze of agony, it seems to register: I just said his name.

He spits out the bark and sags against a tree, his entire body racked with shudders as the pain reaches a crescendo. I smooth his sweat-soaked hair back from his brow. The wound on his torso continues to bleed, showing no sign of stopping.

'Bandages,' he croaks. 'I'll need to bind it.'

'It's no good,' I protest. 'They won't stop the blood.' I wring my hands helplessly. 'Surely there must be *something* in that pile of potions –' Then I stop abruptly and my eyes widen with realization. 'Lachrymortis,' I breathe.

Before Fox can utter a word I'm darting back through the trees towards Cedar and Scout and the pile of supplies. When I return, clutched in my hand is a small glass vial.

Fox shakes his head. 'No.'

'*Yes*. You said in the inn that it can heal any wound.'

Each word is an effort. 'I also ... said ... that I possess ... the last remaining ... vials. I'm saving them ... for something ... worse.'

I stare at him incredulously. 'Look at you. You're bleeding out.'

'I vowed never ... to use it ... on myself.'

'And how do you intend to keep that vow when you're dead?' I remove the stopper and thrust the vial into his hand. 'Take it. There's still one left.'

Fox looks from me to the lachrymortis, torn. His skin is hot to the touch. He screws up his face as the pain persists.

I wrap my fingers round his. '*Please*.'

I feel his resolve begin to weaken. Gently I ease the vial between his lips before pouring the contents down his throat.

Relief clouds his features. The euphoria is almost tangible.

I gasp as the lacerated skin on his chest begins to knit back together. Ragged flesh turns smooth once more; every cut seals shut, scrapes and bruises fading into nothing.

Fox blinks and stumbles slightly. The agony was so all-consuming that I imagine its sudden absence must be dizzying.

Hesitantly, I lay my palm on his chest, right over the spot where the Bear plunged his tooth-spiked fist. I trace the outline of the wound, from just next to his heart all the way down to his navel.

'It worked,' I whisper. 'You're healed.'

That's when I begin to shake, small tremors quickly turning into shudders so violent I can't seem to catch my breath.

Fox looks alarmed. 'What is it?'

'Nothing. Nothing. I'm f-fine.'

I suspect I'm just in shock. It's the adrenaline wearing off, nothing more. To my dismay, drizzle begins to fall above our heads, light and hazy. I curse and turn away, but Fox pulls me back instinctively, his arms locking round my waist.

'Tell me.'

'I thought . . . I thought you were going to . . .'

His lips part in surprise, his green eyes scanning my face. 'It's all right now,' he says softly. 'I'm all right. *We're* all right.'

I nod, balling my hands into fists to keep them from trembling.

Fox tucks a stray curl behind my ear. 'Look at me.'

But I just hang my head, a blush staining my cheeks.

He cups my face, tilting my chin. '*Blaze*,' he breathes, my name as sacred as a prayer on his lips. 'Look at me.'

My eyes flicker up.

Everything else seems to fall away, and I see only him. The boy who broke the world. Beautiful and bewildering and covered in blood, looking down at me as though I'm the answer to a question he hasn't dared to ask. The cloud of drizzle grows warm, falling like ash from the midnight sky. In the light from my brandmark, I watch his pupils dilate.

'This is a very bad idea,' I whisper.

'You're probably right,' he says.

Then he kisses me.

Time seems to slow as his lips meet mine. I'm frozen, suspended somewhere between trepidation and disbelief as I wait to come to my senses. Except I don't. I just melt into him, wrapping my arms tightly round his neck.

The kiss is hot and hungry, almost feverish.

It's not like it was in the maze. This time there are no masks, no case of mistaken identity. This time, I know it's him. I *choose* him.

I let out a gasp as the sharp sting from the knife wound dulls, then vanishes entirely. Some of the lachrymortis must have lingered on Fox's lips.

Fox drops his hands to my waist once more, reeling me closer, banishing any remaining space between us. I think about the first time I saw him. I think about how often I've thought of him. I think about how long he's haunted me, running circles in my mind.

Then he slips his tongue into my mouth and I forget my own name.

He backs me slowly into a tree, pinning me gently to the trunk, kissing my jaw, my throat, nipping at the spot where my neck meets my shoulder. A small sound escapes my lips, and any lingering restraint shatters. My hands move instinctively, running over his body as though committing its shape to memory – my fingers gliding across his blood-slicked chest, digging into his back, tangling in his hair. He tastes like blood and salt and summer rain.

I want to lose myself in his touch, in the soft slide of our mouths. But I'm worried that if we don't stop now, we won't stop at all. And I barely know what I've started.

Fox must be thinking the same thing. He groans softly. Then, with what seems like considerable effort, he pulls back, breaking the kiss.

For a moment we just stand there, panting, staring at one another, our faces flushed and smattered with blood.

I blink, dazed.

Fox leans against a tree. His voice cuts through the silence, low and rough. 'For what it's worth,' he says, 'I rather like your bad ideas.'

38

Elva

I'll never forget the masquerade ball after the second trial.

I'd got ready in Blaze's rooms once she and Spinner had left, marvelling at the dazzling gold-silk gown and delicate mask adorned with tiny crescent moons – a subtle nod to my homeland. Hal had picked them out specially.

My disguise gave rise to a different kind of anonymity than the one I experience as a serf. I didn't go unnoticed but rather blended in, just another masked, gold-clad courtier gliding gracefully through the crowd, gazed upon and admired, yet unidentifiable.

I met Hal in the gallery overlooking the ballroom, too high for prying Eyes. I remember how beautiful he looked, leaning against the wall, waiting for me.

Since I had never been taught, it came as little surprise that I was hopeless at dancing. But Hal only smiled. Lifting me into his arms, he set my feet atop his and danced for us both. And I forgot about his looming betrothal, and the scars of my past, and our uncertain future. We were unburdened, happy. There was nothing else in the world but him and me.

We're going to kill the emperor.

The memory shatters as I recall Ingra's words, broken shards slicing my heart to ribbons as I relive what happened the night before in the broom cupboard. I was frozen in place, unable to move, or think, or form a sentence. The others seemed to interpret my horror as stunned exhilaration, for they all grinned conspiratorially at me.

At long last, when I'd finally regained the ability to speak, I looked straight at Ingra and asked the first of three questions: 'Why?'

'Seriously, Elva? Do you really have to ask?' Ingra snorted derisively. 'Because the Castellions are tyrants who've been enslaving our people for over fifty years. And because the political climate in this Gods-forsaken empire is already so fragile that taking him out will cause it to topple like a house of cards. Killing him will incite *chaos*.' Her dark eyes flashed and her tone grew feverish with excitement. 'His death is exactly what we need – the spark to fuel an uprising decades in the making. Besides, everyone knows he's sickly. I don't imagine he'll live long by the looks of him. Why waste the opportunity to have his death pave the way for anarchy and revolt? If he's going to die, let it be for *our* cause, not theirs.'

Everything she said seemed to tear me apart, right down the middle. More than ever before, I became agonizingly aware of my own duality – that I am made up of two warring halves, forced to conceal one part of myself to preserve the other. And I realized in that moment that I could no longer be one of them *and* be in love with Hal.

My voice was small as I uttered my second question: 'How?'

Ingra understood what I meant. 'Seth made a copy of the key to the armoury, so I'll have my pick of the bunch. Though Ty's right – the weapon should be something long-range.' She smiled, a little sadly. 'My father taught me how to shoot back in Veridia. I don't miss.'

'Let's hope not,' said Seth. 'Because you've only got one shot at this.'

'Literally,' added Pip.

Ingra only smirked at them. 'When it's done, I'll slip into the serf tunnels, where the others will be waiting.'

My eyes widened. 'You mean . . .'

'That there's more of us in on the plan than just this lot?' Ingra finished. 'Of course. But we couldn't risk meeting in large groups.' She gave me an apologetic look. 'I was going to tell you tonight, and ask you to join us.'

Guilt hacked into me like a blunt axe.

'The Etheri have their magic but we have the numbers,' she continued. 'We have weapons and the element of surprise. And most importantly, we have nothing to lose.'

'Well, except our lives,' Clover pointed out dryly.

'What lives?' Ingra shot back. 'This isn't a *life* – this is an *existence*, and a pitiful one at that. If I don't make it home, at least I'll know that because of me someone else might.'

I remembered what she had told me all those years ago.

If I did nothing, I'd become nothing.

It appeared her courage was infectious, for the others all nodded. Not for the first time, I found myself in awe of – and a little frightened by – Ingra's boldness, her bravery, her unbroken spirit. Perhaps I too would have revelled at her words, allowed them to raise me up and rally me to her cause, were she not planning on murdering the boy I love.

What was I supposed to do? Tell them Hal is nothing like his family? Tell them he was already planning on freeing them? And how would I tell them how I knew this?

'We were going to delay a while,' Ingra said. 'But we heard the emperor is back on his feet, so I figured, why wait? Let's strike while the iron is hot.'

It was then I asked my third and final question: 'When?'

Ingra's grin was catlike. 'Tomorrow night.'

Which, despite how much I willed it not to, has now arrived.

I gaze out of the window in Elaith's chambers at the crescent moon bathing Cor Caval in silvery light. King Gethen of Vost, brother to the Empress Dowager and, so far, Hal's only ally, arrived this afternoon. He's here to publicly pledge his allegiance, and presumably to negotiate the terms of whatever incentive Hal has agreed to grant him. Gold, I suspect.

Already I hear the courtiers making their way towards one of the countless gilded ballrooms, where a ball is being held in the Vosti King's honour. Vost is a kingdom rich with expensive fabric and materials. It's also one of the two places Hal said we might find my sister, if she's still alive. I wonder what Astrid would say, if she knew what I'm planning.

I catch sight of myself in the mirror and look away quickly, unable to meet my own eyes. A lifetime of regret will not be punishment enough for what I'm about to do.

Elaith hovers by the door, dressed in swathes of crimson gossamer, her red hair unbound round her shoulders, concealing her necklace of bruises.

'Are you expecting someone?' I ask.

She blinks, then blushes. 'Oh, well, sort of. Cole said he'd come by and escort me, but he must be running late.'

I do my best to return her smile before excusing myself.

The ballroom is teeming, the air thick and close. I skirt the perimeter of the dance floor, searching for familiar faces.

Hal isn't here yet.

If I didn't know what was going on, I might not have noticed the way the serfs keep glancing furtively at one another, shifting on their feet. I can feel it – that nervous energy, the sense of waiting for something to happen.

Where is Ingra?

I spot Clover carrying a tray of empty glasses, watching as her gaze flickers to the gallery above, the same one where Hal and I had danced together at the masquerade ball.

A high vantage point – private, easily concealed. It's the perfect spot.

I don't hesitate before taking off, weaving like a needle through the crowd.

The gallery is empty save for an old golden harp sitting forgotten in the corner. I move to stand beside it, shadows shrouding me in darkness as I wait for her to appear.

A hush falls over the ballroom below.

'His Imperial Majesty, Emperor Haldyn Castellion,' a voice announces.

I peer over the golden railing to see Hal standing in the doorway, dressed in an elegant burnt-gold doublet. To my surprise he looks if not *better*, then not worse. The opium the physicians prescribed must be taking the edge off the pain, for he strides easily through the kneeling crowd, flanked by his mother and King Gethen – a portly, bearded man wearing a fine purple cloak. I feel the scars littering my back twinge – a gift from his daughter, Princess Lira, who thought spilling some wine was deserving of a dozen lashes. I remember it so clearly – the sharp whistle of the whip, my tunic ragged and covered in blood. But I know in my heart I would do it all again just to save Pip from the same fate.

Which only makes what I'm about to do a hundred times harder.

Chatter resumes as the Etheri rise, with several couples taking to the dance floor. I wait with bated breath, my gaze fixed on the door to the gallery.

I hear her before I see her, my ears already attuned to the beating of her heart, thudding in time with my own.

Ingra slips through the door, a heavy-looking crossbow clutched in her arms. She props it on her hip while she wipes at the sweat dewing on her brow. Then, cautiously, she moves forward, sinking into a crouch before the golden railing and scanning the ballroom for her target. As soon as she spots Hal speaking politely with a group of Vosti courtiers, she nocks the single bolt, squeezes one eye shut and takes aim.

'Ingra,' I say, stepping out of the shadows.

She starts, and whips her head round. Then her mouth splits into a gleeful smile. 'Come to watch the show from the royal box?'

'Not exactly.'

Her smile fades.

I realized last night that I had a choice to make, one that would rip me in two as callously as the Earth Cleaver tore apart the realm. It's little wonder I feel emptier than the Rift. For I made my choice, and I choose Hal. Because I'm selfish. Because I can't lose him. Because I *love* him. Even if loving him means betraying my friends and, by extension, my people. Even if it makes me the most despicable person who ever lived.

So be it. I *won't* let him die.

Ingra's eyes are narrowed, and her fingers tighten round the crossbow.

I could've prevented this. I could've blown the whistle on the attack the moment I learned of it. But doing so would have meant confessing how I became privy to it and, more importantly, who was behind it. The serfs involved would've been punished – even executed. No, I couldn't expose their plan, so I'm just going to have to make sure it doesn't succeed.

'Don't do this, Ingra,' I say evenly.

Her voice is acidic. '*Why not?*'

What answer can I possibly give? That it's too dangerous? That she's risking her life? She knows this. Nothing I say will dissuade her now. She's made her choice, just as I've made mine. My only hope is the truth.

I glance over the railing to where Hal, having escaped his entourage, is standing with his back to us, entertaining a group of children by conjuring tiny orbs of light.

Hal is not his grandfather. He is not responsible for the atrocities committed by those who came before. He is good and gentle and kind. He can make things right.

I drag in a breath and say, 'Because he doesn't deserve it.'

This catches Ingra off guard. She stares at me, bewildered. Then her expression shifts, understanding sparking to life in her dark eyes. '*No*,' she breathes.

I say nothing.

'I don't *believe* it.' Her shoulders begin to quiver. It takes me a moment to realize that she's laughing. 'This is just too good,' she snickers, lowering the crossbow a fraction. '*He's* your Emmeric? *Seriously? Him?* The Gods-damned *emperor*? *He's* your secret lover?'

The smallest dip of my chin is my only response.

She sits back on her heels and shakes her head. 'Oh, Elva. Oh, you stupid, *stupid* girl. What were you thinking?'

'It's not like that.'

'Then what's it like?'

'We . . .' I swallow. 'We *love* each other.'

This sets her off again. '*Puh-lease*.'

'You don't know him.'

'I know his kind.'

'He's different. Ingra, listen to me – he's going to free the serfs.'

'Oh *really*? Is that what he told you to get you into bed?'

'I swear it. He's –'

'Dead,' Ingra finishes, raising the crossbow.

No.

My body reacts instinctively. I lunge for her and knock her off balance. The weapon skitters across the gleaming floor, still loaded.

Ingra pushes herself up and shoves me hard in the chest. She isn't laughing any more.

I careen backwards into the harp, barely registering the pain. She's just reaching for the crossbow when I grab hold of her ankle and pull. Ingra snarls, kicking her legs and catching me in the stomach. I stagger drunkenly, then spring forward once more, gasping on impact as we collide and roll across the gallery, tearing and scratching at one another.

I barely recognize her – this girl I grew up with. I barely recognize myself. We are two wild things, all nails and teeth, any semblance of friendship ground to ashes underfoot.

With a grunt of triumph, Ingra manages to pin me to the floor. I struggle desperately, my arms clamped beneath her knees.

'So this is what you want, is it?' Ingra spits. 'To *screw* him and screw us over? You lying, traitorous *whore*.'

'Ingra, please –'

'What about the others? You would betray your own to save the life of a Castellion?'

'I'm saving your life, too. Shoot him and you'll never make it out of here alive.'

'I don't *care*,' Ingra half shrieks, slamming me into the floor. I see stars as she leans down close to my ear. '*I don't know who you are any more*.'

I curl on to my side as the crushing weight lifts. 'No,' I choke out.

Among the white spots crowding my vision, I watch her assume her position by the railing, crossbow in hand, tongue between her teeth as she prepares to fire.

I can't get to her in time. I can't move.

Terror grips me tightly and I think only of Hal.

'I love you,' I whisper.

For a moment there is nothing but the thunderous beating of my heart.

Then, the darkness erupts.

Shadows pour out of me, black as night and utterly impenetrable, enveloping the ballroom in gloom.

I turn rigid with astonishment, watching my magic dance as it takes form, snuffing out the flickering torches, spreading outward. It's . . . it's as if my fear for Hal is enabling me to project my power. This time my shadows aren't protecting me but allowing me to protect *him*.

Over the courtiers' shrieks I hear Ingra's sharp gasp – of shock, of dismay, of bitter, burning rage. I see her, my gaze cutting easily through the dark. I drag myself to my feet and kick the crossbow out of her hands. To my horror, this causes it to fire. The bolt shoots upward, then ricochets off the ceiling. I hold my breath, hardly daring to watch as it plummets to the ground. A split second later, there's a deafening shatter as it hits a ginormous vase of golden roses. I exhale in relief while a chorus of screams pierces the din.

Several orbs of light blink to life, illuminating the ballroom. I can hear Hal calming the crowd, calling for the Ignitia to relight the torches.

Ingra is panting, her hair falling loose from her thick braid. Her hands are clenched into fists as she gapes at the shadows still twining themselves round my wrists.

Suddenly – footsteps. Lots of them, headed our way.

Reflexively, I shrink back into the lingering darkness just as the Imperial Guard burst through the doors to the gallery.

There are half a dozen knights, yet Ingra fights them anyway, kicking and punching until the pommel of a sword hits her squarely in the ribs. I hear the sickening, splintering crack right before she goes limp. As they drag her away, she jerks her head round and stares into the spot where she watched me melt into the darkness, her face twisted with fury and betrayal.

And I know that however much she hates me in this moment, it's nothing compared to how much I hate myself.

39

Blaze

I sit by the fire, watching Fox sleep.

He's lying on his back, his breathing slow and rhythmic, his arm outstretched towards Scout, who stands guard over him like a sentinel. His chest is still streaked with blood, which has dried a dark rust-red. But his wound – those awful ragged gashes – has been reduced to nothing more than a few thin scars to add to his collection.

If it weren't for the lachrymortis, he could well be dead. It terrified me, seeing him like that – golden skin pale, movements slow and staggering. When he screamed, the sound of it ripped a hole in my own chest, and I just kept thinking, *He's going to die*. But then he didn't, and all that terror was replaced by a wave of relief so strong it threatened to sweep me away. I was drowning, and I needed something to cling to, and he –

He kissed me.

He kissed me, and I kissed him back.

It was as if the whole world crumbled into nothing. All I knew was heat, and him. His lips, his touch, his body moulding itself to mine.

Our skin and clothing are still covered with telltale smears of blood that reveal exactly where our hands have been.

I swallow hard then snatch up a wad of bandages, douse myself with water and scrub myself clean, washing away all trace of the kiss.

It's not that I regret it. It's that he knows now. He knows that despite all my protestations, I feel something for him.

I never meant for it to happen. I tried to keep my distance. But the more I learned about Fox, the fewer reasons I found to stay away. He's not who I thought he was. He's not cruel, or heartless, or wicked. He's not exactly *good*, either, but then neither am I.

I wrap my arms round my knees as a tremor runs through me.

I killed someone tonight. I took a life.

I suppose I should be used to this feeling. After all, I have thousands of deaths on my conscience. Yet unlike the storm, this was intentional. I knew exactly what I was doing as I plunged my dagger into the Bear's back. He was a brute, already half-dead, yet he was still a person – a person who, because of me, is now a corpse. But if I'm being entirely honest, I know I would do it again in a heartbeat if it meant saving Fox.

I find myself wondering whether he feels the same about me as I do about him, whether all that shameless flirting and evident protectiveness point to a deeper, more sincere attachment. I think about the way he said my name, his rich, velvety voice laced with the same inexplicable intimacy as his gaze. From the moment I met him, he has looked at me like he knows me. Like I am some riddle only he has the answer to.

And perhaps . . . perhaps that's true.

I slip my hand into my pocket and pull out the Eye of the Past.

I still haven't entirely forgiven Fox for scouring my memories, whether inadvertently or not. I was furious that he eavesdropped on a private moment between his brother and me, even more so to discover that he knew of my anchors. Melding is a secret the Rain Singers protected for centuries – one that, if not for River, could've died along with them. River told me once that he had travelled to Brava to see them for himself, and amid my astonishment I recall feeling a pang of envy, followed by wistfulness. Because the Singers are gone. I am all that is left of their legacy.

The last Rain Singer.

The words have always weighed so heavily. It is the weight of solitude, bone-deep and unquantifiable. It is the knowledge that I am an endling. An anomaly. And there is nobody left to offer any kind of explanation to the question that has plagued me all my life:

Why?

Why am I a Rain Singer? How is it possible that I, a Harglade, a daughter of two pureblood Ignitia Houses, was born with the ability to call the rain? And not only the rain but a storm – one so devastating it almost drowned the empire.

I wind the gold chain round my index finger, my mind awash with unanswered questions. When I asked Fox why he had sought the Eye of the Past, he told me, in his infuriatingly cryptic fashion, that he was searching for answers. Yet what of the answers I seek? I have a right to know who I am. And if Fox knows something I don't, I refuse to be left in the dark any longer. I've spent nearly eighteen years believing myself an aberration, and maybe I am. Maybe there is no explanation for my existence beyond some cruel twist of fate. But then again, what if there is? What if I am a mystery I'm yet to unravel?

I look down at the Eye. That night in Fox's chambers, I remember thinking of all the things I would use it to discover if it were mine. And now it is – at least, until the sun comes up. At this moment I have history at my fingertips. The past spreads out before me like a map of memory. This is my chance to trace my path back to the very beginning. To find the truth, if there is truth to find. To understand who I am, once and for all.

My skin tingles nervously.

I cast a glance at Fox, who's still fast asleep. I'm struck briefly by a twinge of guilt for going behind his back. Then I shake it off. If there are no answers to be uncovered, he doesn't have to know I went looking for them. And if there are, I'd bet the Aquatori crown that he knew and hasn't told me. Because whatever I may feel for him, I still don't trust him entirely. Not yet. So, let this be the test.

I close my hand into a fist round the Eye, then hesitate, unsure how to proceed. I think back to all the times I've seen

Fox use it. There seems to be no clear method to replicate, no incantation to speak. Perhaps I should just . . . ask it?

I gnaw on my lip, feeling slightly foolish, the same as I did when asking the Golden Keep to grant me entry. But I'll never know unless I try.

Taking a deep breath, I close my eyes.

I wish to know the truth about myself.

For a long moment, nothing happens.

Then I almost cry out as the Eye begins to pulsate in my palm, as though I were clutching a beating heart. The darkness behind my eyelids becomes light, refracting over and over until, quite suddenly, I'm looking out across a vast expanse of ocean.

A winged shadow glides over the water, and a creature lands smoothly on the beach beside me. My mouth tips open – I am staring into the bulbous eyes of a giant dragonfly. It's roughly the size of a small horse, deep blue and breathtaking.

They say the Rain Singers used to fly upon dragonfly-back, and that they were sometimes spotted swooping through the clouds above Brava.

Sure enough, a boy with pale-white hair slides gracefully from the saddle and begins to make his way up the beach towards the forest.

Out of the corner of my eye, I spot a girl hiding in the treeline. She's beautiful, with eyes the colour of twilit sea. Only when the boy glances in her direction, she disappears. I wonder briefly whether she's Ventalla, and using her gifts to flit. But no, I can still hear her footsteps, twigs snapping as she keeps pace behind him, vanishing and reappearing every few yards. It's as if she's still there, but I can't see her – as if she's *invisible.*

All of a sudden the boy whirls round, snatching at thin air. The girl lets out a squeak and materializes with his hands clamped on her shoulders.

'Hello, Mage,' he says, grinning.

'Hello, Singer,' she responds, rising up on her tiptoes to kiss him.

I stare at them. How can this be? And what has any of it got to do with *me*?

The visions come thick and fast, and I watch as a story unfolds. A love story. Years pass, and two become three when a child is born – a little boy who inherits his father's hair and his mother's eyes as well as both their gifts: *Demari.*

The scene shifts and the happiness fades. The boy, now around nine or ten, sobs over his parents' pox-ridden bodies. He sits by their bedside night and day, yet they never wake up. Tears drip from his face, forming a small pool on the floorboards. I gasp as the pool transforms into a shimmering portal, and the boy falls through it with a scream.

He emerges on the outskirts of a large province. The day is blisteringly hot, the sun beating down mercilessly upon the barren stone plains stretching out for miles before us. We're no longer in the Otherlands – we're in Ostacre. Specifically, the Firelands.

A few yards away, a girl is perched on the edge of a steaming hot spring, moodily tossing stones into the water. She looks about the same age as the boy, her thick hair unbound, dark eyes narrowed with irritation. She doesn't notice him standing there, tear-stained and bedraggled, until his foot makes a scuffing noise on the rocky ground.

She whips round, flames igniting in her palm as she demands, 'What do you want?'

The boy shrinks back, raising his arms in surrender. 'N-nothing.'

The girl angles her head as she considers him. Then she extinguishes the flames and folds her arms crossly. 'You shouldn't go sneaking up on people. It's bad manners.'

His lower lip trembles.

Her gaze softens along with her voice. 'What's wrong?'

'My . . . my parents are dead,' he whispers. 'And I . . . I don't know where I am.'

Rain begins to fall above their heads – fat droplets sizzling on hot stone.

The girl stares, wide-eyed. 'Rain Singer,' she breathes.

The boy looks frightened. He stumbles backwards, as though about to run away.

'No, wait! Don't go. I've never met a Singer before.'

He hesitates. I can't be sure whether it's rain or tears streaming down his cheeks.

'I'm not going to hurt you,' the girl adds gently.

The boy wipes his eyes, then sits down next to her.

'I thought all the Rain Singers lived in Brava,' she says. 'What're you doing here?'

'Where is here?'

'Valburn, of course. *The flaming heart of the Firelands*, as my father calls it.'

Valburn? Of all the provinces in Ostacre, why is this particular vision taking place in the one I grew up in? Who are these children?

'I sometimes wish my parents were dead,' the girl muses, as if to make the boy feel better. 'My mother is more interested in drinking wine and throwing parties than she is in me, and my father – well, he's in charge of my training. If I get something wrong, he hurts me.' She rolls up the sleeve of her red dress to reveal a nasty burn in the shape of a handprint. 'He says it's for my own good, that it's to make me stronger. He wants me to be queen one day, you see. Only I'd much rather be a knight, or maybe even a pirate.'

The rain eases off as the boy's choking sobs turn to sniffles.

'What about you?' asks the girl. 'What do you want to be when you grow up?'

'I . . . I don't know. I'm not entirely sure what I am, let alone what I want to be.'

'How d'you mean? You're a Rain Singer, aren't you?'

'My father was a Rain Singer. My mother was . . . something else. Sometimes, I think being both feels a bit like being neither.'

'Then *be* neither,' she says, with that childlike conviction that makes everything sound so simple. 'Be whoever you want to be. Think of it as a fresh start.'

The boy blinks at her.

'Rain Singers are Aquatori, aren't they?' The girl nibbles on a fingernail. 'Perhaps you should go to the Waterlands. I've heard it's a lot prettier than here. And a lot cooler,' she adds, fanning herself with the sleeve of her gown for emphasis. 'The only downside is that you'd have to hide your rain, but you could still use your other water gifts. And it sounds a lot more fun than pretending to be Fidra, which would mean you couldn't use magic at all.' She smiles triumphantly, pleased with her solution. 'What d'you think?'

'I . . .' The boy pauses for a moment. 'Aquatori,' he murmurs thoughtfully.

'Of course, to be Aquatori you'll need a brandmark, but that's easily solved. I can brand you myself, if you like. I'm very good at that sort of thing.'

His gaze travels to the Ignitia fire sign seared into her flesh. 'Will it hurt?'

'Yes,' she replies matter-of-factly.

The boy swallows. 'All right.'

The girl nods, then presses her palm to the back of his hand. A moment later, the boy lets out a yelp. When she releases him, the skin is red and inflamed, branded with a perfect Aquatori waterdrop. He closes his eyes, and I watch in astonishment as he lowers the temperature of the hot spring before plunging his hand into the now-icy water.

The girl smiles approvingly. 'I'm Leda,' she says.

The boy ducks his head shyly. 'I'm River.'

My heart seems to grind to a halt.

Grandmother. That's my grandmother as a little girl. And the boy . . . the boy who is half Rain Singer, half Mage is . . . *River.*

The vision changes before I can catch my breath.

I'm in the Waterlands, watching River, now a young man, lugging barrels of freshly caught fish from the harbour to the market. His snow-white hair has been cropped short, and sheathed at his belt is a familiar silver trident. Suddenly the people around him begin looking up at the sky, shielding their eyes from the sun, which, moments later, is eclipsed by the moon, drenching the world in darkness. River drops the barrel balanced on his shoulder, his face a picture of shock as he clutches his glowing brandhand.

The vision changes again, and I'm standing in the banquet hall of the Golden Palace. Eighteen-year-old Grandmother is talking to Prince Caius Castellion, who, with his neatly combed hair and simple gold crown, is almost a mirror image of Hal.

'Ah,' he says, nodding at someone standing behind me. 'Leda, have you met River?'

Grandmother turns and her eyes widen in surprise. River bows, but his gaze never leaves her face. For a long moment they just stare at one another.

Then Grandmother says, 'Yes, Your Imperial Highness. I do believe I have.'

Memories begin to unravel, and I tumble through them.

Secret glances, long conversations, the brush of hands in a crowded room. Walking together to the Keep to train. Sharing a bottle of wildfire wine with Caius, the three of them drunk-eyed and grinning, watching the sunrise. Grandmother's laughter as she runs through the maze, her dark hair streaming out behind her. River kissing her in the statue garden.

I stiffen in shock. I had known they were friends, but not anything more.

As the vision shifts, I think back to my Name Day ball, when I saw them speaking with their heads together. Sitting with them in my tent as I waited to battle Marina. Watching them fight King Balen side by side. Have they really loved each other all this time?

An irate man with golden-brown eyes hurls flames at Grandmother, accusing her of threatening the reputation of House Harglade, demanding that she keep her distance from *that lowborn Fish* or she'll come to regret it. Afterwards, River tends to her burns.

My stomach jolts as the amphitheatre swims into view. I look on helplessly as they both lose their third trials. Now they sit at opposite ends of the Choosing Chamber while Caius is bound to his new Crowned Council.

The next vision is one I've seen before. Grandmother bursts into the Council Chambers, her steely glare fixed on Caius as River closes the doors behind them.

It's not long before the War of the Empires begins.

River begs Grandmother not to fight. She tells him she has no choice – the Noble Houses have pledged allegiance to the emperor and called their bannermen to war. I see her on the battlefield, Leda Flameslinger, her fighting leathers slick with blood, burning her enemies to dust. River watches from atop a high hill before turning and riding away.

Now Grandmother is standing at the altar, dressed in a scarlet wedding gown, while her family watch on proudly. A single tear rolls down her cheek as my grandfather, the Ignitia High General, lifts her veil, his signet ring – a golden swan – glinting in the candlelight.

The vision shifts again.

Letters. So many letters. Grandmother keeps them hidden beneath a loose floorboard, tied up with blue ribbon.

She watches from the window as my grandfather departs for a military posting, accompanied by a battalion of Ignitia soldiers. Two little girls play at her feet. I realize with a jolt who they are – my aunts. Yvainne and Hester.

Rain pours down from a darkening sky. Grandmother rides out of the city walls, her face obscured by the hood of her cloak. River waits for her on the outskirts of Valburn, standing at the edge of the hot spring where they first met. She slides from her horse. Time seems to slow as she takes a step towards him, then another, before falling into his arms.

'I'm sorry,' she whispers.

'I love you,' he tells her.

The scene changes once more.

Grandmother stands before the mirror in her dressing room, a hand on her growing belly, her expression twisted with dread.

My insides turn to stone as the next vision descends.

Grandmother's screams echo through the birthing chamber.

A physician beams as he holds up a squalling baby. 'Another girl, my lady.'

The moment the child is placed on Grandmother's chest, a fire roars to life in the hearth, burning so fiercely that some of the attendants squeal in fright. Even the physician looks alarmed as the candles begin to flare and gutter, followed by the torches in the courtyard beyond the window. Grandmother's face floods with relief, as if she'd feared the flames would not appear. As if she knows the child in her arms is not pureblood Ignitia.

She gazes down at her daughter. 'Analiese,' she murmurs.

My mind is spinning.

River. River is my mother's father. River, son of a Rain Singer and a Mage. Which means . . .

I fall to my knees as the vision shifts for a final time.

It's no longer my grandmother clutching a newborn, but my mother, her jaw clenched with determination as she stumbles through a torrent of rain so violent I can't see where the sky ends and the ocean begins. At the very top of the cliff, the baby holds out a tiny hand and closes it into a fist. All of a sudden, the storm comes to an end.

I look down at the child and see my own eyes looking back at me.

Fox's voice fills my head.

Over the years, there have been cases – very rare cases – of children born half Etheri, half Magi. Children born to those children would then be part *Etheri, part Magi, and so on, forever tainting a bloodline.*

My breathing turns ragged.

Someone with dual ancestry might only inherit one gift. They may appear to be either Etheri or Magi. But their gift could be . . . distorted. Too strong. Too dangerous.

I stare at the utter devastation left by my storm. The empire flooded. Bodies blue and bloated, washed out to sea.

These people . . . they were never supposed to exist. They inherit too much power.

I emerge from the visions as if from icy water. A strangled sound escapes my lips as I fling the Eye of the Past away. But there is no escaping the truth that slams into me again and again like the butt of a knife. History plays on a loop in my head, each memory opening a wound beneath the skin, bruising my heart, colouring everything I thought I knew the deep blue-black of betrayal. My entire life has been a lie – one that was created and covered up by those I trusted the most. It is not so much a question of *who* I am, but *what* I am.

The words dance round my mind, each one given new meaning.

Rain Singer. Storm Weaver. Etheri. Mage.

Demari.

40

Blaze

'Get up.' My voice slices through the air, sharp as freshly forged steel.

Fox grunts and opens one eye. He peers groggily at the dagger brandished at his throat, still half asleep. 'And good morning to you too, Storm Weaver.'

'I said, *get up*.'

'As much as I enjoy it when you threaten me, could it perhaps wait until after breakfast?'

I grit my teeth. Slowly, I sheath Silverclaw and get to my feet.

Fox props himself up on his elbows, bemused. 'Well, aren't you just a ray of sunshine. And there was me thinking we were getting on rather well last night.'

My face grows hot. He's still covered in blood – bone-dry and flaking – but I can pinpoint the many smears and smudges that indicate exactly where I'd touched him, the memory of that kiss imprinted on his body as well as in my mind.

He smirks a little. 'Seems a shame to get rid of the evidence,' he says as he reaches for the waterskin and douses himself clean.

My blush deepens. Faintly glowing embers hiss as I aim a kick at the smouldering remains of the fire. Then I turn away and begin to pace furiously, my fists clenched.

'Are you going to tell me what's wrong or am I just supposed to guess?' Fox asks, sitting back against a tree, his chest glistening in the dappled light.

'I'm surprised you can't work it out given how well you seem to know me,' I snap. '*So well*, in fact, that you apparently knew more about my past than I did.'

I pull Sifa's Eye from my pocket and hurl it straight at his face. He snatches it out of the air before it can meet its mark.

There's an almost seismic shift in his demeanour as he unfurls his fingers.

'What have you done?' Fox demands.

'What have *I* done?' I splutter. 'You're the one who went snooping through my family tree and then just conveniently forgot to mention that for the last seventeen years I have been living a lie. And don't even try to deny it, because while you might know me, I know you, and this wouldn't be the first time you've kept something like this to yourself.'

He grimaces. 'How much do you know?'

'I know that I'm *Demari*,' I spit. 'And that *you* are a liar.'

'I never lied to you. I just . . . didn't tell you the whole truth.'

'That's the same as lying.'

'What was I supposed to do?' Fox shoots back. 'Just tap you on the shoulder and say, *Oh, by the way, remember that storm you summoned as a baby which almost drowned the empire? So that was actually a result of the Magi blood you inherited from your real grandfather, who, as it turns out, is River, the Aquatori trainer.*'

'Yes,' I say fiercely.

Fox gives up sparring with me. 'I should've told you.'

'Why didn't you, then?'

He exhales before getting to his feet. 'I appreciate you're upset –'

'Try furious.'

'– but it felt cruel to just spring this on you. I told you about Demari in the hope that you'd, you know . . .' He gestures wordlessly. 'Figure it out.'

'Oh, I'm *sorry*,' I say in a voice so remarkably like Grandmother's that it's almost frightening. 'But in case you hadn't noticed, there's been rather a lot going on recently, and I haven't exactly had time to sit and reflect on your *cryptic little mind games*.'

'This was never a game to me, Blaze.'

'Then what is it, *Fox*?'

He flinches. Last night I'd said his name like a plea. Today it's a punishment.

'Look, I was waiting for the right time, but now I realize there wasn't one. And if I'm being entirely honest –'

'There's a first,' I interject.

'I told myself that I was merely shielding you from the truth, not concealing it; that I was acting solely in your interests rather than mine,' he says. 'Because I knew that this would change things between us. I know these past few weeks have been hard, but being with you has felt so . . . *easy*.' He swallows. 'And I didn't want to ruin it.'

For a moment I feel myself soften. Yet when I speak, my voice is hard. 'Too late.'

'I'm sorry, all right? I am.'

This takes me by surprise. I don't think I've ever heard Fox apologize to anyone before. 'I suppose you weren't the only one who didn't tell me,' I concede. 'All this time, Grandmother knew what I was, and she knew why. And then there's River . . .'

'I'm sure they were just trying to protect you,' Fox offers.

But that was the wrong thing to say.

'Will everyone just stop *protecting* me?' I half yell. 'I'm sick and tired of being treated like a little girl who doesn't know her own mind!'

He holds his hands up in surrender. 'You're right.'

Some of my rage seems to evaporate, and I lean against Cedar's flank, fingering the tiny braids Fox has woven through the horse's mane.

Silence stretches between us. My mind is spinning. A thousand questions clamour and claw like a flock of birds.

'My mother,' I say eventually. 'She was Demari too, but she was born Ignitia.'

Fox nods. 'The purity of the Harglade bloodline made it the more potent, but when it was mixed with Magi blood . . .' He lets out a low whistle. 'While your aunts could conjure flames, your mother could create an inferno.'

'But then what about her Choosing? Why didn't she win?'

'Given the unpredictable nature of her gift, I believe your grandmother advised her that it might be best if she . . . *didn't.*'

My eyes widen. 'You mean –'

'That your mother lost on purpose,' Fox confirms. 'She let her eldest sister take the crown, then hid herself away on your father's coastal estate where any threat of wildfires was swallowed by the sea.'

My nails cut like little scythes into my palms. 'Did she ever discover what she really was?'

He shakes his head. 'I doubt it. I believe your grandmother would've taken the secret to her grave, all to protect the reputation of her House.'

'If my mother was so powerful, then how did she die in childbirth?' I ask quietly.

'Demari blood is strong. It can withstand a number of ailments and infections. It's why you were able to survive that snake bite, for example. But your mother . . . she lost too much of that blood.'

A cloud of drizzle forms, droplets clinging to my eyelashes.

'As for River,' Fox adds, 'the strength of his blood has weakened with age. That's why he wasn't able to defeat my uncle at the Binding Ceremony.'

'And what of my brothers?' I ask. 'This makes them Demari, too.'

'Like your mother, Flint was born Ignitia. While his gifts were never dangerous like hers, they were exceptional. If it weren't for his more *hedonistic* pursuits –' I glower in warning – 'then he would've been more than a match for Ember. As for Renly . . .'

'He has no gift at all,' I finish sadly.

'Not yet,' Fox points out.

I exhale shakily, feeling my magic stir beneath my skin – potent in its impurity, the product of a secret so big it swallows me whole. I *need* to speak to Grandmother, yet part of me never wants to speak to her again. For years I believed myself to be twisted. A *monster*. And she just let me.

'I'm . . . I'm so *angry*,' I whisper.

Charred logs crunch underfoot as Fox makes his way over to me and runs a hand across Cedar's muscular flank. 'I understand how you feel.'

'How?' I demand. 'How could you possibly understand?'

Fox scratches his neck. 'Here goes nothing,' he mutters. 'Remember when you asked why I was searching for the Eye of the Past?'

'Yes,' I reply. 'You told me there were some questions you wanted the answers to, and when I asked what they were, you said, quite irritatingly I might add, *You can't have all my secrets, Storm Weaver.*'

Laughter catches in his throat. 'I must say, that was flatteringly verbatim. Exactly how many of our conversations have you memorized by heart?'

I flush.

Fox grins. 'Anyway. These answers I was searching for – they were about my family.'

'The Castellions?'

'No,' he says. 'The Calloways.'

'Why?'

'After the Cleaving, when power like I'd never known burst out of me and almost destroyed the empire, I began to wonder whether there was something I was missing.'

I inhale sharply. 'What're you saying?'

'I'm saying . . .' Fox trails off as he rakes a hand through his hair. 'I'm saying that Healer's hands were not all I inherited from my grandmother.'

The ground seems to tilt beneath my feet.

'You're Demari too,' I breathe.

Fox smiles. 'Haven't I always said that you and I are more alike than you think?'

My chest constricts and my arms fall to my sides as I take a stumbling step backwards.

'Like yours, my mother was an Heir,' he continues. 'She too was forced to conceal her true abilities, even from my father.'

He reaches out to brush his fingertips lightly against mine, and I see Kestrel Calloway. I see her strange, beautiful magic. Barren forests bursting into bloom. Flowers enchanted never to die. A pair of falcon's wings springing forth from her shoulder blades.

All I can do is blink.

'Oh, and just one more thing,' Fox adds. 'Do you, by any chance, happen to recall saying that if you didn't know any better you'd think I could . . . *speak* to Cedar?'

I turn my head to stare at him. 'Yes,' I say slowly. 'Why?'

'Well –' Fox clears his throat – 'that's because I sort of . . . can.'

There is a long, stunned silence.

'You . . . you *what*?' I yelp.

'Though I suppose it's not so much speaking as communicating,' he explains. 'We have a shared line of thought which enables us to converse telepathically.'

I think I might topple over.

'I have the same connection with Scout,' Fox continues, trying not to laugh. 'With all creatures, really. My grandfather was Terrathian, but my grandmother came from Serolia. She was a Mage with the ability to communicate with animals.'

'You can . . . speak . . . to animals,' I say weakly.

'Again, it's not really, technically, *speaking*, but essentially . . .' He shrugs. 'Yes.'

Recognition sparks. 'The wolf . . .'

'He begged me to help him. I couldn't just leave him in that cage.'

Any more and I fear my heart may give out, but I can't help asking, 'So . . . so you can communicate with any animal? All animals?'

'Yes and no. Some, like beetles for example, are far less interesting to engage with than, say, a mountain lion. I've learned to tune out the thoughts of less complex animals. Otherwise things would get pretty overwhelming.'

I swallow. 'And Cedar and Scout, you can hear what they're thinking?'

Fox nods.

'Can you hear them now?'

Another nod.

'What're they saying?'

He glances at them, then back at me. 'Honestly, they both think I'm a selfish prick for not telling you all of this sooner.'

I choke on a laugh, which quickly turns into a sob. My legs buckle and I sink to the ground, overcome.

Fox kneels in front of me. 'I've always known I was different,' he says softly. 'My sister too. It's why I never fully accepted that Freya succumbed to the sweating sickness. Such an infection couldn't have killed a Demari. But it . . . it seems our uncle knew what we were. Or at least suspected. I believe Balen would've attempted to recruit us both if Freya's death hadn't been prophesied to unlock the full destructive potential of my power. Besides, she was far too gentle to be of use to him.' His voice is bitter, brittle. 'So he killed her. I created the Rift, but he created a villain – one he could hide behind.'

My chest aches.

'And me?' I whisper. 'Does he know that I'm Demari too?'

'I expect he's known since the day you were born. But if the storm wasn't indication enough, he decided to try a different experiment. D'you remember, at your Name Day ball, when he asked you to . . . perform?'

I cover my mouth with my hands. 'He raised his broken glass to me as Grandmother dragged me away. He was *smiling*.'

'He knew he was right about you,' Fox says gently, prising my hands away from my face. 'He was planning on *collecting* you, just as he intended to collect me – to swell the ranks of his Demari army and use it to take the Imperial crown.'

'*If only you knew what he has in store for you*,' I whisper. 'That's what your grandfather said to me before the Binding Ceremony. He was foretelling the future.'

'He was foretelling *a* future,' Fox corrects. 'The future is an ever-changing tide. The slightest decision can cause it to take a new course.'

But I'm no longer listening. I wrench my hands from his grip, stagger to my feet and begin stuffing things into his satchel, still reeling. 'We can't afford to waste any more time. We have to go to the Lagoon, *now*.'

'And you're still convinced that's where you sent the missing Eye?'

'Why wouldn't I be?'

'Well, what if it's some place even more . . . meaningful?'

'More meaningful than my future home?' I say, a note of irritation creeping into my voice. 'In any case, that's where Flint's headed. Perhaps he's already there.'

'But –'

'We don't have time for this,' I growl. 'I'm going to the Lagoon and I'm going to find my brother. If you try to stop me I'll freeze you where you stand. So, you have two options. You can either come with me, or stay here and make friends with the squirrels.'

Fox rolls his eyes as he bites back a smirk. 'All right, you win.'

I nod curtly before snatching up various pots and potions from the pile still strewn across the forest floor.

'Careful with those,' he warns, taking a small jar of sage leaves from my hands. 'I'll do this. You ready Cedar.'

For the sake of time I don't protest. I fumble with the reins while Fox meticulously packs up the rest of his supplies, slipping the last remaining vial into his pocket.

He crosses to me just as I'm finishing tacking up.

'Blaze?'

My name sounds different on his lips. I like it more than I should.

'What?' I ask, without turning round.

'I want you to know that I'm really sorry about this,' Fox says, before clamping a hand over my mouth and nose.

Something strong and sharp-smelling fills my nostrils. I jerk my head and let out a muffled scream before inhaling even more vapour from whatever insidious ointment coats his palm.

What is he doing?

What is he doing?

I buck and writhe, my fingernails scratching frantically at his arms until my movements begin to grow slow and sluggish.

I stop fighting. My body turns limp.

But before I slip into unconsciousness, my gaze latches on to Fox's, my eyes wide and wild and so full of betrayal that I hope he feels it in his bones.

41

Elva

There's a spider on the ceiling above my head. I watch it scuttle about directionless for a while before it disappears through a small crack in the corner.

I'm lying on my back in my bunk, trying not to think about the empty bed beneath me. I hear the soft jangle of keys at the end of the hall and stifle a sigh. Matron has taken to performing nightly room checks to make sure all the serfs are accounted for.

Unsurprisingly, the attempt on the emperor's life sent the Golden Palace into uproar. Although when I managed to sneak into Hal's chambers later that night, he himself seemed far more concerned about my injuries than his own brush with death. I assured him that the scratches on my face were the work of the rather irritable cat down in the stables, and declined the vial of painkiller he offered, knowing that I deserved to feel the stinging remnants of Ingra's fury.

In the days that followed there were no balls, banquets or gatherings of any kind. Courtiers took to walking the hallways in pairs, shooting distrustful glances at any passing serfs, Marina among them. Her hostility towards me has reached new heights, since she feels certain that, as both a serf and a spy, I must have known about the assassination. She's right, of course, but with Ingra claiming to having acted alone there's little Marina can do to prove otherwise.

Yet nobody could explain the sudden darkness that descended moments before the bolt was fired. There were even whispers of spirits and omens and divine intervention. When it became apparent that no other explanation was going to present itself, Cole – in his own words – *humbly admitted* to having extinguished every flame in the room after catching sight of a suspicious figure high up in the gallery. Naturally, he was showered with praise, and Ember granted him lands and a title. Nobody seemed to recall *Lord Cole* staggering drunkenly into the ballroom an hour after he promised to escort Elaith.

Still, at least his taking the credit prevented any further investigation into the matter. The only person who knows what truly happened that night is Ingra. Now she's shivering in a damp cell awaiting execution, and it's all my fault.

I snap my eyes shut and breathe deeply as Matron pokes her head round the door. I wait until she's gone, then wedge my fist in my mouth, and scream.

I never meant for this to happen. I didn't save Hal to sacrifice Ingra. That was not supposed to be the price of his life. I only intended to stop her. At least the others, having quickly realized something had gone wrong, dispersed before anyone could catch them.

Last night Pip made the mistake of asking Matron

whether he could take some food to the dungeons for Ingra. I can still hear his whimpering sobs all the way from the Pit. I roll on to my side and clamp my hands over my ears to block them out. Self-loathing wraps itself round me and won't let go. Ingra's voice echoes in my head, her words as sharp as knives.

I don't know who you are any more.

In truth, neither do I.

Am I the serf, slipping unnoticed through a world that is not her own? The spy, tangled up in lies and deception? The lover with her golden roses? The little girl afraid of her own shadow? Or the Mage, who used her magic to betray her friend?

I sit bolt upright in bed and hug my knees to my chest.

I have to talk to Ingra. I want to tell her everything. I want to tell her I'm sorry. And that's exactly what I'm going to do.

The passageway is narrow and lined with ugly golden gargoyles. I keep to the shadows, my pockets bulging with food I swiped from the kitchens.

Half a dozen guards stand stationed outside the entrance to the dungeons, the gold pommels of their longswords gleaming in the light of a single flickering lantern. Ever since the mysterious break-out in which King Balen freed a number of prisoners, Hal has doubled down on the already stringent security measures.

There's a collective groan of irritation as the candle is snuffed, smothered by an obedient ribbon of shadow. Before any of the guards can so much as strike a match, I dart past them into the darkness beyond.

Like everything in this place, even the dungeons are hewn from solid gold. They sit right above the mine, where many of the strongest serfs are sent to work – tall, strapping boys like Seth and Ty, breaking their backs mining the empire's principal source of wealth.

I pick my way carefully down the steep steps, pausing on each floor to peer into cells. It's cold. A little damp, too. Silent and eerie and still. I shed my cloak of shadows, having no need for it any more. My heart thuds violently as I spiral deeper and deeper into the darkened cavern, not stopping until I reach what appears to be the bottom level.

The air is thicker down here. It smells like death and decay, unbearably strong thanks to my unparalleled senses. Resisting the urge to plug my nose, I force myself onward.

Some cells are empty, doors ajar. Some contain a handful of occupants, their skin tinged grey, their eyes dull. I scan their faces, searching for my friend.

I'm beginning to lose hope when someone clears their throat startlingly close to me. 'You did the right thing, you know.'

I whirl round.

The voice belongs to a boy sitting cross-legged on the floor of his cell. His skin is sallow and his eyes are a murky shade of yellow, like a cat's. Yet what captures my attention are the manacles round his wrists. They're clear, made of glass. No, not glass.

Crystal.

My knees buckle. This boy . . . He's a Mage. Just like me.

'*Salvos*, Elva.'

I turn rigid. My name. He knows my name.

And he greeted me in Obsidian.

'Who are you?' I whisper back.

The boy smiles. 'I wanted to thank you for your intervention.'

'W-what intervention?'

'With the Castellion boy. You saved his life the other night, yes?'

I nod once, hardly daring to breathe.

'You did the right thing,' he says again. 'I wasn't ready for him quite yet.'

I frown, trying to make sense of his words. He might be speaking my native tongue, but I can tell it's not his. I detect an accent. Soft, yet guttural. Neptan, perhaps?

Fear skitters down my spine. Nepta was an isle once home to Magi gifted in necromancy. So this boy is a Death Mage. Yet why are my instincts screaming at me, telling me that he's something . . . *more*? Something different, something *ancient*, despite him appearing not much older than I am. I can sense it – that strange, haunting otherness. It chills me to the bone, as if I were looking into the eyes of Death itself.

The Mage jerks his head. 'She's over there. Your friend. Hurry, now. Dawn is fast approaching, and daylight chases away little shadows like you.'

I begin to retreat, not stopping until his smiling face is out of sight. My whole body is trembling so violently I feel nauseated.

At the end of the passageway I find a small, poky cell, barely bigger than the Pit. A single prisoner sits with her back against the wall, absent-mindedly tracing shapes in the layer of grime coating the ground. Her hair is matted. It's strange to see it hanging limply round her shoulders rather than woven into a thick braid down her spine. Vicious red lines score her cheeks. I dig my nails into my palms and swallow hard.

'Ingra,' I whisper.

She jerks away from the sound of my voice as though it were the crack of a whip, her dark eyes straining through the gloom. Of course – I can see her, but she can't see me.

I crouch and wrap my hands round the bars. 'It's Elva.'

'What are you doing here?' Ingra snarls.

I deserve every scrap of her ire and more, yet the venom lacing her tone still causes me to wince. 'I . . . I came to talk to you,' I stutter.

'I don't talk to traitors.'

Grimacing, I try again. 'Ingra, please –'

'Go *away*.'

I take a deep breath, wrinkling my nose at the fetid air. I wasn't exactly expecting a warm welcome, but I need her to listen to me. I have to make her understand.

'I'm sorry,' I murmur. 'For what I did.'

'*Tal frakhas*,' Ingra snaps in Veridian.

I know that one. She likes to mutter it behind Matron's back.

Tal frakhas.

Eat shit.

I hesitate, then sit down opposite her. She makes an impatient sound and lets her head tip back against the wall. A vein pulses in her neck.

'Are you all right?' I ask gently.

She makes no response.

I notice two of her fingers are swollen, both bent at odd angles. My heart sinks. 'Did they hurt you?'

Again, nothing.

I reach into my pockets for the stolen food – bread, cheese, ripe plums, treacle tart. 'Are you hungry?'

'How about *I* ask the questions?' Ingra growls through clenched teeth.

I nod, forgetting she can't see me, then quickly add, 'Of course.'

'I thought I must've dreamed it at first,' she murmurs quietly. 'But if I had, I wouldn't be here, would I?'

'Dreamed what?'

'The darkness,' she says. 'It was *you*, wasn't it?'

I steel myself, then answer, 'Yes.'

'*How*?'

'It's a . . . long story.'

'Then you'd better start telling it.'

So I do. I tell her about waking up in the Earth Cleaver's chambers, the terror that consumed me for weeks, about learning how to *use* my magic instead of repressing it.

As I talk, Ingra's hard expression turns to one of astonishment, even wonder.

'You can see in the *dark*?'

'I can,' I tell her. 'I can see you right now, clear as anything. In fact, all my senses have been heightened.'

She leans closer. 'What else can you do?'

'Mine seems to be a defensive gift,' I explain. 'It's like my shadows anticipate danger. They hide me. Protect me.'

I tell her about becoming a spy, the discovery that my sister might still be alive in either Thaven or Vost, and about overhearing the Eyes who plotted with King Balen. When I get to the part about Caius Castellion, she splutters in disbelief.

'You're telling me the man who started the war that drained the Magi of their magic *knows* you're a Mage and *hasn't* tried to kill you?'

'Well, I'm still breathing,' I point out. 'The strangest thing is, he didn't seem the slightest bit surprised. It was like he already knew.'

'Did he tell you how?'

I sigh. 'No, he just spoke in riddles, then recited the plot of *The Tragedy of Emmeric and Irabella*. I think he may be senile.'

Ingra snorts. 'You *think*?' she says, before grudgingly accepting the plum I press into her hand and taking a huge bite.

'He spoke about Blaze Harglade, too.'

'The Storm Weaver? What's she got to do with any of this?'

'*Everything*, apparently,' I say, raising an eyebrow.

'And neither she nor the Earth Cleaver told you *why* your magic was returned?'

I shake my head. Despite the growing web of mysteries that ensnare me, it's this that proves the most bewildering.

'Do you . . .' Ingra begins tentatively. 'Do you think it's just you? Or that others might be able . . . I mean, is there a chance that *I* could . . .'

The dungeon is as black as night, yet her dark eyes seem to glimmer with hope. I think of the Veridian Desert Magi – those with the ability to conjure sandstorms, create mirages, control minds and plant dreams. Not for the first time I consider what it would mean for Ingra if she too were able to reclaim the gifts of her ancestors.

And what of the other serfs, and everyone back home in the Otherlands? If our people were to become Magi once more . . . it would change *everything*. We would no longer be defenceless. We would be *powerful*. A force to be reckoned with.

I had thought I was an anomaly – an unexplained glitch. But then I think of the boy sitting just a few cells away. *He* has power. I could sense it, with or without those crystal shackles.

What if the old magic never died? What if all we have to do is *reclaim* it?

If I could only get some answers; if I could only find out why – and how – I came to be a Mage, then perhaps there's hope for the others too.

Still, I won't make Ingra false promises.

'I . . . don't know,' I answer slowly.

Her face falls.

'But I'll do whatever I can to find out,' I hurry on. 'I swear it.'

'Good,' she says, nodding. 'That's good. Although it'll be too late for me.'

I bite the inside of my cheek. 'Don't say that.'

Ingra scoffs. 'What? You think they'll let me out of here with a slap on the wrist? Come on, Elva. We both know how this ends.'

'*No*,' I insist fiercely. 'No, I'm going to fix this. I'll speak to Hal and –'

I know immediately that this was the wrong thing to say.

'Yes, do that,' Ingra hisses. 'Speak to your precious *Hal* and tell him that I will face death happily, knowing that he won't be far behind me. He looks half-dead already.'

She may as well have slapped me in the face. 'Ingra –'

But she's not finished. 'When did things start between the two of you, anyway?'

I feel the ghost of a lash across my back. 'Not long after the whipping.'

Ingra lets out a harsh, hollow laugh. 'All this time I assumed he was some courtier, your Emmeric. The son of a rich noble. Not the *Crown Prince*. Really, Elva, I think you might have taken the phrase *sleeping with the enemy* a little too literally.'

Heat blooms across my face. 'Hal's not my enemy.'

'Oh, I'm *sorry*,' Ingra snaps. 'What would *you* call the current ruler of the empire that conquered your homeland and enslaved your people?'

I try to keep my voice level. 'It was his grandfather who did those things, not him.'

'He's a Castellion, Elva. They're one and the same. Fine, maybe he didn't *do* it, but I don't see him trying to *undo* it.'

'He *is* trying to. I promise you, he *will* free the serfs.'

'When?'

'Just as soon as he can persuade his advisers and convince the court.'

'And when will that be? A few months shy of *never*?'

'He wants things to change,' I protest weakly. 'But his position is already threatened. He doesn't have the support –'

'*Listen* to yourself,' Ingra cries. 'How can you possibly defend him?'

'Because you've got him all wrong. He's nothing like his family. He's . . . *gentle*.'

'Face it, Elva. You *belong* to him. You're his property.'

'No, I'm not,' I say quietly.

Her eyes widen, then narrow. 'You mean . . .'

'Yes.'

'You're *free*? You're free and you're still *here*? What is *wrong* with you?'

I cringe away from the acidity in her voice. What answer do I give? I'm here because of Hal. Because my parents are dead and Obsidia is empty without them. Because it's my best chance of finding my sister. And because . . .

'I couldn't leave you,' I say quietly.

I've known Ingra for almost as long as I knew Astrid. She's always reminded me of her – bold and bright and fearless. And she's always protected me. In many ways, she's my sister, too.

'You couldn't leave me,' she repeats, nodding slowly. 'So you decided to . . . what? Get me killed instead?'

A wave of guilt slams into me. 'That's not going to happen.'

Ingra rolls her eyes. 'Sure, sure. Forgive me if I don't take your word for it. Only, it seems I can trust you about as far as I can throw you.'

The words cut deep. I'm certain they'll scar worse than the whip.

'Tell me,' she continues, her tone part derision, part disgust, 'was he grateful, the emperor, when he heard how you saved his life?'

I say nothing.

Ingra frowns slightly, confused by my silence. Then her brows shoot upward as the realization dawns. 'Of course,' she half whispers. 'You haven't told him. Because telling him would mean telling him *everything*. And you can't do that, can you, Elva?'

I let go of the bars and wrap my arms round my chest.

'I wonder what he'd do to you if he were to find out,' she muses. 'I doubt he'd be so *gentle* then.'

'Ingra –'

But she cuts me off. 'I just hope he was worth it.'

Her voice is drained of vitriol, yet I still flinch. In that moment I see myself through Ingra's eyes. And she's right – I am a traitor. A traitor and a fool. Of all the people I could've fallen in love with, I fell for the son of my oppressors. Heir to a dynasty of blood and gold, ruler of the empire that vanquished my homeland. The very person I ought to hate.

Shame burns my throat and spills down my cheeks. A quiet sob escapes my lips before I can clamp them shut.

Ingra is unmoved. She turns her back on me and sighs softly. 'Oh, run along, Irabella. Save your tears for your sweet Emmeric. I hope for your sake he never discovers what you truly are, or you'll be swinging from the noose right next to mine.'

42

Flint

Time escapes me. Trees knit together overhead, concealing the sky. I have no way of telling day from night. Not a single ray of light – whether sun or moon – can break through the permanent veil of gloom that hangs over the darkest depths of the Greenwood. Neither Sheen nor I have slept. We've just been wandering the forest, searching for a way back to the Bandits' camp, to no avail. My voice is hoarse from calling Spinner's name, though Sheen had pointed out the futility of this plan – even if she could hear us, she would likely assume it was just another of the dryads' tricks. I comfort myself with the knowledge that if I don't manage to set an example to follow, others can at least learn from my mistakes.

'Keep up, would you?' There's a particularly cold bite to Sheen's usual frosty tone.

'I'm trying,' I mutter, blinking hard in an attempt to stave off the exhaustion seeping into my bones.

A will-o'-the-wisp glimmers to life beside me. I aim a kick at it, but it simply vanishes, another appearing in its place several yards ahead. Only a handful remain, flickering lazily among the trees, which have spent the better part of the night twisting out of shape – gnarled branches twining together to block our path, forcing us back in a different direction. I wonder if their present stillness is indication that the nymphs have got fed up with their games, or whether they sleep during the day like other forest-dwelling creatures.

At the mere thought of sleep my limbs seem to turn to liquid and my pace slows to a disjointed stagger.

Sheen, who's striding swiftly through the undergrowth, glances back over his shoulder, his mouth set in a grim line. 'What now?'

'I'm tired.'

'You're always tired. Or hungry. Or bored. Really, it's like travelling with a child.'

I swallow my irritation. 'Maybe if we could just stop and rest for an hour or so –'

'In case you've forgotten, Harglade, you're the reason we're in this mess. The least you can do is help find our way out of it.' Sheen snorts derisively. 'You seriously believed it was your *sister* calling to you? That she just happened to be here, in the Greenwood?'

'I wasn't thinking about that –'

'You weren't thinking at all.'

I glare at him. 'Do you mean to tell me that if someone you loved was calling your name, you could just ignore them?'

'You forget I possess something called rationality,' says Sheen. 'You're too hot-headed for your own good.'

'I'd rather be hot-headed and irrational than a miserable prick like you,' I shoot back. 'I can't imagine you know how to love anyone.'

His eyes spark with rage. 'You don't know anything about me, Harglade.'

'No, you're right, because you don't *tell* me anything. You don't talk to me, and when you do, it's to make me feel like I'm some airhead you can't stand to be around. I wonder, does it take practice, being that sour all the time? Or were you just born that way?'

Sheen's voice goes deathly cold. 'Are you finished?'

But now that I've started, I can't seem to stop. The anger proves energizing. 'You know, I like to look for the best in people. Always have. But when it comes to you I draw a blank. From the moment we met you've treated me with utter contempt. Do you have any idea what that's like? Being forced to spend time with someone who makes it painfully clear how *repellent* they find you? Because it's not exactly an ego boost.' I let out an empty laugh. 'Seriously, Sheen, I don't know what I did to make you hate me so much.'

A deafening silence follows. My heart pounds as I wait for him to respond.

Eventually, quietly, he says, 'I don't hate you.'

I stare at him, bewildered. 'Well, you certainly fooled me.'

Sheen looks as though he's about to say more, then thinks better of it. I watch as he turns on his heel and marches away through the trees.

'No, just stop a second,' I demand, half running to keep up.

He ignores me.

I lunge and grab his shoulder, yanking him round to face me. 'I said, *stop*.'

He shakes me off roughly, as if my touch burns. '*What is it*, Harglade?'

'Why did you even come after me?'

Sheen blinks. 'What?'

'Why did you follow me into a cursed forest crawling with dryads? You knew the voice was a trick – you knew what the consequences might be, and yet you did it anyway.'

He says nothing, his brow furrowed.

'And that's not all,' I continue. 'When Darrow threw his axe you saved my life with that forcefield. Not even Spinner reacted that quickly.'

He avoids my gaze, looking beyond me into the twisting maze of trees.

'You kept tabs on us – Blaze and me – across the Firelands and into the Ridge. Spinner had cause, but you didn't. At first I thought your being here was out of loyalty to her, but if that were the case you wouldn't have abandoned her in order to come after me. And it doesn't explain why –' I hesitate. 'For days after the third trial I was barely conscious. I don't remember much, but I remember you. Sitting at my bedside, day and night.'

Sheen's face is a careful mask, yet a muscle throbs in his jaw.

I swallow. 'You act like you couldn't care less whether I lived or died, and yet you're always *there*. Why?'

There's a long pause. Several will-o'-the-wisps sputter to life amid the shadows, but I keep my gaze fixed on Sheen.

'Because I'm your chaperone,' he says at last.

'Oh, give me a break,' I snarl. 'The Choosing is over. You have no obligation to me any more. I don't understand it. I don't understand *you*. Just tell me *why*.'

Sheen's chest rises and falls rapidly, his hands balled into tight fists. For a moment I wonder if he's going to punch me.

Then he crosses the space between us in two strides, grabs hold of my face –

And kisses me.

My entire body turns rigid with shock. My arms hover uncertainly, whether in defence or surrender, I can't be sure. I'm rooted to the spot, my lips parting instinctively as he crushes his mouth to mine.

He's kissing me. *Sheen* . . . is kissing me.

Am I hallucinating? I must be, because this can't be happening. It's impossible. Nonsensical. Totally, utterly *wrong*.

Only, it doesn't feel wrong. It feels –

I gasp as his tongue glides lightly over mine, sending a shiver from the nape of my neck to the tips of my fingers.

Sheen clutches me tightly, one hand gripping my waist, the other knotted in my hair. Even the slightest graze of his knuckles sets gooseflesh skittering across my skin. His lips are punishingly soft. I've watched them curl in disgust and tug downward with disapproval, but never once did I imagine how they would *feel*, sliding against my own.

I've been kissed countless times before – by kings and courtesans, poets and princesses.

But I've never been kissed like this.

It's rough, unforgiving, so fervent in its intensity I can't tell whether it's fuelled by hatred or desire. Perhaps both.

The line between the two seems to blur more and more with every spine-tingling sweep of his tongue.

Should I pull away? Push him off? Demand an explanation? Because Sheen can't *stand* me. Nothing about this makes sense. Am I really expected to believe that, underneath all the coldness and disdain and downright hostility, he . . . *likes* me?

My limbs are still frozen in astonishment, yet treacherous heat pulses at my core. Am I *enjoying* this? Is he?

Tentatively, I reach out a hand and let it rest upon his shoulder. Then I tilt my head back further, deepening the kiss, tasting him, breathing in the scent of fresh snow.

Call it an experiment.

But if anything, my response seems to wake Sheen from whatever trance he appears to have fallen into. He jerks away, releasing his grip so suddenly I almost topple over. His shirt has ridden up slightly, exposing a sliver of russet skin low on his hips. He's panting, violet eyes wild as he takes a stumbling step backwards. Gone is that marble-smooth composure, the graceful fluidity with which he moves.

As for me, it's not often I'm rendered speechless. I open my mouth to say something, but the words stick in my throat.

The air around us seems to crackle and thrum.

Before I can recover the ability to string a sentence together, Sheen turns and walks away into the gloom, leaving me alone.

43

Blaze

I float through dark nothingness.

I have no way of measuring how long I've spent in this shadowy place, conscious yet unconscious, suspended somewhere between sleep and waking. Occasionally chinks of light appear, as though shining through cracks in a wall. Other times I hear a voice, deep and familiar, murmuring soothing words. The sound sends my heart racing, yet before I can remember why I slip even further into oblivion.

Dreams morph into one another. I see Flint summoning the flames of a thousand candles from their wicks. I see my mother telling me a story while the fire in the hearth brings her tale to life, burning fiercely, twisting into different figures and faces. I see the storm, the rainfall flooding entire provinces, drowning men, women and children. And I see River, spinning Grandmother around the dance floor, pulling her into the statue garden, his hand cupping her face, his gaze soft, almost reverential.

The orphaned son of a Rain Singer and a Mage. A little boy who met a little girl who played with fire, and decided to trust her.

When I wake, I'm surrounded by water.

The small boat sails smoothly along the Creek, the glassy surface a mirror to the sky, which is pale grey and brimming with swollen clouds. No trees line the banks. In fact there is no greenery in sight – just miles and miles of craggy, treacherous-looking gorge.

My eyes widen, confusion tinged by fascination.

Scout is lying curled up at my side, her coppery-red fur the single streak of colour amid this strange rocky wasteland. And there, his eyes fixed on the horizon line, the corded muscles of his weather-beaten forearms pulsing with each dip and drag of the oars, is Fox.

I lurch away from him and hit the back of my head on the prow of the boat, the memory of his hand clamped over my mouth fresh in my mind.

'You,' I spit. 'What did you *do*?'

'Ah, good,' he says, glancing down at me. 'You're awake. Sleep well?'

I stare at him, my head throbbing like a heartbeat. He drugged me. He *kidnapped* me. And he's acting like I just woke up from a nap?

I reach for Silverclaw, but my boot is empty.

'Looking for this?' Fox glances down at his belt where my dagger is sheathed at his hip. 'Since our dear friend the Baron stripped me of Soulkiller, I was in need of a weapon. And given your rather stormy temperament, I thought it prudent to ensure you were unarmed upon coming to. Don't worry,' he adds brightly, as the oars in his hands grow slick with ice, 'you'll get it back. But for now, just sit tight and enjoy the view.'

I watch him chew on a sprig of mint as he rows. He must've abandoned his bloodied shirt in the forest, for he isn't wearing one at all – just a thin dark jacket gaping open, exposing the golden planes of his chest and the Eye of the Past nestled next to his heart.

Fox smirks. 'I didn't mean this view, though I'm flattered nonetheless.'

I grit my teeth and avert my gaze. We're not in the Wildlands any more, clearly. Nor does the terrain match the rocky wasteland or red-sandstone canyons of the Firelands.

'Where are we?' I demand.

'We're in your kingdom, of course,' says Fox with a grin. 'Welcome to the Waterlands.'

My insides curl with disbelief and frustration. 'But . . . but . . . this is where we were headed all along!' I half yell. 'What possible reason did you have for *knocking me out*?'

'I prefer the term *sedated*,' Fox muses. 'And because, Your Majesty, once you've made up your mind, it's exceedingly difficult to dissuade you.' He smiles fondly, as if he finds my stubbornness enchanting. 'You wished to track down the missing Eye and to be reunited with Flint, and you were convinced that the Lagoon would be where you would accomplish both.'

I grip the sides of the boat. 'Where are you taking me?'

'A place far more meaningful than the Court of Waves, where I believe you may find the Eye of the Soul. Though admittedly not your brother.'

'*Where?*'

Fox lowers his voice theatrically, as if this is all some big game. 'Somewhere very few have dared to tread.'

My head is still a little clouded. What is he talking about?

'You've just learned that you're a Demari,' he continues. 'That the blood running through your veins is not only Etheri but Magi too. But what if you ignored the tangled branches of your family tree and asked yourself which part of your ancestry you resonate with most? Who've you always been, since the day you were born?'

I frown. Since the day I was born? Is he referring to the storm? And me, the Storm Weaver? Except that was a name given to me – one I only learned to accept after unleashing my power and winning the Aquatori crown.

I blink. *Aquatori.* Is that what he means? To categorize myself by the element I wield? I am to be the Aquatori Queen, after all. And I do consider myself a Fish, even if one of my gifts will forever set me apart.

Then I freeze as realization trickles through the sedative-induced haze, which slowly begins to evaporate like morning mist.

What makes me Aquatori is the same thing that makes me the Storm Weaver. Because what I am – *who* I am – first and foremost, is . . .

'A Rain Singer,' I breathe.

Fox clicks his tongue. 'Precisely.'

'So where . . .' My mouth tips open as the final piece of the puzzle slots into place. I shake my head. '*No*. You haven't.'

'Yes. I have.'

'You've brought us to *Brava*?'

Fox nods, pleased with himself.

I've thought about this place so often. I've pictured it a thousand times – but as it *was*, back when the Singers ruled this backwater province like a kingdom of their own. Not as it is now: uninhabited, forsaken, its vast emptiness heavy with their absence.

For a moment I'm torn between wonder, grief and rage. Rage triumphs.

'You *idiot*,' I snap. 'This means we're miles from the Lagoon. I might never have been to the Waterlands before, but I can read a map. You've wasted *days* on this fool's errand. What were you thinking? Are you *insane*?'

'That's not very polite.'

I launch myself to my feet, ice crystallizing at my fingertips. 'How could you?' I snarl. 'You lied to me. You drugged me. You brought me here against my will.'

'I did it to help you.'

'*Bullshit*.'

'Believe it or not, Blaze, most of what I've done these past few weeks has been to help you,' Fox shoots back. 'Now quit sulking and listen to me.'

I curl my hands into fists, squeezing so hard the nails bite into my palms. I can't believe I ever kissed this boy. I can't believe I felt –

Well, it doesn't matter what I felt. I won't allow myself to feel it again.

'I hate you,' I mutter.

'No, you don't.'

I almost choke on my exasperation. 'I *do*.'

'No, you don't,' Fox says again. 'You hate the uncertainty. You hate the lack of control. You hate that you can't figure me out, and you hate that you try to.'

I feel like he's just slammed me into a brick wall. I feel furious. I feel naked.

When Fox speaks again, his tone is gentle. 'Look, you're a Rain Singer. You were a Rain Singer when you could only conjure drizzle, and you were a Rain Singer when you almost flooded that amphitheatre during the third trial. It's who you are, deep down to your core. And yes, you're right – the Lagoon is your future. But surely, *surely*, your subconscious would have a stronger connection to your past. To your roots, your origins, your people.'

'But the Rain Singers are *dead*!' My voice echoes through the ravine. 'They're gone. This place is a graveyard. There's nothing left for me here.'

'You're wrong.'

I hesitate, certain I've misheard him. 'What?'

Fox stops rowing and draws the oars into the boat. 'For months I've been using Sifa's Eye to scour for evidence,' he says quietly. 'Signs of life. But there was no way of telling whether the visions I saw were recent or whether I was glimpsing moments that took place a century ago. That's why Scout was so late in joining us. She was here – in Brava.'

I can't tell whether I'm shaking or shivering. 'And what, may I ask, did you use your Magi gift of *animal telepathy* to instruct her to do?'

He shrugs, as if the answer is obvious. 'To find the Singers.'

My heart seems to screech to a halt. 'What're you talking about?'

Fox's gaze locks on mine. 'Blaze,' he says softly. 'The Rain Singers . . . they're *alive*.'

44

Blaze

For a long time I find myself unable to speak.

Fox tells me that the Rain Singers didn't *die out* all those years ago. Etherian soldiers were sent to slaughter them – a massacre orchestrated by none other than Caius Castellion. His grandfather kept it quiet, of course, just as he disguised the true purpose behind the War of the Empires, and spread rumours about the Singers' extinction.

'He even ordered all books detailing their lives to be burned,' Fox says.

'I used to wonder whether it was an attempt to erase them from history,' I murmur. 'So that all memory of them would eventually die, too.'

'Except while many of the Singers were killed in the attack, many survived. For decades they've existed in secret – depleted yet undefeated.'

'And Scout . . . she's really seen them?' I ask hoarsely.

'It's a lot to take in, I know.' Fox scratches the spot between Scout's pointed little ears, and she licks his knee.

I exhale shakily. 'Any more bombshells you want to drop? Can you read *my* mind as well as your pet fox's? Do Flint and I have some secret Magi triplet we don't know about?'

Fox snorts. 'What can I say? I like to keep things interesting.' He nudges the satchel towards me with his foot. 'Have some food.'

I shake my head as I grip the sides of the boat in an attempt to hold it steady, increasingly aware of the churning in my stomach.

Fox lets out a bark of laughter. 'Don't tell me the Queen of the *Water*lands suffers from seasickness.'

'I've never been on a boat before,' I grit out, glowering at him. 'I'm . . . adjusting.'

'Well, as you can see, travelling on horseback wasn't an option.'

I manage a tiny sip from the waterskin. 'What did you do with Cedar?'

'I sold him,' says Fox.

'You *what*?'

'I sold him,' he repeats. 'How else d'you think I managed to pay for this boat?' He holds my horrified gaze, then lets his face dissolve into an amused smile. 'Don't fret. Cedar bolted the moment we were out of sight. He knows where to find me again.'

The corners of my mouth twitch. 'I imagine his new owners weren't very happy.'

'I imagine you're right,' he tells me. 'Especially since I also swiped their papers to get us through the checkpoints. As of now, our names are –' he pulls two identity cards from his pocket – 'Balthasar and Hortensia Whistlethorpe.'

I stare at him. Then, to our mutual surprise, I start to laugh. I decide I must be having some kind of nervous breakdown, yet the longer I laugh, the lighter I feel.

Fox raises an eyebrow. 'You're laughing. Does this mean I'm forgiven?'

'Absolutely not,' I splutter.

'You wish for me to grovel, then,' he says. 'So be it. I throw myself upon your mercy, Your Majesty. I am yours to do with as you please.'

I clamp my mouth shut, shoulders still shaking. 'Just shut up and row.'

The further we travel into Brava, the harder it is to imagine anyone living here. The terrain is jagged and inhospitable, hewn into deep ravines and endless rocky gorges. According to Scout, the Singers dwell by a sacred lake in the very heart of the province.

Gradually the Creek widens, and soon enough a colossal waterfall comes into view.

'This is it,' Fox announces.

I swallow, my anticipation coiling into a spring. 'You'd better be right about this.'

As we approach the waterfall, I raise my hands and make a parting motion, as though drawing a pair of heavy curtains. Moments later a narrow opening appears. Fox rows hard against the pull of the current, and the frothing surf engulfs us in a cloud of spray as we sail right through the waterfall and out the other side.

My eyes widen as I take in the scene beyond. Not a single ripple shatters the glassy surface of the lake, which sits in the shadow of a rocky valley. The cliff face is pockmarked with caves, yet there is no sign of those who dwell in them. There is no sign of life at all. Everything is perfectly still and eerily quiet, as if this whole place really were a giant tomb.

When the water grows shallow, Fox jumps from the boat and heaves it up the pebbled shore, the sound echoing through the valley. Ignoring his proffered hand, I leap out beside him and glance around uncertainly.

Suddenly an arrow whizzes out of nowhere, skimming close to Fox's neck. I gasp, and he shoves me roughly behind a boulder, shielding my body with his own.

'Believe me now?'

My heart hammers against my chest. 'They're alive,' I whisper.

Another arrow ricochets off the rock and lands in the water.

'We have to show them we come in peace,' says Fox. 'We have to yield.'

Before I can utter another word he ducks into the open.

A third arrow is fired in warning. Fox unsheathes my dagger from his belt and tosses it to the ground. 'We mean you no harm.'

Judging by the twin arrows that whistle past his head, each missing by mere inches, the Singers seem unwilling to take his word for it.

Fox's voice fills the valley. 'We came here to find you, not to fight you.'

'And why is that?'

A woman steps out from a nearby cave. With her pale, lined face, long white hair and authoritative tone, I'm guessing she's an Elder.

'Because I have someone with me I believe you'll want to meet.'

A boy about my age appears next, perched on a jutting rock, his bow loaded. 'The girl cowering behind that boulder, you mean?'

Cowering?

I bristle, then step out into view before anyone else can take a shot at my pride.

More Singers emerge from the surrounding caves. They wear simple, modest garments that blend with the environment – washed-out fabric wrapped several times round their bodies and secured with a length of rope, the kind used to make fishing nets.

I let out a shrill squeak of surprise as two giant dragonflies land on either side of me, cobalt-blue and breathtaking. Weak rays of sunlight glint in their large spherical eyes and off their membranous wings, which gleam like shards of stained glass, a mosaic of every colour I've ever seen and more. I may have glimpsed such creatures once before, but that was in a vision. This is very, very real. Their riders slide from the saddles and regard us warily. I back away, awestruck, until I collide with Fox. He holds out an arm to steady me.

'Perhaps they're spies,' calls a young woman brandishing a driftwood spear.

'Spies for whom, exactly?' Fox asks calmly. 'Everyone thinks you're dead.'

'As you shall be soon.'

'Trust me,' Fox says. 'You don't want to kill us.'

'Give us one good reason,' snarls the boy with the bow.

I draw a deep breath, clench my jaw and clamp my trembling hands into fists. Then I stick out my chin and say, 'Because . . . because I'm a Rain Singer.'

Murmurs reverberate through the caves.

'Lies,' the boy scoffs.

The Elder silences him, then peers down at me through ancient, hooded eyes, her expression unreadable. 'If you speak true – if you really are one of us – then prove it.'

I swallow and glance sidelong at Fox before planting my feet. For a long moment nothing happens.

Then – rain.

It's light at first – a smattering of hazy droplets wrinkling the mirror-smooth surface of the lake. The shower soon intensifies, drizzle turning to raindrops in the blink of an eye. The sky darkens ominously, clouds hanging low and pendulous.

Dozens of Singers have emerged into the open, their frosty disbelief melting away.

Rain spatters across the pebbled shore, whipping the lake into frenzied peaks. Even over the rumble of thunder I hear the stunned gasps.

I raise my arms, my every movement fluid and precise, as though I am stitching threads, weaving my storm like a tapestry.

I hear it then – music like no other, a sound of such devastating beauty that I feel an ache in my chest. It's pure, exquisite, ethereal in a way that seems to transcend realms: a symphony of souls that slips seamlessly between life and death and what comes after.

Rain song.

The Singers all climb down the gorge or take to the skies on dragonfly-back, swooping in and out of sight among the swollen clouds before landing smoothly on the rocky shore, their riders leaping off on to rain-slicked pebbles.

The downpour becomes a torrent. Yet I am shielded from it all.

The eye of the storm.

Lightning strikes the lake in a blinding flash of silver just as I cut the final thread and reel my power in.

The storm ebbs, then ceases entirely.

Hundreds of faces are gazing at me with such deep-rooted wonder that I can almost feel it thrumming amid the heavy silence.

Then, one by one, the Singers drop to their knees.

I'm panting, staring uncomprehendingly at the scene unfolding before me.

The Elder walks forward and kisses my hand. 'I never thought I'd live to see this day.'

'Why are they kneeling?' I hiss at Fox. 'What's going on?'

'You shall know when she has come, for the sky will weep tears of rain upon the earth and all the faithful will hear its song,' murmurs the Elder, as if reciting scripture.

I blink at her, bewildered. 'When *who* has come?'

It's the boy with the bow who answers me, his voice hushed, reverent. '*Om Shikara*.'

I turn rigid. I know that name. I know what it means to these people. The Rain Singers do not recognize Etherian customs. They bow before no king or queen, nor do they worship the Water Goddess, Morwenna. There is only one figure they venerate:

Om Shikara.

A myth, a deity, the one true God.

I gaze out at the sea of Singers, my chest rising and falling, half bemused, half horrified. 'Er . . . no. No, I'm not . . . I think there's been some mistake,' I garble, turning to Fox. '*Why are they calling me that?*'

He rakes a hand through his damp hair. 'It appears they think you're a God.'

'But I'm not a God,' I almost wail. 'I'm just –'

'You're not *just* anything,' he corrects.

My voice is pleading. 'Tell them, Fox. Tell them I'm not who they think I am.'

'I'll do no such thing,' he says with a grin. 'I've never been particularly devout, but if anyone could convert me – it's you.'

Then he, too, bends the knee.

I hold his gaze for a long moment. Then my eyes latch on to a figure behind him, walking slowly through the crowd – a man with dark-blue eyes and frost-white hair. He comes to a stop several paces away, one hand resting on the hilt of his silver trident.

'Hello, Blaze,' he says.

45

Blaze

'River,' I whisper.

Since discovering the truth about my family, I haven't had much time to consider all the ways this moment might play out, and now that it's arrived I don't know how to handle it. I don't know how to handle any of this, quite frankly.

First I find out that I'm Demari, then that Fox is too. Then I wake up after being drugged and abducted to be told that the Rain Singers are alive, and not only are they alive but they truly seem to believe that I, of all people, am a *God*.

Power still hums through my veins. My head is spinning and my hands are shaking and all I can hear is this rushing, whistling sound, like when you hold a seashell to your ear.

For a moment I wonder if I'm going to vomit. Wouldn't that be an auspicious way to mark my elevation to divinity?

'I . . .' My voice trails off limply and I begin to sway on my feet.

Fox reaches for me, but it's River who says, 'Shall we go somewhere quiet and talk?'

And I nod, because I seem incapable of doing anything else.

I let River guide me through the kneeling Rain Singers. I try my best to smile, though in truth their apparent deference makes me so deeply uncomfortable I want to curl into a ball. For I have lived my entire life as an outsider, feared and reviled. I am used to people tripping me up or tearing me down, whispering insults in my presence, not prayers.

I glance back to where Fox is standing with the now-weeping Elder, patting her awkwardly on the shoulder. He gives me an encouraging smile coupled with a shrug, as if to say, *Just own it.* So I hold my head up high until the pebbled beach turns to rough-hewn steps cut into the cliff face, which lead into the mouth of a cave.

River is not dressed like the other Singers, but wears the same crisp blue tunic he wore at the Golden Palace. The last time I saw him it was covered in Queen Hydra's blood.

I follow him through a series of interconnecting tunnels until we come to a large chamber lit by a crackling fire. In the centre sits a low stone table set with an array of food – fish mostly, plump spit-roasted birds, a loaf of slightly burnt bread, cheese. I realize suddenly how ravenous I am. My stomach is tight and hollow, but I don't sit down; I just stand stiffly by the fire, letting it thaw the chill that seems to have crept right into my bones.

'They're not dead,' I say weakly.

River shakes his head. 'No.'

'Fox said that . . . that the rumours about the Rain Singers' extinction were fabricated after his grandfather ordered their deaths. That he sent his soldiers to slaughter them.'

'That's true,' says River. 'Caius disliked their autonomy, their refusal to be governed by Etherian laws. He saw them as a threat. But his attempt to eliminate them, though crippling, was unsuccessful. Thousands were lost, but hundreds survived. Now their existence is not only secluded but entirely secret. They've spent decades training to combat any future attacks. You saw how hostile they were when faced with intruders.'

I nod as I recall the arrows firing down from above, the disbelief and distrust on the Singers' faces. At first they were prepared to kill me. Except now . . .

'What just *happened* out there?'

'The Rain Singers have named you Om Shikara.'

'Yes, I'm aware of that. But *why*?'

'You're the most powerful Rain Singer that's ever lived, Blaze.'

'Even more powerful than you?' I challenge.

Recognition flickers in those deep-blue eyes. He knows that I know what he is, but does he know that I know *who* he is?

'Will you take something to eat?' River asks gently.

I pause, reluctant, then edge towards the table. All restraint vanishes the moment the first mouthful passes my lips, and I devour my plate like some starved animal, ignoring the pile of cutlery. I wonder briefly what Grandmother would say if she saw me eating with my hands. The thought fills me with annoyance, because Grandmother has no right to criticize anything I do any more, given that she concealed my true heritage and let me grow up believing I was some kind of freak, just like my mother before me.

River clears his throat. 'Blaze, I wonder, do you know –'

'That you're my real grandfather?' I say bluntly. 'Yes, I do.'

I realize then that I'm not just angry with Grandmother. I'm angry with River, too. Perhaps it's unreasonable and unkind, but reason and kindness feel beyond my reach right now. I'm hanging on to composure by a rapidly fraying thread.

My voice is quiet, biting. 'All this time you knew and you said *nothing*.'

'Your grandmother forbade me ever to speak of it.'

I scoff, rage sparking. 'Why does that not surprise me?'

'She had cause to keep it from you.'

'It was *your* secret, too.'

'It might've been mine to tell, but it was hers to carry.' River speaks calmly, yet there is a diamond-sharp edge to his tone. 'Your grandmother is of noble birth. She was the jewel of one of the most powerful pureblood families in the realm. Those raised that high have so much further to fall. Do you know what would have happened if word had got out? Her reputation destroyed, the honour of House Harglade forever sullied –'

'You speak of honour, but what of honesty?' I snap. 'What of truth?'

'Truth can be dangerous, Blaze. Your grandmother wasn't just protecting herself but her children, and their children. If Analiese was named a bastard, the legitimacy of the entire House could have been called into question.'

I recall what Fox told me about growing up illegitimate: sneered at and disregarded by the court, a child held accountable for the circumstances of his birth – a fate my mother was spared, shielded as she was by Grandmother's deception.

'Did she ever learn who you really were?' I ask quietly.

River's face is pained. 'I don't believe so. My visits stopped before she was old enough to ask questions.'

'Visits?'

'I would often steal into Harglade Hall,' he says. 'Your grandmother would bring Analiese down to the crypt, where I'd be waiting. She was . . . *extraordinary*.' River smiles softly. 'She was still in her swaddling cloth, and yet fire itself was in tune with her every breath. When she smiled, the flames danced; when she cried, they blazed; and when she slept, they burned low, as though waiting for her to wake again. I would sit there for hours, just holding her.' His voice cracks and I look away. 'As she got older, the risks proved too great, so I kept my distance. But when your mother was branded an Heir, I couldn't resist travelling to Cor Caval with the Court of Waves. I had to see her, just as I had to see you and your brothers. It's why I came to your Name Day ball, why I volunteered to be the Aquatori trainer. I wanted to be near you, even if you had no idea who I truly was.'

I think back to what River said that first day of training at the Keep.

We meet at last.

I never understood the depth of those words until now. I swallow hard, my gaze fixed on the fire as more memories descend – River defending me before the other Heirs, telling me of the book about Melding, escorting me safely from the throne room just as my panic was about to spill over, giving me a clue for the first trial, carrying me back to my rooms after the second, sitting in my tent with Grandmother before the third.

He's always been there, through everything. More than a mentor – a protector, a guardian, someone I've trusted, listened to, cared about.

Emotion wells in my eyes and I blink it away.

'Blaze,' River says gently. 'Knowing you has been one of the greatest joys of my life.'

I can feel the anger splintering. River was sworn to secrecy. He vowed never to reveal that he was my grandfather, and yet he found a way to be one without ever breaking his word. And for that, I'm grateful.

'I understand how unsettling this must be,' he continues. 'But please, don't blame your grandmother. All she's done, she did for you.'

'No, all she's done is *lie*.' I hear some of the viciousness creeping back into my tone. 'To my mother, to my brothers, to me. Clearly she didn't trust us to keep our mouths shut.'

'Blaze –'

'Why are you defending her?' I demand.

'Because I love her.'

There is no hesitation. He says it so simply, and yet the words are steeped with such ardent intensity that they seem to scorch the air between us.

'Still?' I ask quietly, as if the answer is not obvious.

River smiles sadly. 'Until the very end.'

I feel a tug beneath my ribcage as my reluctant heart expands. I watch him trace the brandmark on the back of his hand – a gift Grandmother gave to him so that he might have a choice in who he could become. Her fire forged his future, and he wears it proudly.

'I . . . I saw you,' I confess. 'Both of you. I saw the moment you met. I saw you at the Choosing. I saw your lives, intertwined.'

'But how?' River asks in surprise.

'With the Eye of the Past.'

'I thought King Balen –'

'His is a fake. Fox has the real one.'

A corner of River's mouth twitches. 'Smart boy.'

'That's certainly one word for him,' I mutter.

River laughs, and soon enough I find myself telling him everything. About the Eyes, about Elva, about the escape from Fire Mountain, the Ridge tunnels, the Wildlands, what happened in Wellwall. He listens with unwavering patience, letting me talk until my voice is spent. He tells me of unrest among the courts, the break-out from the dungeons, Hal's waning authority, the attempt on his life and the chaos left in its wake.

'And you believe that you'll find Syla's Eye here, in Brava?' River asks.

'Yes, or at least Fox seems to think so. He reckons wherever I sent the Eye will have a stronger connection to my past.'

'And exactly how much do you know of *my* past, Blaze?'

'I know your father was a Rain Singer and your mother was a Mage. That you possess all four water gifts and the ability to turn invisible.' I pause, suddenly curious.

River's eyes sparkle with mirth. One moment he's folding a blue handkerchief, the next he's gone. Yet the handkerchief continues to move, tucking itself in neatly at the corners, smoothed by a pair of unseen hands. I gasp. Seconds later River reappears.

'And the Rain Singers – do they know that you're Demari?' I ask.

River nods. 'I travelled to Brava during the war. I refused to kill my mother's people, so I sought refuge with my father's. I couldn't bear witness to such atrocities any longer.'

A vision slips into my mind – River riding away from the battlefield after begging Grandmother not to fight.

'The Rain Singers could sense I was different,' he continues. 'But they accepted me. Given their history with the Aquatori, they would never seek to persecute another for their gifts. They embraced me, for many among them still remembered my father. He was one of the best dragonfly riders our people have ever known.'

'Your father,' I say. 'Why . . . I mean, *how* did he meet your mother?'

'Even before the Singers' existence was a secret, they lived independently of the rest of Ostacre,' River begins. 'They were self-sufficient in every way. The Creek is home to a plentiful supply of fish. Many birds roost high on the cliffs, and a number of mountain goats provide both meat and milk. A few miles south of here is a small expanse of fertile land used to grow grain and crops. Only supplies like weapons, coal, fabrics, oil and medicine were necessary for survival and yet beyond their reach. After centuries of bad blood, pride prevented them from stooping to trade with the Aquatori. So every year a number of riders were selected to travel to distant lands and source what the Singers needed to sustain themselves here in Brava.'

'And your father was one of them?'

River smiles. 'He was a curious man. Though I suppose he

was just a boy when he left for the Otherlands. He wanted to see more of the world than his own small corner of it – a wanderlust I believe you share.'

I rest my chin on my knees as I think about the years I'd spent dreaming of sailing across the Second Sea, of becoming someone new.

'My father flew to Thresk, and it was there he met my mother,' says River. 'He would return year after year to see her. And then, one day, he never went back to Brava.'

'Thresk,' I say quietly.

The isle from which the Magi sisters hailed. A connection with Syla I never knew existed.

'They built a life together. Only I knew from a very early age that I was not like the other children,' River continues. 'I always felt . . . out of step. When I was ten years old, a pox swept the land. It took my parents, along with countless others.'

'But you survived,' I say.

For a moment River looks regretful, even guilty. 'Thanks to the strength of my blood, I was able to burn off the infection before it managed to spread.'

I swallow as I recall the snake bite and the way my body fought the venom. 'And then you came here, to Ostacre.'

'I conjured the portal accidentally, or perhaps subconsciously. With my parents gone, I knew I couldn't stay in the Otherlands. My gifts made me powerful, but they made me different. I didn't belong to the Magi, yet nor did I belong wholly to the Rain Singers.'

'Both, and therefore neither,' I murmur, remembering his words.

River nods. 'Quite. And so I chose freedom and a fresh

start. I chose to be Aquatori, and to leave my past behind. The rest is history.'

He snaps his fingers and the water in the teapot begins to boil. As he passes me a cup of honeyed tea, all I can think about is Queen Hydra and our lessons. A ragged lump forms in my throat. I clear it sharply, then ask, 'What's your anchor for simmering?'

'Fear,' River says simply.

I nod and tuck the information away for later use. That's when I recall something else – a vision of a little boy sobbing over his parents' bodies, rain streaming down overhead.

'And your rain . . . it's Melded to sadness, to grief, isn't it? Just like mine.'

For a moment I regret asking such a deeply personal question. But River only nods. 'Certain anchors run in families, just like gifts can sometimes skip a generation.'

I think about all those years of drizzle, how I didn't let myself cry after my mother died. I used to want to feel nothing. At least that way I wouldn't feel all the bad things – the heartache and anger, misery and despair. But Melding changed that. My anchors are an outlet, a means of channelling and processing emotion, of turning pain into power.

I take a scalding sip of tea, then murmur, 'Did you really mean what you said? That I'm the most powerful Rain Singer who's ever lived?'

'Blaze, as a Demari, your gifts are exceptional,' says River. 'Mixing blood doesn't dilute magic – it strengthens it. But even among Demari your power is unparalleled. You are a descendant of the Fire Goddess Vesta, hailing from a long line of pureblood Ignitia. You descend from Rain Singers, the strongest of the Aquatori, possessed of the ability to manipulate water in all its forms. And you descend from Magi, magical beings as ancient as the earth itself. You are the sum of your parts and of your past.'

His words send a shiver skittering along the notches of my spine.

'It is because of the strength of your bloodline that you are the Storm Weaver, and it is because you are the Storm Weaver that you have been named Om Shikara.'

'But I'm *not* a God,' I protest. 'I mean, look at me.' I gesture to my tattered clothes and tangled hair.

'They believe you are.'

I try very hard not to roll my eyes. I spent my life being told I was Gods-*damned*, for crying out loud.

'This is ridiculous. My birth killed people, River. Thousands of them.'

'The Singers consider your birth an act of vengeance – drowning the empire that conquered another.'

I clutch my cup so hard my palms blister. 'So I'm . . . what? A punishment?'

'A punishment and a gift.'

'You're telling me that the very reason I'm reviled by some is the same reason I'm revered by others?'

'Om Shikara has long been a myth, a folktale,' he says. '*She who brings destruction, then peace*.'

'Well, I don't believe in any of it,' I reply stubbornly.

'Then don't,' says River calmly. 'But they do. They will pledge allegiance to you and you alone. No Aquatori sovereign has ever had the loyalty of the Rain Singers. And there may come a time when you need them.'

We talk for hours, until the tea has gone cold and the fire is reduced to embers.

'You should rest,' River tells me. 'Quarters have been prepared for you.'

He leads me to a cave that overlooks the pearlescent surface of the lake. In one corner sits an ovular tub carved from pale stone, the steaming water scented with jasmine and citrus. In the centre lies a large bed fashioned from driftwood. Lying atop the sheets is a swathe of fabric the colour of water and sky – the same garment worn by the Singers.

'I'll leave you now,' says River, hovering by the door. 'But we'll talk again tomorrow.'

'Wait!' I call, struck by a sudden thought. 'You said you came to Ostacre by accident. What place were you thinking of when you fell through the portal?'

River's eyes burn as bright as sapphires. 'Something I wished to find. Somewhere I could finally belong. *Home*.' He smiles softly. 'Though as it turned out, mine wasn't a place.'

I feel a twinge of understanding. I see sun-bleached plains, a bubbling hot spring, a little girl in a red dress, extending her hand.

I'm Leda.

The moment the door shuts behind River, a single tear rolls down my cheek. I fall asleep to the sound of rain and awaken to a golden dawn.

46

Flint

Sheen doesn't return.

If it weren't for the erratic throbbing of my heart and my swollen lips, I expect I would've begun to wonder if I'd imagined it – the way he'd held me against his chest and kissed me like he hated me. Hard and rough and mind-bendingly intense.

But there was *want* there, too. A bitter, burning desire. I could taste it.

Is that why he can hardly bear to be around me? Have I truly got under his skin, in more ways than one? Has he really wanted me all this time? I don't know how I'm supposed to feel. Bewildered, of course. Furious that he left me here alone. Because who treats someone like dirt, kisses them like *that*, then pisses off without a word? I should be fantasizing about punching him in the face, not running my fingers through his hair.

When at last it became evident that Sheen was not coming back, I gave myself a little shake, adjusted my bow, and set off in the direction he'd vanished into the gloom.

I'm not sure how long I spent tripping through the undergrowth. Hours? Days? I know it can't have been weeks or else I'd have starved to death. After a while I came across a thin stream. The water was cold and fresh, and I drank my fill, then carefully soaked my burns, dousing my filthy eyepatch and wringing it dry. I stopped to rest a few times, curling up on a carpet of moss and gritting my teeth against the chill. Sleep was elusive, and when it did come, so did the nightmares. Blaze was there, calling out to me. But no matter how hard I tried, I couldn't reach her. Then there was Ember, her face twisted with glee as she prised my fingers one by one from a ledge, laughing as I fell into a lake of fire, as I was roasted on a spit, burned at the stake. I almost bit through my tongue in an effort to stop screaming.

This morning – or perhaps this evening, I can't tell day from night in this Gods-forsaken forest – my pace has slowed to a lurching stagger. I walk hunched over, my body curling round the hollow ache in my stomach, which grows worse with every step I take. As for my eye, the pain is nauseating, and the packet of dillweed Iris gave me is almost empty. All in all, the idea of knocking myself out against a tree is growing increasingly appealing. Maybe I should just ask the dryads to finish me off, since my hopes of making it out of the Greenwood alive are dwindling by the hour. At this rate, a quick death would be mercy. But then what about Blaze? Renly? Grandmother? What about Spinner – did she find her way back to the Bandits' camp? What would she say if she knew what happened between Sheen and me? And is it wrong that I'm thinking about kissing her, if only to compare what it felt like kissing him? Quite possibly, though I doubt I'll ever get the chance.

I kick at a tangled clump of weeds, which instantly transform into pretty pink-and-silver blooms, stretching as tall as my waist. It appears the nymphs have not had their fill of taunting me. I jump at the sight of a beautiful elfin face peering out from among the stems, but it disappears before I can do so much as scowl.

The growling in my stomach reaches a crescendo and I sag against a tree, sliding down to the ground. This seems as good a place as any to curl up and die. Tipping my head back against the trunk, I let my eye fall shut.

When I was young, I used to sneak into the throne room in Fire Mountain. I'd climb the rough-hewn steps to the enormous stone throne, gaze down at the chamber below and imagine the day it would be filled with my adoring subjects. I dreamed of a glittering future, one that had been promised to me from birth. If I'm being entirely honest, I could never quite work out whether being king was something I wanted or something I was conditioned to want. Either way, want it I did. More than anything, in fact. It was my true and unwavering purpose. Yet what purpose do I serve now? I'm not an Heir. I'm not *anything* any more. I'm the runner-up. Once a prodigy, now a punchline.

The idea of *serving* Ember, of being granted a position in *her* court and watching her sit on the throne that should have been mine . . . I can't imagine anything worse. So in some ways, the fact I'm most likely going to die here brings me a modicum of comfort. At least I won't have to live with the shame of losing both my crown and my eye to my cousin for evermore.

I realize I'm shivering and wrap my arms round myself. The cold is biting, but the idea of attempting so much as a spark sends my stomach roiling.

I take a long, deep breath and begin to count – the leaves, the trees, my arrows.

What would Aunt Yvainne say, I wonder, if she knew I could no longer use my gift? I think back to all those years of training, the pains she took to ensure that I was without equal and would one day take her place as the rightful ruler of the Ignitia.

It's what you were made for, she told me after the second trial.

Except I threw it all away on girls and boys and parties. I let her down. I *failed* her. If only I'd applied myself, I might not have underestimated my cousin. But who am I kidding? I was blinded by my own arrogance long before Ember's fireball met its mark.

I drift into a restless sleep, my dreams filled with soft lips and fresh snow.

I'm woken sometime later from a blow to the head.

'Sheen?' I croak, blinking blearily into the shadows.

It's not Sheen. Sitting in my lap is a small dark object, which I realize upon closer inspection is a piece of fruit. Purplish-black in colour, resembling a fig. I glance up at the branches above and see that I am indeed slumped beneath a fruit tree.

Maybe it's not my time to die after all.

I cradle the fruit in my hands and take a large bite, then another, and let out a groan of relief as the hollow hunger eases with every mouthful. I'm too weak to climb, so I shoot down some more, gorging myself. It's only when I lean back against the tree, my palm resting over my stomach, that I recall another of Iris's warnings about the Greenwood.

Never eat anything that grows in there.

Bile rises in my throat. I curse the star I was born under, and then every constellation in the sky. She never told me why, but I get the feeling I'm about to find out.

47

Blaze

I open the door to my quarters before Fox has the chance to knock. His dark hair is tousled from sleep, and his buttonless jacket reveals a sliver of golden torso.

'Oh,' I say, startled. 'It's you.'

'It's me.' He grins as he sinks into a half-bow then lets his gaze rake upward as he straightens, for gone are the blood-stained shirt and tattered trousers – I am dressed like a Rain Singer. The swathe of blue and dove-coloured fabric is modest in length but cinched at the waist with a thin piece of rope which I've tied in a neat bow.

Fox swallows, then extends his arm. Naturally I ignore it, but fall into step beside him as we make our way out of the cave tunnels and down the gorge, with Scout darting ahead.

The Singers beam as I pass. They dip their heads or reach out to clasp my hands, and their excited murmuring bounces off the stone walls.

Om Shikara, Om Shikara, Om Shikara.

I try not to look as mortified as I feel, but smile and nod as graciously as I can.

'First Heir, then Queen, and now God,' says Fox. 'Talk about rising through the ranks.'

A little girl toddles up, holding out a tiny dragonfly whittled from driftwood.

'Thank you,' I tell her, admiring the figurine before slipping it into my pocket alongside Renly's wooden knight. 'It's beautiful.'

The girl ducks her head, pleased, then skips back to her mother.

It isn't long before River appears and carefully extracts us from the throng. We follow him across the pebbled shore and into the mouth of a large cave, from which faint whirring and clicking sounds emerge. Scout's ears prick up in interest.

The Elder, Harana, is already waiting for us. 'I understand that you're looking for something,' she says, plucking a torch from a bracket. 'And that time is of the essence.'

'That's right,' Fox and I answer in unison, then glance at one another, bemused.

'River suggested that having your own mounts would allow you to cover more ground,' Harana continues, holding the torch high to illuminate the cave beyond.

It takes a few seconds for my eyes to adjust. Then I see them. Dragonflies – around two dozen of them, their slender bodies a bright cobalt-blue, their long gossamer wings intricately veined and shimmeringly transparent.

I blink. 'You mean, we'll be . . . *flying*?'

Harana gently nudges two of the dragonflies awake; their

bulbous eyes flicker open and fix on us. 'I assure you, it's perfectly safe.'

'Provided we don't fall to our deaths,' I mutter.

Fox smirks. 'Scared, Storm Weaver?'

Yes.

'No,' I snap, but inch ever so slightly closer to him and lower my voice. 'Can you hear their thoughts?'

He nods.

'And?'

'Oh, they're planning all kinds of tricks. Nose-dives, feinting, loop-the-loops.'

I elbow him in the ribs.

River, who's readying the saddles, watches this exchange with amused curiosity. He finishes adjusting the stirrups, then beckons me forward. I edge towards him nervously and reach out to stroke the dragonfly's ridged flank. Her eyes are as large as my head.

Fox follows suit, approaching his mount slowly. After a silent exchange he bows respectfully and swings up into the saddle.

I let out a squeak of protest as River half lifts me into my own.

I grip the reins tightly. 'Aren't you . . . you know, going to give us some lessons first? You are my trainer, after all.'

'The greatest lessons are taught through experience,' River replies with a smile.

At that moment Harana gives a short, high whistle and the dragonflies take flight, shooting out of the mouth of the cave and soaring up, up, up into the sky.

Fox whoops, jubilant, while the sound of my scream is

snatched by the wind. Fear quickly morphs into adrenaline and, though I'm still clinging on for dear life, my mouth curves into a smile. I've never known anything like it – the rush, the ecstasy. It's as though I left all my burdens in that cave and now I'm unencumbered, weightless. It's almost childlike, this sense of wonder – so palpable it takes on wings of its own.

My mind gradually relaxes into a state of utter calm. Up here, safe in the quiet fortress of the clouds, gazing down upon the patchwork of blue and grey, I feel utterly serene. The Rain Singers have named me Om Shikara, and perhaps this is what it feels like to be a God – untroubled and untouchable, watching the world from above.

I doubt even sailing the Second Sea could feel this *free*.

Fox's dragonfly glides beside mine, their iridescent wings gleaming blue-green in the morning sun. They have four wings apiece – two sets working independently in a blur of motion.

We spend the next several hours in the clouds, occasionally swooping down between the gorges, waiting for a sign, a tug of recognition.

I've almost given up hope by the time something catches my eye. I stab my finger at an expanse of ragged rocky plains nestled between tall peaks. 'What's that?'

'Let's find out,' Fox calls.

Hope sings in my chest as the dragonflies plunge towards the cliffs, hovering a couple of feet above the ground. I hesitate before dismounting. For we appear to be standing in a sea of graves. Thousands of them, the headstones carved from slate.

'What is this place?' I breathe as I slide from my saddle.

Fox traces the names with his finger. 'I think . . . I think these must belong to the Rain Singers who died during my grandfather's attack on Brava.'

My heart sinks, folding in on itself as I gaze out at the sprawling graveyard, a cloud of drizzle forming overhead.

We walk among the headstones, sobered by the scene before us. The euphoria of flying is replaced by a heavy, melancholic silence we both seem reluctant to break. The graves stretch on and on. So many people: mothers and fathers, brothers and sisters, all dead and buried. Entire families gone. Generations wiped out and unavenged.

My stomach twists the way it often does when I think of the storm. I didn't mean to almost drown the empire, the same way Fox didn't mean to cleave the earth in two. Yet Caius Castellion knew exactly what he was doing when he sent his soldiers to slaughter the Rain Singers. This was intentional, premeditated. A cold-blooded massacre.

'How could he do such a thing?' I whisper.

'Because he's despicable,' says Fox simply. 'Deranged. The worst man who's ever lived. Though I doubt you'll find many emperors who aren't morally bankrupt. Power tends to suck the goodness out of you. That's if there was any to begin with.'

'Hal's an emperor,' I argue. 'He would never do anything like this.'

'No,' Fox agrees. 'But then, he never does anything at all.'

I hesitate before asking quietly, 'What really happened? Between the two of you?'

'You know what happened,' says Fox. 'I accidentally killed our father. My brother exiled me. The end.'

I shake my head. 'I know there's more to it than that.'

'Do you now?'

'Yes, I do. Hal hated you long before the Binding Ceremony. Why?'

'Families are complicated, Storm Weaver. You of all people can understand that.'

I hold his gaze defiantly.

Fox sighs, defeated, and my heart thumps in anticipation. 'You really want to know why my brother hates me?' he asks bluntly.

I nod tentatively.

He drags in a deep breath. 'It's because I told him he was going to die.'

I recoil in shock. Of all the things I thought he might say, it isn't that. 'What're you talking about?'

The tendons in his neck are stretched tight.

'Fox?' I urge.

Green eyes shutter at the sound of his name. He runs his tongue over his teeth. Then he says, 'You remember Senna, the fourth Magi sister?'

I nod, bewildered. 'What about her?'

'She didn't have an Eye, nor was it thought that she possessed any magic,' says Fox. 'But after Syla died, Senna's power awoke.'

I blink in surprise. 'But . . . how? If the Magi had been stripped of their gifts, then how could . . .' I inhale sharply as understanding dawns. 'She was Demari,' I say slowly. 'Senna. She was like us, wasn't she?'

Fox dips his chin. 'She had a different father – one with Etherian ancestry.'

I take a moment to process this. Though I still don't see what it's got to do with Hal.

'What . . . what was her gift?'

'She was a Cursemaker,' Fox replies gravely.

'A Cursemaker?' I repeat.

'Yes. And she told my grandfather that he would pay for what he'd done.'

I shiver as Fox brushes his fingers against mine and I hear a voice – it belongs to a girl, yet it burns with age-old fury.

You took my sisters. I will take your sons.

'She cursed the first-born sons of his House,' Fox says quietly. 'Cursed them to slowly sicken and die until the Castellion line died out.'

I lean heavily on a headstone as a memory surfaces – the emperor. I remember thinking he looked so gaunt, so ill. Fox told me he suffered from a *hereditary ailment*. Now I realize this was more or less true, for Emperor Alvar had inherited his father's punishment.

And that means so did . . .

'Hal,' I breathe.

'Hal,' Fox echoes.

A tight knot lodges in my chest.

'As one might imagine, he didn't take it well,' continues Fox. 'At first he thought it a cruel joke. A vicious lie meant to unsettle him. But then . . .'

'I remember,' I whisper. 'He had those dark circles beneath his eyes, as if he hadn't slept in weeks. His hands would shake. I assumed it was all the pressure he was under . . .'

Fox clenches his jaw. 'The curse was designed to make my grandfather suffer. To strike his Heirs down in their prime, forcing him to watch as they withered away to an early grave. For years he searched for a way to break the curse. And suddenly . . . there you were.'

There is a long, loud silence.

'*Me?*' I choke. 'What? *Why?*'

'Think about it,' says Fox. 'Why d'you suppose he told you about the three sisters? What did he want you to find?'

Realization strikes, lightning-bright. '*The Eye*.'

'You were always going to find it, Blaze,' Fox says. 'Seera must've foreseen it, and so did my grandfather. There is nothing – *nothing* – more important to him than his legacy. Haldyn is the last Light Wielder. If he dies, the Maker's gift dies with him. Our grandfather will do anything to stop that from happening.' He laughs hollowly. 'Believe it or not, Caius Castellion is on our side.'

I exhale shakily, stunned. 'What are we going to do?'

'Find the Eye. Break the curse. Kill my uncle.'

I rub my scar, hard enough to bruise the skin. 'Why didn't you tell me before?'

'There was already so much depending on you,' Fox answers quietly. 'How could I tell you that Haldyn's life does too?'

My eyes widen hopefully as I'm hit by a sudden idea. 'What about lachrymortis? There's still one vial left.'

'Lachrymortis is designed to heal wounds, not break curses. It wouldn't work.'

'Then Hal's really . . .' I swallow. 'He's . . .'

'He's dying, Blaze,' Fox says softly. 'My brother is dying.'

48

Elva

The floor of Hal's chambers is strewn with an assortment of open books and rolls of parchment. He's pacing back and forth through the middle of them, clutching a dog-eared scroll, his dark brows pulled together in concentration. Several orbs of golden light drift after him, floating lazily above his head and illuminating his face. His fair skin is moonflower-pale, his under-eyes still blotched with bruise-like shadows. My gaze lands on the empty vials of opium littering the large writing desk. I'm glad it seems to be allowing him to function, but the drug is not curing his pain – only dulling it – and growing reliant on such substances would be unwise.

I pick my way through the sea of papers. Hal's head snaps up as I approach and a distracted smile softens his sharp focus. My heart squeezes tight as I imagine that smile sliding from his face when he hears what I came here to say.

I begin to make a list in my head – a List of Lasts.

The last time he'll ever look at me like that.

The last time he'll pull me close.

The last time he'll kiss me.

His lips are soft and taste of lemons, and I linger longer than I should, savouring him. He draws back first but keeps his fingers twined with mine.

I take a deep breath and jerk my chin towards the floor. 'Is there any particular reason you decided to ransack the library?'

Hal's expression turns intent once more. 'You remember the Eyes you overheard discussing my uncle's plot to steal those prisoners? Well, after Marina got a tad ... *creative* with her persuasion, one of them finally cracked. A single word – that's all he let slip.'

'Which was?'

The orbs above our heads drift closer, as though listening in.

'*Demari*,' Hal says.

'Demari?' I repeat, unfamiliar with the word – in Ostacrian, at least. 'What's that?'

'That's what I'm trying to find out.' He taps the scroll against his leg, then lets it fall into the pile at his feet. 'I'll call a meeting in the observatory tomorrow. Maybe I'll give some of these books to Elaith to sift through. It might help distract her.'

'From what?' I ask, stricken.

Does Hal know about Cole? About what he's doing to her?

'I had word this morning,' Hal says. 'It turns out Blaze isn't in that safe house, and neither is Flint. Their grandmother was using decoys, if you can believe it.'

'Decoys?'

'To cover up the fact the twins are missing. It seems they disappeared shortly after the attack on Fire Mountain.'

Unease coils in my stomach. 'But why?'

'Search me. Anyway, one of the stable boys sold the information to the highest bidder. I imagine half of Ostacre knows by now, including my uncle.'

I swallow. I only hope Blaze knows what she's doing.

Hal's raven eyes meet mine, and whatever he sees there causes him to ask the question I've been dreading. 'What is it?'

My mouth turns very dry.

He reaches out to touch my cheek. I add this to the List of Lasts.

'We need to talk,' I mumble.

'Is this about your sister?' Hal guesses. 'I'm sorry I don't have more to tell you yet. You know I have to be incredibly careful about the Eyes I assign to find her.'

'Yes, I know. That's not –'

'I never thanked you properly for what you managed to uncover at Ember's banquet,' he continues. 'It's because of you that we now know what my uncle was looking for. And once I figure out exactly what these *Demari* are, then we'll know why, too.'

'Hal.' Barely a whisper.

'I knew you'd make an excellent spy. It's a pity there haven't been more feasts or balls since the . . . *incident*, but with any luck there'll be some intel to gather in a few days. Honestly, the people love an execution almost as much as they love a wedding.'

I go rigid.

'Alator said they're anticipating a large turnout,' Hal goes on, oblivious. 'I thought it a little unsavoury, but he assured me that a public spectacle is the most effective way to make an example out of the girl.'

Slowly, I untangle my fingers from his.

Hal lets me go at once. 'Has something happened? Are you all right?'

I answer his questions internally – yes, and no.

'Elva?' His tone is anxious.

The words emerge in a strangled gasp. 'I came to ask you to spare Ingra's life.'

Hal's expression shifts, just as I knew it would. His mouth clamps shut, his jaw locks, and his eyes – slightly glazed, whether from confusion or opium or both – blink twice, then narrow, tightening at the corners.

When he speaks, his voice is low, almost inaudible. 'What?'

'I'm asking you . . . to spare her.'

'You know I can't do that.'

'You can do anything,' I insist. 'You're the *emperor*.'

'Which is precisely why I can't do what you're asking. What sort of message would that send – to my enemies, to my allies, to the entire realm?'

'That you're merciful.'

'No, that I'm *weak*,' Hal corrects. 'Not to mention delusional and spineless. An assassination attempt by a serf? It's made me into a laughing stock.' He sighs. 'Look, I take no pleasure in it. But what she tried to do – that's not something I can just let slide.'

'So don't,' I say quickly. 'Don't pardon her. Say that her execution took place privately to avoid turning her into a martyr. Say that you killed her yourself, if you must. Then we can smuggle her out.'

There's a pause, and for a moment I almost manage to convince myself that he's considering my proposal. Then he takes a step back. 'No.'

'Hal –'

'Elva, listen. I can't . . . I *won't* pardon the person who plotted to kill me. I won't do it.'

'You said you wanted things to change. That you wanted to be better.'

'I did, and I do.'

'Then *prove* it.' I take a step towards him. 'I know you intend to free the serfs. What's one more?'

Hal scrubs a hand over his eyes.

'*Please*,' I urge. 'She's my friend.'

A muscle pulses in his neck. 'I understand, and I'm sorry. I am. But, Elva, she committed *treason*.'

'No, she didn't.'

I barely register the words until they are out of my mouth, suspended in the space between us. Hal stares at me and I feel my face flood with colour.

Don't be a coward, I tell myself.

I clear my throat and stand my ground. 'It's only treason if you're betraying your own country, your own sovereign. Ingra is Veridian. You may be a ruler, but you are not *hers*.'

Hal looks as if I've just reached out and slapped him. For two years there have been certain subjects we've tried to avoid, thinking that never talking about what makes us different – what separates us – would mean we could go on pretending. I was a serf and he was the Crown Prince, but sometimes I could convince myself that it didn't matter. That he was nothing like his family and that I was more than what had happened to me. Because when we're together, the rest of the world seems to fade into the periphery like a bad dream. But it's time to wake up now.

'Do you remember how we met?' I ask. 'You saw me cover for a boy who spilled wine on your cousin. Well, that boy's name is Pip. He's twelve years old, and he's currently locked in a damp, dark hole called the Pit, all because he asked to take Ingra some food.'

Hal's eyes shutter in horror. 'Have you . . . ever been . . .'

'Thrown in the Pit?' I finish. 'Yes. For the crime of speaking in my native tongue.'

He swallows, pained. I'd never really thought about it before – how we fell in love in *his* language.

'I was forced to learn Ostacrian,' I continue. 'Like the rest of the serfs.' My heart pounds. 'Don't you see? You *own* them, Hal. Just as your father owned me. They are your *property*, not your subjects. Is it really any wonder Ingra wanted you dead?'

The silence is heavy, almost suffocating. It squeezes the air from my lungs.

'You say you won't spare her, but I won't let her die,' I whisper. 'Not when I'm the reason she's in that cell in the first place.'

Hal frowns. 'What're you talking about?'

I inhale jaggedly. 'If anyone committed treason, it's me. Because I betrayed my friends – my *people* – to save *your* life.'

Confusion twists his features. 'I don't understand.'

'*I* stopped Ingra.'

'But . . . How?' Hal frowns, trying to make sense of this. 'What about Cole?'

Irritation claws at my insides. 'You really think that arrogant brute was sober enough to notice an assassin all the way up in the gallery, or powerful enough to extinguish every flame in the room? He's not the reason that ballroom went dark, Hal. It . . . it was me.'

'What do you mean, *it was you*?'

I look away. Panic descends, hot and sharp, and I'm overcome with the desire to backtrack, to make an excuse, to turn and run and hide.

I hear my mother's voice in my head.

Don't shut fear out, Elva. Invite it in.

I feel my shadows begin to coil beneath the surface, ready to spring.

Ingra said that Hal would kill me if he discovered the truth about my magic. There's only one way to test that theory. Because how can I continue to give my heart to somebody who might ever wish it to stop beating? How can I expect Hal to love me – *truly* love me – when he cannot fully know me?

The shadow emerges slowly, a ribbon of ink-black smoke twining lovingly round my wrist. Hal staggers backwards, his mouth dropping open just as another shadow materializes and hovers protectively in front of me, curling itself into different shapes.

'I . . . I don't understand,' he breathes.

A third shadow is unleashed, spiralling upward to dance among the glowing golden orbs above our heads.

I meet Hal's gaze, take a deep, trembling breath – and tell him the truth.

49

Elva

Hal is staring at me like he's never seen me before. His eyes are wide, jaw slack, knuckles white, voice a raw, scratching stutter as he says, 'W-what? Why? I mean, *how*?'

I drag in a breath. 'The magic of my ancestors was returned to me.'

Hal gives several small, jerking shakes of his head. 'That's impossible.'

As if in retort, one of my shadows darts forward and curls itself round his ankle. He gasps, shakes it off and backs up until he collides with his bedpost.

I resist the urge to reach for him and force my tone to remain steady. 'That night you found me unconscious in Blaze's chambers . . . I know your memory is hazy because of the sedative, but do you remember the darkness? Do you remember . . . my eyes?'

Hal's chest rises and falls rapidly, and the orbs of light hovering above his head blink frantically in warning. His brows knit together in concentration as he sifts through his recollections, all of them clouded by whatever substance Fox had administered.

Then something shifts and his mouth falls open. 'Your eyes,' he says slowly. 'I had a dream that they glowed in the dark. At least, I *thought* it was a dream.'

I glance down at the floor as I let a strange but familiar tingling take root, similar to the hot prickling of tears. When I look up again, Hal blanches, and I know that my eyes must be glowing as bright and luminous as amber stone.

Then I squeeze them shut, and the feeling fades away.

Hal's horror is almost palpable. For one terrifying moment I wonder if Ingra was right. A beam of light to the chest, a letter opener to the throat – that's all it would take for him to dispose of me. My shadows would try to defend me, but I couldn't fight back. And what's more, would I even try to? Would I let him hurt me just so I wouldn't have to hurt him? As twisted as it sounds, I don't know the answer.

Hal takes a long, shuddering breath, then says, 'Explain.'

I swallow hard. 'When I woke up, your half-brother –'

But Hal cuts me off, his voice burning with rage. 'Fox is a liar. A *murderer.* Whatever he told you –'

I interrupt him back. 'He said it was my body's response to the power . . . awakening. Decades' worth of raw magic entering my system.'

'But *how* can this be?'

I sigh. 'I don't know. He only told me *what* happened, not *why*. It makes no sense to me either.'

Hal looks as if he's vibrating. I decide not to mention the Death Mage in the dungeons just yet, for fear of giving him some kind of heart attack.

'Who. Else. Knows?'

'Blaze,' I say.

He makes an impatient sound. 'Of course she does.'

'Ingra.'

'Brilliant. That's just brilliant. Anyone else?'

I bite down on my lip so hard I taste blood. 'Your grandfather.'

Hal sways on his feet. '*What?*'

More shadows begin to curl from my fingertips. 'He knows. He knows about me, about us, about everything.'

Hal runs a hand through his hair. His previously pristine appearance is no longer at odds with his slightly crazed expression. 'You're . . . you're not safe here,' he mutters.

'He's not going to hurt me.'

'Elva,' Hal grits out, 'don't you understand what my grandfather is capable of? What he'd *do* to you if he –'

'If he was going to do anything, he'd have done it by now. Anyway, it's not my life that concerns him. It's yours.'

'What do you mean?'

'He spoke of . . . of your health.'

Despite the floating orbs of light, Hal's face darkens. There's a long pause, during which his hands begin to tremble. Cursing, he reaches into his pocket and retrieves a vial of opium. He pulls out the stopper, turns away and drains the clear liquid before tossing the tiny glass cylinder on to his desk. I flinch as it lands, clinking sharply against the others.

'Tell me what's wrong with you,' I plead.

'I'm just under a lot of pressure, that's all.'

'Hal –'

'No,' he snaps, his voice almost unrecognizable. 'Not this *again*. I told you already, it's *nothing*.'

'Except it's not.'

I move closer instinctively, my heart splintering as he tenses. With a deep breath, I banish my shadows and lay a hand on his arm.

Hal swallows, but doesn't shake me off. 'Maybe it's for the better,' he murmurs.

'What is?'

But he only clears his throat and takes a step back from me. 'Look, it doesn't matter what my grandfather said. You can't stay here. It's not safe.'

'I'm not leaving,' I insist.

'You have to.'

'I *can't*.'

'Elva, it's too dangerous.'

'For me or for you?' I ask quietly.

A longsword could not cut through the silence that follows.

The shock has drained from Hal's eyes. His mouth is set in a grim, determined line.

'Fine,' I say, my voice cracking. 'I suppose I should be grateful that you haven't tried to kill me yourself.'

The expression that flits across his face is one of pure agony. 'How can you say that?'

'Because I'm a *Mage*, Hal.'

He looks as though he's about to reach for me, but his arm swings back to his side, dangling loosely. My chest aches.

'I knew that telling you would change everything,' I say thickly. 'So end it. Banish me, like you did your brother. But I won't abandon the serfs. I *won't* let Ingra die here.'

'She threatened the crown!' Hal half yells. 'I *have* to make an example out of her.'

'Spoken like a true Castellion.'

Hurt – real, raw hurt – dulls the dark spark of rage kindling in his eyes. A muscle flickers in his jaw. 'If I were to spare your friend, it would be considered a sign of weakness,' he says roughly. 'My position is tenuous enough as it is. I could lose *everything*.'

'But what of Ingra?' I demand. 'What of my people? Everything they have lost? Everything that was *taken* from them? You might not have the power to erase all the terrible things your grandfather did, but you can be *better* than him. You could make a difference, Hal. Not in a year, or two, or ten. *Now*.'

His face twists with pain and indecision, his fingers flexing then curling into fists.

And for a brief moment I recall the boy I first met – the one who begged his brother for a salve to soothe the lash marks on my back, who found a way to give me a golden rose every single day, who introduced himself shyly, as if I had no idea who he was. Who looked at me as though I was his sweet deliverance. His shining salvation.

'*Please*,' I whisper.

Hal reaches out, his thumb tracing my cheekbone. His voice is soft. Tenderly resigned, like gently closing the door to a place you once called home.

'I love you, Elva. I have loved you since the first moment I saw you, and I will love you until my last breath.'

I catch his wrist and feel his pulse race in response.

'My heart is, and always will be, yours. Whether you're a serf, or a spy, or a Mage. Whether you're at my side or lost to me forever.'

His eyes are sombre. I can read the guilt in them, the longing, the finality.

'But my hands are tied,' he says. 'I can't do what you're asking of me. I . . . I'm sorry.'

And with that, my Hal is gone. In his place stands an emperor, Heir to House Castellion, destined to marry a golden-haired princess and uphold the blood-stained legacy of his grandfather. I was a fool for ever daring to hope that he could right the wrongs of the past, that we might have some kind of future together. He was never mine to lose.

I feel something crack deep inside.

A stray shadow emerges from my fingertip and glides gracefully into the air before twining round the golden orbs floating overhead. One by one, they are snuffed out.

I look at Hal and watch as a tear slides slowly down his cheek.

We were always doomed, right from the very beginning. And now, it seems, we've reached the end. He is my greatest love, and my worst regret.

He is a secret I have kept, and will keep, for the rest of my life.

50

Flint

The Greenwood is on fire.

Flames lick up the sides of trees, burning leaves to ash, rising taller and hotter. Smoke spreads through the gloom, forcing itself down my throat. Terror sinks its talons into me, pinning me to the spot. I can't move. I can't breathe.

A ragged scream tears from my mouth as a blazing sapling snaps in two and falls to the ground, igniting the carpet of moss. I screw my good eye shut as I choke and gasp, my heart thundering so hard it could burst through my chest.

The forest is filled with the sound of my nightmares – the snarling, snapping crackle of fire, threatening to devour me.

No.

A surge of adrenaline rips through me, and I realize I don't want to die. I don't want to die like *this*.

I stagger to my feet and collide hard with the thick trunk of the fruit tree. My limbs seem to be working one step faster than my brain, for I'm already climbing, my bow slung across my back, scrabbling desperately for footholds, grabbing branches and heaving myself up. Smoke rises with me, obstructing my vision even further.

When I glance over my shoulder, I see that the forest floor is now entirely ablaze. Panic lodges in my stomach, scratching my insides.

There's no way down, but the trees in the Greenwood grow so closely together they almost intertwine. If I could just manage to swing myself into a neighbouring tree . . .

A blast of heat billows upward, engulfing me, and my foot slips. There's a wrenching in my shoulder socket as my whole body lurches.

I dangle helplessly from a branch, just metres above the inferno.

My palms are slick with sweat. I feel myself sliding.

'Flint.'

Over the roaring flames I hear my name. His voice is a winter's breeze, crisp and inviting, and I hold on to it even as I lose my grip.

I fall down, down, down, and flames swallow me whole.

I'm burning alive, writhing in agony as the flesh melts from my bones. The world is nothing but smoke and suffering. Death will be a kindness. I welcome it with open arms.

'*Flint!*'

Cool hands cup my face.

'Flint, listen to me. Whatever you're seeing, it isn't real. You're hallucinating.'

And suddenly, as quick as a finger-snap, the pain recedes. The blazing heat evaporates, followed by the deafening crackling.

I open my eye to find that the flames are gone, leaving no trace behind. The Greenwood is just as gloomy and empty as ever, except for –

'You,' I breathe.

Sheen scans my face, his throat bobbing anxiously, his white-blonde hair tousled and streaked with dirt. I lie flat on my back, staring up at him, shaken and bewildered.

He breaks his gaze, glancing up at the fruit tree. His tone is teasing, yet for once free of malice. 'Got a little hungry, did we?'

That's when I put it together. 'The fruit,' I croak.

He nods. 'It's hallucinogenic. I've heard it forces those who eat it to relive their greatest fear.' There's a pause. 'You were screaming. What . . . what did you see?'

My mouth goes dry. My skin smarts. Sheen's face blurs out of focus.

Can I really admit the truth? Can I say it out loud? This secret I have kept hidden – a source of shame and torment and self-loathing so visceral it rips me apart from the inside.

My voice is barely a whisper. Even the word burns.

'*Fire.*'

That's when the tremors take hold. My whole body begins to convulse, wracked with awful, jerking shudders. I gasp as my airways constrict.

Panic descends, and there's nothing I can do to stop it.

'Flint?' Sheen looks stricken.

'Can't . . . breathe . . .'

He slides an arm under me and props me up. I'm shaking uncontrollably, fingers bunched in his shirt, knuckles white.

There's a crushing weight pressing on my chest. No matter how hard I try, I can't seem to catch my breath.

'Breathe with me,' Sheen orders, placing one hand on the back of my neck to keep it steady. 'Like this, see?' He inhales, long and deep. 'Now you.'

Rasping, choking sounds escape my lips. 'I . . . can't . . .'

'You can,' he says. 'It's going to be all right. It'll pass. I've got you. Just breathe.'

Tears sting my face. I grit my teeth and do as he says. The tightness eases somewhat, loosening with each jagged drag of air.

I begin to count.

His heartbeats.

The scatter of tiny freckles I've rarely been close enough to notice.

His eyelashes – every single one.

And when I finish counting, I can finally breathe again.

Sheen doesn't let go of me and I don't want him to. My bones feel brittle. My head aches – a dull pounding throb.

His brow is crumpled with concern. 'How long has this been going on?'

'Since the third trial,' I admit, my voice hoarse.

He closes his eyes for a moment. 'Why didn't you tell anyone?'

'How could I?' I demand, suddenly defensive. 'How could I admit that Flint *Flameborn* is terrified of fire?'

Sheen's face softens. It's remarkable how different he looks – how unguarded.

'Only, in the Ridge tunnels . . .' I swallow hard. 'I have no explanation for that explosion, other than it was fuelled by a desperation to save my sister. Except, it felt so . . . Well, that's just it. I didn't *feel* anything. It was almost as if . . .'

'As if?' Sheen prompts.

'As if the fire wasn't mine at all. Of course – it must've been. It's not like Blaze conjured those flames.' I let out a shaky laugh, which soon peters out. 'I . . . I've always been so *self-assured*. But now I don't know who I am any more. I don't even recognize myself.'

A strained silence falls and I instantly regret my words.

Then Sheen says, 'I'm sorry.'

'For what?'

'For what happened to you.'

My throat tightens. Most people assume it's best never to mention it, as if treating me the same as before could somehow counteract the fact that I am forever changed. I didn't know how much I needed to hear those words until he said them.

'Do you want to stand up?' Sheen asks.

I nod and let him pull me to my feet. The transition is dizzying. I stumble, and he catches me by the shoulders.

'I'm fine,' I lie.

Sheen raises an eyebrow. 'No, you're not. But we shouldn't have far to walk.'

My jaw drops. 'You mean . . .'

'When I left, I marked a path. Dryads are pesky things, but they can be outsmarted. By some of us, that is,' he adds wryly. 'The treeline lies a little over a mile from here.'

Relief floods through me. *We did it.* Or rather, *he* did it. I was too busy having an existential crisis and consuming hallucinogenic fruit.

The ghost of a flame skims my skin. I shiver. What might've happened if Sheen hadn't found me? Would I still be trapped in that nightmare, burning to death in my mind?

I open my mouth to thank him, but instead I say, 'You came back.'

He nods, a little stiffly. 'I should never have left.'

I look up into his face, for once not opposed to our notable height difference. In spite of everything, a smile tugs at my lips. 'I didn't hallucinate that kiss too, did I?'

Sheen clears his throat uncomfortably, his expression slightly pained. I'd always assumed it was because he couldn't stand being so close to me. I expect I was right on that count, only not for the reasons I imagined.

He moves to step back, but I don't release my grip, suddenly struck by the strangest feeling that as soon as we leave this place he'll disappear. This version of him, anyway. And I'm not ready to let go just yet. What would he do, I wonder, if I moved closer? What would I do if he leaned into me? I'm loath to admit it, but I'm more than a little intrigued.

Slowly I drop my gaze to his lips.

At that moment there's a crashing sound, followed by a shrill voice. 'Flint! Sheen! Oh, thank the *Gods*.'

We spring apart mere seconds before Spinner bursts through the trees. Her shirt is ripped as though she's caught it on one too many branches, and there are a number of twigs and leaves sticking out of her hair. She makes a sound somewhere between a sob and a laugh and then launches herself into my arms. Before I know it she's kissing me. My hands move instinctively, sliding round her waist, but my eye remains open, fixed on Sheen. I watch his expression shutter, then smooth over, growing distant and unreadable.

And although he doesn't walk away this time, I find myself thinking, *He's gone.*

51

Blaze

Over the past few days I've searched Brava high and low for the missing Eye. I've combed crags and clifftops and rocky mountain passes, shallow pools, hollows and caves. I waited desperately for a sign, a pull, a whisper – anything at all to indicate it was nearby.

Nothing.

I'm beginning to wonder whether the Eye is even here, or, worse, whether it's *anywhere*. During my lessons with Queen Hydra the furthest I ever transported that silver teacup was to the opposite side of the room. Was I a fool to believe I had somehow managed to subconsciously send the talisman halfway across the empire?

Hope is a dangerous thing. It can be misleading – a trick of the light.

Still, I'm not ready to give up. Not yet.

The sky is a painting. Colours bleed into one another, smudging the canvas with shades of lilac and gold. Another day is drawing to a close. The sun refracts through my dragonfly's gossamer wings, turning them from transparent to kaleidoscopic.

I grip the saddle with my knees, my curls streaming out behind me as we plunge down a steep cliffside before gliding through an echoing gorge, our elongated shadow skimming silently across the surface of the Creek far below.

I began my search at dawn. Alone, this time. It was Fox who suggested splitting up. He said we would cover more ground that way. I agreed, especially since with the Eye of the Past round his neck Fox is just as likely to be drawn towards Syla's talisman as I am.

Though part of me wonders whether his sudden desire for solitude has anything to do with our conversation in the graveyard.

I shudder.

Hal, *cursed.*

Hal, *dying.*

Now more than ever before it is imperative I find the Eye. I might be airborne, but the weight of that responsibility seems to pull me down towards the very depths of the earth.

At that moment I feel . . . *something.*

I tense, scarcely daring to believe it, but there it is again – a faint tug on an invisible tether.

My heart leaps.

Tightening my grasp on the reins, I steer my dragonfly over a rocky valley and land smoothly on a jutting ledge. I slide from its back, anticipation pounding in my chest. I'm standing on the verge of a small cliffside pool. The water is perfectly still, glittering emerald in the evening sun. Only that's not what makes my breath catch in my throat.

Fox is facing away from me, elbows propped on the stony edge of the pool as he gazes out at the view beyond. His dark hair glistens, droplets clinging to each curling strand. I can see the muscles cording his golden, scar-flecked arms, rippling up his back. Heat spikes in my stomach when I notice he's wearing nothing but his undershorts.

'Are you going to stand there staring all night, or are you going to come and join me?' Fox asks without turning round.

A blush stains my cheeks, as warm as the setting sun. 'The Eye . . .' I begin.

His tone grows hopeful. 'Have you found it?'

'No, but I felt it. Or at least, I think I did. Whatever it was, it led me here.'

Fox finally turns. I concentrate very hard on not letting my gaze flicker any lower than his chain. He glances down at the pool, then back up at me. 'Here?'

I nod.

'I don't see anything,' he says slowly.

To my disappointment, neither do I. The water is clear enough that I would be able to spot a glimmer of gold at the bottom. Perhaps the Eye is lodged under a rock?

I untie the rope at my waist and let it fall to the ground. 'Turn round,' I order.

Fox's vaguely puzzled expression shifts. He blinks twice, then his lips curve upward.

'And lose the grin,' I add as I kick off my boots beside his own discarded pair. 'I just need to make sure.'

He raises his arms in surrender and swivels back round. My mount makes a low clicking sound, then soars up to join the second dragonfly circling lazily high above.

I keep my eyes fixed on the back of Fox's head as I undress. I decided to dress like the Singers as a mark of respect, but the truth is I feel at home in these garments. The swathe of pearly fabric is a nice change from the scratchy linen of Fox's old shirt, even if it does lack that fresh-mint-and-pine scent I've grown worryingly attached to.

I step out of my clothes and wet my lips nervously as I peer down at the slip beneath, which is as thin and white as paper.

I'm simply looking for the Eye, I tell myself as I perch on the edge of the pool. *As soon as I ascertain it's not here, I'll go.*

The water is silken and cool. I let out a gasp as it licks up my stomach, then fold my arms across my chest as Fox turns to face me. The last dregs of golden sunlight glance across his face, illuminating the angular ridge of his cheekbones and the shadow of his lashes. His green eyes latch on to mine and linger. A muscle pulses in his jaw.

I duck beneath the surface before I can make the mistake of blushing twice.

As expected, the Eye isn't in the pool. Maybe I was mistaken? What if that curious tug I felt was merely a figment of my imagination, brought on by sheer desperation?

I break the surface, breathless and disgruntled, and toss my dripping hair over my shoulder.

Fox is leaning against the edge of the pool. 'It doesn't matter. We'll try again tomorrow.'

'Except it *does* matter, and we don't have an infinite supply of tomorrows,' I snap. 'I'm beginning to wish I'd never found the Eye in the first place. Why did it call to me, anyway? Why did Syla choose *me*? Is it because I'm Demari, like Senna? Or that our ancestors hailed from Thresk? Or because the Singers have decided I'm some divine saviour?'

'Perhaps,' Fox muses. 'If Seera saw you coming a long time ago, maybe Syla felt . . . connected to you in some way.'

'Your grandfather told me I reminded him of her,' I say, unable to suppress a shiver.

'Did he?' Fox winds his gold chain round his forefinger, the Eye of the Past glinting as it catches the light. 'I wish I could speak to him.'

'Why?'

'Because I can't shake the feeling that there's still something I'm missing. One final piece of the puzzle. But since I don't know what I'm looking for, I can't find it.'

'You mean to say there's something you *don't* know about me?'

Fox rolls his eyes. 'How many times do I need to tell you that I'm sorry?'

'Once more wouldn't hurt.'

He lets out a long-suffering sigh. 'Fine. *Sorry.* Better?'

'Not really.'

'Listen, Blaze – I've told you everything I know. That is, everything I know about *you*.'

'Oh, and how many other people's secrets are you carrying around like a bag of coins?' I ask derisively.

He smirks. 'Are you jealous? I'd rather like it if you were.'

'Would you?' I challenge. 'And why is that?'

Fox's amused expression fades. He rakes his fingers through his hair, his gaze charged with such clear-cut sincerity it seems to spear me straight through the chest.

'I think you know why,' he says.

My heart throbs, each beat as loud and furious as a thunderclap.

The shock must be written across my face, because Fox raises an eyebrow ever so slightly and adds, 'Come on, Blaze. It's not like I tried to hide it from you.'

I stare down at the jewel-green water.

It's true that he never attempted to conceal his . . . *interest* in me. From the moment I met him he has sought me out, watched me with an intensity that felt intimate. No, his interest was undeniable. It was the motivation behind it that I questioned.

I used to wonder whether Fox's attentions towards me were his way of provoking his brother. A game, a ruse, but never *real*. Then I considered whether he was simply using me to get to the Eye, but he had every opportunity to take it for himself and didn't.

Yet during all this time spent alone with him in the Wildlands, I found myself wondering whether his feelings might, in fact, be genuine. I've caught him stealing glances at me, his eyes soft and searching, and when he kissed me in the forest I felt the racing of his pulse beneath my palm, the hunger with which he crushed his lips to mine.

He has healed me, comforted me, cared for me, fought for me. But he has also goaded me, tricked me, abducted me, and worst of all – he's *lied* to me.

'I can't trust you,' I mumble.

'Then tell me how I can prove myself,' he counters. 'I already bent the knee. What else do you require? A blood oath? A vow of allegiance?'

'*Honesty*.'

'You want me to be honest?'

I nod, a little warily.

'All right.' Fox draws himself up to full height and moves closer.

I don't back away. I hardly dare breathe.

'If I were being honest I would tell you that I think about you all the time,' he says. 'I'd tell you that I think about your hands and your mouth and that little crease you get between your eyebrows. I'd tell you that I think about the way you say my name and the way you're looking at me right now. And I'd tell you that I reckon you think about *me*, too.'

His words scorch my skin. They burn right through to the bone. I press my lips tight together and say nothing, which is a bit like saying everything.

Fox shrugs a shoulder. 'You said you wanted honesty.'

'This isn't . . . We're not . . .' I trail off weakly, eyes downcast.

He angles his head. 'What're you so afraid of?'

You, I think.

But it's not quite as simple as that. I'm not afraid of Fox the way I used to be, when he was nothing more to me than the Earth Cleaver, the most dangerous boy in all the realm. Now I know that boy. I know his secrets, I've seen his scars, and in spite of everything I care about him. And admitting that feels an awful lot like handing him the power to hurt me. How could I possibly entrust him with my heart when he's proved himself all too capable of dishonesty and deception?

I gaze out over the ledge at the watercolour sky, the peach-pink clouds, the dragonflies circling the summit of the rocky mountain. All in all, a rather fitting setting, since being with Fox has always felt like balancing on the edge of a cliff. Yet these past few weeks something has shifted, and I can't seem to work out whether I fell, or if I jumped.

Either way, I'm falling.

'Blaze,' he says softly.

I swallow, tilting my chin to look at him, then wish I hadn't. I might be unwilling to trust him, but there's no use in denying how devastatingly beautiful he is. So beautiful that sometimes, when he looks at me like that, my traitorous mind wanders to forbidden places.

Slowly, he reaches out a hand, fingers sliding through my damp hair and cupping the nape of my neck. He strokes the pad of his thumb along my jaw and my eyes flutter shut, my lips parting – whether in surprise or invitation, I can't be sure.

I should fight this, I think, as I lean into his touch.

I should push him away, I think, as I pull him closer.

His other hand finds my waist. I can feel every ridge and groove of his chest, smooth and hard like marble. I'm dizzyingly aware of just how little clothing separates our bodies – my slip is indecently translucent, clinging to every inch of me.

He'd let me go if I told him to. I could leave right now if I wanted. But what would be the point? I might be able to run from him, but not from how I feel.

'What've you done to me?' Fox murmurs.

I could ask him the same question. My heart writhes the way it does when I'm faced with danger. How foolish must I be to want something that frightens me?

This is a risk. *He* is a risk.

His gaze drops to my lips. 'Scared, Storm Weaver?'

'*Yes*,' I whisper, and kiss him.

This kiss is gentler than the others – tentative and feather-light, sending sparks skittering across my skin.

Of course I'm scared. I'm scared to trust him. I'm scared this is going to end in regret. But most of all I'm scared of how much I want him.

Because I do. I do want him.

I want him so badly I could die.

Suddenly, without warning, the pool begins to churn, the water turning from cool to warm to piping hot.

I gasp and lurch backwards. At once the temperature drops.

Fox is staring at me, his eyes wide with astonishment. 'Was that . . . Did you just *simmer*?'

I blink, dazed. Of the four water gifts, simmer skimming is the only one I haven't mastered, since I still haven't been able to figure out which emotion it's anchored to.

My mind wanders back to my conversation with River when I asked him what his anchor was for simmering. He said some anchors tend to run in families. And right now, what did Fox just say to me? What did I just admit to feeling?

Scared, Storm Weaver?

Understanding cascades through me. That's it. That must be my anchor – *fear*.

Only, it doesn't quite make sense. I've experienced fear plenty of times before now. What was it about this time that . . .

And then it hits me.

I think about the way Fox makes me feel. The heat that flares in my cheeks, burns at my core, builds to a blazing inferno with every kiss, every touch.

I was wrong. It's not fear itself but a fear *of* something. Something feverish and devouring that I've tried to suppress. Something that, just now, I finally surrendered to.

My anchor to simmering – it's *desire*.

The corners of Fox's mouth quirk upward. Either he's figured it out too, or he's simply amused by the mortified expression etching itself on to my face. But before I have time to decide which it is, his arms encircle me, lifting me up against his chest so that our eyes are level, his glinting wickedly, mine painfully unguarded. So much for burying my feelings.

The next kiss steals the air from my lungs. I feel a tightening in my lower stomach as I wrap my legs round Fox's waist, his tongue dancing against my own. To my horror, the water responds with enthusiasm, roiling and frothing as it begins to heat. I curse, and Fox chuckles softly as he trails his mouth down my throat before nipping at my shoulder.

His lips are just brushing mine once more when I draw back with a chastising look. 'Lie to me again, and I'll make you wish you'd never been born.'

He scoffs as he hooks a stray curl behind my ear. 'That's not very inventive.'

'Fine,' I say, lacing my fingers round his neck. 'Lie to me again, and I'll drown you in this pool. Or feed you to my dragonfly. Or strangle you with the cord of my dress.'

Fox's answering smirk makes my toes curl. 'That's more like it.'

52

Elva

The day of Ingra's execution is ushered in by a molten dawn studded with sea-foam clouds.

I watch from a window as the gallows is erected, a noose dangling from the wooden crossbeam. Already the sprawling courtyard is filling with people.

Hal and I haven't seen each other since *that* night. Or rather, he hasn't seen me. I've been keeping tabs on his movements, his deteriorating health, and the resultant increase in his opium intake. I followed him when he stormed into the library to confront his grandfather, only to find a few orbs of light floating lazily above an empty armchair. I watched his usually pristinely kept chambers grow more and more disorderly, littered with rolls of parchment, glass vials and golden roses. It appears his research has extended beyond the Demari, for I've also found him poring over books detailing the War of the Empires and the Magi, desperately seeking answers – about my magic, about *me*.

It seems neither of us has been able to let go. Yet what I'm about to do today will undoubtedly cut the last thread binding us together. Because I'm not going to let my friend die up there, choking and helpless, at the hands of her oppressors.

I suspect the only reason Hal has allowed me to remain here, roaming the palace freely, is that he believes me too much of a coward to strike back. I used to think myself a coward. A trembling, fragile little flower, afraid of her own shadow. Then I became a Mage, and there was a sweet kind of irony to my gifts. If fear is a response to danger, then my magic is a response to fear. And I'm not shutting it out any more. I'm inviting it in. Because without fear, there cannot be courage.

I think of protecting Pip from the lash, of risking exposure to save Hal, and of what I'm about to do today. For what is courage if not the impulse to stand up for another?

I've realized that I *can* be brave.

I *am* brave.

When the horns are blown, I join the throngs of spectators moving towards the gold-paved courtyard. I walk with my head down until I'm just a stone's throw from the scaffold. There's no breeze, and yet the noose seems to quiver, as if in anticipation.

A sudden hush falls, blanketing the excited chatter.

My skin grows cold as two members of the Imperial Guard drag Ingra into view. Her hair is matted with grime, her skin ashen and covered in bruises. Bile rises in my throat as I notice more of her fingers are bent and swollen. Yet her face remains a perfect mask of defiance – jaw rigid, chin in the air, wearing an expression that is almost bored. The knights fasten the rope round her neck and leave her standing upon a wide trapdoor.

I try to regulate my breathing, but the attempt proves futile, for someone is already climbing the steps to the scaffold.

Hal is dressed in a pale-gold doublet with solid-gold epaulettes, a grand ceremonial cloak fastened at his shoulders. His father's, I think. The finery only exacerbates his gaunt appearance. I'm close enough to see his hands trembling as they reach up to straighten his crown. Not the Imperial Crown, since the coronation still hasn't taken place, but his old simple circlet, gleaming against his neatly combed dark hair.

He doesn't so much as glance at Ingra as he moves to the centre of the scaffold. I can barely hear his greeting over the thundering of my heart.

After the answering applause has died down, Hal clears his throat. 'We are gathered here today to witness justice prevail,' he begins. 'The prisoner you see before you conspired to commit a heinous crime.'

Ingra stares off into the distance. Her eyes are clouded, far away. I wonder where she's gone. Veridia, I bet – racing across the sand dunes towards a glittering mirage.

'She sought to take a life,' Hal continues. 'My life. And, in so doing, she threatened the future of House Castellion.'

The crowd respond angrily, shaking their heads.

'A serf who plotted to kill an emperor.' Hal holds out his arms. 'Who here would see her punished? Who here demands her death in retribution for seeking mine?'

Cheers ripple through the throng, with many of the Etheri stamping their feet. Ingra's gaze flickers to Hal, and for a moment hatred like I've never seen flashes across her deliberately blank expression. She's bleeding; the rope binding her wrists has chafed her skin raw. I press my lips tight together, balling my hands into fists before my shadows can spring free.

Not yet.

I grit my teeth and concentrate.

Before, I chose Hal. Now I choose Ingra. I choose my friend, my people and myself. I know what I have to do. I doubt I'll make it out alive, but I will not falter. I will use my shadows to block out the sun. I will condemn Ostacre to darkness if I must.

'As emperor, I will not stand for acts of violence. I will not tolerate brutality or intimidation.'

Ingra's lips begin to move, as though she's muttering a prayer. The crowd lean forward eagerly, craning their necks to watch hers snap.

'I wish for my rule to be the dawn of a new era, one free from tyranny and oppression. And that is why . . .' Hal finally turns to face Ingra and takes a long, deep breath. 'That is why I have decided to spare her.'

The sound that escapes my lips is drowned by the collective gasp of the spectators.

Then uproar.

All around me the air grows thick with voices, exclamations and yells of protest. Up on the scaffold Ingra's mouth has fallen open in shock.

Hal raises a hand for silence. 'This girl is not our enemy. Yet *we* are hers. We, the sons and daughters of those who conquered her homeland and persecuted her people.'

'It was the Magi who started the war!' someone yells.

'A war that ended more than fifty years ago,' Hal answers. 'In any case, there are no Magi left.' I watch the almost imperceptible bob of his throat as he swallows the lie.

More clamour ensues. It takes a blinding beam of light from Hal to subdue the crowd.

He raises his voice for all to hear. 'Why should we continue to punish one another for the enmity of our ancestors? We cannot change the past, but we can change the future.'

My heart beats violently, flipping over and over inside my chest. The man standing next to me spits furiously on to the ground.

'I once thought mercy to be a sign of weakness, but now I see it is a mark of strength,' Hal continues. 'My reign will not be one of terror, but of peace. We will be better. *I* will be better. This is my promise to you. All of you.'

It takes everything I have not to sink to the ground, but Hal isn't finished.

'This brings me to my final decree.' He draws himself up to full height. 'I, Haldyn Castellion, rightful Emperor of Ostacre, do hereby declare that from this day forth, all slavery is prohibited . . . and all serfs shall go free.'

53

Blaze

Today's theory is that the Eye is sitting at the bottom of the lake.

The idea came to me last night, after a conversation with River, who told me that the Singers believe it to be sacred – oaths are sworn on it, newborns bathed in it, and it's traditional for newlyweds to drink from it as a means of sanctifying their marriage.

We've exhausted countless other theories. I have a good feeling about this one.

'You've *got* to be kidding,' Fox says incredulously.

I turn from my heaped pile of rocks. 'What?'

'What d'you mean, *what*? You're about to jump into a lake with stones in your pockets. Shouldn't I be a little concerned?'

I roll my eyes as I bunch up the sleeves of his old shirt. My Rain Singer garb didn't seem best suited to swimming – or, in this case, diving.

'It's the fastest way down,' I explain. 'I'm being practical.'

'No, you're being an idiot,' he says. 'What if something goes wrong?'

I sigh impatiently, even as the corners of my mouth quirk upward. 'Then I'll carve a few waves, and you have my permission to come and rescue me. Happy?'

Fox pushes off from a boulder and sidles over to me. I straighten up, regarding him warily, as if half expecting him to toss me over his shoulder and carry me away from the water's edge. He looks tempted. Instead, he reaches out and runs a finger along the ridge of my jawline. I flush, mindful of the dozen or so Singers scattered across the rocky shore – sharpening weapons, washing clothes, and stealing less-than-subtle glances in our direction.

Fox smirks. 'I'm surprised I haven't already had an arrow through the back for the impertinence of laying a hand on their beloved Om Shikara.'

He speaks in jest, but there's truth to his words. The Singers are adoring, if a little too reverential, and fiercely protective. For the first time in my life I feel as though I belong. When I'm not searching for the Eye, I'm learning the histories from Harana, or taking long walks across the mountains with River. Fox and I have barely had a moment alone since that night in the cliffside pool. My heart thuds at the memory, then again as he impulsively trails his finger over my throat, along my collarbone and down the side of my arm, calling to mind the ghost of other, more toe-curling touches, each as gentle as it was explorative. His hands were clever, mine a little clumsy, though he didn't seem to notice.

I look up at him, his face framed by the veil of clouds hovering overhead. There's a glint in his green eyes that tells me he's remembering too.

My breath hitches as he shamelessly tugs me closer.

I arch a brow. 'Are you finished?'

'Not quite,' he says. At that moment the vine curling slowly round his forearm shoots out from beneath his sleeve and wraps itself round my ankle.

I yelp indignantly and a few of the Singers jump to their feet in alarm.

'What d'you think you're doing?' I demand, tugging at the thick green rope binding us together.

'I'm making sure you don't drown. Consider it a pre-emptive rescue measure.'

I scowl darkly and reach for Silverclaw to cut myself free, but Fox has already swiped it from my belt.

'Unbelievable,' I mutter.

He grins as I stalk back to my rock pile, the vine lengthening with every step. It's perfectly ridiculous, of course. He's being unnecessarily overprotective. I purse my lips disapprovingly in an effort not to smile while I toss stones into the boat.

'Want me to teach you how to row?' Fox asks as I push it out into the shallows and clamber inside.

'No, thank you,' I say waspishly.

Honestly, how hard can it be?

The answer is *very*.

I zigzag haphazardly through the water, almost dropping an oar.

'Don't think about me too much while you're in there,'

Fox calls from the shore. 'You don't want to be responsible for boiling all the fish.'

'Piss *off*,' I yell back, which only makes him laugh.

The vine extends between us, curled securely round his wrist.

It takes an age, but eventually I reach what I judge to be the deepest point of the lake, midway between the rocky beach and the waterfall.

I rest my oars across the bench and pick up two large stones.

If I found the Eye at the bottom of the training pool, then why shouldn't I find it again at the bottom of a holy lake? It's worth a try, and at this point I'll try anything. I think of Senna, cursing the Castellion line as an act of vengeance. I think of Hal, weakening by the day just like his father before him, condemned to die for a crime he did not commit.

The boat rocks as I get unsteadily to my feet. I glance back to where Fox is teaching a little girl how to skim. He's already lost one sibling. I won't let him lose another.

I steel myself, then jump, silver bubbles streaming from my nose as I sink fast towards the lakebed, which is carpeted in a fine layer of silt and festooned with tall, translucent plants billowing eerily in the sway of a phantom current.

Squinting blearily, I turn my head from side to side, searching for a glimmer of gold, a sharp tug on an invisible thread, anything to indicate that the Eye is here. I crawl on my belly, feeling my way through the underwater wilderness until my lungs scream for air.

Frustrated, I release my grip on the stones and swim back towards the surface, grasping the side of the boat and grabbing two more from the pile.

As I sink downward a second time, my mind paints a picture of the future I cannot let come to pass – a future in which Hal will be dead, the Maker's gift along with him, leaving King Balen to claim the Imperial throne, flanked by his army of Demari. How many are able to wield the gifts of both Etheri and Magi, like River, or are possessed of one gift that's no match for their pureblooded counterparts, like me? How many agreed – or were coerced – to fight for the Ventalla King? And how long before he makes his next move?

Suddenly, without warning, the lake seems to quiver.

It happens again: a violent, pulsing tremor that wracks my body. I drop the stones and kick my legs hard until I break the surface.

Something is wrong, yet nothing looks amiss. Then I catch sight of Fox. He's standing stock-still, staring straight at me, one hand clasped round the Eye of the Past. I watch, stricken, as his gaze snaps upward. My stomach lurches and I tilt my face towards the pale sky.

A single feather floats lazily down towards the lake, cradled by a gentle breeze. Sleek and black, flecked with grey, it lands not two feet from where I cling to the boat.

Whispers ricochet across the surface of the water, two words repeated over and over in warning.

He's coming.

He's coming.

He's coming.

That's when the wind begins to blow.

I barely have time to gasp before the vine round my ankle grows taut, then reels me into shore at lightning speed. A pair of arms scoops me out of the shallows.

Fox's voice is rough with dread. 'He knows. He knows about the decoys. He knows we're here.'

At that moment the first Ventalla soldier materializes out of thin air.

He is followed by another, then another, each flitting into view, their armour gleaming like freshly sharpened knives. My eyes widen with terror as somewhere high in the cliffs a bell begins to clang. The sound of it reverberates through my very bones.

The Singers leap into action. After herding the children to safety, they sprint for their weapons, launch themselves on to the backs of dragonflies and soar high into the sky as the squalls howl through the valley. Rain splatters down in great sheets. Arrows begin to fall.

Fox severs the vine, grabs my hand and pulls me towards the caves. Scout darts ahead of us – a streak of copper through the chaos.

Seconds later, we're surrounded. The soldiers' faces twist with frenzied glee as they circle us. Fox doesn't hesitate. The first vine winds itself round a man's legs, swiping his feet out from under him, while a second snakes round his comrade's neck, growing tighter and tighter. A third vine seizes another soldier and flings her so hard into the cliff face that her spine snaps on impact. I follow suit. One soldier lets out a strangled cry as his rain-slicked armour begins to freeze, while another screams in agony as her own begins to heat, burning her skin. A blast of wind nearly knocks me off my feet, but Fox catches hold of me before I'm thrown backwards, then sends a rock the size of his fist straight at the culprit's face.

The rain grows heavier still. The Singers fight using their weapons as well as their water gifts. Dragonflies swoop overhead, their riders armed with bows and spears and fishing nets designed to ensnare. A stray arrow flies straight at Fox, but my reflexes are faster than they once were, and I send a shard of ice up to meet it, knocking it off course.

My ears fill with a cacophony of screams and voices and clashing metal until, all of a sudden, a silken whisper slips through the din.

Hello, little dove.

Everything inside me seems to buckle. I whip my head round, straining my eyes against the torrent. He is standing right in the thick of the battle, yet is somehow set apart, as though protected by an invisible forcefield or a dense current of air.

King Balen.

His lips curl into an amused smile, as if to say, *Surprise.*

Beside me, Fox goes very still. I reach for him, and as soon as my hand makes contact with his skin I see Emperor Alvar lying in a pool of blood. I see the Council dropping like flies round the golden dais. And I see his sister suffocating to death.

The expression on Fox's face chills me to the bone. It is fury untethered, bloodlust unquenched. Vengeance itself.

King Balen inclines his head. '*What are you waiting for, nephew? Come and play.*'

Fox doesn't hesitate before taking off through the fray, cutting down any who stand in his way, carving a path through the throng of bodies. I follow him, encasing a group of Ventalla soldiers inside a frozen wave and shattering it to pieces.

We're barely ten yards from King Balen when two figures emerge from behind him. One man, one woman, both dressed in long silvery cloaks. They wear no armour, carry no weapons, yet all around us the air seems to thrum with powerful, dangerous magic.

Demari.

The man brandishes something in his palm. It looks like fire, only it's as black as coal. I stare at it uncomprehendingly until the pieces fall into place, and I realize what it must be.

Shadow flame.

A gift born from inheriting the magic of both an Ignitia Etheri and an Obsidian Mage. Victims would burn blind, engulfed in blazing darkness.

King Balen's smile widens as his second companion steps forward. I watch in horror as the woman flicks her wrist in the direction of a fallen soldier. The dead man shudders, then lurches to his feet like a puppet on strings, his face a vacant mask.

Death Magi possess the ability to communicate with the departed. Yet this Demari can *resurrect* them.

Fear fills me to the brim. Fox's eyes are wide, yet he shows no sign of retreating.

King Balen's gaze lands on the talisman round his neck. He chuckles. 'Oh, nephew. Always one step ahead. And yet think of all you have lost, how much more you have to lose.'

I move closer to Fox, ice crystallizing at my fingertips.

'My spies tell me poor Haldyn is almost at death's door,' his uncle continues. 'How sad that you won't be able to save him, just like you weren't able to save your sweet sister.'

With a howl of rage Fox lunges. But the female Demari snaps her fingers and the dead soldier raises a sword to block his advance.

King Balen's raven eyes gleam as he turns his attention to me. 'I do so enjoy a family reunion, don't you, little dove? Tell me, how are those dear brothers of yours?'

I clench my hands into fists and the sky rumbles with thunder.

Seconds later a shimmering wall of ice erupts from the ground, separating us from King Balen. Then River is there, trident in hand.

'You have to get out of here,' he shouts over the tumult.

'We're not going anywhere!' I yell back, as the airborne Singers rain arrows down on the other side of the barrier.

Fox snarls as he attempts to hack his way through the sheet of ice.

'This is what Balen wants,' says River. 'He's protected. You're outnumbered.'

Far above, a Singer is thrown from her mount by a powerful gust of wind.

'You can't win, Blaze. Not like this.'

I hear the truth in his words. King Balen planned this attack. It is to his advantage. He has the element of surprise on his side, as well as two lethal Demari and an army that is not only disposable but also able to be resurrected. I watch as the fallen Singer's body is dashed against the cliffs, and I know the same can't be said for our own.

My resolve begins to weaken, and I catch hold of Fox's arm. 'River's right.'

He shakes me off and slams the butt of Silverclaw into the frozen barrier. I try again, my eyes burning into his.

'Fox,' I say. '*Please.*'

He looks down at me, his face twisted with anguish. Scout appears at his ankles. He picks her up, and I watch him unravel.

River doesn't waste a second before drawing a portal – a watery sphere glistening blue and boundless at our feet.

I shake my head in alarm. 'But – but Queen Hydra only taught me how to transport objects. I'll get us both killed!'

'No, you won't,' River tells me. 'Concentrate. Clear your mind. Think only of your destination and will yourself to go there with every fibre of your being.'

I swallow.

'*Now*,' River demands.

At that moment the wall of ice finally shatters. King Balen's furious scream barely has time to pierce my ears before the portal swallows us whole.

54
Blaze

Fox and I tumble together through the churning portal, swept along by a powerful current. I can't breathe, or hear, or speak, but I can see. Images appear like mirages through the crystal-clear water – the steel gates of Harglade Hall, the rocky cove beneath Bartell Manor, the sprawling front steps of the Golden Palace. Yet none of them is the place I'm searching for.

The thing is, I've never actually *been* to my destination. I've only glimpsed it once, fleetingly. But it lodged itself in my mind, a safe haven coloured by memory. *Fox's* memory.

I hold on tightly to his hand, scared that if I relax my grip even a little I'll lose him. That's if I don't manage to drown him first.

Focus, I tell myself.

My chest grows taut and my lungs scream for air. As I screw my eyes shut, I think of nothing else but where I wish to be, and will myself to go there with everything that I am.

It works.

The portal spits us out on to solid ground, then melts away into the earth. I'm flung on to my stomach, still clutching Fox, who lies sprawled on his back, Scout tucked under his arm, blinking up at the canopy of trees above. Chinks of honeyed sunlight filter through the branches, which sway gently in the warm breeze, casting dancing shadows across the forest floor. The air smells of damp wood and pine needles. Birdsong mingles with the babbling of running water and the soft tinkling of windchimes.

'You did it,' Fox says.

'I did,' I agree, a little breathlessly.

'Are you all right?'

'I'm fine,' I assure him, letting go of his hand and flexing my fingers. 'But *what* just happened? *How* did King Balen discover where we were?'

'One of the stable boys, by the looks of it. He knew you and Flint were missing and sold the information to a Ventalla spy. It seems all loyalty can be bought.'

I grimace. Grandmother's never had much tolerance for turncoats. I imagine Caleb is now nothing but bones and ash.

'Once my uncle realized you weren't at a safe house, he began his search. Perhaps he knows of your connection to River. Perhaps, like me, he believed you may have sent the Eye to Brava. Regardless, he figured it out. Then he used the wind to spy for him.'

A shiver runs through me.

As Fox props himself up on his elbows, his gaze lands on something behind me. He stiffens in surprise. Slowly, I turn round.

I know at once that we are in Thorndale, a small, forest-wrapped province near the Wildlands border. I know this because there, nestled in the clearing with a moss-covered thatched roof and a faded buttercup-yellow front door, stands the Calloways' cottage.

I feel myself clam up, suddenly nervous as I try to predict his reaction. Maybe this wasn't such a good idea after all. This place is personal to Fox. It might dig up old grief he'd prefer to keep buried.

I'm so busy worrying that I may have overstepped the mark that I don't notice the horse emerging from the trees, his dark mane still threaded with small braids.

'Cedar!' I exclaim. 'What – I mean, how –'

'I told you he knew where to find me again,' says Fox.

'So you were always planning on coming here?'

'Yes, I was.' His voice is light with incredulity. 'But I didn't realize *you* were.'

'Are you angry?' I ask tentatively, as Scout fixes her beady green-gold eyes on me.

'I . . .' For once Fox seems at a loss for words. 'I presumed you were taking us to the Lagoon,' he says at last.

I shake my head. 'Too obvious. Besides, you were right about there being a stronger connection to the past. You took me to Brava, so I . . . I thought I would bring you here.'

Fox gets to his feet. He rests his forehead briefly against Cedar's, then walks away from me towards the cottage.

I curse myself. This was a mistake, a foolish misjudgement. If only I'd –

'Aren't you coming?' Fox calls over his shoulder.

I exhale deeply, relieved.

As I get closer, it becomes clear the cottage is no longer lived in. The varnished wood is chipped and crawling with rampant ivy, and the door is so swollen with damp that Fox is forced to slide Silverclaw along the length of the frame just to prise it open. Several of the crooked windows are cracked, spidery veins spreading out across the panes, which are made from stained glass in varying shades of green, violet and sunset orange. A narrow path snakes through the overgrown grass towards a tiny outhouse I recognize as Fox's grandmother's workshop. Behind it, dangling from the overhanging branch of a tall oak on the bank of the Creek, are two rope swings. My heart twists painfully.

Fox shoulders open the door and the wood groans in protest. 'After you.'

The inside of the cottage is as quaint as the outside, filled to bursting with handmade furniture. The largest room contains a soot-blackened hearth, mismatched lace curtains and an oblong table surrounded by spindle-legged chairs. Slightly threadbare rugs carpet the wooden floor, and the whitewashed walls are lined with dozens of willow-patterned plates, each covered in a thin layer of chalky dust. The sun pours through the stained glass, bathing everything in kaleidoscopic light.

Fox is looking at me, his expression guarded, as though half expecting me to sneer.

'It's beautiful,' I tell him earnestly. 'Your grandfather really built all this?'

He nods and sets my dagger down on the table as Scout curls up in an armchair. A column of horizontal markings has been scored into the wall beside it. Above the notches someone has etched two names – Fox and Freya.

Fox sees me looking. 'She never grew much taller than that.'

'I'm sorry,' I whisper.

'My sister was happy here. She adored our grandparents. We both did.'

'They must've loved you very much,' I say quietly. 'When did they . . .'

'My grandmother died a year or so after Freya, and our grandfather a few months later.' A ghost of a smile flickers across Fox's face. 'They could never bear to be apart.'

I'm overcome by a desperate wave of sadness as I think of my own grandparents, bound by fate, divided by circumstance, forced to love one another from afar.

'River,' I say suddenly. 'Is he –'

'Hold on.' Fox reaches up to grasp the Eye round his neck, his forehead lined with concentration. After a minute or two he seems to resurface. 'He's alive. It looks like the Ventalla retreated soon after we disappeared through the portal.'

I sag into a chair, rendered boneless with relief. 'And the rest of the Singers?'

Fox grimaces, and my stomach churns. 'Most survived.'

Most, but not all. I ball my shaking hands into fists.

He sinks into the seat opposite, his face twisted in anguish and dappled with soft violet light. 'I should've stayed. I should've killed my uncle while I had the chance.'

'And what if you'd got yourself killed?' I challenge. 'You saw what those Demari were capable of.' I shudder as I recall the shadow flame burning ink-black, the dead soldier moving disjointedly like a puppet on strings.

'If I'd managed to take Balen down with me, it would've been worth it.'

'Not to me,' I tell him.

His eyes are so full of warmth that when he glances away I realize how cold I am.

'Here.' Fox fetches a slightly moth-eaten blanket and drapes it round my shoulders, then sets to work building a fire in the hearth.

My thoughts return to River and the Rain Singers. If only I'd achieved what I set out to, I could have prevented this. How many were lost in the attack? How many more deaths am I responsible for? And what if it's all been for nothing?

Suddenly I feel impossibly, painfully small. *Useless*. Tears prickle, threatening to spill. A cloud of drizzle forms over my head, hazy droplets kissing my cheeks.

Fox turns instinctively, sets aside a box of matches and kneels in front of my chair.

My breathing is jagged. 'This is all my fault.'

'No, it's not,' he says, blotting a tear with the pad of his thumb.

'I'm the one who threw the Eye into Queen Hydra's portal. I'm the one who failed to find it again. Because I can't, all right? I can't find it. I can't stop your uncle. I can't save Hal.'

Fox arches a brow. 'Really, Storm Weaver, this defeatist attitude doesn't suit you. The Blaze I know wouldn't give up so easily.'

I sniff pathetically. 'And who is she exactly, this *Blaze you know*?'

'Let's see now,' he muses. 'She's stubborn. Impatient. Impulsive. Occasionally hot-tempered. Incredibly cutting when she wants to be.'

I open my mouth in indignation, but Fox isn't finished.

'She's also resilient. Thoughtful. Kind. Clever – almost frighteningly so. She's brave too, not to mention distractingly beautiful. And I'd follow her anywhere.'

My heart stutters. 'You would?'

'I would do anything for her,' Fox says simply. He smiles a little, then amends, 'I would do anything for you.'

For you.

The words stick out to me, hovering in the space between us – the echo of a memory. Two ordinary words, and yet, when put together, undeniably familiar.

'It was you,' I whisper. 'The gifts in my chambers, the notes. It was you all along.'

Drizzle clings to Fox's eyelashes. He makes no attempt to deny it.

I sit there, stunned. Even when I began to doubt they were from Hal, I never considered the alternative. Or perhaps I just hadn't wanted to.

I make a list in my head, sorting through each gift in turn, starting with the curved leather sheath designed to fit a dagger. *My* dagger. I think back to that conversation in the library when Fox confessed to watching my first trial. He'd been impressed with the way I had fought that beast, wielding the pain it inflicted like a weapon. Even before Silverclaw was used to kill the Council, I'd considered it a twisted souvenir from the arena. But now I realize it's so much more than that. It's a reminder of what it felt like to *win*. To triumph over hatred. To defy the odds, even when they were stacked against me.

Then there was the mask – the one I wore to the masquerade ball, the one I was wearing in the maze. It can't have been a coincidence that it was shaped like a dragonfly – the symbol of the Rain Singers. Such a thoughtful gift. Meaningful. Intimate.

And finally, the burn ointment. I remember how instantaneous it was: the cool salve leaching the heat from my skin, expertly crafted by Healer's hands. Except . . .

'Hold on,' I say, puzzled. 'You weren't there that day in the Keep. You weren't even in Ostacre. How could you have sent the ointment?'

Fox smiles mysteriously. 'Oh, I have my ways.'

'But how did you even know I'd been burned?' I press.

He reaches up and gently taps the talisman round his neck.

'I see.' I try to sound accusatory. 'Perhaps I'll overlook the spying, just this once.'

Amusement glints in those green eyes, then it's gone, replaced by something earnest, almost soul-baring in its sincerity.

'I meant it when I said it was unintentional, Blaze,' he says. 'I didn't search for you. You were always just . . . there. Like you were waiting for me.'

He brushes his fingertips lightly against mine, and an image floods my mind – a girl in a blue dress, sitting by the window in Harglade Hall, a book propped open in her lap.

Me.

'At first all I got were glimpses,' Fox continues. 'Fragments of you. I've spent years trying to piece them together.' He smiles again, softly. 'You see, I've known you for a long time. It just took a little longer for us to meet.'

My heart threatens to burst out of my ribcage.

No one has ever looked at me the way he is.

At that moment wildflowers begin to sprout up from the cracks between the floorboards, filling the room with purplish, thimble-shaped blooms – foxgloves.

I don't remember leaning forward, but all of a sudden his lips are on mine and I melt into him. The kiss is slow. Tender and deep. It seems to say everything I can't.

Fox pulls me off my chair and into his lap. He doesn't let go, not even as he lights the fire.

It's not long before weariness comes to claim me. I fall asleep on his shoulder in front of the crackling hearth, and as I drift off into dreams, I find myself thinking that never have I been held more gently than by the same pair of hands that tore apart the world.

55

Flint

We lie side by side in the long grass, watching each other.

Moonlight gleams silver in Sheen's pale hair. Slowly I trace the shadows along his cheekbones, his jawline, the curve of his lips, biting back a gasp as he catches my finger lightly between his teeth. He angles his head a fraction, releasing me, violet eyes appraising.

It's hard to believe there was ever a time I found his beauty vexing – when the mere sight of him didn't jolt through me like a lightning bolt to the chest.

My next thought vanishes before it has the chance to form as Sheen lets his hand trail lazily across my ribs, over my waist and down my thigh, tightening his grip on my leg before hitching it up and round his hip in one smooth movement. He rolls on to his back, pulling me on top of him. His body is solid beneath me. It's a bit like sitting astride a marble statue, but I'm not complaining. I run my palms across the hardened contours of his chest, breathe in the scent of fresh snow and cold, cloudless nights, then give in to temptation. His mouth is just as soft as I remember, sliding slick and hot against mine.

I sit bolt upright, the dream disintegrating. Blood pounds in my ears, keeping time with the thudding of my heart. There's a chill in the air, but my skin feels flushed, as though I'm running a temperature. I swallow hard, swivelling my head round cautiously.

Sheen is asleep several yards away at the edge of the wind shield, his breathing rhythmic, one arm resting behind his head. I feel my stomach lurch as I look at him – a dizzying swoop followed by a gentle fluttering sensation.

Are those . . . *butterflies*?

I shudder, horrified. What is *wrong* with me?

Scrubbing a hand over the peppering of stubble on my jaw, I glance down to where Spinner is sleeping soundly, her body angled towards mine. Seized by a jarring pang of guilt, I get to my feet and head for the Creek. Perhaps a morning swim will help to drown the swarm of accursed butterflies. Or at the very least it'll help to cool me down.

The meadow is as pretty as a painting, carpeted by blades of grass as tall and thick as barley. I strip down to my undershorts and dive into the water, slipping my eyepatch over my head and letting the bracing cold leach the heat from my burns. Then I tip backwards and float, staring up at the brightening sky.

Since making it out of the Greenwood, Sheen has barely said one word to me. He's reserved, distant. At this rate I'd take his scorn over his silence. I've never craved someone's attention so much in all my life. Last night I even offered to refill his waterskin, just so that our fingers might brush when I handed it over.

I scoff. This is stupid. Pathetic. Yet I can't seem to stop thinking about him, and not just in *that* way, but the way he held me as the world felt like it was closing in.

I used to think that being intimate with someone meant letting them put their hands on me. But this was something else entirely, raw and vulnerable. And that's not to say that I don't want his hands on me – I do. Much to my surprise and more than I care to admit.

I'm startled by a sudden tinkling laugh, followed by a splash. I quickly pull my eyepatch back on before Spinner resurfaces, smiling as she winds her arms round my neck.

'Found you,' she says, then presses her lips to mine.

Kissing Spinner is very different from kissing Sheen. I tried not to compare the two, I really did, but it was impossible to keep my mind from wandering. With Spinner, it's sweet. Light and playful and easy. There's desire there, though not the kind that seems to twist my insides out of shape. I find her attractive. Endearing. She makes me happy. But Sheen . . .

'Flint?'

I blink. 'Sorry. Still half-asleep.'

'Sheen sent me to fetch you.'

At the sound of his name, the butterflies perform a series of loop-the-loops. I cross my arms over my chest, trying to squash them flat. 'And why am I being summoned?'

'He thinks we should set off. Best not keep him waiting. You know what he's like.'

Another lurch. 'Uptight, bad-tempered and miserable, you mean?'

She punches me on the arm. 'Be nice.'

'Why do you put up with him, anyway?' I ask, more out of curiosity than anything. 'I've never understood your friendship. I mean, he barely speaks to you.'

She rubs absent-mindedly at the layer of panstick covering her tattoos, smearing it across her cheek. 'He wasn't always this way.'

My heart gives a disjointed thud. 'What d'you mean?'

Spinner bites her lip, her expression regretful. 'It's not mine to share.'

'Oh, come on. Out with it.'

'Flint –'

'Tell me,' I order.

She looks surprised. 'Well, all right. But this stays between us.'

I mime sealing my lips shut and tossing the key over my shoulder. But any remnants of bravado are swept downstream as Spinner's next words sink in.

'Sheen's entire family died from the sweating sickness.'

I open my mouth, then close it again.

'He was only fourteen, and he was all alone. I think . . .' She hesitates. 'I think it haunts him – being the one left behind.'

The butterflies scatter, their wings withering like dead flower petals as they fall through the pit in my stomach.

Words dart across my mind, cutting and cruel.

I can't imagine you know how to love anyone.

I'd spoken in anger, furious that he'd berated me for following Blaze's voice deep into the Greenwood, unable to understand his cold criticism, his grim rationality. But I do now. It's little wonder he never fell for the dryads' tricks. There's nobody left to call his name.

All those times I mocked him for being so sour, so morose, when all the while . . .

You don't know anything about me, Harglade.

The guilt is almost painful. A well-deserved gut-punch.

'He and I, we grew up together,' Spinner says. 'He might not always be a barrel of laughs, but he's as loyal as they come. You'll see.'

I just nod, not trusting myself to speak.

By mid-afternoon the sprawling meadow has melted away and we find ourselves back among the trees. Thankfully, this forest is nothing like the Greenwood. Birds trill merrily, perched on ivy-wrapped branches, and the sun shines brightly through the canopy above.

Only a couple of provinces lie between us and the Waterlands border. If all goes to plan, and we manage to stow ourselves away on a boat or barge, we should reach the Lagoon in a matter of days. My heart leaps at the thought of being reunited with my sister. I picture her there, waiting for me, the Eye round her neck.

As usual, Sheen is striding a little way ahead, his shoulder blades protruding through the thin material of his shirt.

I'm still reeling from what I learned of his family. I want to tell him how sorry I am, how much I wish I could take back every taunting gibe I threw his way.

The silence stretching between us is so heavy it's almost tangible. Even Spinner's constant stream of chatter can't make a dent in it. I wonder if Sheen keeping his distance has more to do with not wanting to hurt his friend than a desire to stay away from me.

At that moment, he slows to a stop, scanning our surroundings.

'What is it?' Spinner calls, looping an arm through mine.

His voice is quiet, but I detect a slight hint of triumph in it. 'We're here.'

'And where is *here*, exactly?' I say, frowning. 'Because I know my sight's impaired and all, but this doesn't exactly look like the Aquatori Court to me.'

Spinner only grins, her eyes alight with excitement.

'What're you up to?' I ask. 'What's going on?'

They share a look. Neither answers me. I'm about to demand an explanation when something coppery-red and bushy-tailed streaks through the undergrowth, darting right between my legs. I yelp in surprise and jump about a foot in the air.

'This way,' says Sheen, pointing through a copse of trees.

Warily, I edge closer. In the clearing beyond sits a small thatched cottage. The crooked windows are made from stained glass and the chimney belches smoke. There's a tiny outhouse, and a swing set dangling from a tree branch overhanging the Creek, where a handsome chestnut-coloured horse is munching his way through a patch of reeds.

'What is this place?' I murmur, utterly bewildered.

Suddenly the door to the cottage opens. Instinct kicks in – I grab my bow, nock an arrow and take aim.

The figure that emerges is also armed, slowly unsheathing the silver dagger at her hip. Her olive skin is sun-kissed and unruly curls spill in a dark curtain down her back. She's a little thinner than I remember, but there's a newfound strength to her too – a confidence that wasn't there before. I see it in the way she carries herself.

As I lower my bow, my knees almost give out beneath me. My voice is hoarse with shock and relief. '*Blaze.*'

56

Blaze

'Flint?!'

Silverclaw falls from my hand, landing with a soft thud at my feet. Then I'm running, launching myself into my brother's arms, unable to tell whether I'm laughing or sobbing.

He catches me with a whoop and whirls me round. 'There you are!'

'Here I am,' I mumble into his chest.

Waves rear and arc along the surface of the Creek, splashing on to the bank and soaking a disgruntled Cedar.

Flint chuckles. 'Miss me?'

I draw back slightly, drinking him in, hardly daring to believe my eyes. 'What're you doing here? How did you find me? Where have you –' That's when I catch sight of his companions. '*Spinner?*' I splutter. 'Sheen?'

My chaperone blows me a kiss while Sheen nods stiffly.

I blink several times, bemused. Suddenly Flint turns rigid – his gaze is fixed on something over my shoulder. Or rather – someone.

I twist round to see Fox up in the tree, lounging across a thick branch.

'Right on time,' he calls.

Flint's grip tightens protectively, but I wriggle free. 'It's all right. I can explain.'

Fox gets to his feet, walks the length of the branch, then drops lightly to the ground, landing at my side. Flint's expression darkens. I brace myself as a beaming Spinner comes bounding over. Only it's not me she throws her arms round. Sheen is close on her heels, looking happier than I've ever seen him.

I don't realize my mouth is hanging open until I see my expression mirrored in Flint's, both of us speechless as we take in the scene.

Fox, Spinner and Sheen are locked in an embrace, all three of them grinning, talking fast and excitedly over one another.

I stare at them, unable to process what I'm seeing, then turn back to my brother, who tilts his head to the side, mystified.

After a minute or so, Flint clears his throat loudly and they break apart. Fox's gaze finds mine. He smiles a little sheepishly as he claps Sheen on the back.

'Care to explain?' I prompt.

'Ah,' he says. 'Did I forget to mention that these two are my best friends?'

'*What?*' Flint and I chorus.

Spinner giggles.

My mind races. 'But . . . but I've never even seen the three of you have so much as a conversation before.' Then my eyes widen as I remember an altercation at the Golden Palace during Marina's party. 'You forced Spinner to give up her seat,' I accuse Fox. 'You were awful to her, and she called you an arrogant bastard.'

The two of them burst out laughing.

'I meant it, too,' says Spinner, elbowing him playfully in the ribs.

Fox smirks. 'Think about it, Blaze. Think about who I am. The reputation I have. Now tell me, why would I want people knowing where my true loyalties lie?'

I frown as I dissect his words. He's got a point, I suppose. Information like this could be used against him – or them. Not to mention that it would undermine the role he plays. All things considered, concealing his friendships actually makes a lot of sense.

'How did *this* –' Flint gestures in their general direction – 'even happen?'

'Well,' Spinner begins, 'when I was young, I was selected by Empress Goneril to be playmates with Hal.'

'He told me about that,' I interject. 'He said that his friends were chosen for him – junior Eyes sent to report back on his every move.'

Spinner makes a face. 'As the Castellion Heir, the prince was kept under close observation, even at so early an age,' she admits. 'Only as time went on I found I preferred his surly younger brother's company.' Her grimace melts swiftly back into a grin.

'And you?' Flint says, jerking his chin at Sheen. 'How did you begin rubbing shoulders with the Earth Cleaver?'

Sheen makes no attempt to answer. I might be imagining it, but I could swear my brother's face seems to flush under the gaze of those eerie violet eyes.

I break the silence, glaring at Fox. 'I'm guessing it's no coincidence that they were assigned to be our chaperones?'

'None whatsoever,' Fox agrees, entirely unabashed.

I fold my arms. 'That's no better than the empress asking Spinner to spy on Hal.'

Spinner looks wounded. 'I wasn't spying on you, Blaze. It wasn't like that.'

'My grandmother always told me never to trust an Eye,' I say accusatorily.

'I just made sure you were safe, that's all,' she wheedles. 'And I may have *occasionally* passed along some gifts.' She winks conspiratorially at Fox.

I shake my head, incredulous, recalling her words as I admired the dragonfly mask.

He must like you very much, you know.

Only now I realize she wasn't referring to Hal. I try to scowl.

Flint is staring blankly at us all, as though we are speaking a different language. 'Will someone *please* tell me what's going on?'

'Well,' Flint says several hours later as I finish telling him everything. 'That was unexpected.'

We're sitting on a grassy verge, dangling our feet in the Creek.

'It's a lot to take in, I know.'

My brother huffs a laugh. 'I'll say. In truth, I'm not sure what I'm more shocked about – the fact that we're part Mage or the reason why.' He tuts, grinning. '*Grandmother.* My, my. Talk about skeletons in the closet. How deliciously scandalous.'

I roll my eyes.

'It certainly explains a great deal,' Flint continues. '*You*, mainly. What am I supposed to call you now, by the way? Om Shikara? Your Holiness? Goddess Divine?'

'Oh, shut up,' I say, splashing him.

'Fine.' He shakes his wet hair like a dog. 'Then I'll settle for *Your Majesty*.'

I feel my expression twist into a grimace. I haven't given the whole becoming-queen business a huge amount of thought of late. I've felt so far removed from that future out here, and after weeks of freedom the image of the crown I hold in my head is beginning more and more to resemble that of an ornate golden shackle.

'Enough about me,' I say quickly. 'What happened to *you*? Spinner mentioned something about bandits and *forest nymphs*?'

'Put it this way,' Flint says. 'I for one will be glad to return to civilization. Won't you?'

I glance down at my feet, letting a curtain of hair swing between us. 'Mmm,' I mumble unconvincingly.

'Come on, don't tell me you *enjoy* it out here in the wilderness,' Flint scoffs.

'It's not so bad.'

That's something of an understatement. These last few days with Fox have been so ... *peaceful*. As though this place were a fortress and the rest of the world can't touch us. Here, we don't have to be the Storm Weaver and the Earth Cleaver. We can just be Blaze and Fox. We can just *be*.

Flint pulls my hair back to look at me. 'This is about *him*, isn't it?'

'Who?' I ask, feigning innocence.

'Who d'you think?' He purses his lips. 'It's not escaped my notice that the two of you seem to have got rather *cosy* of late.'

'I don't know what you're talking about.'

'Oh, give it up, Blaze. I can see the way you look at each other.'

'What's your problem?' I demand.

'My *problem* is him.'

I grind my teeth together. This is another inevitable downside of returning to reality. I knew that my ... *involvement* with Fox was hardly going to be cause for celebration, but I thought I could prolong the onslaught of objections for at least a while longer.

'He's not good for you,' Flint continues. 'He's not *good*, full stop.'

'You don't even know him.'

'I know enough. In any case, isn't he supposed to be in exile for – oh yes, that was it – *murdering the Council*?'

'I already told you – what happened at the Binding Ceremony was an accident.'

'Regardless, Hal's hardly going to welcome him back with open arms.'

'So I'll talk to him, tell him the truth.'

'And if he doesn't listen?'

'Then we'll *show* him the truth using the Eye of the Past.'

'Well, good luck with that. Though speaking of Eyes,' Flint says, momentarily sidetracked, 'do you still think you'll find Syla's at the Lagoon?'

I gnaw on my lip in consideration. I meant what I said to Fox, about losing hope of finding the Eye altogether. Yet my reasons for believing it could be at the Aquatori Court still stand – it was Queen Hydra's home and it's going to be mine.

For a moment all I can think about is that the queen never got to go home again.

As I will away the drizzle that threatens to fall overhead, I lean back on my elbows and watch the last rays of sunlight glinting off the water.

Queen Hydra told me once that she felt ill at ease in Cor Caval because her connection to the Lagoon was severed. She was referring to the Creek, which flows through every province except the Imperial, given that it was cut off from the rest of Ostacre when Fox cleaved the empire in two. It's little wonder the Queen of the Waters disliked spending any great length of time in what was effectively a landlocked island.

I remember her words that day.

Know, child, that when you leave this place, no matter what path you might tread, so long as you follow the Creek, you will always find what you are looking for.

My body turns stock-still.

'Blaze?' Flint prods my shoulder. 'What is it?'

The blood has rushed to my face. I sit bolt upright. It was Queen Hydra herself who taught me about portals and their different uses.

One can use a portal to send an object to a destination, but also have it remain there, hidden . . . accessible only to someone who knows exactly where to find it.

This whole time I've been so busy picturing the Eye at the Lagoon, or nestled at the top of a cliff in Brava, that I never once stopped to consider that it wasn't somewhere to be discovered, but revealed. That it wasn't lost, but *concealed*.

I think back to the night I was called to the Keep. The Eye hadn't just been sitting at the bottom of the training pool for decades. I found it because I *knew* it was there – the same way I pulled that silver teacup from the portal in Queen Hydra's chambers.

At the Binding Ceremony I was trying to get the Eye away from King Balen. But what better way to ensure that it would be out of his reach than to hide it somewhere only *I* could find it?

Queen Hydra's words have a way of sticking in my head, influencing my subconscious.

So long as you follow the Creek, you will always find what you are looking for.

The Creek has kept us company this past while, guiding us from province to province. I have drunk from it, *bathed* in it. But I never, not for one moment, imagined that it was the key to everything – the destination, the hiding place, the *portal.*

'*No*,' I breathe.

'What're you doing?' Flint asks as I roll up my sleeve and plunge my arm into the water.

I say nothing, not trusting myself to speak. The Creek is cool and clear, and I let it claim me, praying that I'm right.

Please. *Please.*

I squeeze my eyes tight shut, concentrating hard, heart hammering against my chest. A painful moment drags by, all hope hanging precariously in the balance.

Then I see it – a glint of gold beneath the surface. Seconds later my fingers close round something small and cold and unequivocally familiar.

Slowly, I retrieve my hand.

There, sitting on my palm, is the Eye of the Soul.

57

Elva

I lean against Hal's shoulder, gazing out at the swathes of black-silk night. The moon is just a crooked sliver, but the stars burn bright, speckling the sky like tiny white diamonds.

These past few days have been a period of adjustment – for everybody.

The liberation of the serfs marks an end to over fifty years of tyranny, but for many it marks the beginning of a new age, a new life. The hours following Hal's decree passed in a dreamlike blur. Ingra was released and taken to the medical wing while the rest – some smiling, some weeping, some in a state of dazed disbelief – began streaming out of the palace gates, piling into carts and carriages headed for the fleet of Ostacrian ships waiting in the ports, each vessel crammed with chests of Castellion gold and bound for the Otherlands.

Pip hugged me tightly before joining Seth, Ty, Clover and the others. I watched them go, these people I grew up with – all of us casualties of a war we did not start, guilty of no crime beyond being descended from the vanquished.

So much was stolen from us. Our stories will forever stain the pages of history books. We are human scars, and we may never truly heal. Yet while what Hal has done cannot erase the past, it does promise a future. One that is free from oppression and bloodshed. One that is *free*.

I thought about Obsidia and felt a wistful pang of longing for the life I left behind. I know that one day I will return. But when I do, it'll be with my sister.

Though it seems I was not the only one who chose to remain. For some, Ostacre is all they've ever known. *Home* is not always a straightforward concept. But now they are free to choose. Several have even decided to stay on at the palace, where they'll be paid fairly for their service as attendants.

As for Matron, she was discovered filthy and hysterical at the bottom of the Pit.

Mostly, opinions are divided. After the initial shock wore off, many courtiers felt that Hal's display of mercy was a testament to his character. Others, including his advisers, were furious, saying it only served to demonstrate poor leadership and lack of judgement. Word continues to spread like wildfire. Soon the whole of Ostacre will have heard the news, and no doubt King Balen will use it to kindle yet more support. To my surprise, Caius Castellion has made no attempt at retaliation. The last I saw of him was in the library, sitting in his armchair, muttering feverishly to himself.

Hal believes it's only a matter of time until King Merrick of Thaven withdraws his daughter's hand, since freeing the serfs was certainly not what the king had in mind when he demanded Hal prove he was the more powerful ally. It seems that liberating my homeland may just be the downfall of his own. Politically, Hal is balancing on a knife edge. He *needs* Thaven's support in order to defeat his uncle. That, or a miracle.

Hal slips his hand into mine – his skin is as cool as the night air caressing my face. Part of the observatory's domed roof has been slid open to reveal the constellations.

I shouldn't be glad that his betrothal may soon be brought to an end, not when it could destabilize his position even further. And yet, however selfish it might be, I cannot bear to think of him with another now that he has never felt more like *mine*.

I watch a wisp of shadow curl fluidly round one of the floating orbs of light in front of us, then dart away again before it can extinguish it. Hal smiles a little. He's still coming to terms with my being a Mage, just as I'm slowly getting used to this strange new dynamic between us. Strange, but good. Because now I am free to love him without guilt or fear. Now, there are no more secrets between us.

Well – apart from one.

Slowly I reach out to trace the dark circles under Hal's eyes, my fingers grazing the small criss-cross scar on his cheek. 'Tell me what's wrong with you.'

His jaw tightens and one of the glowing orbs flickers slightly. 'Elva, I . . .'

'Tell me,' I whisper again. 'Please.'

He gets to his feet and moves to the edge of the observatory, as if he can outrun the question. I follow him.

We stand there, face-to-face.

There's a long, tense, painful pause. Then Hal seems to deflate, as though someone has stuck a pin in his chest.

'It's not what you think,' he begins. 'I'm not suffering from some common affliction. This is no virus or disease.'

I frown. 'Then what?'

'I'm not ill,' he says quietly, looking away.

'I don't understand.'

'I . . . I'm . . .'

'*What?*' I plead. 'You're what?'

He takes a deep breath. 'Cursed.'

The word is barbed and jagged. It hooks into me, burrowing deep, reverberating over and over inside my head.

Cursed.

Cursed.

Cursed.

For a moment my mind turns blank. An empty, echoing chamber. And then, all of a sudden, a flash of light, a finger-snap, and everything begins to slot into place.

Caius Castellion. The statue garden. The story.

Noble, handsome Emmeric was born into a powerful family.

I stare at Hal as if seeing him for the first time. He holds my gaze, a thousand different emotions dancing across his face.

Irabella was a rare beauty, with hair like cornsilk and eyes as bright as jewels. But she was also penniless, a mere servant.

Emmeric and Irabella – that's what Ingra teasingly called my secret lover and me. It was her little joke. Rich boy, poor girl, divided by circumstance, united by love. Yet never once did I imagine our resemblance to these characters extended beyond that. But now, I understand. The old man wasn't talking nonsense. He was trying to tell me something.

Because Emmeric was *cursed.*

'It was a . . . a Mage.' Hal grimaces, then shoots me an apologetic glance. 'I believe it was her act of revenge for what my grandfather did during the War of the Empires.'

He was cursed by a vengeful witch who blamed his family for her people's ruin.

'The curse fell on the first-born sons of House Castellion. The Light Wielders. It was my grandfather's punishment – that the Maker's gift would die along with his line.'

In destroying their legacy, she took away their dominion.

'In some ways what happened to my father was a kindness. He was dying anyway, growing weaker every day.' Hal closes his eyes. 'I . . . I can't stop it, Elva. The opium seems to slow it down, numb the pain, but I'm only delaying the inevitable.'

Irabella was forced to watch her love sicken and die, knowing there was nothing she could do to stop it.

No. *No.*

We are all stories, girl. Just as we are all of us bound by this curse of blood.

My knees finally give out. Hal catches me in his arms and we sink slowly to the floor.

'How do you know?' I choke out.

A hollow laugh. 'Fox. Of course, I thought he was lying until I realized he wasn't.'

Tears blur my vision. *Hal.* The dutiful prince, condemned for the crimes of his grandfather.

Terror becomes tinged by fury as I remember what Caius Castellion said:

Every story needs a villain, you know.

I suppose that explains why he would take this stance – painting the vengeful Mage as the enemy rather than Emmeric's tyrannical family.

'For so long I clung to the hope that there was a cure,' Hal murmurs into my hair.

My heart gives a sudden lurch.

A cure? Or . . . a *key*?

'Blaze,' I breathe.

Hal draws back, one eyebrow raised. 'What about her?'

'Your grandfather seems to think that . . . that she has the power to break the curse on Emmer– I mean, on you.'

'He does?' Hal considers this for a moment. 'I don't see how Blaze has anything to do with this,' he says slowly. 'But if somehow she does – she's still missing. Her brother too. We won't know anything until she returns. *If* she returns.'

The orbs of light shrink smaller and smaller until they extinguish completely.

Hal sighs, weary and defeated. 'At least now I know that my rule – my life – wasn't entirely wasted,' he says. 'If I am going to die, then I'll die knowing I did something good.'

'Don't talk like that.' I take his face in my hands and force him to meet my gaze. 'This is not the end. There has to be a way to fix this, and we're going to find it.'

His answering smile is unconvincing, but he pulls me close and kisses me softly – and that kiss feels like a promise.

58

Blaze

The night air is thick with the scent of liquor and triumph.

We sit round the bonfire clutching cups of Fox's grandmother's juniper-berry gin. She kept it for special occasions, which is why he thought it fitting to fetch a couple of dusty bottles from the kitchen cupboard. I've lost count of how many toasts we've raised – to Queen Hydra, to Syla, to me. I haven't stopped grinning since finding the Eye in the Creek. It's back where it belongs now, hanging from the chain round my neck.

Flint and Spinner are in the middle of a slurred rendition of some ballad about a pirate and a prince, their voices loud and off-key. Beside them, Sheen winces and holds out his hand for another bottle, which sails over to him, carried on an obedient stream of air. Fox laughs and slides an arm round my waist.

The drunken singing falters as Flint breaks off mid-verse to glare at us. Ever since his arrival he has left us in no doubt as to his opinion of our attachment. Once Fox had finally managed to convince my brother that, firstly, he was not holding me hostage, and, secondly, that he truly was a Healer, he offered to tend to Flint's burns. Naturally Flint refused, but grudgingly accepted a vial of painkiller at Spinner's insistence.

I notice he stays well back from the bonfire, angling the left side of his body away from the crackling flames. I also notice him stealing glances at Sheen.

I swirl the contents of my cup. The liquor is not nearly as strong as the relief that continues to cascade through me, intoxicating in its intensity.

'I can't believe we did it,' I say.

'*You* did it,' Fox amends, tucking a stray curl behind my ear and ignoring Flint's low growl of protest.

I smile as I pinch my chain between thumb and forefinger, letting the talisman swing back and forth like a pendulum before adding thoughtfully, 'It's strange, though.'

'What is?'

'Only that the first time I found the Eye, touching it felt like being struck by lightning,' I muse. 'Except this time – nothing. It's just as cold as when I threw it into the portal.'

'What?' Fox asks sharply.

I glance up at him, startled by the edge to his tone. 'When I touched it before, it was incredible but *agonizing* too. I remember seeing stars. I thought I might die from the pain. I could feel the power racing through me, as if it were in my blood.'

'You've never mentioned that until now.'

'Didn't I?' I arch a brow and take another swig from my cup. 'Well, it makes a nice change – knowing something you don't.'

Fox jerks his chin towards the Eye. 'Can I see that a moment?'

I shrug and pull the chain over my head. As I drop it into his palm, I attempt to translate his curious expression.

'I know!' Flint announces. 'Why doesn't Blaze give us a show?'

I turn to him. 'What d'you mean, a *show*?'

'Oh yes,' says Spinner. 'Let's see what the Eye can do, Blaze.'

'I don't actually know how to *use* it yet,' I admit. 'Returning Elva's gifts was an accident.'

'What about the third trial, when you summoned that storm?' Flint asks.

'I suppose I just sort of . . . willed it to happen. I asked for my power to be returned to me and it was, though that power was already mine to begin with. It's complicated. I've still got a lot to learn. Fox says it took him years to figure out the complexities of Sifa's Eye.'

'Oh, come on, Blaze. What've you got to lose?'

I sigh and scramble to my feet. 'If I agree to try, will you stop pestering me?'

Flint nods sagely. Spinner leans forward eagerly, but Sheen's gaze is fixed on Fox, who tosses me back the Eye.

'Here.'

I catch it, wobbling slightly, my reflexes somewhat clouded by liquor. Furrowing my brow, I begin to concentrate.

A whole minute passes. Then another.

'Are we sure it still works?' Spinner whispers loudly.

Flint shushes her.

At that moment the bonfire suddenly glows bright blue, the flames leaping higher and higher, spitting out sparks that glitter like sapphires.

Flint lets out a whoop while Spinner bursts into raucous applause. Even Sheen raises his cup in approval. I blink several times and the enchantment comes to an end. I stare at the carpet of powdery blue ash round my feet and feel my face split into a triumphant smile, but it fades abruptly the moment I catch sight of Fox's expression.

'What?' I ask. Then, more defensively, 'Not impressive enough for you?'

'It's not that.'

'Then what is it?'

The others have turned to stare at him too.

He fights to keep his voice neutral. 'A . . . complication.'

Flint frowns. 'Spit it out, Earth Cleaver. What's the problem?'

'The problem,' he begins slowly, 'is that Blaze just cast an enchantment without using the Eye of the Soul.'

'What're you talking about?' I brandish the talisman in my hand. 'It's right here.'

'No, it's not. You're holding the Eye of the Past.' Fox gestures to the talisman round his neck. '*This* is Syla's Eye.'

I cross my arms impatiently. 'I'm not following.'

'I swapped them.'

Flint makes a derisive sound.

'Why would you do that?' I ask, perplexed.

'Because of what you just said about the first time you touched the Eye. The way it felt. How it's felt ever since.' Fox glances away and murmurs, 'Why didn't I see it before?'

I throw up my hands in frustration. 'See *what*?'

'Most things I put down to you being Demari,' he continues. 'Surviving that snake bite, turning the forest to ice. And the portal from Brava. The Aquatori spend years learning how to use portals, and yet you got us here, safe and sound, on your first try. But it didn't *all* fit. Take the Eye of the Past, for example. It took me a long time to figure it out – you just said so. Even now there are things I miss, memories I can't seem to find no matter how hard I try. Only you got it to show you exactly what you wanted to see – your entire history, just like that.'

My skin tingles nervously.

'Then there's Elva,' Fox goes on. 'The night you returned her shadow magic, you told me you'd cut yourself.'

'What's that got to do with anything?' I demand.

'*I could feel the power racing through me, as if it were in my blood*,' he repeats. 'Well, what if it was? What if the source of the Eye's power wasn't sitting round your neck but running through your veins? Elva bandaged your hand, remember? She didn't get her gifts back because she touched you – she got them because she came into contact with your *blood*.'

My gaze flickers.

'Think about it. Both Sifa and Seera tried to hide their Eyes so they could never be wielded by another, but they were still discovered. Doesn't it make sense that Syla's last enchantment was not only designed to hide her talisman but to ensure that it would never belong to anyone else?' Fox pauses. 'That is, except for someone she had chosen.'

I'm shaking my head, but as his words land each new realization pummels me in the ribs before slotting into place.

'The Eye called to you. It wanted you to find it. Not so you could possess it but so it could possess you. When you touched it, all that power – it must've been . . . transferred.'

My voice is barely a whisper. 'What are you saying?'

Fox takes a long, deep breath. 'Blaze, I think . . . I think you *are* the Eye.'

59

Blaze

For a moment there is silence.

Then everybody starts speaking at once.

'As if,' scoffs Flint.

'Are you out of your mind?' Spinner demands.

'Seems plausible,' muses Sheen.

But Fox is looking only at me.

I stare back at him, dumbstruck. My limbs seem to be made of rubber. I lean heavily against a tree to avoid keeling over into the pile of glittering ash.

I was only just beginning to come to terms with the fact that I'm Demari, let alone that the Rain Singers believe me to be some kind of *God*, or that, in a few short days, I'm going to be crowned Queen of the Aquatori. But *this*? Me? The *Eye*?

'That's impossible,' I murmur.

'Why?' Fox asks calmly.

'Because ... because ...' I search desperately for an answer, but the liquor clouding my head is making it difficult to think clearly. 'Because it just *is*, all right?'

'I agree with Blaze,' my brother announces, loyal to the bone.

'Harglade,' Sheen says, his voice unexpectedly soft, 'think about what happened in the Ridge tunnels.'

Both of us turn to stare at him. Then I watch as understanding sparks in Flint's right eye. His mouth stretches first into a taut line then curls into a grimace.

'Oh,' he mumbles.

'What is it?' Spinner asks, her gaze flicking quizzically between him and Sheen.

'I . . .' Flint clears his throat. 'I couldn't explain it before.'

'Explain *what*?' I splutter.

'The explosion.'

Fox closes his eyes.

'I thought *I* was the one who killed that snake,' Flint continues. 'It was the only logical conclusion. Only, deep down . . .' His face flushes.

'What?' I demand.

'I knew . . . I knew it couldn't have been me.'

'I don't understand,' I say through gritted teeth.

'I didn't conjure those flames, Blaze.'

'Why not?'

'Because I –' He glances at Sheen, who nods once. Flint then swallows hard, inhales, exhales, and says, 'Because I *can't*.'

For a long moment we just look at each other.

My stomach churns violently. 'What d'you mean, *you can't*?'

'Ever since the third trial, I . . . I haven't . . .' He looks as if he might vomit.

And then it hits me. All his excuses and deflections. His reluctance to ignite so much as a candle. Even Aunt Yvainne's funeral when he couldn't face lighting the pyre.

I think back to the Ridge and how desperate I was for those flames to erupt, almost as if I'd willed them into existence.

I stand rooted to the spot as realization burns through me. In one last-ditch attempt to smother it with doubt, I drag my gaze from my brother and glare at everyone in turn.

'Is this some kind of joke? Because it's not funny.'

'No one's laughing,' Sheen points out quietly.

Spinner twists her fingers together nervously.

'Well, I don't believe it,' I snap. But if that were true, then why is my heart pounding so fiercely I fear it may break a rib?

I glance down at the talisman clutched in my fist. Even in the flickering firelight I can see that the chain is ever so slightly thicker, the clasp a different shape to my own. Fox was telling the truth. This is the Eye of the Past.

I bite the inside of my cheek until I taste blood, the salt-iron tang coating my tongue.

I see Elva's hands – streaks of red across her porcelain skin. I hear Caius Castellion's voice in my head, telling me the story of the three sisters, telling me about Syla.

Power belonged to her. It ran through her veins.

'Remember when I told you that the Eyes are drawn together?' Fox says in a voice one might use to calm a wounded animal. 'You could've emerged from any of the Ridge tunnels, yet you stumbled right into my arms. In Brava, you felt pulled towards something, only it was me you found in that cliff pool. Or rather, the talisman round my neck. Do you see? The Eyes can sense when another is near. *That's* why you were drawn to me.'

His words pierce my heart.

I don't realize I've dropped the Eye of the Past until it hits the ground, bouncing twice before rolling to a stop at Fox's feet.

'Blaze,' he says, but I shake my head, backing away.

Flint moves forward but Sheen places a cautionary hand on his chest.

The forest grows darker with each staggering step I take from the bonfire.

Fox's footsteps make no sound as he follows me through the trees. 'Blaze.'

I ignore him.

'Please. Just talk to me.'

His hand brushes my shoulder. I shrug it off roughly and whirl round to face him. 'I bet you knew this whole time, didn't you?'

He flinches as if I've struck him. Then he composes himself and meets my gaze, holding it carefully as he says, 'I *swear* to you, I didn't.'

But the problem is I don't know whether to believe him. He's hidden so much from me in the past. Does his pledge of honesty still stand? Or is he lying to cover his back?

'I'm sorry,' he says. 'I should've pieced it together the day we arrived here, when . . .' His eyes shutter. 'Like Flint, I thought it must've been me. That I'd done it subconsciously.'

'Done what?'

But he doesn't need to respond. I see them in my mind, sprouting through floorboards, blooming brightly all around us.

Foxgloves.

Heat prickles, blurring my vision. The rain is light at first but grows heavier with every painful thud of my heart.

Was it all a lie? This. *Us*. Everything he said. Everything we felt. Were we really only drawn to one another because of the Eyes?

I always knew we were a bad idea. I was so reluctant to trust him, right up until the moment I surrendered my heart. Perhaps it was not my trust in Fox I should have questioned but the connection we shared. The intimacy, the *intensity* of it.

I used to struggle with my emotions. I used to bottle them up, bury them deep – until I learned to control them. But my feelings for Fox were never something I could control, no matter how hard I tried. What if this is why?

The thought rips me to shreds.

My throat is tight, my voice abrasive. 'It wasn't real, was it?'

Confusion clouds his features. 'What wasn't?'

I don't answer him. I don't trust myself to speak. The heartbreak from Hal's betrayal was nothing – *nothing* – compared to this.

How could I ever be with Fox now, when I have no way of telling whether the way I feel about him, the way he feels about me, is true? I'd be living a lie.

'Blaze, you're not thinking clearly. Calm down, and then we'll –'

'*No.*'

I feel myself splitting apart, coming undone. Droplets cling to Fox's eyelashes and spill down his cheeks like tears.

He reaches for me. I don't shake him off this time but turn very still, rigid, like a statue, and he lets go at once, his hand falling back to his side.

I don't want him to touch me. I don't wish to be held or comforted.

'Blaze.'

My chest aches at the softness in his voice. The rain intensifies, falling heavy and cold from a starless sky.

I never asked for this. It's not *fair*. The gravity of it all weighs me down, sinking into my bones. My body is paralysed, yet my mind is spinning.

'Leave me alone, Fox,' I say flatly. 'I need time to think.'

'Why don't you come back to the cottage and we'll –'

'I *said*, leave me *alone*.'

Rain turns to hailstones as the anger returns, cutting through the pain.

I always wanted it – power. I *revelled* in my water gifts. Only possessing power is one thing. To be possessed, quite another. When I found the Eye, I thought I held the key to power itself. But I was wrong. I don't hold the key – I *am* the key.

A prize to be won. A weapon to be wielded.

I don't belong to myself any more.

Perhaps I never did.

60

Blaze

There was a time I found solitude suffocating. Now, I welcome it.

It helps me think.

About Etheri and Magi and Demari. About the three sisters and their talismans. About Senna's curse and how I'm supposed to break it.

I think about my mother.

I think about fate and prophecy, life and death, about the past, present and future – a tangle of golden threads. I think about who I was and who I wanted to be.

But most of all, I think about what I have become.

The Eye dangles uselessly from the chain round my neck. I considered hurling it right back into the Creek. Now that its power has been transferred to me, it's nothing more than a piece of jewellery. A shiny relic. But something made me slip it over my head, where it's remained ever since, sitting cold and empty between my collarbones, the sole witness to my self-imposed isolation.

Having long given up trying to get me to *talk about it*, the others eventually – mercifully – agreed to let me have some time to myself. Flint had Sheen cast a powerful wind shield around the perimeter of the cottage for my protection. It was the only way my brother would consent to leave me here unguarded, since I refused Fox's suggestion that Scout or Cedar remain behind to watch over me. So, after several anxious looks cast in my direction, they all reluctantly left for the palace. I didn't say goodbye.

Perhaps I'm being selfish. Fine, I *know* I'm being selfish. But the way I see it, I've spent weeks caught up in a fool's errand, risking life and limb to find the Eye of the Soul, when all this time – *all* this time – the very thing I was searching for . . . was *myself*.

If my sense of humour hadn't abandoned me along with my appetite, self-conviction and general worldview, then I'm sure I'd find the whole situation rather amusing.

But then I recall the Rain Singers back in Brava, mourning their dead. Yet more deaths on my conscience.

In my dreams I see their broken bodies littering the beach. I wake shivering, drenched in cold sweat. No arms reach out to comfort me, and I remember I'm alone.

My only visitor is fury. It drops by every so often, arriving in sharp bursts that frost the leaves and crystallize the water lapping at the bank of the Creek. Sometimes it spreads wider, coating the trees with thick layers of ice that I shatter like glass in the absence of a real target – one with raven eyes and a voice softer than silk.

I wonder how long it'll be before King Balen learns of my new . . . *identity*. I imagine most people will think me triumphant. Even smug. After all, who wouldn't want the ability to wield power itself?

So it may come as a surprise to many that the answer is *me*.

Because I don't. I don't want it. I wanted *my* magic. Power that belonged to me and me alone. But the power running through my veins is not mine. Already I feel drained by it, as though it were some kind of parasite, and I its involuntary host.

And the worst part is I can't seem to tell where I end and it begins. Did I succeed in opening that portal because I'm a gifted Aquatori, or because I drew from power itself? Did I survive that snake bite because of the strength of *my* blood, or because that blood was steeped in ancient magic? Did I turn the forest to ice because I'm Demari, or because I'm the Eye? It's little wonder I never figured out the truth. In a way I'm grateful for these past few weeks of ignorance. The responsibility of possessing this much power is a burden too great to fathom. As for becoming queen . . . if the crown is starting to resemble a shackle, then the Golden Palace is no better than a prison. Even the Lagoon – my court, my link to Queen Hydra, this shimmering ideal of a new home and a fresh start – is beginning to tarnish.

Gilded cages still have bars.

I never wanted this, just as I never wanted to be an Heir. All I've ever wanted was to leave Ostacre far behind. To see the world and become someone new.

But it doesn't seem to matter what I want.

There's a sense of being pulled backwards through door after door, each clanging shut behind me. The future I'd planned for myself is now forever beyond my reach.

I feel bitter and bruised and small.

So maybe that's why I'm still here, sitting aimlessly on a rope swing in the Wildlands, stewing in my own misery. Maybe that's why I'm acting like a petulant child rather than the soon to be Queen of the Waterlands.

Though I just wish it were the only reason.

I pluck a leaf from a branch and tear it into tiny pieces, letting them drift down into the Creek below.

Fox might be gone, but those spring-green eyes are all I can see. This place is his. Everything about it calls him to mind. I started sleeping on the floor to avoid the ache-inducing mint-and-pine scent clinging to the bedsheets. Yet it seems to linger on the air, taunting me. Haunting me. I can't stop thinking about him. I've tried. I even drank up the last of the liquor in pursuit of a moment's reprieve, to no avail.

The Earth Cleaver burrowed his way into my heart and, quite unintentionally, broke it in two. He said himself that the reason we were drawn to one another was the Eyes. Which means that whatever I feel for him, whatever he appears to feel for me, I have no way of knowing if it's real. Which means I can't trust my own feelings any more. Which means we can never work, he and I.

And it hurts. It hurts so badly I can barely breathe.

But soon – very soon – I'm going to have to face him. Face everybody.

Part of me wishes I could just stay here forever, indulging my suffering, hiding from the world like my father did. Or sprout wings like Kestrel Calloway and fly far away. Only that would be the coward's way out, and I'm many things, but I am not a coward.

I vowed to do whatever it took to save Hal. I won't turn my back on the crown I won. I have to see this through.

King Balen was right – this is only the beginning.

And I am the beginning that brought the end.

61

Elva

They arrived as dawn broke, appearing out of thin air in the Council Chambers.

Spinner, Flint, his sullen-looking chaperone and the Earth Cleaver, who wore a slightly tortured expression and held a small copper-coloured creature in his arms.

Hal, who'd fallen asleep with his head on a stack of papers, woke with a start and almost toppled from his chair. He was on his feet in an instant, his gaze locked on his half-brother, a beam of light materializing in his palm.

Fox made no effort to defend himself, but to my surprise the two Eyes positioned themselves protectively on either side of him.

Flint, who was too busy staring open-mouthed between Hal and me, blinked hard, then carefully manoeuvred himself between both parties. 'Well,' he said genially, 'I think several explanations are in order, don't you?'

Countless conversations ensued, each one more astonishing than the last. I could hardly believe what I was hearing – about Rain Singers and Demari, Magi sisters and enchanted talismans, the truth about the Rift and the storm and the Binding Ceremony and . . . Blaze. I understand now why Caius Castellion called her the key.

Flint's jaw almost hit the floor when Hal told them how I became his spy, about the break-out from the dungeons, his grandfather's return, the attempt on his life and the liberation of the serfs, and, finally, about the curse. For hours he barely looked at his brother, until Fox calmly suggested they speak alone, and the rest of us filed out.

'We haven't been formally introduced,' said Blaze's twin, extending a hand. 'Flint Harglade – reformed playboy, Ignitia runner-up, and newly discovered Demari.'

'Elva,' I mumbled.

'The Shadow Mage.' He nodded thoughtfully. 'Now I guess you know why.'

'Where is she?' I asked.

Flint grimaced slightly. 'Blaze just . . . needs some time.'

This did not surprise me. I imagine the discovery that you're the embodiment of power itself would take some getting used to.

Hal and Fox didn't reappear until dusk. This was no loving reconciliation, but a tentative truce. An old alliance made new again. Fox watched me step out of the shadows and shot me a rather half-hearted wink. The next morning Hal revoked his brother's banishment and pardoned him before the court. The news was met by gasps and whispers, and even cries of protest, yet all fell silent when Hal made his second announcement: those who still felt any kind of allegiance to King Balen should know that, thanks to the Storm Weaver, we now possessed a weapon powerful enough to match whatever army he might raise to usurp the throne. Whispered speculation followed, with courtiers trading rumours like currency.

When Blaze showed up several days later, emerging suddenly from a portal in the centre of the banquet hall, many screamed in fright and backed away, staring at her with a mixture of terror and curiosity. Her grey eyes were dull, her clothes tattered and ill-fitting. She did not look like a future queen, much less any kind of *God*. She looked haunted, tense, uncomfortable in her own skin, as if all too aware of the power running through her veins.

Fox tried to follow her, but Spinner caught his arm. I couldn't help but wonder what might've happened between them.

The Earth Cleaver is almost unrecognizable. I'm still a little scared of him – that deep-rooted arrogance is hard to shake, but he also seems more *real* somehow. Less of a myth and more of a boy. There's a gentleness to him. I see it when he hands Hal a fresh vial of painkiller, or when he speaks to me in Obsidian. He even paid a visit to the medical wing, waving the flock of physicians aside so he could examine Ingra. After she'd hurled some very choice words in his direction, and only after he managed to convince her that he was not and never had been the Prince of Slavers, she let him tend to her injuries, biting down hard on a strip of leather as he realigned her finger bones.

As for me, I've barely left Hal's side. While our involvement – and my magic – remains a secret to all but a few, I am now officially an Eye of the Imperial Court and a personal spy to the emperor. I've been given my own quarters, a silvery thoroughbred and more gowns than I can count. The one I'm wearing now is the same one I wore to the masquerade ball – swathes of glittering gold silk. Elaith insisted on dusting some shimmering powder across my eyelids and along my cheekbones, and my hair swings in a buttery curtain down to my waist. She said it was important I look my best.

It is coronation day, after all.

The palace is filled with flowers and swarming with guests. Hundreds of guards line the corridors and are stationed throughout the grounds, just in case King Balen decides to make an appearance. Yet Hal believes his uncle wouldn't be stupid enough to attack, not now he suspects that we have all three of the enchanted Eyes.

I notice Spinner as soon as I enter the throne room – she's engaged in a one-sided conversation with Sheen. It was all I could do not to throw my arms round her when she volunteered to lead the search for my sister. My heart swells at the thought of being reunited with Astrid, then it lurches as my gaze falls on Caius Castellion. He's talking quietly with River, the Aquatori trainer, who I now know to be Blaze's real grandfather. Next to them, leaning heavily on her cane, is Lady Harglade, her brow creased with sorrow. Blaze still refuses to speak to her. She will see no one apart from her brothers.

Standing stiffly beside Blaze's grandmother is a man I don't recognize. He's tall and broad-shouldered, with dark auburn hair and brown eyes. I imagine he was handsome once, but now his face is weary-looking and engraved with deep lines. I wonder who he could be.

Elaith nudges me in the side. 'Look!'

I turn to watch the new Supreme Mother of the Valla Jakartis sweep into the room. She's younger than her predecessor, who died at King Balen's hand, yet she sports the same long robes that trail behind her like a wedding gown. As head of the ancient sisterhood of Etheri who preside over various rites and rituals, she's here to oversee the coronation, since for the first time in history there will be no Binding Ceremony. Given that Blaze has yet to discover a means of breaking the curse, Fox feared what might happen if she were to bind her power to Hal's. He said the force of it could kill him.

A hush falls as Hal appears in the doorframe. Though still pale and drawn, he's no longer utterly bowed under the crippling weight of despair, and this newfound hopefulness, along with Fox's tinctures, seems to be allowing him to function – for now at least. He wears the same ceremonial cloak he wore for Ingra's execution, yet as he walks through the crowd my gaze falls on the hem, where some embellishments have been made. Stitched among the tiny golden suns are a number of silver crescent moons. My heart swells. He catches my eye as he passes and his mouth curves briefly into a small, secret smile.

I watch him make his way towards the dais, where five thrones await.

Zephyr is next to appear, dressed in a thick cloak the colour of sea-smoke. Since King Balen still occupies the Windlands, Hal has offered his friend – and all loyal members of the Ventalla Court – the east wing of the Golden Palace for the time being.

He is followed by Ember, wearing a rust-orange gown and a smirk. A muscle twitches in Sheen's jaw as she skips smugly up to the dais.

A collective gasp ripples through the onlookers as the fourth member of the Council strides casually into the throne room – an official pardon was not all Hal granted his brother. Even in a fine green-velvet doublet, leather trousers and shiny new riding boots, the Earth Cleaver still manages to look unkempt. He chews lazily on something as he mounts the steps two at a time, the Eye of the Past gleaming gold round his neck.

The crowd seems to be holding their breath.

Fox doesn't so much as glance at them. His gaze is fixed on the door while he absent-mindedly twists his signet rings, waiting.

The whole palace is waiting.

Waiting for *her*.

62

Blaze

A glance at the golden clock on the wall tells me I'm already late. I can't find it in me to care. Let them wait. I can only hope my tardiness is perceived as a reluctance to attend rather than a desire to build suspense. Though I doubt I'd have to try much on that front.

My return to the palace caused quite a stir. I think one courtier even fainted. I forced myself to walk slowly through the crowd, and only when I reached my old chambers and shut the door behind me did I allow myself to exhale. Since then I haven't opened it to anyone except Flint, who provides distraction, and Renly, who offers comfort – and chocolate. My little brother greeted me with a kiss on each cheek and a kitten in each hand.

'I missed you,' he said, rather reproachfully.

'I missed you, too,' I told him.

'How much?'

'A lot. More than a lot. The most.'

This seemed to mollify him.

Mouse, who's quite a bit bigger now, curled herself round my neck like a fur scarf and started purring in my ear.

I thought Grandmother was going to blast the door off its hinges the first time I refused her entry. Pleading, bribes, threats, endless lectures, emotional blackmail – I've had it all. Yet nothing she said persuaded me to let her in. I'm still angry with her. I'm not ready to talk about the fact that for seventeen years, she let me live a lie. *Her* lie.

So I began playing the music box Flint gave me to drown her out.

I also denied myself River's company, since I knew he'd only try to convince me to speak to Grandmother.

That's one good thing about becoming queen – I don't have to answer to anybody.

Others have attempted to visit me. Flint told them not to bother, but they tried anyway. Elaith. Spinner. Elva. Hal.

And Fox.

He sits on the other side of the door for hours at a time. Sometimes he says nothing at all. Other times he'll try to reason with me.

'Look, I know this has come as a shock, and it's not something you'd have ever chosen for yourself. But I don't understand why you won't talk to me.'

Because I don't know if what we had was real, and it feels like my heart is breaking.

The words formed and died on my lips.

'Tell me what I've done wrong and I'll fix it. Whatever it is, we can work it out.' Fox's voice was soft. Pleading. 'Just open the door, Blaze.'

The ache in my chest was unbearable.

During a moment of weakness I sat with my back pressed to the door, wishing it wasn't there at all. Then I locked that thought away inside the box I keep in my head and smashed an ornate golden vase into a thousand sparkling pieces.

I picture Fox standing on the dais with the rest of the new Council – the Earth Cleaver, soon to be King of the Terrathian. I wonder how he feels about it.

I think back to what Grandmother said on the morning of the eclipse.

Make no mistake, the real game begins when the winners take their thrones.

Well, if I know anything about Fox, it's that he likes to win.

Syla's Eye looks back at me in the mirror, dangling from the chain round my neck. My coronation gown glints sapphire-blue in the sunlight; the expensive Vosti fabric is supple and fluid, studded with pearls. My curls are unbound, spilling down my back and framing my face, which is pale and pinched and carefully schooled into a mask of . . . forbearance? Resignation? Do I look grateful and graceful, just like Grandmother always taught me? I'm half tempted to send my decoy in my place. She seemed to do a pretty convincing job of pretending to be me until Caleb the stable boy saw an opportunity to earn a few coins. My life, his loyalty – it seems everything has its price.

Minutes trickle by and still I make no move towards the doors.

What would my mother say to me if she were here? Would she hold me close? Tell me everything's going to be all right?

A cloud of drizzle forms above my head, hazy droplets landing on the mirror, scattering my reflection. Then there's a crackling sound as the water turns to ice.

I refuse to appear weak. Not now that I own – that I *am* – power itself.

Yet while I may possess it I still haven't attempted to *use* it. Perhaps once I've figured out a way to save Hal and, if I can, return what was taken from the people of the Otherlands, I'll reject it entirely. Let the magic lie dormant until it eventually dies with me. One person should not have this much power. It isn't right.

At that moment a light breeze caresses my face.

It happens again – softly, running through my hair, skittering down my spine.

That's when I hear a voice. Smooth like silk, eternally amused, whispering in my ear.

Hello, little dove.

I stiffen. The hairs on the back of my neck stand on end.

The breeze picks up, causing the gauzy curtains to billow outward. An elongated shadow pools on the floor, merging with my own. I whirl round, choking on panic, my hands raised defensively. Yet there's no sign of the Ventalla King.

Is he really here?

I came to wish you luck on such an auspicious day.

The sound is directionless.

'Where are you?' I breathe.

A gust of wind ripples through my skirts. I jerk backwards, gasping, trying to focus on the power coursing through my veins. But what am I supposed to do? I can't attack thin air. I can't fight a phantom.

Dear Haldyn must have forgotten to invite me. Perhaps his mind is beginning to decline just like his body. It can only be a matter of time before the sun ceases to shine.

Fury undercuts fear. I grit my teeth. 'Show yourself.'

I feel a tap on my shoulder and recoil, stumbling backwards into the dressing table – but once again, King Balen is nowhere to be seen.

Whispers flit around my head, darting from ear to ear.

I know what you are. I know who *you are, too. You've tried to hide it, even from yourself. But I have seen it in you – that appetite for vengeance. The quiet pleasure you take in hurting those who have hurt you. In making them pay.*

The words chill me to the bone. 'You're wrong.'

I meant what I said, little dove. You and I – together we could conquer all.

My voice is a sharp scratch. 'What do you want from me?'

I want your power. I want your loyalty.

I swallow hard. 'Never.'

King Balen laughs, soft and silken. *We shall see.*

And this time, when I turn round, it's to find a pair of raven-black eyes boring into mine. I try to speak, to scream, but the sound is ripped from my mouth. I reach inward, fumbling desperately for my anchors, preparing to unleash my ice.

'You know, I believe anyone is capable of changing their mind,' King Balen murmurs, his cool fingers gently grazing the Eye round my neck. 'All it takes is the right . . . motivation.'

Suddenly there's a loud knock on the door to my chambers.

The Ventalla King smiles. Less than a heartbeat later, he is gone.

I sag against the wall, my breathing jagged. King Balen – he was *here*, in the palace, in my *room*. Bile crawls up my throat.

His words linger on the air.

I have seen it in you – that appetite for vengeance.

'Blaze! Open up!'

Ten seconds – that's all I have to compose myself before crossing the reception room and wrenching open the door.

'What time d'you call this?' Flint asks in mock-disapproval. 'Everyone's waiting.'

'I know,' I say, voice trembling. 'I – I'm sorry.'

My brother is dressed in a rich scarlet doublet complete with a matching eyepatch. Renly clings to his back, adorable in a little orange-and-gold tunic. He slides to the ground and launches himself into my arms.

'Blaze,' he says, 'your face is very white. Like a ghost. Are you frightened?'

I feel the frantic pounding of my heart as I hold him tightly, breathing in the calming scent of fresh linen and chocolate.

'Nerves are totally understandable, sister mine,' says Flint sagely, 'but Hal's beginning to look a tad unsteady on his feet and our dear sweet cousin is seconds away from throwing a tantrum, so best shake a leg.' Then he pauses, tilting his head to one side. 'Hm. On second thoughts, hand me that brush.'

Mouse crawls sleepily on to my lap as Flint dusts shimmering powder along my cheekbones and lines my eyes with slicks of gold.

It's only when I glance down that I see a sleek black feather perched atop the vanity next to the wooden knight from Renly. My skin crawls. I don't trust myself to speak. I can't tell Flint what just happened, not with Ren here. But more than that, I'm still reeling from the Ventalla King's words. From the awful, twisted truth of them. And what did he mean when he spoke of *motivation*?

'There,' my brother says with a flourish. 'That's better.'

Ren beams. 'Pretty.'

A phantom breeze kisses my face as the door to my chambers swings shut behind us.

I clutch Ren's hand. Blood rushes in my ears.

All too soon, we reach the throne room. I can hear the low rumble of voices beyond the towering golden doors.

My knees knock together.

'Chin up,' Flint instructs. 'Shoulders back.'

'*Stand up straight*,' Renly says, mimicking Grandmother.

'Oh, and whatever you do, don't trip,' Flint adds helpfully. He glances at Ren. 'Remember what I taught you?'

I watch, utterly speechless, as my brothers bow deeply in unison.

Then Flint straightens up and punches me lightly on the arm. 'All right, sister mine. It's time. Knock 'em dead.'

With that, he ushers me gently through the doors.

A thousand heads turn in my direction. Hiding my shaking hands in the folds of my dress, I make my way slowly through the crowd of onlookers towards the dais where the new Council await. A pair of green eyes snaps to mine, burning holes in my skin. My stomach tumbles and I force myself to look away before I lose my nerve entirely.

Whispering fills the hall.

It's madness.

The emperor must be out of his mind.

I don't care if she wears a crown. I'll never bend the knee.

What d'you reckon this weapon of hers is, then?

I just hope it's not another storm, or we're all dead.

She looks like she's going to vomit.

Excellent.

I spot Elva, beautiful in a glittering gold dress. Next to her is Elaith, bouncing up and down excitedly on the balls of her feet. My friend and former training partner, Kai, gives me a little wave from where he stands with a few Aquatori courtiers, all craning to get a glimpse of me. I catch sight of Sheen, who looks as sullen as ever, and Spinner, who blows me a kiss. Cole gives me a look that suggests he'd prefer it if this were my funeral rather than my coronation. As for Marina, I can practically hear her grinding her teeth from several rows away.

Then my gaze lands on Caius Castellion and my insides turn to ice. Beside him, River nods in encouragement, his silver trident catching the light. Grandmother is gripping her ruby-encrusted stick, her expression unreadable. And there, standing at her side, is –

My breath catches, my already-fraying resolve unravelling until it hangs by a thread. It's all I can do not to come undone.

My father looks back at me with hollow, haunted eyes. Seven years of soul-shredding grief have rendered him almost unrecognizable, a ghost of the man I once knew. Emblazoned on the pocket of his carmine doublet is his House emblem – a silver peacock.

Pain flickers across his face as I pass. If he found my resemblance to my mother torturous before, what must it be like for him now, with my dark hair flowing freely to my waist, the same age she was when they first met here in the Golden Palace?

I wonder what Grandmother said to convince him to leave the confines of Bartell Manor. I doubt his attending the coronation came from a sudden desire to see his children.

By the time I reach the dais the whispers have been replaced by thick, smothering silence. The Supreme Mother of the Valla Jakartis purses her lips. Zephyr inclines his head. Ember fixes me with a sickly-sweet smile. Hal looks relieved. And –

My heart twists out of shape.

I stare at the floor as I take my place beside Fox.

The Supreme Mother bids each member of the new Council to kneel before the five thrones and the ceremony commences. I only half listen to the recital of ancient scriptures. I'm too busy talking myself out of making a break for the doors.

I can feel Fox looking at me. It's almost painful, the urge to meet his gaze – to be close to him. Is it real, this feeling? Or is it just a response – a result of the talismans drawing us together like a magnetic force? I don't know. And that's the problem. It's *killing* me.

I swallow a gasp as my brandmark suddenly glows blindingly bright – so bright I can hardly see – before extinguishing entirely.

The Supreme Mother presses her fingertips together in prayer, then signals for us to rise. One by one we take our thrones.

Hal is crowned first. The Imperial Crown is magnificent – an intricate fusion of golden feathers, flames, leaves and waves set round a glimmering sun. He had a second Ventalla crown made for Zephyr, since the original is still worn by King Balen. Tension coils between my shoulder blades as the King of the Air's soft laughter echoes in my ears.

Ember is up next, grinning triumphantly at Aunt Hester. Then Fox, who's still looking at me. I grip the arms of my throne as the Aquatori crown is produced – a circlet of curling waves nestled on a gold-silk cushion. I recall that night after the second trial when I overheard those courtiers discussing my prospects in the hedge maze.

Mark my words, the Veridian Desert will turn to ice before the Storm Weaver is crowned Queen of the Fish.

Perhaps if I felt less like I were about to self-implode, I'd take a moment to revel in spite.

The crowd stare up at me – a sea of gold, grey, green, red and blue. I see fear in their faces. I see hate and horror, anger and awe. I feel it, too, deep down to my bones.

Murderer. Changeling. Freak.

The words are always there. I can hear them in the silence. The Riftkeeper once told me that I understood the value of a name. Unsurprising, really, since I'm known by so many.

Storm Weaver.

The girl who wove the storm that shook the world. Responsible for almost drowning the empire on the day of my birth.

Rain Singer.

I think of my people back in Brava, still alive after all these years. I am no longer the last of my kind. I never was.

Demari.

Part Etheri. Part Magi. The product of a love that changed the tides of fortune.

Eye.

Power hums beneath my skin, raw and restless, a caged beast fighting to break free. When I touched Syla's talisman, I became the key.

And now, today, I become something new.

The Supreme Mother clears her throat. 'I hereby pronounce you, Blaze Harglade . . .'

The whole world seems to hold its breath as the final crown is placed upon my head.

Queen.

Acknowledgements

I always read acknowledgements. Maybe it's because I'm nosey, or sentimental, or both. But it fascinates me just how many people have shaped a book – and a writer – into what they are today. I've often thought of acknowledgements as a kind of love letter. So, here's mine.

This is my second book, so it feels fitting to first thank the readers. Thank you for following Blaze into the next adventure. Thank you for making me happy-cry on the way home from events. Thank you for every message, video, gift, post, picture, piece of art and friendship bracelet. I feel so lucky to be a part of such a kind and supportive community.

Thank you to my agent, Catherine Cho – measured, insightful, ever supportive, a true powerhouse and the fastest replier known to man.

Thank you to my editors, Carmen McCullough, Kate Meltzer and Emilia Sowersby, who saw this book at every stage and never stopped believing in it – or in me.

Thank you to the team at Penguin – Chess Vincent, Shreeta Shah, Awo Ibrahim, Faith Young, Alice Todd, Maeve Banham, Beth Fennell, Millie Lovett, Magdalena Morris, Clare Braganza, Ellie Williamson, Stella Dodwell, Tom Rubira, Alicia Ingram, Libby Thorton, Millie Street, Katherine Whelan, Rebecca Mason, Lottie Chesterman, Adam Webling, Alice Grigg, Katy Adams, Elsie Regan, Rachael Hughes, Susanne Evans, Rosie Pinder, Aisling O'Toole, Cande Rivero and Chloe Traynor. It really does take a village, and I'm endlessly thankful for mine.

Special shoutout to Sarah Doyle and Nina Douglas, who were not only fantastic publicists but also lovely friends – thank you for calming me down, cheering me on and always being up for a Swiftie debrief.

Thank you to the team at Macmillan – Connie Hsu, Allison Verost, Tatiana Merced-Zarou, Gaby Salpeter, Julia Bianchi, Samira Iravani, Kathy Wielgosz, Jennifer Healey, Celeste Cass and Eleonore Fisher. Watching US readers discover my books brings me immense joy.

I'm very grateful to my international publishers, editors and translators for allowing me to share Blaze's story with the world. Special thanks to the team at Éditions Milan, my French editor – and Ember defender! – Noémie Coutant and my French translator, Marion Segui. The *Heir of Storms* France tour was truly magical and so are all of you.

Thank you to the booksellers who have championed this series, and to every teacher, librarian and blogger who has read and recommended it.

Thank you to my family for supporting me in everything, for keeping me (moderately) sane and for loving me through it all. Mum, Nan, Bubba and Nisey. Dad and Grandad. My brother, Sam, and my sister, Rebecca. My cousin Hayley. My dogs, Hux and Ziggy.

Thank you to my best friends, Sam, Kirsty, Amy, Tia, Emma, Emily, Mhairi, Beth and Amber, for never failing to make me laugh and for always being my lighthouse in the storm.

Bea Fitzgerald, what would I do without you? First-rate author, first-rate friend.

My love to the Wadees, the Mackies and the Keanes.

And to my second family – the Wrights.

But most of all, to Gill, who I see in every smile, sunflower and small act of kindness. She never got to read this story, but she'll always be a part of mine.